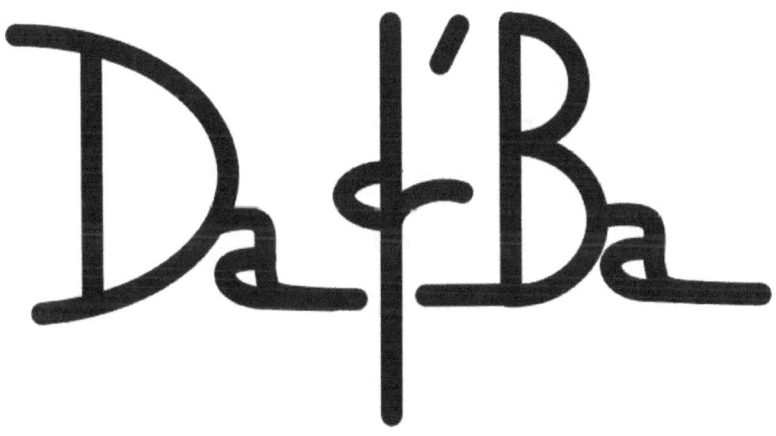

By

Tetsu'Go'Ru Tsu'Te

Ah'Ma'Go Publishing
Honolulu, Hawaii

This book is dedicated to Su'Zi

Published by Ah'Ma'Go Publishing

Dadr'Ba Copyright © 2015

Ah'Ma'Go Publishing

Cover Art by Tetsu'Go'Ru Tsu'Te

Library of Congress Control Number: 2015959731

ISBN: 0-9817327-8-X
ISBN-13: 978-0-9817327-8-7

First Edition: May 2016

Prolog – The Future Remembered

Our world has become uninhabitable, unchecked technology, industrialization, overpopulation, greed and war had poisoned our world.

The uncommitted attempts, distrust of our neighbors and unwillingness to make sacrifices that would through necessity cost the lives of millions of people forced our species into that age old philosophical debate; do we forfeit the few to save the many? Or even forfeit the many to save the entire species? If we allow ourselves to get backed into that corner, is our species even worth saving? We had made the choice, and it was doubt, delay, and inaction. Though not intentional, we chose to risk sacrificing the species. All because the world couldn't agree on what to do, when to do it and who would pay the cost, in money, labor and lives.

This by itself would not have forced the launching of the arks, that we came to call, "Dadr's." Had it not been for two natural events.

Our world's magnetic field was weakening and moving, signs that the world's magnetic field was going to reverse, as it had reversed in the past. This time it was in conjunction with a steady increase in solar flare activity that if predictions held true, would together with our weakened magnetic field, strip off a significant portion of the world's atmosphere, and threatening us with extinction.

Our technology enabled us to send out ark's destined for exoplanets that had been identified as habitable and without intelligent life. The targets were examined closely with a variety of instruments and proven absent of mechanization or industrialization indicative of intelligent life and quite as peaceful as a deserted isle.

Chapter 1, Kr'T's Demise

Kr'T[1] pulled himself along the suspension line past the strategically spaced explosive armor meteoroid shields, towards the damaged section of the number one shield. The number one shield suffers the most frequent damage, and has increased in frequency since the ship began nearing O'M's[2] Oort Cloud. The number one shield, due to its location usually suffers the kind of damage that can't be repaired by the automated systems.

Having reached the edge of the number one shield, Kr'T unclipped from the tight suspension line and let himself fall out, or more accurately, thrown out to the end of his safety line. A dangerous move but one that allowed him a better view, but an action that he knew would bring a challenge from the monitors at job control that watched his every move. He didn't care much about job control, they've worked with him long enough to expect him to stretch the limits, but can be relied on to get the job done.

At the end of his tether, Kr'T turned the adjustable attachment on his harness around so that he faced outward toward space, his tether straining under the centrifugal forces and causing blood to surge to his head. He immersed himself into the universe passing in front of him and around him. He spotted his favorite constellation and then started naming them to himself as they slowly passed in front of him, like the last time he and his daughter Su'Zi[3] visited their private observation port.

Seconds later, job control broke the moment of solitude. "Four-Tango-Seven-Three, is everything okay?" Job control, like all guards monitoring the inmates, is prohibited from using the inmate's real names, required instead to use "the last four" of their alphanumeric conviction number, but the tone was cordial.

Kr'T, irritated by job controls interruption, responded with "everything's fine, just backing off to better assess the damage." Job control could see everything Kr'T could see from Kr'T's helmet cam and knew that he had looked but wasn't now looking at the damage. They already knew approximately where the damage and its extent by the visual monitors and impact sensors placed at key positions on the structure. Seismic data helps to assess the magnitude of the damage and general location. However, seismic data is perturbed by mining operations and fluctuations in the fusion rocket engine output caused by the ship passing through dust or a gas cloud creating a kind of space turbulence. The number one shield is the only one that has

---

[1] Sounds like Kirt.
[2] Sounds like Home, means home.
[3] Sounds like Suzie.

1

limited angles of view, and only a personal visual examination can precisely assess the damage.

Turning back, Kr'T radioed in what Job Control already knew, that the damage is confined to a single explosive panel.

It's been three years since his capture and sentencing and over seven hundred years since the half way point, the braking maneuver and the Touch of God Event.

Had this grain of sand hit, seven hundred years ago, when the ship was traveling at its peak velocity, the damage would have been a thousand times greater. Fortunately, the halfway area of space was tens of light years away from any system, and devoid of anything much larger than hydrogen atoms and cosmic rays.

The ship has slowed down dramatically since and a grain of sand meteoroid only packed the energy of a hand grenade. A large meteorite that can't be detected, avoided or destroyed in time can punch through several of the shields each causing an explosion the size of a house.

Each layer of the shield protects the main body of the ship; the outward direction of the explosion disperses the energy of the meteoroid strike and simultaneously helps to slow the forward motion of the ship. Repairs are made by Kr'T and the other convicts on Kr'T's work detail.

Upon Kr'T's conviction his choice was simple "volunteer" for hard, dangerous work or be "forcibly retired" the CA's (Central Authorities) pseudonym for execution. There's no wasted labor aboard a starship in interstellar space.

As much as Kr'T hates the CA and its oppressive totalitarian regime, knowing that this work is helping to bring himself and his family to their new home on a new world is comforting.

This ship, the only home they have ever known has been traveling for almost two thousand years. They are now only around one hundred years from arrival, and most of his family and friends will step foot on a new world. Kr'T will see it, he's only one hundred thirty-seven, young by most standards, most people on Dadr'Ba[4] live well into their two or three hundreds. Kr'T could expect the same… providing he survives his sentence.

Doing this labor, although benefiting the CA is essential for the survival of his people.

He had taken a risk dangling at the end of only one safety line that kept him from being thrown out into interstellar space. If that line were severed and he wasn't caught by the safety nets shot from catapults along Dadr'Ba's perimeter, he could be lost in space forever. His space suits systems would eventually run out of resources, and he'd slowly expire, never to retire.

A more likely fate would be to get caught in the ship's powerful magnetic field and slowly drawn into the fusion rocket engine intakes. A horrible process that meant risk getting beat up against the sloped meteoroid shields,

---

[4] Sounds like Dah-Dur-Bah, or Daw-Der-Baw, means gift of God number two.

not having the kinetic energy needed to detonate them, then mashed against particle collection plates on his way to annihilation in nuclear fire.

More likely, due to his relatively slow velocity and large mass, he would fly fairly well centered, guided by the ship's artificial electromagnetic field. He would skirt passed the particle collection plates into the electrostatic fields that focus and accelerate the input to the engine, straight into the ultra-strong electromagnetic fields that contain the front edge of the fusion reaction. The heat increasing as he passes each stage he would first fry, then vaporize and finally ionize. His plasma would be squeezed, heated, channeled and accelerated through increasing strong energy fields until finally, his lighter atoms will be squeezed together with so much force that will fuse. Causing the release nuclear energy, the same energy that powers stars, impossible to contain but instead focused out the ships rocket exhaust.

As expected but forgotten, job control came alive over the radio, the noise shattered the intense silence, causing Kr'T to recoil out of the solitude he was experiencing. Kr'T activated his space suits HUD (heads up display) that he had turned off to clear his view of the universe and checked his suit. His suit, a tightly fitted, millimeters thick material that uses direct contact against his skin, and constriction bands to compensate for the intense vacuum of the interstellar space. A compressed air system is necessary only for his face plate and breathing apparatus.

Kr'T thought he could feel a tingling through his suit, imagining the attack of the vacuum, or more accurately the nothingness hid underneath the vacuum. Nothingness so intense, that, over time, acts as an acid, striving to rip away every molecule it can from the intruder. It being nothings way of saying "you don't belong here." Space, especially interstellar space, hates matter, and anything to do with it and at every turn tries to eliminate it. Kr'T then realized that the tingling must be a side effect of him being head first at four G's at the end of a safety line.

Kr'T began to make his way back toward Dadr'Ba and in front of him Kr'T saw the nuclear fusion engine exhaust in the distance, it's small diameter, only meters across, yet impossibly bright giving the appearance of it being many times further away than the five hundred meters that separated it from him. Kr'T could feel the heat and noticed his suit's systems adjust in response, its surface, changing color from a near black to a metallic silver facing the heat, reflecting the thermal radiation as the thermoelectric membrane compensated for the heat that was able to penetrate. Kr'T noticed that the suits thermals were acting a little slow, he'd need to report that later.

The fight between the energetic photons, high kinetic energy ions, and Dadr'Ba's magnetic field produced a kaleidoscopic light show of blues, turquoise' and purple's, with a rare red and orange in front of the slowly decelerating ship.

Kr'T followed up the beam with his eyes as it stretched out as far as his eyes and his suits HUD with its built-in camera system could see. The wave effects causing ripples or bands to run down the beam of super-heated plasma, in turn causing it to disperse slowly. Kr'T used his suits camera and filters to zoom in and see a light show as small perturbations in the plasma jet, causing it to splinter, sending off small jets making the pillar of fire appear to sparkle.

Farther out and very faint today, Kr'T could see the Aurora, waves of color passing across the plasma perhaps thousands of kilometers distant. Caused by the plasma interacting with clouds of hydrogen, (if you can call hydrogen molecules separated by meters a cloud) all to be captured in Dadr'Ba's magnetic field and fed into its nuclear fusion engine.

Kr'T could see occasional streaks of light as the plasma gobbled up larger molecules and meteorites, some perhaps like the one that caused the damage he was now repairing. It must have been one lucky meteorite to have made it through or around the plasma beam pushing out in front of Dadr'Ba. The plasma beam that everyone on Dadr'Ba lives to support, the beam that's retarding Dadr'Ba's velocity preparing it for gravitational capture in our new O'M's system.

Dadr'Ba's artificial magnetic field pushes charged particles out of the impact zone Kr'T is repairing and down around into the fusion rocket intake on the other end of the massive ship. The glare from the blast is so bright that even at five hundred meters away it makes it difficult for Kr'T to see his repair job. His helmets automated shielding system is blocking out too much of his view. He may have damaged it by looking directly at the plasma beam for too long. Job control didn't complain; they must have appreciated the view too. Kr'T adjusted his helmets mechanical shield and pressed on.

Kr'T pulled himself back to Dadr'Ba struggling against the four G's of centrifugal force from the ships spin, thankful that he had been genetically engineered to handle the four G's here at the outer edge of the spinning ship. The force declining to a more comfortable one to two G's where the bulk of Dadr'Ba's population resides within the ship. Kr'T examined the damaged shield brackets and supports and notified job control what components are needed for the repair.

Kr'T secured the damaged plate and mounting bracket then maneuvered on the suspension rails to position himself in the right spot to release them. They fall away, caught on the retention cables and returned for recycling or repair via the same cable and rail system that brought him to the site and deliver the replacement parts.

Once the bracket system is fixed, the blast plate management system will promote the number two plate into the now vacant number one position and number three promoted to number two, and so on until the meteorite shield system is complete and fully functional once again.

The damaged number one plate and brackets fell free dangled on the cable retention system and began their trip back to the ship's maintenance airlock. Kr'T would have a little break waiting for the transport system to return with the repair brackets. Kr'T relaxed to admire the view, wishing he could share this spectacular view with his wife and two children, sending them a mental message of love and how much he missed them.

Then it happened, a larger than average sized grain of sand meteorite, hit the plate nearest to him and the explosive armor material detonated. The odds of this happening twice in the same place so quickly was astronomical. The armor is made to explode in sections and only when struck with very high-velocity impacts. The blast totally obliterated the particle, the force of the blast directed in such a way as to assist with the desired motion of the ship.

A significant portion of the plate exploded in a blinding flash of light. The explosion and blast occurred so close to Kr'T that it made a sound inside Kr'T's helmet in spite of it being in the noiseless vacuum of space.

Had this meteorite struck Kr'T it would have ripped through the flexible layered ceramics that make up the outer layer of his suit, easily penetrating the carbon fiber ballistic material making up the inner shell of the tight fitting suit.

The damage would be catastrophic; hydrostatic shock on his flesh would explode the fluid-filled vessels of his body, possibly sending a shock wave to his heart causing it too, to explode. Depending on the location the exit wound could rip a hole the size of a person's head, or tear off limbs, it would be instant death.

As it was, he and the remnants of the blast plate were exploded out into space with the added boost by the G forces generated at the edge of the rotating ship.

The once taught retention cables flailed freely in the vacuum; useless because the retention cable Kr'T was using was now part of the damage. The remainder of the damaged and detonated plate now came free; its mounting brackets some of which Kr'T had removed for the repair fell free, along with Kr'T. The plate a severely twisted, mangled outline of a shell with many jagged edges and scarred with blast marks followed Kr'T out into space.

Kr'T stunned, unable to move, the echo of the explosion still reverberating through his senses, suddenly weightless, no longer felt control of his body. The ship seemed to cartwheel and fly away as if launched by a gigantic catapult. The remnant of the distorted blast plate spun end over end, a large ragged hole through its center. The spinning plate intermittently blocked Kr'T's view, providing a brief glimpse of the ship. On each rotation, the ship grew further and further away.

The blast had propelled Kr'T at a higher velocity than the plate which just fell away from the ship. The plate began to grow small.

Kr'T had little to do but wait and hope that the catch-net system could target him and Drag him back to the ship. He had no individual rocket propulsion. Dadr'Ba's rotation made using rocket packs complicated and wasted fuel. Individual rocket propulsion fell out of favor for routine extra-vehicular work, replaced by retention cables and the catch-net system that can recover an overboard person up to several kilometers away.

Kr'T was now, thanks to his initial momentum and the blast, traveling away from Dadr'Ba at tens of meters per second. A jagged plate the size of a large conference table cartwheeling between Kr'T and Dadr'Ba with a large hole in the middle, the lifesaving catch-net system on the other side.

Kr'T's helmet camera continued to function, whose wide-angle view showed Dadr'Ba, which up close seemed like scaling a mountain, fell silently away with the blast plate spinning in between blocking most of the view.

The people monitoring the catch-net system frantically worked to solve the life and death problem, the supposedly automated system was having trouble deciding what to do, the programmed priority being to recover Kr'T but the blast plate barred the way making it impossible to target him.

Kr'T's helmet camera automatically switched from normal to low light to Starlight mode, then to infrared bands. His helmet camera sent images of the Starship Dadr'Ba, sent back in a large combination of colors. It's natural and crafted beauty, showed a relatively small comet, as comets go, still over three trillion kilograms, shaped and compacted while soft near the sun into a cylinder shape, a kilometer diameter and over five kilometers long.

The ships core is a fusion rocket engine. Integrated down the central core of Dadr'Ba's bulk, the engine burns over ten kilograms of fuel per second[5]. The rocket produces an exhaust mass accelerated to a significant percentage of the speed of light. Though this thrust may seem large, it's imperceptible to the crew operating a ship with a mass of trillions of kilograms.

This comparatively tiny engines saving grace and real power resides in that it's been running for almost two thousand years. During the first millennium, it pushed Dadr'Ba to a velocity of over ten percent the speed of light and is now working to slow Dadr'Ba down.

Dadr'Ba for all of its operating life has been traveling fast enough for even small meteoroids a problem, even now after decelerating for hundreds of years, it's still going plenty fast enough to turn a grain of sand sized meteoroids into high explosive missiles.

Dadr'Ba's cylinder-shaped main body is capped on each end with meteoroid blast plates designed to sacrifice themselves to protect the ship. On one end of the ship the blast plates are designed to help accelerate it, the explosion is delayed and positioned to blast behind the plate and to blast outward, protecting the main ship while adding a minute amount of thrust and destroy the offending meteoroid.

On the other end of the ship, the end that Kr'T was working on, the blast plates are designed to slow it down, they detonate at the impact point or forward side of the plate, destroying the offending meteoroid and providing in the process a little reverse thrust.

Kr'T's helmet cam now showed Dadr'Ba in its entirety, its main body rotating slowly, enough to provide artificial gravity to its occupants. Counter rotating bands near the ends and midsection became clearly visible, containing the ships docking bays, observation decks, and catch-net systems, shrinking in the distance. It's unlikely that anyone but the watchful on the observation deck would have noticed Kr'T flying away, there wouldn't have been any sound,

---

[5] Though not all of it is fused.

maybe the flash when the plate detonated caught someone's eye, but now he was only a speck in the distance.

The catch-net system finally fires and is quickly wrapped up in the spinning plate; the catch-net line goes taught, almost to the breaking point then slowly starts to draw its haul back to Dadr'Ba.

The Milky Way slowly engulfs Dadr'Ba it shrinks in the distance.

Kr'T is too far away now for the catch-net system to reset and reach him. Had they been prepared for this sort of thing they would have caught the plate right away, and then been able to reset and catch Kr'T but now they don't even waste the energy to try. Someone made a note to send the catch-net programmers a memo to make the change.

Dadr'Ba fades into black against the relative brightness of the Milky Way, and Dadr'Ba begins to move slowly against the Milky Way's starry tapestry, not due to Dadr'Ba's movement but due to Kr'T's capture in Dadr'Ba's magnetic field and is slowly drawn toward the fusion rocket engine's intake.

Dadr'Ba looks small, a short laser pointer held out at arm's reach, firing in a mist, its jet, piercing into space, an iridescent line drawn out into infinity. At this distance occasional ripples different than those seen from close up, move across its length, only noticeable from this distance, probably caused by slight variations in its fuel. Dadr'Ba's fuel contains in part molecules vacuumed up by Dadr'Ba's gigantic magnetic field, mostly hydrogen molecules, collected as it fly's thru space, the rest of the fuel, provides the bulk of the rockets exhausted mass comes from the fuel that is mined and processed out of Dadr'Ba itself.

Visible at this distance Dadr'Ba's exhaust looks laser-like, a shimmering, pulsing, jet scintillating from what must be the result of the rocket exhaust interacting with Dadr'Ba's magnetic field. Creating an energetic conflagration, as the relativistic jet passes through a thin cloud of gaseous particles. Particles and waves working at cross poles, attempting to break the speed of light barrier annihilating each other in the process.

The result is a manufactured Aurora. Seen from this angle, Kr'T can see colors and designs he didn't dream possible and thinks how beautiful it is.

Kr'T remains motionless, one of his retention lines almost caught on a jagged shard of the blast panel as the catch-net wrapped around the panel, stops, then slowly starts to draw it back. It catches Kr'T's line only for a moment, then gave way, but it stopped Kr'T's spinning.

Now Kr'T, deathly still, his helmet cam focused on Dadr'Ba as it passes, or more accurately Kr'T passes by, moved by Dadr'Ba's magnetic field. Kr'T has moved in a long arc around Dadr'Ba toward the trailing end, the intake of the fusion engine.

During the acceleration phase of Dadr'Ba's journey, this engine intake is the front, and the plasma jet trailed out the back pushing it along. Now decelerating Dadr'Ba has turned around and the plasma jet pushing out the front of its path slowing down Dadr'Ba's tremendous mass.

Kr'T can now see Dadr'Ba's fusion rocket engine intake, it looks like a gaping mouth within mouths, the layered edges of sloped blast plates surrounding a throat leading to a fiery gut of nuclear fusion fire.

Further in Dadr'Ba's throat, not far from the fire are catch plates designed to collect precious elements, guided by electrostatic forces that guide some of the heavier elements too big to burn, onto the catch plates. Recovering valuable elements and refining them at the same time.

Kr'T is too massive, and is moving too fast, to deflect to a capture plate, and finds himself looking down the engines maw to a fusion fire. His helmets visual filters strain to protect his vision and allow him the view.

The arch that brought Kr'T to the mouth of a furnace hotter than the surface of the sun was wide enough to prevent a second attempt to save him with the catch-net system. Assuming that the catch nets recovery wasn't intended just for the plate.

It's one of the core tenants aboard Dadr'Ba that nothing is wasted. Kr'T wondered if the remnants of the plate might have been deemed more important than he by the Central Authority.

Most of Kr'T's mass will burn in the fusion fire as well as his tightly fitted Carbon fiber spacesuit and life support system. The CA would have undoubtedly preferred to save the metals and electronics that helped the magnetic field bring Kr'T to this end, but for that to work they would have to be free pieces and particles not integrated into his suit.

Kr'T's path down the throat of Dadr'Ba's fusion rocket engine intake included some high-speed bumps that separated some of the metals and other precious compounds from his suit and life support system. The bumps, his momentum, and inertia along with the electrostatic fields helped to center him in the bore of the intake and kept him from splattering against the heavy element catch plates lining the innermost throat of Dadr'Ba.

It's been a very long time since anyone was lost to the fusion engine; Kr'T may even be the first, at least in official recorded history (since the Touch of God Event and the braking maneuver) to be devoured by Dadr'Ba's engine.

Kr'T's body clips against a particle collection plate, causing him to spin uncontrollably. He's stretched and squeezed by powerful fields. He makes no attempt to struggle, apparently at peace, possibly paralyzed, not having moved since the initial explosion that launched him on this last odyssey.

Kr'T's body reflexively rebels against the forces. Kr'T, through an enormous strength of will, forces his body to relax. His muscle tension eases and his body returns supple, as it slips through the electrostatic fields. Kr'T's heart rate slows as he lets go of his body, and takes back control of his mind. Then gives up control, looking for a way out. It's over in milliseconds, as Kr'T's battered and crushed high-velocity body passes into the fusion fire, and whats left of his body winks out of existence.

Chapter 2, The Birthing

Waking up refreshed, the lovemaking from the night before fresh in his mind, the little death, having released its grip feeling wide awake and refreshed Tu'Tan[6] opened his eyes and turned to see Le'Ta[7] looking at him smiling. "You cheater" He said, trying unsuccessfully to pout; it was supposed to be a win-win. "I know," Le'Ta says, "but I felt that you needed a ten or eleven more than both of us a nine."

She was right, Tu'Tan's parents, having passed only a week before, had taken a heavy toll and although he hadn't fully realized it Tu'Tan had been under a lot of stress. The burden of dealing with his parent's estate was tremendous. The transfer of ownership, fighting with the CA, who seemed to think they had more right to his parent's possessions and credits than the family, was too much.

The CA was trying to impose tax and fees on what little was left, imposing charges for each time A'To[8] had changed jobs throughout his entire life. It was terrible and prevented Tu'Tan from concentrating on his obligation to carry his parent's seed, to give, together with Le'Ta, a birth, a life.

Gathering his thoughts Tu'Tan said: "Last night was great, and I probably needed it, but we were supposed to be practicing to give birth." "I know, but we can always do it again" was Le'Ta's reply, and with a closed lipped smile moved towards Tu'Tan. She reached her arms around Tu'Tan, and they embraced, and then began to make love.

Although their sexual parts were aroused, the focus of their lovemaking wasn't on those small pieces that can be so consuming. They concentrated on the whole body, a whole of existence experience, erasing the thought of separate bodies. They became one and then gradually their minds joined, becoming indistinguishable, they lost awareness of their existence, joining as one, and found themselves cast out into the inky darkness of space with no method of propulsion except their will and their thoughts.

Only vaguely aware of the other, and trying to without trying to move together, failing at first, stretching their connection and nearly breaking their link. Then finally moving together, searching, finding others, but keeping distant, because it's not time yet, this is only practice.

They turned inward and became aware of a feeling, a rhythm, beneath their thoughts they recognized the clear echoes of A'To's and Ba'Ni's[9] rhythm, but don't name them; they are in a world beyond names.

---

[6] Sounds like Two-Tan.

[7] Sounds like Lee-Tah or Lea-Taw.

[8] Tu'Tan's Father's name sounds like Aw-Tow or Ah-Toe.

[9] Tu'Tan's Mother, name sounds like Baw-Nee, Bah-Knee, and Bonnie.

The only way they could move without breaking their tenuous link was to lose everything tangible, solid, anything that can be described with words disappeared. Their world now is intangible, indescribable, encompassing emotions, love, and trust. The fullness and satisfaction from being loved and feeling hearts join, adjusting, accommodating and incorporating two heartbeats into one, feeling whole, complete.

They were in another universe; the rhythm matched the physical selves in the old universe, but here the physical doesn't matter, it gets in the way, it needs to disappear and be forgotten. To think about pushing the physical away, only grasps it, drawing it closer.

No, it's better to ignore the physical and let yourself synchronize with the other, and as the waves of existence beneath the thoughts align, a new pattern emerges, different from the old, a new original pattern where the peaks and the valleys match, magnifying each and where the peaks and troughs align, cancel each other. What remains is a new pattern recognizable, different and similar, like and unlike, at the same time. Working without thought maintaining the new synchronicity achieved and letting go of parts of you, and accepting new found patterns, forgetting your old self and feeling turned inside out. Then much faster than it was achieved the pattern slips away and they found themselves transported back to reality. Sad as if awakening from a dream they didn't want to end they woke as if they just lost a true reality.

After a long pause, Le'Ta says "I think that's what it must be like" and Tu'Tan responded, "I think we're ready."

It was unusual to wait so long; the norm was to perform the birthing as soon within days after a retirement, assuring the grandparents imprint is as strong as possible. But Tu'Tan had to delay the birthing; the CA had been giving him trouble over the settlement of his parent's estate, making it impossible for him to concentrate.

Everyone thought the estate was settled before the retirement, but the CA came back after the retirement, rejecting the award of most A'To's overtime credits, forfeiting them to the CA. Tu'Tan had to dig up documentation that his father, had luckily, kept, then Tu'Tan had to file an appeal.

The last thing a birthing needs is even the slightest emotional stress and issues dealing with the CA over a parent's retirement and the settlement of their estate.

Tu'Tan's emotional stress dealing with his parent's retirement began with the most important episode of his life to date. Important not in a good or bad way, only in that it changed his life and the way he looked at life from that moment forward.

It was the day that his parents retired; it was a beautiful and profoundly meaningful moment, the moment they passed. Hand in hand, side by side, their lives ended in the same instant. Tu'Tan couldn't help but feel a deep loss, and a profound gain.

He lost their company, but in a larger way, he felt they became part of him. In the physical sense, their existence stopped, but at the same instant, they passed to him, those parts of themselves not connected to or dependent on their physical selves.

The love his parents had for each other, and their children passed to him. It was now his turn to carry the families love, name, and values forward. It was his task, duty, and honor to pass as much of what made his parents who they were and who he is to his children.

His parents had a long and productive life. They eventually grew tired and fatigued. To have lived a quarter millennia and without seeing a change or improvement in their lives for over a century fosters a feeling of despair. That's when the thought, then the hope, then the dream of bringing new life into existence takes hold, not only to make room for it but to be part of it, becomes a goal in itself. A'To and Ba'Ni sacrificed their lives to give him birth rights so that Tu'Tan and Le'Ta could have children in Dadr'Ba's zero population growth society.

Then, someday after a lifetime of being head of the family and setting the example, Tu'Tan and Le'Ta will pass from existence. He and his love, his life mate, will pass the baton of love and life, like what was given to him, to their children, not unlike the birthing ceremony that started their children's lives so many years ago.

Retirement, instead of giving life to something that wasn't living before, is synching with the living, and leaving behind tired and worn out bodies. A'To and Ba'Ni hadn't synched with Tu'Tan since his birth. This time, Le'Ta witnessed and participated, Le'Ta had become part of Tu'Tan long ago and couldn't be separated.

This time, the synching was very different, this time, they didn't synch to give strength to initiate life in unanimated flesh, they were too old and too tired for such an arduous task. This time, they synched and allowed their tired, weak selves to be cradled and carried away, leaving behind empty unanimated flesh.

Their flesh became still, the life that was within their bodies faded to nothing. They found peace and tranquility, passing their lives to those that love them.

After his parent's retirement Tu'Tan felt truly mature. All the while his parents were alive there was always "someone there" Ma and Ba, although being for all practical purposes beyond ever needing their help they were there and insisted that they would always be his parents, and he and his sister, their children. Now that they're gone Tu'Tan was beyond their help, even when it became apparent that they had become more dependent on him than he on them, the parent-son relationship was always there. Now that had all changed.

There is no better end to life than to die with family and close friends present, to share the experience. Those witnessing can bid a fond farewell. The one's passing, gives family and friends a final seed or the impression that will live on with them and through them all their lives and perhaps beyond, a kind of immortality.

Tu'Tan's parents lived an average life span, two hundred fifty-three years and two hundred forty-seven years for A'To and Ba'Ni respectively. They married early, both of them in their early fifties and perhaps because they married early, they had more troubles with settling down than most couples. A'To changed jobs as often as the CA would let him until he was nearly one-hundred and seventy-five then finally seemed to settle down and stayed at the same job until the end.

Perhaps bouncing from job to job for one hundred twenty-five years, then to be stuck doing the same job for seventy-five years straight aged A'To early. It's not uncommon for people to live to three or four hundred spending their entire working lives at the same job, yet for all their years they can't claim to have done all the things or gone through half the rewards and hardships (although some self-inflicted) that was experienced by A'To and Ba'Ni.

By the end of three or four centuries, most of these people stuck in the same job are little more than robots satisfying their standards or quotas and going through motions that on the surface would appear rewarding activities but in the end make them empty shells with happy faces painted on them. A'To and Ba'Ni pursued life with a passion for most of their lives, had they not and become robots they may have survived for another hundred or more years. There's no physical reason they couldn't have, the crew of Dadr'Ba being genetically locked clones in a sterile environment means there's no such thing as natural death or death due to age or disease.

Nobody ages, nobody gets sick, and all except for a few dangerous jobs (really dangerous jobs are done by robots and convicts) the CA ensures nobody gets hurt. The age record holders among the commoners seem to top out near five hundred, by that time their minds are gone, they begin to fail standards and quotas and the CA comes in and retires them, or convinces them to retire.

Once selected or approved for retirement, they only have a few weeks free from work to devote to getting their affairs in order before the prescribed termination date even then the time is charged against vacation time earned, deducted from their children's inheritance and the families ranking based on mileage earned from work contributed towards O'M.

Retiree's body parts are said to be donated to those few that have suffered injury, or they may get frozen for possible use later. A'To and Ba'Ni could probably have held out for another twenty-five or fifty years, but the cost they would have paid in mental and emotional ability would have been great. It's better to retire voluntarily while your mental faculties are intact while you still care, while you still love, and while others love you. There is nothing so sad as to see living machines retired, who are not cognizant of what is happening; not knowing that they are leaving anything or anybody behind, incapable of leaving a thought, a wish, a desire, a little piece of themselves, anything, behind. A'To and Ba'Ni had plenty to give to Tu'Tan and Le'Ta.

The birthing was going beautifully, Tu'Tan and Le'Ta were bonded and synced, they could feel the presence of A'To and Ba'Ni, and now together they found what was to become P'Ko[10] like a quiet, secluded pool of crystal blue water on an isolated island in the middle of a vast ocean. As they had practiced so many times before, they gathered their collective being, and like shimmering translucent specters each overlapping and joined. Not just synchronized, but unified, allowing the natural additive and subtractive focus to run their course without complaint, freely sacrificing and accepting self and losing all sense of being, replaced with a feeling of belonging and that belonging, with a common goal of seeking out the still pool of P'Ko.

P'Ko is laying on a cushion on a dais between Tu'Tan and Le'Ta in the Churches birthing chamber. His breath slow and regular, monitored by the med-tech, but dead or more accurately as are all preborn, without brain function, their bodies warmed, and their hearts started for the first time minutes ago, not ever alive.

Exactly where preborn come from is one of the CA's secrets. The prominent theory is all pre-burns had been on board since launch, stored with the passengers in suspended animation, frozen. The minority theory says that they're created as needed in a three-dimensional printing process.

Being GLC's (Gene-Locked Clones) they cannot be born in any normal biological way, their cells don't divide so they cannot grow. They come into the world physically fully developed, but with minds that are, aside[11] from what their parents impart to them during the birthing process, initiating their cognitive functions, a blank slate.

Of course, the people whose work exposes them to harsh environments show signs of wear and tear, but not age. When the wear and tear affect's performance, they can go in and have the worn parts replaced, even whole skin transplants, (the most common repair/replacement) since everyone is genetically the same transplants are easy to perform. Since a certain percentage of people are always retiring there is a ready supply of spare parts; nothing is wasted on a starship.

The MedTech, assisting with the birth had brought P'Ko's body up to the proper temperature, started P'Ko's heart and breathing but could do nothing for P'Ko's brain. Starting P'Ko's brainwave and cognitive functions would be up to Tu'Tan & Le'Ta, with the recent memory echoes of A'To and Ba'Ni providing subtle but recognizable undertones. A'To, Ba'Ni, Tu'Tan and Le'Ta

---

[10] P'Ko sounds Pee-Ko or Pea-Kow. Male names customarily end with o or u and sometimes n; female names normally end in a, e or i. Though P'Ko had not yet chosen a gender, nor would he for twenty-five years Tu'Tan and Le'Ta already thought of P'Ko as a he.

[11] There is also a protected almost hard wired autonomic portion that controls maintenance functions like heartrate and respiration.

need to as one, find and enter P'Ko's pre-born mind and provide the seed of life, of self.

To join like this is exceedingly difficult because it's dependent on the relinquishment of all individual will and acceptance of belonging. The problem is that without will, action is impossible. All participants must at the root of their self, want to perform the act, the act of finding the pre-born and starting its life. The process has to be automatic like a mental muscle memory process, shared by all participants. This process is so complicated that successful firstborns (the successful birth at the first attempt) are rare. It's common for couples to have to make multiple tries and much joining practice to achieve a successful birth.

The composite Tu'Tan, Le'Ta, A'To, and Ba'Ni, is formed, a waveform unlike any of the individuals, yet carrying their most important and powerful traits, good and bad. It moves towards the still pool of P'Ko's lifeless mind and settles upon it and slowly as wind upon water causes ripples and waves, to begin to appear. Slowly the processes of brainwave functions start to initiate, barely perceptible at first, with some intermittent pauses but then slowly grow in duration and magnitude until a clearly recognizable pattern begins to emerge based on the composite mental image of the parents and grandparents.

Initially, P'Ko felt Tu'Tan, Le'Ta, A'To, and Ba'Ni as a single painful stimulus, but gradually came to recognize it as something familiar. Like an excellent massage, he began to feel his body awaken, becoming at first awake, and then aware of body parts he hadn't realized before that he possessed. But something was missing, P'Ko couldn't define it, but the lack of something important made it feel strange. Finally, even without the missing piece, P'Ko came to become comfortable with Tu'Tan and Le'Ta, forgetting there ever was something missing.

P'Ko remembered the peace and solitude from before, before these friendly invaders, little did they know or realize that they had corrupted the serene nothingness from before, before he was alive. This was the beginning of what P'Ko was and could have easily been the beginning of the universe; it was certainly the beginning of the universe for P'Ko. Even empty space before it can be called space existed as nothingness, a pure nothingness, not even corrupted by dimensions, let alone energy or matter.

Why do energy and matter seek to invade something as pure as nothing? First forcing nothingness, to become an empty space by stretching and ripping dimensions into existence, then tearing open a place to enter. Taken as a whole all the universe equals nothing, so why does the universe need to tear itself apart in order to exist? As much as the universe exists, in its totality, it must equal nothing. It's a balance.

P'Ko realizes that being is as important as not being and slowly allows being to come into focus. Without knowing the words to express all that has happened begins to recognize the internal universe and opens the sensory organs that will be known later as eyes.

Suddenly, from nowhere and everywhere was felt an impact, a thump followed by a thump-thump-thump, each impact growing in magnitude, though it was a mental/psychic impact Tu'Tan and Le'Ta felt it as physical impact jarring them and the echoes of A'To, Ba'Ni. Tu'Tan and Le'Ta. They find themselves struggling in a psychic storm, barely hanging on, finally, after several painful, frustrating failed attempts; they find P'Ko in the middle of the tumult and start to draw him out.

Tu'Tan and Le'Ta were told that sometimes the preborns resists birth, but they felt that P'Ko was cooperating, that something had happened to interfere, something from outside.

P'Ko was in a lot of pain and discomfort; it was difficult to see and feel P'Ko in so much distress. They had been told that some preborns fight birth when they suddenly become aware of so many stimuli coming from places unknown, it takes time to sort out what is pain and what isn't. Everything, at first, is pain. Tu'Tan and Le'Ta felt it at the same time as P'Ko; it was pain, and it came from outside, not from his awakening senses.

Tu'Tan and Li' Ta's concentration is so severely shaken that they wake from their concentration, fighting hard to maintain their link to P'Ko but unable to.

Consciousness and back in this universe Tu'Tan and Le'Ta sense and see the intrusions and the psychic impact's effect on P'Ko. It altered P'Ko's pattern with a sharp and distinctive rush, like a strong wind or more like an explosion or concussion on the waves that they built with their combined efforts. The last thoughts imparted on them by the impact before awakening back to the physical world was that of shock, and terror followed immediately with pain and anguish. They realized they couldn't help but reflect this mental energy towards P'Ko, even as he experienced it himself.

Tu'Tan and Le'Ta's greatest fear was that P'Ko was dead, or worse, in some catatonic vegetable state and that P'Ko would have to be forcibly retired. The disaster erased A'To and Ba'Ni's echoes from Tu'Tan and Le'Ta's completely. Another attempt at birthing would not include their presence or participation, a tragedy, and a mortal sin in the religion of Dadr'Ba because it represents a break in the parental lineage[12] and a break with the first Touch of God event[13].

P'Ko's body lay in convulsions, twitching uncontrollably with occasional moments of seizures, his body so tense it would be easy to imagine muscles tearing loose from their anchors. P'Ko's grown body belies the fact the he's a

---

[12] Dadr'Ba society honors ancestor's very highly, due to a couple's decision to retire being decided in no small measure at a time to ensure maximum chance of passing their imprint, their psychic genes to their grandchild and achieving in a small way an afterlife.

[13] All the crew aboard Dadr'Ba are survivors or descendants of the survivors of the Touch of God event, a massive Gamma Ray Burst striking Dadr'Ba half way through their voyage killing the majority of the crew and wounding or maiming the rest. It also marked the birth of Dadr'Ba's official religion.

newborn, conceived and brought to consciousness just moments ago. P'Ko is alive and breathing, but Tu'Tan and Le'Ta are terrified sensing that something terrible is happening, and incapable of doing anything about it. What could be going on in P'Ko's mind? Was P'Ko alive or in some terrible process of dying?

The MedTech looks up from her monitors to Tu'Tan and Le'Ta, and as calmly and compassionately as she could muster, said that she has never seen or heard of anything like this, even the many failed first born attempts never ended like this. The MedTech softly asked if she should terminate P'Ko, suggesting that they could try again another day.

They looked at P'Ko, the expression on P'Ko's face was one of fear and pain, at that moment his eye's wide open, seeing some unknown terror with tears streaming down his cheeks. Tu'Tan and Le'Ta looked at P'Ko and in spite of the obvious trauma P'Ko was experiencing, felt an enormous bond to P'Ko. They psychically examined to the best of their ability and could sense through the dark cloud that enveloped him, that they had succeeded, they were able to recognize the important parts of themselves and A'To and Ba'Ni, that they had implanted on P'Ko. But there was something else, the source of the terror, but it was beginning to quiet down. Tu'Tan and Le'Ta both felt hope beyond hope that P'Ko would recover and be all right.

They empathically tell the MedTech, no! Don't terminate! And take P'Ko up in their arms, comforting him. P'Ko's seizures slowly subside, and he finally falls asleep.

P'Ko remains comatose and unresponsive for a very long time. Unable to eat the MedTech is forced to install a feeding tube to prevent P'Ko from starving to death. Tu'Tan and Le'Ta take turns juggling their work schedule and their saved up CA approved parental time off[14].

The MedTech that attended P'Ko's birth comes to Tu'Tan and Le'Ta wanting to report the anomaly that occurred during the birth. Saying that she did some checking and that it qualifies as what the CA calls a "Touched Birth"[15] The MedTech fearing that P'Ko might have a latent memory from before the Touch of God, and that is what brought on the spasms of terror. If discovered the CA would come down on everyone involved with unbelievable vengeance and P'Ko could very likely be tested, analyzed, forcibly retired and dissected.

Tu'Tan and Le'Ta convince the MedTech that even if they had reported it immediately, the CA would have come down hard on them. Now since she waited, punishments would certainly result. They bribe the MedTech to

---

[14] Parental time off is earned in excess of normal vacation hours, reluctantly authorized by the CA because parents are raising a future crew member that will work, on average, over two hundred years toward the goal shared by all crew members, to take Dadr'Ba to their new home.

[15] A loosely defined term meaning, something that the CA doesn't understand and can't be explained. Touched births include births with suspected latent memories.

remain silent about P'Ko. Tu'Tan and Le'Ta, in their desperation pay more of their hard-earned credits to have P'Ko evaluated by a Doctor, who performed an illegal Bio-Mod (all Bio-Mods before the age of twenty-five are outlawed) in an attempt to help cure P'Ko's affliction, with no apparent effect.

After several weeks, P'Ko regains consciousness and is taken off the feeding tube and begins progressing, although more slowly than his peers.

Despite physical/genetic equality, the personality traits and cognitive capacities, including IQs vary widely. Personality, temperament, and cognitive ability differences are the core of the birthing system, the passing of mental/personality imprints from generation to generation, and is believed to be a product of the Touch of God Event.

The Touch of God Event is credited too with a crucial element of the birthing process, and that is psychic abilities, which varies from individual to individual, like people's cognitive capabilities and personalities. It's said that this ability is what enabled the crew to survive and to recover from what should have been the death of all on board Dadr'Ba and the failure of their mission.

P'Ko survives his rough childbirth and eventually begins school and begins what seems to be a normal childhood.

Chapter 3, A Families Loss

Su'Zi, Kr''T''s daughter, burst through the doorway to the converted cargo container turned camp trailer home, having run the short distance from the community school with her brother as soon as they sensed something wrong.

Hysterical and crying, Su'Zi exclaimed, "Somethings happened to Ba[16] I think..." and couldn't finish the rest.

Ln'Da[17], Su'Zi's mother, already knew, Ln'Da felt something wrong before the psychic impact hit alerting Su'Zi, and had already started searching for her husband.

As soon as Su'Zi saw her mother and felt her mother's search, Su'Zi realized that she needed to find her brother, Sa'To[18], he'd been right behind her a moment ago.

Su'Zi didn't have to look far; Sa'To was outside not far down the alley leading to their camp trailer home. He was sitting, staring out into space with a pained expression on his face. Sa'To being Yng'Gr[19] sensed Ba's trouble even before Su'Zi.

Sa'To was already looking for his Ba but based on his psychic aura, the expression on his face and his trembling hands; he was unsuccessful. Su'Zi got Sa'To's attention and together went to be near and join Ln'Da in her search.

They have no idea what exactly happened, only that Ba suffered a violent end, they don't know where to look for his psychic remains, and there's little time before they fade or become lost.

Ln'Da, Sa'To and Su'Zi searched, like individuals with candles wondering caverns looking for the last ash glow of a candle that had just gotten blown out. Their job was to find the smoldering remains of a husband and father before he's lost forever.

With joined forces they're able to cover more ground faster and detect greater detail. They try using their combined forces to do the psychic equivalent of a shout, hoping, that for a brief instant, it may brighten the output of what remains of Ba's candle, but to no avail.

As they search, they sense others, unfamiliar to them, and avoid them. Even though they desperately want to find Ba they couldn't afford to compromise themselves and be discovered by the CA. Though doubtful that a casual observer could perceive an individual's psychic exploring, a novice would be able to discern a group search, shouting into the ether.

---

[16] Ba rhymes with Pa, meaning Dad or father.

[17] Sounds like Linda.

[18] Sounds like Saw-Tow.

[19] Sounds like and means younger, the youngest and second born to a couple and with the strongest psychic ties the parents.

Psychic searching is by necessity an opening and revealing process. It is voluntarily exposing one's psyche, which is the only way to leave one's physical existence. It is an accommodating process which allows you to get close enough to recognize someone psychically. It also makes it impossible to hide or disguise oneself, or avoid being interrogated. Stealth and deception are impossible; any deception would require extraordinary abilities and even then a good psychic interrogator should find it easy to detect a deception or charade. The extraordinarily difficult effort to deceive would shout out to those present, when engaged telepathically a person is psychically naked.

Kr'T's physical death caused a brilliant psychic burst as he first smashed against a collection plate, was squeezed, crushed, burned and almost instantly atomized, leaving his psyche baseless, foundationless, adrift and slowly dispersing. Unless he could find a friendly host or hosts to join with, he would pass into oblivion, a fate akin to Hell.

What Ln'Da, Sa'To and Su'Zi, attempted was a spontaneous, unrehearsed retirement ceremony at a great distance, in a bid to save some portion of Kr'T's psyche and prevent the mortal sin (in Dadr'Ba society) of Kr'T's passing into oblivion.

Psychic energy like any form of energy has a place, a time, a direction and a magnitude, but it is impossible to tell if psychic energy has momentum. Once foundationless, no one knows if a psyche would get quickly left behind. Since the ship is traveling three thousand kilometers per second, a momentum-less psyche would almost instantly be left behind and lost forever.

Retirement ceremonies are planned far in advance and conducted in a slow coordinated, synchronized way so that everything that happens is known. Yet this didn't stop Ln'Da, Sa'To and Su'Zi from trying. They thought for a brief moment that they found him, but it turned out to be someone else with a similar pattern to Kr'T, and who at the same time they tried to make their presence known seemed to flee in pain and terror. They realize to their dismay that they stumbled on a birthing, and their searching probes may have caused a premature birth or mental damage to the child even producing a stillbirth.

With the shock and dismay about what their frantic search may have caused still echoing the psyche-sphere around them, helpless to do anything about the damaged birth, they turn the quest outside the ship as a last resort, attempting to find Kr'T adrift in interstellar space.

It's a slim, desperate hope, interstellar space is second only in its hostility to intergalactic space, it's a cruel acidic environment that continuously strives to shred whatever ventures into it, of its very existence.

Now Ln'Da, Sa'To and Su'Zi, have to deal with the reality that for whatever reason, be it consumed in fusion fire, cast adrift and left behind, or evaporating under the forces of the nothingness of interstellar space. Kr'T was gone, the worst fate possible for a Dadr'Ba crew member, is to be wasted... on a starship where nothing is wasted.

Chapter 4, Su'Zi's Mourning

Su'Zi wondered the labyrinth matrix of shafts and tunnels, her mind adrift, unable to focus; oblivious to the dangers, hazards and threats her inattention placed her in.

She wandered a vast maze; the result of centuries of mining operations, the T'Bm's[20] resemble giant worms working their way throughout Dadr'Ba. Starting near the core and slowly working outwards in levels, each colder than the one above it, edging toward the outer skin of Dadr'Ba.

Dadr'Ba is slowly consuming itself for the fuel to power its main engine that provides both propulsion and primary power needed to operate.

The infrastructure necessary to operate and maintain Dadr'Ba and its engine is massive. There is mining equipment to collect the raw fuel cometary material. Then there is the material transport system; belts, elevators and vehicles, and the processing plant that refines the raw fuel, separating valuable byproducts and producing a light element rich mixture easy for Dadr'Ba's fusion fires to consume.

There is a multitude of essential life support and ancillary equipment, storage tanks, vats, silos, pumps, kilns and reactor vessels. There are asteroids buried within Dadr'Ba that are mined for minerals and metallic ore and metal refineries and fabrication plants needed to produce everything else needed by Dadr'Ba.

Now with the voyage, almost complete, Dadr'Ba had consumed a third of its three trillion-kilogram mass for fuel.

Dadr'Ba's light weight, almost hollow status meant little to Su'Zi as she wandered deep, down, following the ten-meter diameter tunnels left by the T'Bm's. The tracks run away from the warm core of Dadr'Ba towards its cold outer regions, closer to the frigid hostile expanse of space.

Su'Zi wishes she could go back in time, back to a time when Ba was still alive, but she reminds herself that only fools think of time as a dimension.

Su'Zi doesn't use the light built into the eSuit (environmental suit) she was wearing. She doesn't even echo click; the method miners can use for hearing their way down dark passages. She feels her way, guided by the curved bottom of the tunnel and the steady breeze of Dadr'Ba's circulation system. The system carries warm air from near the center of Dadr'Ba, assisted by massive fans, out to Dadr'Ba's edges and the cold emptiness of space. There it liquefies in stages and gets pumped back to the core as a cryogenic liquid.

Dadr'Ba is a living thing, and like all living things must maintain a delicate balance to stay healthy. Dadr'Ba uses its circulatory system to balance between

---

[20] Sounds like Tea-Bum or Tee-Bim, what Dadr'Ba's call T'Bm's or Tunnel Boring Machines.

the near absolute zero of interstellar space and the fusion fire that propels it through space and provides the energy to support life.

In between the two extremes lay its internal organs, the structures, processes and technology and the thousands of people operating and maintaining it all. The challenge is to maintain the critical temperature balance necessary within each zone to ensure the structural integrity of Dadr'Ba's water ice, frozen organic and gaseous body.

All Life in Dadr'Ba exists solely to support the fusion fire that drives Dadr'Ba. It seems strangely fitting that Ba lost his life there, his molecules burned and fused in the atomic fire that is the life of the ship. It is even likely, that the atoms that made up Ba would be recycled and burned yet again since the exhaust of the engine is rocketing out the front of Dadr'Ba slowing it down.

Dadr'Ba will eventually catch up to this exhaust and with the help of its magnetic field draw many atoms back into its nuclear fire until it can be burned no more, yet still supply exhaust mass. Finally creating a cloud that Dadr'Ba must pass through providing resistance further slowing Dadr'Ba. It may be possible that the atoms that once made up Ba would stay with Dadr'Ba, continuously recycled and make it all the way to O'M.

Su'Zi let her mind wander, unable to focus on anything, not conscious of herself, blindly walking, like a wandering out of body experience, taking strange solace in the feel of the increased chill and gravity as she descends.

T'Bm's have removed vast volumes of ice, frozen gasses and an assorted mixture of various other elements, leaving a skeleton of a structure engineered and reinforced to be strong enough to frame and support the ship while taking every available kilogram for fuel and raw materials to be processed into the necessities of the ship.

The place she was walking through now had walls resembling the ribs on the inside of an ancient sailing vessel, the ribs, crafted for extra strength. In Dadr'Ba's early days the builders hollowed out areas to make temporary living quarters, some of these had been abandoned and forgotten over time.

Some cellar areas of Ol'Tn[21] once occupied by people before the Touch of God are avoided and sealed off, thousands of people died in those spaces, and even though their bodies had been processed in a manner consistent with the time and custom, many believe ghosts still inhabit those areas. They all died without retirement, without passing their psychic seed to their descendants.

Su'Zi wonders if Ba survived the calamity as a spirit, a lost reflection of one's self, surviving somewhere in this reality. Wondering too, if his spirit was lost in space or was he able to make it back to the ship?

Su'Zi passes the active mining zone and now knows where she wants to go; she begins to reflect on the events that have led to this point while her body grows heavy with each step towards her destination forcing her to slow down.

---

[21] Sounds like Ol-Tin a shortened form of Old Town. Each sector has an Ol'Tn.

The artificial gravity induced by Dadr'Ba's spin was set for Zone Two, one hundred to two hundred meters from the core, where the greatest population of the crew works and resides.

She'll soon be approaching Zone Four, and the outer shell of Dadr'Ba, that keeps Dadr'Ba's atmosphere in, and the ravages of interstellar space out. The air Su'Zi is breathing is recirculated inside the eSuit she donned as she passed from Zone Two to Zone Three.

Dadr'Ba is by necessity a cold place made predominately of ice, the insulated personal quarters and work modules of Zones Two and Three originally in place when Dadr'Ba exited Or'Gn[22] have since been rebuilt out of sturdier materials and Zone Two is now entirely above freezing. Su'Zi being born a Mi'Nr[23] has spent the bulk of her scant sixteen years in the lower or non-insulated portions of Zone Three where few except for Mi'Nr's like herself and her family dwell and work.

She plods along, each step becoming an effort due to the increased gravity, without regard for personal safety, oblivious to the dangers almost as if she were already dead.

She thinks of the Se'Ro'Bs[24], disappointed that she hasn't encountered one. The mysterious and deadly creature or creatures are known to roam these zones. Rarely seen, and then only in glimpses, the monsters are responsible for gruesome deaths by disembowelment. They consume their victim's soft internal organs and suck every drop of blood from the unfortunate prey. Few bodies of those gone missing are found.

Su'Zi psychically challenges such a confrontation, welcoming the chance to face down a Se'Ro'Bs or be devoured, and perhaps join Ba. She descends further and slows in the increasing G-forces as she nears her destination, these tunnels are not lit and she uses her light, but set at the lowest intensity, she navigates an obstacle course, along small maintenance and service passages occasionally crisscrossed with beams, struts cross members and scaffolding. The Se'Ro'Bs that had been following her stops at the edge of the obstacles waits a moment, then as if deciding the prey is not worth pursuing through an obstacle course turns and slowly walks away.

She had now passed through and neared the outer edge of Zone Four, the Death Zone. Her weight is nearly more than double the norm of zone two, and she fights to keep from going down on all fours.

The heating systems of the class two eSuit she's wearing are maxed out; it was designed for the temps of Zone Three not zone four. If she weren't exerting herself so much to keep moving and creating body heat, the cold would surely take over.

---

[22] Sounds like Ore-Gin, shortened form of origin, the name Dadr'Ba has for the world they came from. The real name was in the Touch of God and since banned by the CA.

[23] Sounds like and means Miner, one who works in mines.

[24] Sounds like Say-Row-Bus.

She was able to see frost and an occasional frozen patch of some frozen gas at her feet and on the walls. If she didn't keep moving and didn't reach her goal soon, she would perish. Her eSuit, at the edge of its safety margin, began to make a crackling sound as she moved.

She had long since silenced the audible alarm of the suit, but the automated flashing body recovery light had no switch. It irritated her, and she wished she had a wrap to cover it. The flashing caused the eerie sensation of a time stop sequence of movement. The repair patch on one of the pockets of the suit would have been large enough to cover the light sewn into the arm, but she doubted that it would stick as cold as it was.

In the mood she was in, if she died or collapsed, she would rather not be found. After hours of searching and failing to find her father, she only told her mom that she was going for a walk along with a mental reassurance that it was safe for her to be alone. It was only after she walked for a while that she decided on this dangerous course.

She couldn't feel her hands or her feet as she arrived at her destination. She cycled the airlock and stepped inside. Then turned to the panel on her left and toggle on the radiant heat as she closed the airlock.

As the temperature of the suit slowly warmed, the crackling sound the suit had been making stopped and the emergency recovery light stopped its irritating flashing. Su'Zi's Mi'Nr eyes quickly adapted to the infrared light.

Su'Zi paused for a moment, allowing her eSuit to warm up and the feeling to come back to her hands and feet, and reflected on what she had just accomplished. It would have been fatal for anyone but a Mi'Nr. Of the three racial divisions aboard Dadr'Ba; Mi'Nr's are uniquely designed to operate in the harsh environment of the mines. Mi'Nr's are short, stocky, thick skinned, and strong, with the best twilight and infrared vision of all the races.

The most populous race, the "U'Te's[25]" short for utilities, are the most common and perform the majority of jobs aboard Dadr'Ba, they have no special strengths or abilities.

Then there is the management, technical, engineering class or race, they are genetically superior in the areas of memory, and intelligence. They call themselves the guardians or "D'En's[26]," they make up the ruling class, smallest in number, but every one of the five Central Council members are D'En, and the Commander is D'En. D'En's make all the decisions, and they are keepers of and "guardians" of the detailed knowledge needed to run the ship.

The development of the races was a necessity dating back to Or'Gn. Races ensured the right numbers of people with the right abilities were available to run the ship, but only made sense if people were treated like machines.

There's no way for one race to do the job of another race without wasting resources in the form of expensive body modifications. A D'En or U'Te couldn't be a Mi'Nr without significant, modifications and for a Mi'Nr to

---

[25] Sounds like "You Tee" or "U T"
[26] Sounds like "Dee in"

become a D'En or U'Te would be a waste of existing mods. And it's unknown what mods are necessary to become a D'En, but there has never been a Mi'Nr or a U'Te that's been able to pass the application exam for a D'En position.

The D'En's are by far the minority and are rarely seen in the common areas. It's been said that they keep an unusually low profile since the equal job rights revolt. Almost five hundred years ago, there had been an uprising because of the unfair treatment between the races. Some strikes threatened to slow the progress of Dadr'Ba, and the CA had to make an official statement that all races were equal and that anyone no matter what race could hold any job they qualified for.

The CA was forced into authorizing costly Bio-Mods. The CA was able to circumvent what they had permitted by stipulating that the applicant had to be otherwise qualified before the Bio-Mods. This effectively prevented Mi'Nr's and U'Te's from becoming D'En's and most Mi'Nr's didn't want to do U'Te work and those that did seemed to have trouble passing the qualification exams.

And there had, so far never been a D'En or U'Te that wanted to apply to be a Mi'Nr. Mining is looked down upon as hard, dirty, work for the less intelligent and Mi'Nr's are viewed as unfriendly, harsh and belligerent.

The CA was able to guarantee racial status quo by restricting the budget allocated for body mods making it impossible to do a cross-racial body mod, claiming that most of the mods fall into the category of "elective" thereby forcing the individual to pay for the mods from their personal funds.[27]

In the end, the equal job rights protest resulted in no real change in the way people were treated or treated each other, and only further alienated the crew and drove a wedge deeper into the gulf between the races and between the crew and the CA.

Su'Zi wondered if Ba might still be alive had the CA handled the equal job rights situation differently or any number of other situations where CA's response was inordinately harsh. Like why criticisms of the CA are considered a crime? It's understandable that a starship needs discipline, but why can't the CA be freer with the wage scales, medical procedures, spices, and why are there so many secrets? What is the CA hiding?

Su'Zi wondered about these things as she worked her way down the slope towards the command compartment of what was once one of the last crew supply ships to make it to Dadr'Ba before it left Or'Gn's solar system. This ship had instead of delivering its cargo and returning to a dying world, crashed itself into Dadr'Ba becoming semi-buried and the crew rescued.

The carcass of the crashed ship was found by accident years later by Mi'Nr's surveying Dadr'Ba using ground penetrating radar to map Dadr'Ba's density for structural integrity and the safety of future T'Bm operations. The

---

[27] All crew members get a small allowance of ration credits they can use what food, clothing, and incidentals this is the only pay they get. Most people use their credits for food, spices, cheap cosmetic surgery or entertainment. It's also possible to gain incentive pay and bonus paid credits

discovery was kept secret, and a path to the ship was created, the ship and others like it were repaired enough to turn into a network resistance safe houses.

Su'Zi walked down what once was the ceiling and opened the command compartment hatch and stepped inside. It was as she remembered it, this was Su'Zi's and her father's special place. She hadn't been there since she and Ba visited shortly before his capture and arrest by the CASS[28]. She went over to the control panel and activated the command compartment auxiliary power and turned the lever, retracting the forward command compartment shield and the inky blackness of space opened beneath her feet.

The cold vacuum of space lay on the other side of a few centimeters of an optically transparent liquid metal specially molded and constructed to stand up to the extreme conditions of space. The super-cooled metal hydride retains its shape yet still acts like a fluid, virtually impervious to damage by electromagnetic radiation and self-healing even when punctured by micrometeorites.

After nearly two thousand years, the command compartment main viewport remained optically clear showing little damage from its exposure to the ravages of interstellar space, albeit most of that time it was physically protected by the much stronger and thicker outer cover the clear metallic liquid held the vacuum at bay.

Su'Zi took one of the thick mats that had been rolled up next to the bulkhead and laid it out at her feet, and slowly settled her nearly four times normal weight onto the mat and relaxed, staring out into space.

The view and the weight gave the illusion of floating outside the ship, held in the tight grip of an invisible hand. Su'Zi eyed the ocean of stars drifting past. Each time the vast river of the Milky Way passes, Su'Zi imagines the sensation of gravity pushing her toward it. Then as she rotates away, her back to the Milky Way, she faces the sparsely populated diamond studded inky blackness of intergalactic space.

Strangely, she feels comfort looking away from the crowded dust obscured center of our galaxy, while looking away, she gets the urge to turn on her side and curl up, wrapping herself in the blackness of space and sleep. She wonders if that is what death is like and if so, that it wouldn't be such a bad thing at all, especially if Ba might be there.

She thinks about time, about traveling or going back in time, and then the thought struck her that she's doing it now, by coming here. She laughs inside at the novelty of the thought, how at one time the whole of the scientific community thought that time travel was possible.

The fools confused the relative aspect of time; that of keeping track of the ordered movement of things in space, occurring in the present, with a person's mental ability to record past events and predict future events, based on experience, blending the laws of physics with people's perception.

---

[28] Central Authority Security Service.

A rational being, living in the present remembers or can record the events and motion of things and can "travel" in their mind anywhere along the time scale of their memory of the past and their imagined future that they choose.

Su'Zi's memory of the last time she was here with Ba, allowed her to come here, resurrecting in her mind that past, when Ba was still alive, and they were there together. Coming here only assisted with that "memory" time travel.

True time travel would involve the travel of "all" elements involved. To stop time means to stop all the forces of nature responsible for the movement of matter and energy. To stop time means to stop gravity and momentum, the planets orbiting around the sun. To stop time means to stop electromagnetism, the strong and weak nuclear forces, to stop the sun from shining.

To reverse time or to go back, or to set it back, would mean reversing all the forces that control the movement of energy and matter. Turning back time means to rearrange all things back to a previous state. For scientists of all people to think that is possible to move the stars, planets, people and things back to a previous state is clear stupidity, but at the time it was sold to the public, and the scientists profited greatly. Having convinced even themselves.

The reality was, is and always will be, that time travel as once depicted is impossible. The closest that can be achieved is little more than what Su'Zi has already done, and that was to rearrange the present to reflect the way it was once in the past.

These thoughts tugged at Su'Zi making the pain of the loss deeper and more poignant because of the futility of ever getting Ba back. She imagined Ba there, as he once was pointing out the constellations as they flowed by like a repeating River. They made a game out of naming the constellations as they appeared. Su'Zi found herself playing the game with an imaginary Ba and the game becoming a chat or a mantra as she dosed off to sleep.

Chapter 5, P'Ko at School

P'Ko looked up into Dan'Zu's carefully made up eyes, his extra dark under eye makeup and sharp pointed eye arch, aside from saying, "I'm wealthy and can afford expensive makeup" succeeded in adding to Dan'Zu's intimidation factor.

P'Ko shouldn't have had to look up, being clones based on the same stock; they should have been the same height. It was blatantly obvious that Dan'Zu had had an illegal bio-mod[29]. Dan'Zu's family got away with it due to their status as D'En's and paid someone off to accept a made up medical necessity or accident repair.

Dan'Zu had three of his cronies with him, had he not P'Ko thought he may have had a fighting chance, he'd been secretly practicing martial arts, on his own with imaginary foe's, but it's hard to tell what other unseen bio-mods or what training Dan'Zu might have.

P'Ko knew what Dan'Zu wanted; Dan'Zu wanted P'Ko to submit to Dan'Zu's domination. Submit like the three cronies that were acting as his goons.

Dan'Zu was a D'En, one of only a few at school; most D'En's are private schooled, home schooled or tutored. P'Ko knew that Dan'Zu must have done something wrong to get punished by getting sent to a public school. If Dan'Zu got into a fight and it was discovered Dan'Zu would be in even more trouble, but if someone picks a fight with Dan'Zu it wouldn't be his fault.

P'Ko didn't let the ten centimeters height difference intimidate him and while staring at Dan'Zu kept his focus on the surroundings watchful for an opening to escape.

"What's the matter Bo'Ba?"[30] Taunted Dan'Zu using the colloquial term for a baby, usually a friendly reference among family members to refer to a newborn, still in diapers and not yet toilet trained, Dan'Zu turned it into an insult.

P'Ko was almost ten and wore the ninth year, patterned school uniform; name tag, smock, short pants and slippers, marking him as a Ko'Ka[31] or child, when he turns ten next week he'd be a To'Ta[32] or a teenager, having made it to double digit age. The new school year would bring a new uniform.

Being called a Bo'Ba was an attempt to provoke him, P'Ko knew that this spot was in view of the camera at the top of the dome over town center and if he pushed or hit Dan'Zu it would appear that P'Ko instigated the altercation and Dan'Zu and his cronies would finish it, and avoid any blame.

---

[29] Bio-mods are not authorized until coming-of-age at twenty-five.

[30] Sounds like Bow-Bah.

[31] Sounds like Koh-Kaw or Kow-Kah, a pre-teen child.

[32] Sounds like Tow-Tah.

P'Ko remained silent and after a slight pause Dan'Zu followed up with a "Ha! It's as slow and defective as ever; I don't know why his parents ever kept this piece of crap. They should have sent him back for another, or even better, recycled him as soon as he was born". This was particularly hurtful because, though Dan'Zu had no way of knowing it, there was an element of truth to it. The birthing process is far from perfect. Some births fail, and the failed pre-born is either held back for another birthing attempt, or, if the failed birthing is determined to be from a damaged or corrupted pre-born, the pre-born is "recycled." "Recycled" is a nicer, cleaner term for retired, reprocessed and reutilized.

There had been a few times P'Ko had walked in on his parents talking, only to witness an awkward pause and a subject change. He knew they were talking about him.

There was no doubt that his parents loved him. He could feel it psychically, and though they seem to favor his younger brother, P'Ko knew that they had taken a big risk keeping him. All this ran through P'Ko's mind as he faced Dan'Zu and his goons. P'Ko's emotions began to build, he was on the verge of a break down, or exploding.

Then, summoning all his will, P'Ko took a lunge toward Dan'Zu. Then at the last instant when Dan'Zu stepped back and started to block, P'Ko dodged past Dan'Zu's left side to escape through the gap between Dan'Zu and the weakest looking crony and took off running as fast as he could.

Dan'Zu yelled some insults after P'Ko, then seeing the dumb looks from his cronies, shouted to them, "Don't just stand there, let's get him!" and they took off running after P'Ko.

P'Ko, puffing heavily, muscles aching ducked behind the service panel beneath the escalator servicing the stadium lower level. It was close; his pursuers were close enough that had he been a second or so slower they would've spotted him entering his refuge.

The kids chasing him were especially mean today, as soon as school had let out, they gathered near the alley he planned to use to get home. P'Ko tried to take a different route home each day, but this time, they got lucky.

Picking on P'Ko was a game to them, but it was terrorizing to P'Ko because when they caught him, they always made sure they outnumbered him and P'Ko wouldn't have been the first to get beaten up by Dan'Zu and his gang.

Getting into a fight meant the instigator and his family would have to pay for the medical treatment to repair the damage for everyone involved, which can be costly, because being GLC's cuts, scrapes and bruises don't heal but have to be repaired by special medical treatments. Dan'Zu was always very careful to make it appear that "the other guy" started the fight.

A few years ago P'Ko had gotten into a 'friendly' hand slap contest with one of the older members of the gang pursuing him today; it wasn't even Dan'Zu. P'Ko got beat terribly, and it took weeks for the skin repair lotion P'Ko snuck from his mother to mend his damaged hands.

Dan'Zu was a new arrival, this being only his first year, but he's been making good use of his time. Dan'Zu took over the hand-slappers gang and expanded it.

P'Ko's teachers weren't very sympathetic, most of them being D'En, only a couple teachers' aides were U'Te and P'Ko has never seen or heard of a Mi'Nr being a teacher. He had been slow learning to talk and read, so much so that his Yng'Gr began speaking and reading before him.

This wasn't the first time he'd been called a Bo'Ba, other kids when he was younger called him Bo'Ba too when the teachers were out of earshot and even sometimes when P'Ko thought the teachers should have been able to hear.

In a society of clones, uniqueness is prized above just about everything else, but being unique by being labeled below standard is a curse. How can a clone like P'Ko be less than the norm when physically and genetically everyone is identical?

When P'Ko started school, aside from being slow learning to talk and read, when he got older he'd get ridiculed for asking "inappropriate" questions according to the teachers, "dumb questions," according to his classmates.

Questions "like what is good?" and "what is bad?" The questioning, coming from a child, is excusable and perhaps even expected. But when the answer given to P'Ko by his teachers was "the CA is good." and "Anything that brings Dadr'Ba closer to O'M is good." "Bad is anything against the CA." and "Anything that interferes with Dadr'Ba getting closer to O'M is bad." The children are then expected to let it go at that[33].

What got P'Ko into trouble was his refusal to accept the first answer and go no further, P'Ko then asked: "why is the CA good?" The frustrated teacher replied, "because the CA brings us order, but most importantly the CA is bringing us O'M." P'Ko's naive counter of "it's not the CA but the ship and the crew that is carrying us O'M" got P'Ko suspended from school, grounded at home and one of those father-son talks about not questioning authority. In this talk, his father cautioned P'Ko not to draw attention to himself; the CA could open an investigation into what might be wrong with P'Ko, trying to discover why he's asking 'inappropriate' questions. If the CA found out about his birth touch, they wouldn't hesitate to move in to punish the adults involved with hiding a birth touch and take P'Ko way for "study."

Still hiding in the service space, P'Ko's allowed his eyes to get used to the darkness; turning on a service light might tip his pursuers to his hiding spot.

P'Ko's eyes were genetically identical to those of his pursuers, but he had trained himself to see or sense better in the dark, allowing him to navigate in these tight spaces and avoid bumps, bruises and most importantly not get caught in the machinery, which could easily sever a limb.

The crews genetically modified skin was tough, and gene locked to resist radiation and age, but it meant that self or natural healing is out of the

---

[33] Beyond tolerating innocent questions by children the CA has outlawed Philosophy for adults.

question. Healing means going to a MedTech or in severe cases, such as those dealing with the loss of function of an organ, limb, joint, or muscle, a doctor is seen.

Minor cuts and scrapes can be treated with special Nano-bot lotions or salves, but these are strictly controlled and limited, especially among U'Te's like P'Ko. There should be no need for a U'Te to have or need such a thing, the repair lotion P'Ko pilfered from his mother was authorized since she was a tailor making and altering the clothes and uniforms the crew wears. She sometimes injuries or wears down her fingers handling the sewing machines and needles they use.

If the injury is not normal wear and tear or due to an accident caused by one's negligence, the person or his family will be charged for the repair and possibly fined, to discourage the risky behavior that brought about the injury.

Dadr'Ba society is based largely on equality, at least superficially, which children like P'Ko often see through in an instant. There are inequalities throughout all of Dadr'Ba society; between the Mi'Nr's and the U'Te's and between the U'Te's and the D'En's.

Mi'Nr children don't go to the same schools or day care as the U'Te's, they home school or have community volunteer centers where parents take turns working extra to run it. Mi'Nr's don't even live in the same neighborhoods as the U'Te's; their homes are almost always in Ol'Tn or below, or in mobile housing camps near where the mining operations are.

There are even inequities within races. P'Ko knows little of the inner workings of the Mi'Nr's or D'En society but having observed much of U'Te society noted that laborers, like sanitation and food service workers, are treated below that of the knowledge workers, like power and foundry technicians. Mechanics like P'Ko's father and tailors like P'Ko's mother are somewhere in the middle. The kids picking on P'Ko are from the knowledge worker class.

The stratification of Dadr'Ba society is obvious to P'Ko even at age ten and because it's necessary to maintain zero population growth and only enough crew to run Dadr'Ba - families tend to be tied to a job class for generation after generation.

In history class, P'Ko learned of an equal job rights protest that forced the CA to allow for job mobility within and between races. A job application selection and assignment process had been implemented. But it was nothing but show.

The D'En's still held the upper-level management, engineering, scientific and education jobs. The U'Te's were still the utility workers doing the broad-spectrum the utility work needed to run the ship, and the Mi'Nr's worked the mines.

If Dadr'Ba were a living being, the D'En's would be the brain, the U'Te's, the body and the Mi'Nr's, the gut, processing the fuel needed to support the rest. P'Ko admired the Mi'Nr's greatly, of all the crew members of Dadr'Ba P'Ko, felt the Mi'Nr's deserve the most credit for the advancement toward

O'M they've made so far and the ultimate success when they reach O'M, yet Mi'Nr's are the most looked down upon segment of society.

P'Ko made his way through the darkness using only his memory and his practiced night vision to guide him. He made his way up many levels climbing access ladders and structural braces. Feeling the artificial gravity lessen as he made his way up to one of his favorite spots; it lay in the upper tiers of the stadium shielded from the view of the gigapixel panoramic security camera that P'Ko knew to be at the apex of the dome over Nu'Tn[34] center invisible to the naked eye.

P'Ko's spot provided a view over most of Nu'Tn and allowed P'Ko to watch Dan'Zu and his gang search for him. The stadium, a multi-tiered oval with seating for the entire population of sector three, (over five thousand people), provided a spot for P'Ko to enjoy un-surveilled freedom and solitude and a view of most of the dome covered Nu'Tn center.

The buildings around the stadium are comprised of mostly of light pastel-colored, prefabricated structures, arranged in a regular pattern around the town center's two distinctive, key features, the Church, and the stadium. Distinctive in that these are the only structures under the Nu'Tn dome without square angles.

The Church, a large white steep-sided dome, whose sides are covered with Penitentes, tall, thin blades of ice, closely spaced with the blades oriented upward toward star twinkling at the dome's peak. The star above the Church is dazzlingly bright but small enough that it's actually pleasing and inviting to look at.

P'Ko watched as several people walked through the tall arched entrance to the Church. The stadium, constructed by the CA looks to P'Ko like a large shallow cradle, peaked on either end and sloping down toward the middle with gated entry ways in the middle and both ends. Four enormous rear panel transparent displays arranged at each quarter provided universal viewing.

From his vantage point, P'Ko could clearly see Nu'Tn's curved deck arching up on both ends, the inside surface of a cylinder two hundred meters from Dadr'Ba's core, the location of Dadr'Ba's fusion engine heart. P'Ko watched for a moment as people came and went through the portals around the town center towards "capsule flats" the apartments at the domes edge, repurposed and renovated from old fuel excavation tunnels.

P'Ko's gaze drifted up, nearly level with his vantage point to the balconies of high-class apartments. P'Ko wondered what they look like inside; each separate balcony stretched the length of the flat that he shared with his parents and brother. P'Ko Looked up at the higher class balconies, several large and small balconies grouped together with a rib providing privacy from their neighbors.

Directly above him some distance away he could see the tens of meters of specially treated ice, and the dull glow of the fusion engine beyond along with

---

[34] Sounds like New-Ton, variation of New-Town. Each sector has a Nu'Tn.

a multitude of associated machinery, machinery needed to keep Dadr'Ba alive and on the move.

It slowly began to get dark as end shift approached; the multitude of lights from around the machines surrounding the engine began to shut off and the light, diffused by the translucent specially treated ice, began to fade drawing to a close the end of a Dadr'Ba work day in sector three.

P'Ko, forgot about the time and his pursuers as he scanned the scene below him, the Church, the commissary, the sector exchange and its vendors. Then in the fading light, he thought he could make out his mother closing up her tailor shop. He would have to hurry if he was going to beat her home.

P'Ko took one last admiring glance at the fading glow of the massive engine, above, then seeing that Dan'Zu and his cronies had given up their search, the only activity now visible, preparations for a graduation ceremony inside the stadium later that evening. He made his way home.

Chapter 6, Su'Zi's Graduation

Su'Zi could hardly believe where she was, or what was happening, she was seated in the last seat in the last row. But she was here, and she was graduating!

Her class sat in chairs lined up adjacent to the speaker's podium, on the opposite side sat the many officials and teachers that claimed some credit for this graduating class of fifty students.

Where Su'Zi sat reflecting on her family status and overall academic ranking in the class according to standardized test scores. She grew up in mining camps and had been community home schooled in the impromptu classroom that moved with T'Bm as it worked its way around and through Dadr'Ba. Su'Zi felt good about the standardized test and knew that she scored higher than her friend, Ro'Sa, also a Mi'Nr, seated next to her ahead, ahead in the ranking. Ro'Sa's family status was untarnished, Ro'Sa's father had not been a convict accidentally killed on a work detail. Su'Zi was lucky she was allowed to walk; the CA could have just updated her graduation status online and sent her a graduation notice.

Su'Zi felt proud of her schooling, and especially of her teachers who were volunteers from the mining community. There are always many volunteers to teach the mining community's children. In Mi'Nr society teachers are held with the highest regard.

Teachers in a very real way participate in the collective life of the Mi'Nr's on Dadr'Ba. In a way, teaching mirrors the retirement and birthing process. Just like birth and retirement there is a passing of a part of one's self by teaching a child, it's the passing of knowledge and experience from the teacher to the student.

While it's difficult to put a finger on what exactly is passed from parent to child during retirement or birthing, it is often very easy to recollect who taught you something or where you learned of or experienced it. Mi'Nr's seem to recognize this and treat it with an almost religious fervor.

Mi'Nr's view the Up'Lndrs[35] who have allowed their children's education to be programmed under the control of the CA, with disdain and their opinion is that Up'Lndrs are uncaring toward the education of their young. Mi'Nr's feel that their educational system is far superior, though it's not reflected on the standardized tests that the CA creates and administers to assess academic accomplishment.

The speaker, a D'En with a rounded face and a pot belly (from eating too much), was droning on about how important this moment is, marking the

---

[35] Up'Lndrs, sounds like Up-Landers, the Mi'Nr's name for the U'T's and the D'En's who live a soft life in zone two.

transition from being carried to being one of the carriers, from not contributing, to contributing to the forward motion of Dadr'Ba.

This ceremony marks a change of status, an increase in the level of respect, and an increase in responsibility. Su'Zi felt her face flush and heat boil up inside her when the speaker bestowed thanks and compliments to the CA as if the CA had been the ones mining the fuel and raw materials needed to sustain the ship.

The speaker made it sound like the CA single-handedly performed all the functions carried out by the crew. Su'Zi felt her blood boiling and almost ready to explode. She felt as though a hot spotlight was directed at her; she forced her tense muscles to relax. She can't blow this; this is the proudest moment of her life. Her family and friends were watching, and the CA would probably love for a convict's daughter to spoil a graduation. Just so the CA can use it to further their propaganda campaign to undermine the resistance. The resistance is the only thing that stands against the CA and tries to keep them in check.

Su'Zi knew she was on a watch list, and the CA was undoubtedly monitoring her closely, waiting for her to crack, gauging her reaction to the speaker.

Slowing her breathing, Su'Zi forced herself to calmness, still incredulous that anyone could assert that the CA was anything more than a gigantic parasite that had taken control of Dadr'Ba.

Su'Zi saw Dadr'Ba as a living organism, a living thing with people and machines fulfilling the functions of its internal organs, interdependent and cooperating on their own. They don't need to be lied to and oppressed by the CA, an entity that serves no practical purpose in the life that is Dadr'Ba, other than to perpetuate and guarantee its own existence and dominion.

The speaker, having been indoctrinated with the centuries of propaganda and political correctness, equivocated the CA with the crew and Dadr'Ba, when nothing could be further from the truth. The CA imposes a totalitarian system of control that directs all activity on Dadr'Ba giving the crew no visibility or say in the CA's decisions. The CA twists reality, asserting that the crew couldn't run the ship if the CA weren't there to tell them what to do each step of the way. The crew is treated like pawns, slaves, and robots.

The CA claims credit while giving recognition only to those that serve and support their authority. The speaker, a CA official that oversees education makes a damning remark about the resistance and how the resistance is an anti-forward element that has cost Dadr'Ba millions of kilometers of forward motion, and thousands of work-years.

Su'Zi raged internally and forced herself not to psychically, or physically attack the speaker. She felt as though the speaker was speaking to her trying to provoke her, though the speaker faced the stands in the multipurpose stadium. Sector two's entire available population watched; a close up of the speaker displayed on giant screens above, occasional cut screens showed views of the podium, the attending officials and of select graduates.

She looked around at the crowd seated in the stadium wondering what they thought of her, if anything at all, of her being one of few Mi'Nr's in the graduating class and being the very last, the bottom of the social and academic scale. She wondered if they knew anything at all about her situation, was embarrassed for her, or pitied her.

Fortunately, the CA doesn't publish convictions for participating in the resistance. They don't want to call attention to the numbers or penalties involved and inadvertently bolster the resistance. The CA prefers to rely on rumor and word of mouth, reasoning that the resistances informal network communications will target only the resistance and their sympathizers.

Su'Zi projected her attention toward the crowd listening and feeling their response to what the pudgy D'En was saying. At first, she felt a cold chill from the crowd, but as the CA rep continued to drone on, she overcame the chill and allowed herself to feel deeper, she realized the cold chill was directed toward the D'En. Directed her way, she felt a warm breeze, with only a few isolated cold spots like scattered sprinkles of cold water hitting her skin.

Su'Zi felt a wave of heat and recoiled, she sensed one of the cameras recording the event panned across where she was sitting. She tried to close her mind and thought of Ba. He died while working literally on the front line of Dadr'Ba's progress through interstellar space. Instead of getting recognized for his sacrifice, his entire family was penalized, because Prz'Nrs (and the dead) don't accumulate seniority and mileage, which define the families' status in society.

Ba was doing what he believed in, was caught, convicted and died while still helping Dadr'Ba reach its goal. He's helped more than any of these pompous blowhard D'En bureaucrats, even if they lived to be a thousand. Ba's life was cut short, which contributed to the reason she was in the last seat.

The CA notice for her to graduate had made it clear that it would be very easy to arrange for her not to. She would not graduate and not to get the CA funded body mods that come with this milestone in Dadr'Ba society.

Although born with basic Mi'Nr body mods, without the CA funded mods Su'Zi would remain, not an adult, without recognition as a real mature person, no matter how many distance credits she collects or age she reaches. Su'Zi wouldn't even be a "she" though, in her mind, she sees herself as one[36], the body mods that accompany coming-of-age are too costly for her or her family to afford, she would always be a "U'Ne"[37] or a "Per[38]" neither a him or a her.

---

[36] From childhood kids are allowed to assume whatever sexual orientation they like and often switch back and forth, experimenting especially in the Ko'ka years, usually settling down in the To'Ta years. The fact that the physical equipment doesn't get installed until after the Touch of God Initiation Ceremony after graduation doesn't stop kids from gender experimentation.

[37] Sounds like you-knee, without sexual organs.

[38] Sounds like purr.

Su'Zi needs these body mods to become a fully functioning Mi'Nr, without them; she'd only be capable of menial work, be pitied by everyone and could wind up an outcast.

Outcasts are a shunned people, 'ordinary' people are afraid to associate with them, they're considered physically or mentally defective or deficient. And many believe outcasts are criminally insane.

Some outcasts scrape together or steal enough credits to do some cheap black-market body mods, but the mods are usually of such poor quality and workmanship that they look even more out of place and deformed after the mods.

Outcasts often wind up withdrawing or dropping out of society and may fail to meet quotas in their menial jobs which could lead to forced retirement, some just disappear. A few outcasts can be found living in the dark corners of Ol'Tn possibly forgotten by the CA, but most likely left by the CA as a reminder of the brutal power the CA wields.

Ro'Sa nudges Su'Zi with her foot; startled back to the graduation ceremony Su'Zi follows Ro'Sa up to the stage. It's almost her time to be recognized, the CA rep that had been talking earlier; the extra pudgy D'En has long since gone from the podium. He and the sector two's school superintendent, also a D'En but not chubby exchange the student's juvenile/school badges for crew member/vocation badges.

The announcer identifies each student by name and their new profession, along with their academic record and family seniority. When it came time for Su'Zi, she was announced as an apprentice carpenter and surprisingly, her higher than average academic record, no mention whatsoever was made to her family's seniority.

Her apprenticeship assignment as a carpenter meant she'd be working in the mines.

Su'Zi returned to stand next to her seat, she and Ro'Sa hugged and patted each other on the back then waited, and on cue as a group, sat down watching anxiously as the announcer read the closing remarks.

Su'Zi's heart rate finally began to return to normal, and she thought of her parents, wanting to call them, but the graduation organizers made them leave their TaC-B's[39] at home.

As if on cue Su'Zi felt a comforting psychic connection as she thought of her parents, her brother, aunts, uncles and cousins and she responded in kind. She took comfort in that privately, within the small, tight circles of the resistance she'd be honored and above all she knew beyond all doubt that Ba would be proud of her.

As with all Ol'Dr's or firstborns, Su'Zi's alignment is more tightly linked through the parents to the grandparents, who she never met. Parents see or feel a similarity between the Ol'Dr and their own parent, so Su'Zi's parents treated her more maturely, almost honorably and expect more from her as well. Yng'Gr's usually born a year or so later are much more tightly aligned

---

[39] Sounds like Tack-Bee, Tracking and Communications Button.

with the parents. Su'Zi is confident that next year when her brother Sa'To graduates, her parent's pride will have a different flavor.

Sa'To was the Bo'Ba of the family, got more favors, more lenient treatment for infractions, and more displays of affection than Su'Zi got. But Su'Zi received a more mature kind of love, almost as an equal and perhaps in some ways more profound.

It was time to exit the Stadium, Su'Zi's stomach was grumbling; the graduates were told not to eat for ten hours before the ceremony. She noticed the group in front of her beginning to rustle preparing to stand.

No one that Su'Zi talked to would say anything about what happens next and from what Su'Zi could tell nothing was told to any of the other graduates as well. All the graduates know is that they leave the Stadium and go to the Church for the Touch of God Initiation Ceremony. Nothing is told about what happens in this Ceremony, it's not a CA secret, it's a Church Secret, even more than that, it's a Dadr'Ba secret, one linked to their very existence, and one that every citizen of Dadr'Ba learns upon adulthood.

They all stand and begin filing out of the stadium to a standing ovation. Su'Zi recalls the last words from her mother before leaving for the ceremony; she said: "learn from what you don't know and think twice before acting."

Chapter 7, Su'Zi's ToG Ceremony

As the initiates grouped up outside the stadium, Su'Zi spotted something that froze her with fear. Then she desperately looked for a way to escape as five soldiers moved in from quickly opening gaps in the crowd of onlookers that met them outside the stadium. The soldiers quickly formed a perimeter around them. They were armed with riot batons, dual wielded, one in each of its primary arms, which in the hands of soldiers can be lethal. Su'Zi wanted to run but knew it would be useless.

Soldiers are rare, the last time she saw one was during the early morning raid when her father was apprehended and arrested, having already been convicted by the CA council without ever being able to present a defense.

The soldiers swept into their home in the middle of the night, using their great strength to force the door locks like they had been made of putty. The soldiers rushed down the narrow hallway of their cargo container turned camp trailer home closing and sealing Su'Zi's and Sa'To's bedroom doors with some strange material that held fast for hours then just crumbled away.

They knew just where to find Ba, who knew better than to try to resist. Even though they didn't resist the soldiers stunned both Ma and Ba, and took Ba. They were in and out in less than a minute.

The raid had been totally unexpected. It was at a mining camp filled with psychically aware miners at the lower reaches of zone three. The CASS soldiers got away with it by using stealth mode soldiers wearing special suits that dampened the sound of their muscles firing, and being robots, were undetectable psychically. There were none of the usual D'En handlers accompanying them whose psychic presence would have tipped the community off to their approach.

All they left was their stench and an arrest warrant/conviction/notification tag that provided the computer link to view the referenced documents which had large sections conveniently blanked out, marked classified.

Su'Zi had never before seen a soldier up close like this, the expected response from Mi'Nr's is to turn away or even cower, not to look directly at it. She studied the one closest to her, looking for a weakness and planning to report her findings back to the resistance after this was over. Assuming that the soldiers weren't here to apprehend her.

Soldiers are robots; they're bipedal with two primary arms and two secondary arms. The two secondary arms are usually folded neatly against the body and come into use when the soldiers need to go to high G areas, forced to go down on all fours.

The secondary arms, then allow the soldiers, to handle weapons while retaining the full range of movement while on all fours. Su'Zi noted that these soldiers had a vest or harness that could be used to carry additional weapons or supplies all within easy reach of both the primary and secondary arms.

At first glance or maybe in the distance their silhouettes could be mistaken for an ordinary person, but on closer examination, it becomes quickly apparent, by the way, they move, their arm positioning (always ready to strike) and extra wide stance that they are machines.

They stand on a ball joint ankle on four broad toes that serve as an omnidirectional foot, which has no front or back. Their mechanical arms and legs are also extendable meaning that as needed they can grow in height to more than three meters.

Soldier's hands are composed of reversible opposable digits on the end of arms that function equally well forward or backward. They're topped with a head that can tilt but not turn, it has no need to turn, it has forward, backward and sideways sensors, enabling three hundred and sixty-degree view of their surroundings without the need to pivot, and makes it impossible to sneak up on one.

The batons they wield (the same can be said for any of their weapons) can be used equally well forward and backward on double jointed arms.

There was no way of telling for sure if the soldiers are protecting the initiates or preventing their escape, Su'Zi couldn't even say whether the soldiers were facing the initiates or the crowd. Su'Zi gathered her courage and stepped out of the group of initiates toward a gap between the soldiers and in what seemed like a millisecond the two soldiers closest to her hyper-extended their arms, the riot batons also extending with a snap becoming a staff, blocking her path. She feigned naive astonishment and embarrassment "Oh! Excuse me" and retreated back into the group. As quickly as her way was blocked the soldiers retracted their arms and batons and returned to an on-guard posture.

When interacting with a soldier, it's impossible to tell if they're paying attention or not, it's always safest to assume they are.

Neither of the soldiers that blocked Su'Zi's path made a sound, except for the snap of their batons as they locked into the extended position. They only move when necessary and remain still as statues, their omnidirectional sensors enabling them to monitor their entire environment without moving a millimeter.

And they stink, these soldiers smell as bad as the ones that took Ba. It made Su'Zi's empty stomach churn, a wave of nausea came over her, and she got light headed. Ro'Sa appeared at her side and guided Su'Zi back to the center of the group of initiates, away from the stench.

Su'Zi realized there was no way out, and she must not be in any immediate danger, telling herself that this must be part of the Coming of Age Ceremony that's been going on for hundreds of years but not talked about. Then she remembered her mother's advice "learn from what you don't know and think twice before acting." She must restrain herself, watch carefully, and learn, starting now she's in new territory, she knows that she will survive and when it's all over she will be a different person, an adult and a full member of the crew.

As she was coming to the realization that the soldiers are programmed to "escort" them, she heard the Church Elder that had greeted them at the front of the group confirm her deduction. "The soldiers are here to provide us a safe escort to the Church and into the Ceremony Chamber, there's nothing to be afraid of." The initiates formed up two abreast and led by the elder along the path to the Church, the soldiers forming a perimeter around them.

The initiates made their way the short distance to the Church following the Church Elder who walked with a limp. There they meet up with several Church Ushers that accompanied them inside. All the Church officials, were easily identifiable by their long white robes and inky black tunic's with a small, single four pointed star and halo on the left breast and a much larger one centered on the back. Su'Zi, last, pauses a moment and looks back, which elicits a red warning glow from the crown of the soldier following up the rear. She turns and hurries to catch up with the rest.

They enter into the Church without the soldiers and file along the side wall to the back, then through a doorway, then halfway down a hallway through another door to a set of stairs. Down three flights and through a door and a corridor that seemed to cut back under the central part of the Church above, all this under the escort of the ushers.

They finally enter a large room nearly as large as the main chamber of the Church they first came into. This one they entered through the back and onto its raised dais. Facing across from them stood a large arched doorway with double doors.

Su'Zi could see that the door in front of them looked as though it had been closed and hastily barricaded. The barricade looked a jumbled mess, haphazardly constructed, using materials from inside the Church, mostly piled and broken pews.

This barricade was old, the surface sealants and plastics of the barricade were decaying, peeling and cracking, all appearances indicating that it hasn't been touched in many years. Su'Zi began to think that this place must be a remnant of the Touch of God Event eight hundred years ago, a Holy Place.

It had been a long day, and the initiates had been told not to eat or drink anything after breakfast, it was now late evening, and Su'Zi was tired, hungry and thirsty. She hoped that after all the accolades from the graduation at the stadium that some dinner or feast was in order, but there was no sign of food and the ushers were nowhere in sight.

The Church Elder, a kind looking U'Te limped to the center of the stage. She introduced herself as Ra'Chl[40] and asked the initiates to be seated in the chairs on the right-hand side of the dais, old metal chairs bolted to the floor, reinforcing Su'Zi's impression that this is a ceremonial place. Every effort made to keep the chamber the same for hundreds of years, preserving the look, feel, and orientation of the site for the ceremony that is to come. The initiates

---

[40] Sounds like Ray-chill, Rachel.

seated themselves and Ra'Chl congratulated them on their achievement and said that the ceremony was about to begin and soon after they would be able to eat and drink.

Ra'Chl continued, explaining that they were now in an ancient section of Dadr'Ba one of the few places where survivors gathered after the Touch of God. Ninety percent of all life on Dadr'Ba perished instantly on that day, and the rest were sick or injured to the point that many of them died of their injuries. But some survived, and we are the descendants of those survivors.

That day changed Dadr'Ba forever; no-one escaped the Touch of God, and the Touch of God raised the consciousness of all, and bound the survivors together with a shared purpose, through shared struggle and pain. Together they helped each other recover from their wounds and restarted the main engine that executed a fail-safe shutdown, having left the ship running on emergency and auxiliary systems.

The survivors became the seed of a new civilization. They became a society of the tough, and the strong, that know how to work together and sacrifice. They came back from death, helping each other rediscover the lost knowledge needed to run the ship and overcome the hardships and the pain of losing friends and family.

I will now show you a glimpse of that moment and with that, Ra'Chl limped behind a curtain on the other side of the stage. The lights dimmed, and everyone expected a holograph or something to appear out over the central part of the Church they were facing where the congregation would normally sit.

Instead, there was pain, excruciating pain, paralyzing seizures and gut-wrenching spasms. Su'Zi could see nothing but a bright field of light as electricity raced up and down her limbs and her spine, her head feeling like exploding. All that was left in her supposedly empty stomach surged upward spraying the back of the chair in front of her. Su'Zi doubled over and collapsed to the floor, the pain vanished, but the effects remained; her body was in convulsions as she felt the floor hit the side of her head again and again. Finally, the convulsions subsided as she and all the other initiates faded into blackness.

P'Ko having been sound asleep in bed suddenly woke, overwhelmed with a feeling of vertigo, the room spun and twisted, P'Ko trying to reach out and stabilize himself rolled himself off of his bed onto the floor where he remained splayed out until the spinning stopped. Afterward he sat up wondering what happened for some minutes, and then crawled back into bed; feeling exhausted and fell back asleep.

Su'Zi didn't know anything. If you asked her, she wouldn't have even known her name, time had no meaning, but she gradually became aware. Not yet self-aware because, she was unable to recognize her body, or even if it existed, it seemed like she floated as if in deep space and that nothing existed in the universe. She gradually got the sense that she was tumbling. All was still pitch black, the tumbling increased changing from a tumbling in one plane into tumbling in many planes. Nausea came over her; a mental nausea building up pressure in her mind, ready to burst. Then she spotted what she thought was a light, flying past at crazy, changing angles. She focused on the light, grasping for it with all her will. It was difficult to spot, often she'd miss it as the tumbling caused the light to appear almost in random places and it was very far away.

Slowly, requiring all of her concentration she was able to catch and mentally grasp the light, the tumbling slowed and finally stopped. All that was in her universe was the light; she focused all of her concentration on it. She gradually realized that the light had been out of focus, that made it appear larger than what was, now as she focused on it, it became smaller and brighter.

Continued concentration began to yield information, Su'Zi thought of the light like a distant star in the vast expanse of black space. She just knew these terms with no worded definition, voice or idea, spoken or remembered came to her, from outside her existence, wordless, but the meaning was clear "Learn from what you don't know" all these words or ideas she comprehended but would be unable to describe. She resumed her concentration on the light, as she concentrated and focused on the light it seemed to grow larger, brighter and closer.

It must've been a great distance away; there was no concept of time passing, she just concentrated on the light. The light being the only thing in her universe. The light gave her comfort and an inviting feeling, like there was someone there, a friend, waiting for her. The light guided her through the darkness, voicelessly calling to her and seemed to provide energy.

After a while, she was able to discern an edge or crescent as the light got brighter and closer. It began to look like a spotlight, and she could see the light, like a star, a sun, and feel the warmth from its rays. Su'Zi relaxed and basked in the rays of the friend, the light, the guardian, and the light engulfed her and along with that came her memories of Ba, Ma, Sato, Ro'Sa and others. Su'Zi realized the light friend was not Ba, but something or someone else. As she came to that realization, the light began to fade, along with the feeling of nearness to the Guardian's presence, God?

As the light faded colors began to appear and from these colors, shapes began to form, the realization that she had a body and that she was lying face down on the floor in the old church, where many of the survivors of the Touch of God gathered and she wondered if there was a God? She felt she was certain that there was somebody, a presence, a will behind the light that guided her back in from the blackness that the pain had taken her to because she was able to remember everything.

She hated the trick that was played on them but was thankful for the experience. She blinked her eyes and the smell of her stomach contents she was laying in filled her senses and another set of spasms radiated up from the pit of her stomach but produced nothing. She struggled to her hands and knees and sat upright, taking in her surroundings.

She was one of the first ones to recover, fear that some of the other initiates were dead or lost in the abyss swept over her, and she crawled from one to another of her grad-mates finding each breathing normally with a strangely composed almost pleasant expression on their faces. She left them untouched to finish their journey with the help of the mysterious Guardian.

Several other grads had awakened and were coming to grips with what had just happened and what the others had and were going through. Each one quietly contemplating what had happened taking in their surroundings.

Everything looked different, as the color, hue and intensity had been increased Su'Zi even became more aware of her peripheral vision and with a sudden realization looked around and saw Ra'Chl and the Ushers had returned and were standing quietly watching with a calm approving expression on the faces.

Su'Zi sensed that they wanted this event to complete naturally, without interruption or modification and she sat quietly soaking in her surroundings contemplating what had happened. Soon, in spite of her surroundings her hunger pains returned and one of the ushers as if on cue went to a table and picked up a biscuit and a small energy drink and offered it to Su'Zi, still sitting on the floor, near where she fell. Su'Zi accepted it gratefully as the usher gave her an approving pat on the shoulder.

It took several hours for everyone to recover, yet Su'Zi was in no hurry, as were the rest of the awakened, the biscuit and energy drink quelled the hunger pains, and a peaceful warmth took its place.

Once everyone was awake, Ra'Chl asked everyone to get up and step down the stairs and to wipe themselves off, using a cleaning towel handed to them by an usher at the bottom of the stairs and to take a seat on the pews. Once sitting in the pews, the Ra'Chl began to speak.

First of all, Ra'Chl, apologized for the deception. Explaining that the original Touch of God didn't give any warning either. The Touch of God happened just as suddenly, and even more unexpectedly, since the grads, as off guard as they were, knew or anticipated something was going to happen, just not what. And said that they could believe what she was saying because "I was there, during the First Touch of God." A gasp ran through the gathered grads, that would make Ra'Chl over eight-hundred years old.

Ra'Chl went on to say the First Touch of God was more painful than what they had just experienced and sickening to the brain. And included long-lasting systemic effects, numbness, tingling, tremors, paralysis. It was then that the initiates noticed the trembling of Ra'Chl's fingers, it wasn't that she was nervous, it was that she carried a mark or sign from the Touch of God, and it also explained her limp.

"The electronic shock that was used to give you a glimpse of the Touch of God was real and carefully calculated to bring you to the edge of death so that you may know God, and that if God is willing, return you to life." "Rest assured that though the success rate for this process is high, there are no guarantees. We were lucky this time; Sector Two had no losses. But there was a loss in Sector One and Four. We make no attempt to interfere with God's choices." "Had you tried to interfere we would have prevented you."

"I'm sure you can understand why it's important that the sacred knowledge that you've gained here today must remain a personal secret and never, ever be shared with an un-awakened, penalty for disclosure of the sacred knowledge is severely enforced without exception or hesitation." And then, as if answering Su'Zi's mental question Ra'Chl added, "This is a Church secret not a CA secret."

They were then made to swear an oath of secrecy under the penalty of death, never to reveal the nature of the Touch of God Ceremony they had just experienced.

They were told that God's will is God's will, and that there've been instances of lost grads. God chooses not to appear, or the initiate cannot find God, and the initiate is lost, never finding their way through the darkness, to die lost in the darkness and never knowing God, retiring without passing a piece of yourself on to your descendants. Su'Zi thought of Ba. The Elder concluded with the reminder "The Church suspects that God refuses to appear to those with advanced knowledge of the ceremony."

The Awakened were now guided to another section of the Church and allowed to clean and shower, then given a clean, white robe. Their old soiled undergrad clothes were bagged for recycling. All the grads were careful to keep their crew member badge and displayed it proudly on their new, clean, white robes.

Each of them was given an appointment for their bio-mods and taken upstairs to their waiting families. To Su'Zi's surprise, there was a crowd waiting outside the Church, unlike graduation, where the whole sector attended, there was only the immediate family of the awakened, there was loud applause and occasional cheers as each of the awakened strode out into the broad light of a Dadr'Ba midday. Su'Zi didn't know how much time had passed, but she guessed that it wasn't the following day, but more likely the one after that. She walked out to a cheering crowd, and almost immediately was almost knocked over as out of nowhere; she was grabbed and hugged by her mother and brother. Su'Zi chocked up, short of breath as all she could think of was that Ba was missing this.

Chapter 8, Su'Zi's Bio-mod

Su'Zi having already been apprenticing as a carpenter went directly to work the after she got home from the Touch of God Ceremony, she'd have to wait her turn for her bio-mod appointment.

Su'Zi's primary task in the days before her bio-mods was securing and sealing the tunnel close behind the tunnel boring machine cutter head this work was internal to the T'Bm and in a somewhat controlled environment.

Once Su'Zi has her bio-mods, her duties would include maintaining the high-pressure duct system that carries raw fuel to a staging silo and the elevator up to the fuel processing facility. These tasks meant spending most of her time outside the protection of the T'Bm inspecting and maintaining kilometers of ducts and raw fuel transport systems.

She anxiously awaited her bio-mod appointment. When the day finally arrived, it was the same as with graduation; hers was the very last appointment of all the graduates in sector two.

Su'Zi selected her bio-mods with great care and deliberation. In a society of clones, individuality is highly regarded and sought after, which results in some pretty unique and garish combinations of bio-mods.

Permanent hair is viewed by many as a must. Hair has the practical aspects of insulating and cushioning the critical components of the head. It also offers clones, striving to be individuals, a huge variety of colors, textures, and styles which, along with permanent tattoos and cosmetic facial structural modification can have a dramatic effect, often changing the person's whole personality.

Given the birthing process is equally divided between genders and the necessity for zero population growth, both prospective parents have an equal incentive for picking the perfect mate, which would ideally mean finding a pairing that complements each other while enhancing their strengths at the same time minimizing their weaknesses.

However, this is rarely the case, the vast majority of couples choose their partners based on love.

Gender role development in Dadr'Ba society is unique. Many children like Su'Zi know very early on what gender they want to be, there's no explanation for it, they just know. Early gender self-recognition is common, but sometimes it just takes time and children are free to experiment and behave in whichever gender role they choose. Children that don't resolve their gender identity sometimes run into problems when they near coming-of-age, undergo the Touch of God Ceremony and are awarded their CA sponsored bio-mods.[41]

The norm is that the graduate upon selecting their body mods and their sex will pick an individual or couple to teach them how to use their new equipment. These mentors will guide the Lr'Lng[42] in the ways of sex.

Sex is for many a recreational activity, particularly among the young. Since sex is not involved with birthing, (the whole crew is biologically sterile), there is no risk of unwanted pregnancies and the associated paternity issues. And since DadrBa is a sterile environment, there's no danger of the spread of disease (although climaxes or resets occur, there is no exchange of body fluid). So sex aboard Dadr'Ba is a physical activity used as a physical, mental and psychological stress relief and is often linked to self-image and esteem and group/pair bonding.

Choosing a partner for a mate and forming a committed relationship, is for grownups, those people that have reached a level of maturity, usually at least fifty, more often a hundred or more years old. The joining ceremony at the Church, registering the union with the CA and moving from the single dorms to the family apartment is a significant milestone in a person's life.

Mate bonding is a commitment that often involves a level of sexual monogamy at least until the couple has been together long enough to cement their relationship and build a level of trust, and to become perhaps a little bored, often several decades or more. A mated couple is together for a century or more, and the bond of trust, love and commitment goes far beyond the physical.

Su'Zi had chosen for her mentors, Pri'Api[43] and Ti'Reso[44] a married couple that had been together for over a hundred and fifty years, had birthed two children of their own, had been mentors to dozens, and possessing an outstanding reputation. When Su'Zi asked them to mentor her, they gladly accepted and offered advice on the best sexual bio-mods. In the end, Su'Zi took their recommendations and picked her skin tone, hair color, permanent tattoos, facial features. She had less control of the job-related enhancements, particular ones were mandatory, others optional, allowing her to withstand better the cold, dark, harsh environments, especially in the lower part of Zone Three where current mining operations have progressed to and eventually the "death" zone, zone four.

Su'Zi reported to the Med Clinic at the appointed date and time. Su'Zi would be asleep for the procedure and wake up at Pri'Api and Ti'Reso's place

---

[41] The one time in a person's life the CA authorizes a fixed amount of credits for bio-mods including sexual assignment, which is usually enough for a male or female bio-mod, but not both.

[42] Sounds like Ler-Ling, rhymes with learning and yearling, an apprentice to a sexual mentor.

[43] Sounds like Pre-ah-pee.

[44] Sounds like Tee-Rez-Oh.

and get her first lesson on the use of her new equipment. She checked in and was provided a sedative, after which she remembered nothing.

Chapter 9, Dr. Pan'Ju[45] Performs Su'Zi's Bio-mod

The surgeon, Dr. Pan'Ju, studied the bio-mod order on the screen. Then, with a swipe of his hand panned down to the mentor section "I knew it," he said to himself, noting the mentors, Pri'Api, and Ti'Reso in the mentor block.

Although not always the same P-T's (Pri'Api and Ti'Reso) bio-mods are personalized based on the individual yet have a certain flamboyancy to them that Pan has come to recognize.

P-T has performed lots of mentorships and provided many more bio-mod recommendations. This tops them all; it pushes the envelope of their flamboyant standard to the limit. It's a little over the personal discretion bio-mod budget, but as the surgeon in charge, he has some discretion and knows how to get past the CA's audits.

P-T must be doing something right, though; Pan hasn't had a single request paid or not, to reverse or undo any of their recommendations. There have been a few requests after the fact to add more to the bio-mods that P-T has recommended, but Pan suspected that it was due to a reluctance on the individual to go all the way with P-T's initial recommendations and not the recommendations themselves.

The sexual mods on this one are extensive P-T must be getting feedback from some of their other clients, the cosmetic mods were standard enough, hair, skin tone basic eyeliner a little extra fullness here, no reductions. This one wants to accentuate a shapely figure, much more than the latest trend; this one will be a real looker even spotted from a distance, more of a classic almost retro look.

Nowadays the emphasis is trending to a slimmer, demure look. Pan checked the family status... very near the bottom. No wonder she was the last on the list of the graduation bio-mods. Ordinarily, this bio-mod order would be over the authorizations for someone of her class. The scheduler should have probably not allowed this order to go through, but undoubtedly left that decision to the attending surgeon, which is sometimes the case.

Then he checked her job classification, which ordinarily would've been the first thing he checked, but the sex mod had distracted him. She's going to be a Zone Four Mi'Nr and requires the deep mining package, extreme cold, low light vision, High-G joints, reinforced skeleton and core muscles and, of course, endurance. She's going to be working down near the outer reaches of zone four, the death zone. She's going to need all the help she can get; a little extra volume here and there will provide room for the additional strength, energy, and insulation she'll need to survive.

---

[45] Sounds like Pan-Jew, his nickname or familiar name is Pan.

Before he closed the order narrative and submitted the requisition that would automatically retrieve the parts from the automated warehouse, he noted the scheduler comment. "Thank you" in the comments area.

Pan will make this an extra special mod, this being the last of the grad bio-mods and with no others scheduled; he won't have to deal with the pressure of other anxiously waiting graduates and their families. Today will be one of those occasions when he will be able to set aside the mechanic, and become the artist, the sculptor of living art and life.

He frequently touches people's lives, emotionally as well as physically and on rare occasions like today can create living art, he'll be able to take his time on this one and make it special.

Later that day, Pan walked briskly toward his apartment proud of the day's work he had accomplished. He wondered if he would ever see the work of art he had created that day again.

The e'TaC-M[46] (enhanced Tracking and Communications Module) fused to his skull accessed his front door and his flat panel displays activating in all his rooms, his wife Nu'Wa[47], wouldn't be home for several hours.

They realized, like many other couples that, each needed some quiet time alone, to muse and unwind, and although his job wasn't necessarily stressful he often felt the need for quiet and to ponder life's questions, particularly since he faces the realities of their existence so much during each day.

Nu'Wa also faced the realities of life on Dadr'Ba but from a different angle, her job as a retirement coordinator brought her face to face with the grim facts of life aboard Dadr'Ba and she had many appointments in the evenings.

Both Pan and Nu'Wa are active participants, essential even, in the lifecycle of Dadr'Ba. Nu'Wa at the end of life and he, at the first major milestone when a new person finishes Level I programming and is configured to go online and become an active component in this giant machine that is Dadr'Ba.

Maybe it's because Nu'Wa is female or perhaps it's just her personality, but Pan thought Nu'Wa seems to be able to handle the realities of their existence better than he. She didn't appear to need as much alone time as he after a hard day, instead she seemed to, just need, to be close to him, and he needed to be prepared to support her.

Pan sat unwinding in his favorite chair, staring at the large flat panel as O'M approached at three thousand kilometers a second, still about a light year away. Pan mused that there really must be a God. Because it really is a miracle that they are alive and can appreciate the gifts that life can give, and soon, within their lifetime, though still decades away, they will reach O'M.

---

[46] Sounds like eee-Tack-EM, enhanced Tracking and Communications Module

[47] Sounds like New-Wah.

Pan felt incredibly lucky to be with Nu′Wa. They′re so well matched, with common interests, compatible and complementary in their differences. And both with the same security clearance. Lucky too, that their parents are both healthy and well, though it′ll probably be at least a century, possibly longer before he and Nu′Wa will be able to have children of their own, their children will be born not out here in space but on O′M.

It′s hard to think of themselves as Thinking Machines, but every day Pan opens up and looks inside sometimes three or four people. People as he′s come to know them, people as they′ve come to know themselves.

He single-handedly performs the operations; there′s no need to have a life support system and all the associated equipment and techniques, the machines in his office are ancient and only for show.

He simply puts the brain into standby mode and shuts down the respiration and circulation altogether. There′s no pain, no bleeding it′s not like having to fix a living biological person or a piece of machinery in operation.

He′s alone in the operating room, sometimes he′s the mechanic with a machine and sometimes an artist alone with his canvas, like today. He′s got a large display for reference, but it′s unnecessary. He′s been doing this for over a hundred years, and he′s gotten outstanding at it.

He rubs his chest, the left side containing his heart and the right side containing his brain and memory store, respiration only needed to provide cooling for these internal components. He has as with all the other D′En′s, twice the processing capacity and four times the memory as the most advanced U′Te or Mi′Nr in existence, but does capacity equal intelligence? Who′s more intelligent? The D′En, who only uses ten percent of their capacity or the Mi′Nr that uses half of their processing capacity? Pan can think of many people that fit that situation, shouldn′t that make them equal?

Pan felt proud of today′s job, the last of the graduation season. He spent the whole day making sure everything was perfect, even tuning up the systems that were not part of the work order. This girl, he thought is going to have a tough life, he′d do what he could to make it a little bit easier.

Nu′Wa would be glad to hear that the parts she recovers are being put to good use, being made to last, most are barely worn when they come into Nu′Wa′s custody.

Regardless of the component′s source, D′En, U′Te or Mi′Nr each person gets dismantled and each component gets refurbished and thoroughly checked out then warehoused. Pan has never rejected a part for not meeting standards but occasionally will requisition another if he′s not comfortable with it for any reason. A good example would be like today one of the muscle modules installed passed the one hundred N (Newton) standard for that group, but knows they′re capable of a hundred fifty N sometimes two hundred N, since components need to be balanced. He made sure that this system as a whole was balanced, capable of operating at a hundred fifty percent of officially rated capacity.

Nu′Wa may question him on his multiple returns to stock today, but after he explains, Pan is confident that she′d agree he did the right thing. It′s not as if they need any bonus credits for exceeding parts' conservation standards; they have everything a couple could want, credits in the bank a level four apartment, robotic maid service, flat panel's in every room, full premium channel access and well-filled spice, tea and liquor cabinets.

Now the grad season is over. Maybe they should go on a vacation Pan will ask Nu'Wa when she gets home.

Chapter 10, Nu'Wa Comes Home

Staring at the screen showing Dadr'Ba's advancement toward O'M, Pan thought deeply about Nu'Wa. She never shows her frustration, but Pan is concerned about her, he knows she has an essential role to play in the circle of life aboard Dadr'Ba. She handles all the arrangements before and after the retirement ceremony, but she's not allowed to participate in the retirement ceremony itself. The Church has a firm grip on that process.

She has on rare occasions mentioned to Pan her frustration about having a closed door between her and the retirement ceremony. Aside from reviewing the retirement application, making sure everything is ordered, and the production schedulers have signed off. Nu'Wa interviews the applicants and schedules the room and coordinates with the Church, which performs its own interview and preparation sessions.

Nu'Wa is then in charge of the postretirement processing which occurs after the retirement ceremony. Only when the systems have totally cooled and show no detectable brainwave activity are the systems turned over to Nu'Wa for processing.

Nu'Wa sees them now utterly devoid of life after having interviewed them alive and well only a few days before. When Pan performs his "operations" he knows that they will live again. Nu'Wa sees the retirees as real people, tired and burned out with their lives. Still the retirees have love and hope and dreams of a better life for their grandchildren and being able to be part of their grandchildren's lives.

But when Nu'Wa sees them the second time, it's difficult, even painful, she only sees the once animated, as corpses that will never activate again, at least not in whole.

She removes the outer protective, sensory membrane, Pan knows the process, which in turn gets refurbished or reprocessed, then packaged and warehoused as does the other components; the muscle modules, joints, respiration system (used for cooling). The pump and hosing truss used for pumping the battery fluid which fuels the system, it circulates from the gut to the various active components and storage locations, then special filters remove the spent fuel, which in turn gets collected and defecated, collected and piped to waste treatment facilities and reprocessed back into useable fuel.

The miners have the most fuel storage capacity followed by the U'Te's then least of all the D'En's, but all have roughly the same operations capacity based on expected workload.

A retiree's central processing unit and memory don't get recycled, which forces the printing of new components or the extraction of dwindling spares from those supplies stored in cargo modules at launch. Their "brains" are considered Holy and the tenuous relationship between the CA and the Church remains carefully balanced. A retiree's brain is returned to the Church which keeps them in a sacred, secured, catacomb monitored by both the CA and the Church.

The Church supports the CA by encouraging the people, the system, to work hard and long, obey the CA's rules and not to retire too early. The CA in return stays out of the Church's business and allows them a level of autonomy as long as they don't interfere with the operation of Dadr'Ba or CA business.

Together the Church and the CA have agreed to withhold the true nature of the crews "biology," the crew believes that they're biological clones. The knowledge that they are "just" machines, robots or androids is considered too dangerous to reveal.

The "people" of Dadr'Ba look down robots, like the soldiers and consider themselves to be superior.

The Church's reason for keeping the secret is religious and philosophical. They maintain that the Gamma-Ray burst that struck Dadr'Ba eight hundred years ago and killed all the biologicals, many of whom really were clones, was truly an act of God. This act of God gave life to the people, a miracle, a Holy Act. No less a miracle or Holy act than any dealing with biolgicals, making androids self-aware, it transformed them from machines into people and provided them a soul.

The CA reason for keeping the crews' true nature secret predates the Touch of God. The CA guards evidence that some of the androids, even before the Touch of God, were questioning their maligned treatment as non-biological machines.

Before the Touch of God, a different class structure existed. The pure biologicals were on top, there were only a few animated at a time and they were only able to operate safely in a few restricted areas of the ship due to radiation levels, and they were expensive and difficult to upkeep. They ate specially prepared food derived from algae grown in lighted vats, textured and seasoned to make it palatable. Not unlike the processing done to the battery fluid fuel used by the crew today. The pure biologicals didn't live very long either and died at best around a hundred years and constantly had to be replenished out of the ships stockpile which numbers in the tens of thousands (in preparation for arrival at O'M). But they held the keys to the kingdom, holding the highest offices and controlled all the functioning of the ship.

Then there were the GLC's, back then there was only a single class, and they didn't have psychic ability and were unable to birth. None of the GLC's back then were D'En's or Mi'Nr's; they were all what we'd call today, U'Te's. They ate the same food as the pure biologicals but were radiation resistant and lived much longer, as needed spares were pulled out of the ships stockpile, (this time numbering only in the thousands) thawed and revived. GLC's felt superior to the pure biologicals but had minimal interaction with them.

Finally, there were the androids, which were not ranked, but considered a piece of equipment, part of the ship. They were divided into the three classes that exist today (except the D'En's were not called D'En's then, but were called Sci'Tech's). To add insult to injury the androids were stronger and more radiation resistant than the biologicals, including the GLC's, and even the lower models had computational ability exceeding that of the biologicals, but they were never considered conscious. Not even entitled to person status, the world was upside down.

The Gamma Ray Burst changed everything when it happened, many androids recovered, though some did not, but those that recovered and survived believed that they were alive.

Some of the survivors, the Sci'Tech's mostly, an Android model with higher processing and more robust memory systems, knew or figured out the truth of their nature. But after the Touch of God, it was impossible to convince the Mi'Nr's and the U'Te's that they weren't "biologically" "alive".

When forced to face the reality of their true existence many of the "people" became unstable or fell into a deep depression or melancholy that almost always ended in death. The same that survived the discovery of the truth fell into a robot status that after a while under the new post-Touch of God social order meant that they weren't accepted by the new "society" and eventually got shut off or terminated.

A new class system replaced the old, and the new D'En class quickly realized that to continue Dadr'Ba's mission meant accommodating the crew's 'aliveness' was the most effective and efficient course.

Now, eight hundred years later, we're almost to our goal. We're alive, and as real as any biological there ever was, we love, laugh, cry, want, desire, hope, we pair bond and even thanks to techniques learned from the Touch of God have children that inherit real, tangible traits from generation to generation.

We've even evolved taste and smell, that along with the development of spices, and a cadre of cooks, have made eating the processed "food" needed to sustain our lives more tolerable. Beyond that, we've evolved gender mods and methods of sex that align with gender identities that manifested themselves almost immediately after the Touch of God.

Pan didn't know for sure, though he suspected. Nu'Wa had stopped by the school on her way home and watched the exercise yard as the Ko'Ka's ran and played games with each other. Providing her solace, knowing that these youngsters are the descendants of the people she counsels, and she's part of the system that brought these Ko'Ka to life.

Pan still deep in thought, stared at the panel showing the image of O'M when Nu'Wa entered the room. She stood watching him for a long while, oh how much she loved him, after a while she went over to Pan and wrapped her arms around his neck and kissed him on the cheek and then on the neck. Pan reached up and caressed her arm and said to Nu'Wa "I think we're due for a vacation."

Chapter 11, Su'Zi Wakes After Bio-mod

Su'Zi woke refreshed; it took a moment for her to realize where she was and for what purpose. She slowly realized she was at Pri'Api and Ti'Reso's, in the room they showed her that she would awake in. Where she had met ahead of time and talked at length with Pri'Api and Ti'Reso about how to conduct the lessons.

She looked down at her body, not believing what she was seeing or experiencing. She moved without effort; everything felt lighter, and she looked "good." There was a mirror on the wall across from the spare bed where she woke. She stood up and looked at herself amazed how beautiful she had become. She stretched and turned watching herself in the mirror and let out a little squeal of joy.

Then hearing voices in the next room reached over to the dresser and picked up the robe she had been provided and putting it on slowly walked out to meet her mentors for her first lesson.

The first lessons were exploration and familiarization. Gradually the lessons evolved into stimulation, and on to different methods and combinations. How to arouse, maintain, wane, ebb, and re-excite. How to tease, maintain control and finally to let loose and lose control. To guide, coax and push others to reset. To bring on and send a reset command from your core, cascading out to your extremities, casting yourself adrift as in space. To experience the mental and physical reset, the little death, that, when performed correctly, can result in momentary unconsciousness. Finally, to wake feeling fulfilled and refreshed.

Pri'Api and Ti'Reso were good teachers and also showed Su'Zi how to introduce variety and play, and most importantly, how sex fit into Dadr'Ba socicty, not to take it too seriously and not to cross the line reserved for your life mate, and your birthing partner. This line is where sex stops being sex and crosses from the physical to the mental joining of mates for the purpose of pair bonding and birthing.

Pri'Api and Ti'Reso only once allowed Su'Zi to witness their mental pairing psychically. Though physically intimate, what Su'Zi witnessed focused not on physical pleasure and gratification but something much, much deeper, a oneness that Su'Zi couldn't put into words, and had trouble comprehending.

Su'Zi wasn't allowed to participate, but witnessed from afar, and from that distance couldn't distinguish the two. She psychically preserved only one, a small bright point off in the distance, not cold but warm and one she could tell, felt right and good. Su'Zi was awestruck.

Chapter 12, P'Ko Turns Sixteen

Ever since P'Ko turned ten and his parents upgraded his TaC-B[48], from a restricted call out model, to an unrestricted call out model. P'Ko figured out how to remove it from behind his ear, stash it in his room and forward calls to his old TaC-B that he now wore and had disabled the tracking function on. He was thus able to roam and explore as he pleased with the tracker indicating he was cloistered in his room studying.

P'Ko would disguise himself using one of his father's mechanic uniforms, carefully obscuring the hash marks across the shoulders[49].

His favorite, most interesting and safest from detection, haunts are the back alleys and shadows of "Ol'Tn". Ol'Tn lies thirty meters beneath Nu'Tn[50] (where P'Ko lives with his parents and brother) and is the original living area for Dadr'Ba's crew.

Ol'Tn is crisscrossed with all sorts of ancient equipment, space barges, portable habitats, cargo containers, and a plethora of run down and broken equipment that had been dragged into the original construction tunnels and lashed together during the metamorphosis of Dadr'Ba's from a migratory chunk of intra-solar ice and dirt into a starship.

P'Ko thought back to six years ago, when he first ventured down to Ol'Tn by himself, not sure of himself, making his way through the darkened streets. P'Ko had visited Ol'Tn even before that, with his father to get repair parts from the D'Po[51], P'Ko was impressed and amazed, he fell in love with Ol'Tn and the D'Po.

Despite the fact that for more than five hundred years, it's been mostly inhabited by Mi'Nr's, P'Ko felt comfortable there. The narrow semi-dark alleys and assorted space debris some turned at odd angles to provide structural support seem to P'Ko like art, he didn't like the stark pastel and off-white, straight lines of the structures in Nu'Tn, they felt cold and uninviting, despite the fact that Ol'Tn was much colder than Nu'Tn.

P'Ko having never met a Mi'Nr before was at first terrified during his first encounter, but that fear was short lived as the Mi'Nr's he and his father encountered treated his father kindly. And P'Ko, discovering that Mi'Nr's possessed an enhanced psychic ability, feeling fond amusement directed at him.

---

[48] Sounds like Tack-Bee.

[49] Found on all clothes and uniforms, that allow for easy tracking by the overhead surveillance system. The surveillance system won't flag the obscured shoulder hash as a problem as long as he stayed out of trouble and didn't draw attention to himself.

[50] Ol'Tn was built over by Nu'Tn sometime after the ToG Event.

[51] Sounds like and means Depot, a space ship junk yard.

At first, the dim light of Ol'Tn frightened and intimidated P'Ko. His father warned him not to stray off, warning that outcasts and criminals hide in the shadows and roam the back alleys of Ol'Tn. Adding that "the surveillance systems we take for granted in Nu'Tn and keep us safe are virtually nonexistent in Ol'Tn."

The Mi'Nr's that inhabit Ol'Tn have natural night vision that makes it unnecessary for Ol'Tn to have brighter lighting. Now the dimmer light suited P'Ko; he had spent a lot of time training or discovering and exercising his night vision, although many in the medical community would have argued it an impossible task.

Self-trained or discovered his night vision wasn't good at colors and had little effect on his day vision, not impacting his color resolution at all but it did improve his depth perception and distant vision.

He kept his enhanced vision a secret because all throughout his life he had been accused of being strange and different. He was even persecuted for it, which is very ironic because in Dadr'Ba society (being comprised of clones) people place a high value on being different.

As soon as most people are able, they make dramatic changes in their appearance and even pay hard-earned credits to change themselves to fit the latest fashion. Some even forgo spending credits on food seasoning, to save enough for the latest hair or skin color, or tattoos, or eye, nose or ear job, or some other form of body mod.

P'Ko, now sixteen, like lots of To'Ta's his age was already talking about bio-mods they would like, and many of P'Ko's classmates had prepared lists of what they want, having experimented with makeup, wigs, removable tattoos and even some (for those well to do) prosthetics from an early age.

But unlike his friends P'Ko favored himself with less obvious bio-mods. He liked the idea of hyperspectral vision (special CA authorization required), strength and cold resistance (not authorized for workers, like most U'Te's assigned primarily to zone two), and cognitive abilities, (only permitted for certain knowledge workers) memory capacity, high on his list.

 P'Ko would find out later, that his parents had paid under the table for a cognitive boost when he was very young, thinking that it would help him with his slowness in learning to speak and read but it didn't seem to help and was highly illegal.

His parents and those involved could've been fined, censured, restricted or reduced in status[52]; even restricted or confined. All these years later they could still get in trouble because the CA doesn't have a statute of limitations, for anything.

All this made making any further cognitive changes, like increased memory impossible, if his earlier childhood-mod were discovered everybody would be in trouble, just as if the crime were committed yesterday.

---

[52] Having mileage taken away from family standing.

The CA justifies its totalitarian attitude, with its many rules, and equally many secrets, by saying that it is necessary to provide for a disciplined, well-ordered and functioning crew.

From the ordinary person's perspective, the rules and secrets are applied unequally, and have driven a wedge between the different classes of people and created an enormous gulf between the CA and everyone else.

The privileged aren't held to the same standards as everyone else. Resources, beyond the modest collective living standard, aren't earned or distributed according to the level of effort, merit or impact, but assigned according to family status and position.

Dan'Zu is a glaring example, he doesn't even attempt to be discreet about his illegal, underage body mod, but brazenly employs his extra height to bully and intimidate his classmates. And it goes unnoticed by the teachers and school administration who are all D'En.

Dan'Zu's case can be viewed as comical. P'Ko first noticed this watching Dan'Zu leading his gang from his perch in the stadium. Dan'Zu's height job was cheaply done; it's a legs only mod which puts his whole frame out of proportion. He walks awkwardly looking as though he's walking on stilts and behind his back P'Ko has noticed some of the other kid's make fun of him. Yet this didn't make Dan'Zu less intimidating when looking up at him centimeters away and listening to his insults.

Other times the situation is so minor, and the reactions are so severe that it's on the verge of bizarre. P'Ko's mother, Le'Ta, sees this often, being a tailor, she has customers from across Dadr'Ba society. With only rare exceptions, all of her D'En clients insist on preferential treatment of their requests. She faces frequent threats, like "if you don't get my alteration done by" such and such a date "I know someone that can make your life miserable and your husband's job more difficult".

These situations and so much more like them have caused a growing discontent, and most people are beginning to complain (mostly psychically). The result has led to an increase in the number of scattered malcontents and groups coalescing into a growing resistance movement, something that hasn't occurred since the equal job rights protests. The CA's response has been to seek out and clamp down on the resistance as "anti-progressives," (like Su'Zi's father).

P'Ko didn't look forward to what he expected the years ahead to be like, more than ever, all of the To'Ta's his age are begging their parents to pay for experiments in the way they dress, different makeup, temporary tattoos, and for those still undecided, trying out different gender roles.

Only school issued uniforms are provided free to students and standardized work uniforms are issued to adults, stylish clothes, and clothes alterations are a common method of displaying the much-prized individuality a society of clones prizes and help keep tailors like P'Ko's mother busy.

P'Ko had to acknowledge that regardless of what he thought of Dan'Zu and his stilted legs, Dan'Zu dresses well and is good with makeup. He

(Dan'Zu) seems to have a ready supply of stylized clothes, makeup, and temporary tattoos. And he's wicked smart when it comes to school work.

P'Ko saw that many To'Ta's, boys, girls and pers (undecided) alike, appear to like Dan'Zu and even pump him with compliments which Dan'Zu relishes, not seeming to notice the coincidence that complements are often followed with requests for help with school work.

People can be so shallow, and impressionable, though Dan'Zu's height job made him look ridiculous, he had a lot going for him, his obvious edge in scholastics, especially when it comes to calculation speed, memory speed, bandwidth, overall throughput; sort, search, and retrieval, is plain. The other students realize it too and take advantage of it.

Realizing that there are centuries of having to deal with Dan'Zu and his gang ahead, not just school years, but post-graduation, P'Ko would have to be careful how he deals with Dan'Zu. Dadr'Ba is a relatively small, closed society, and most people have long memories, especially regarding opinions they have of other people.

Although there's a zero tolerance for violence, and a low tolerance for bullying, or similar misbehavior, it never seems to slow Dan'Zu in his pursuit of P'Ko. Dan'Zu treats bullying like it's the way it's supposed to be. Bullying and intimidation are the natural state of affairs, a cruel game and he laughs about it frequently, even in P'Ko's face.

P'Ko knew he could get Dan'Zu to stop picking on him as soon as he submitted to Dan'Zu's dominance. All P'Ko would have to do is play nice, load him up with compliments and always agree with him, but something in P'Ko refused to let him.

As much as P'Ko dislikes Dan'Zu and despises him, P'Ko knows that he must, somehow come to terms with this bully, and potential enemy, P'Ko's stomach tightened and churned at this realization.

P'Ko avoided the clean, well-lit public ramp that offers vehicle and pedestrian traffic down to Ol'Tn. It and the others like it in the neighboring sectors were covered by extra surveillance that logs who and when people passed from Nu'Tn to Ol'Tn. His disguise, a bump helmet and an old pair of his dad's coveralls provided a passable cover for the inattentive, but his obscured shoulder hash and partially disabled TaC-B would create an alarm with the automatic system when it tried to match the shoulder hash to the disabled tracking function in his TaC-B.

The CASS would probably not send forces to respond, but the data from an alert would be databased indefinitely whereas ordinary traffic data stays active for only a few weeks before being overwritten.

It crossed P'Ko's mind that at least some surveillance systems were operating during the Touch of God Event, the thought of what they might reveal made him shudder.

P'Ko accessed the stairwell adjacent to the auxiliary maintenance elevator which ran all the way from the upper decks of Nu'Tn down past Ol'Tn deck one and its main street to the airlock that provided access to the mining zone.

P'Ko looked up at the landing above and noted the access door on the landing above was closed, as it should be. Dadr'Ba's survival depended on a tightly controlled ventilation system. Even the vandals respected the need to carry heat from Dadr'Ba's core quickly enough to prevent Dadr'Ba's melting from within.

The only light came from the emergency exit signs, this stair, and its accompanying maintenance elevator rarely gets used now, its purpose is only for emergency backup when the new elevator and stair which is well-maintained breaks or is closed for repair.

P'Ko wondered what the CA must be thinking, how can they justify not maintaining an "emergency system." He hoped that the other emergency systems, like power, are better kept.

The lack of attention did have its benefits, though, the camera outside the stairwell entrance was pointed away from the stair entrance toward the closed elevator door and loading platform.

Before exposing himself to the surveillance camera field of view in the stairwell, he used his pocket inspection multi tool and checked the camera positioning making sure it was safe.

Inside the stairwell P'Ko looked over at the surveillance camera dangling from its broken mount and pointed at the deck, scrawled on the wall beside it, along with a crude diagram, was graffiti saying what the CASS can do with its cameras. P'Ko chuckled to himself recalling how years ago, his first time through this way, he ever so carefully and slowly moved the aim of that same camera to allow unobserved access to the stair.

P'Ko exited the stairwell on the main street of Ol'Tn; it was safe from surveillance at least from cameras. All the surveillance cameras in Ol'Tn have a nasty habit of breaking, so much so the CA has given up on trying to keep them fixed.

P'Ko felt comfortable; he's become a regular here having visited almost weekly for six years. Now, rather than going directly to the D'Po office to report for "work" he walked down the busy street, tool bag over her shoulder.

It was his favorite day of the week in Ol'Tn; it was trading day and everyone that had something to sell or trade or needed something was there. People staked out spots, showing their wares and hawking their offerings. P'Ko would occasionally pause if he spotted some old mining equipment, a tool, or scientific instrument.

His height, lack of hair, self-done skin tone cosmetics and the rest made it easy to pick him out of the crowd, but this was "Ol'Tn", a lot of strange looking people walk the streets, and nobody asks questions.

He inwardly blushed and quickened his pace as he passed Fa'Na and La'Na, a couple of prostitutes not currently hawking their wares, aside from the way they dressed, but bartering with a spice vendor over some food spices.

The "ladies" being ever watchful, noticed him, and one said, "Hey Mr. Mechanic. I've got some broken plumbing; can you fix it for me?" P'Ko knew they weren't serious; they were only having a little fun with him. He knew both of them and had even fixed the door latch on the apartment they shared a while back. Not yet being equipped to be a client they promised an extra good time in repayment, once he came of age and was properly equipped.

He laughed at their joke and threw back at them that he'd need to get an extra big tool for that job, and kept moving, watchful for anything that might catch his eye.

Mindful that he only had a few hours to work with, he made his way down almost to the end of the street and stepped into Mi'Ka's Curio shop, under a glowing red All-Seeing Eye sign. The place remained much the same as it had been six years earlier, during P'Ko's first visit, except that time it wasn't a trading day.

That day, P'Ko was supposedly home alone sick, but in reality, he was just overly anxious to test out his modified TaC-B system, the street was quiet then, almost deserted, most people somewhere at their jobs. And that day P'Ko had spotted the sign in the near dark (even at midday) and felt a strong compulsion to go inside.

Much to his surprise, upon entering he heard a feminine, slightly cracking voice say "Welcome, P'Ko my name is Mi'Ka[53] I've been expecting you." At that instant P'Ko panicked, unseen and un-introduced this person knew his name and must know he shouldn't have been there. Still not seeing the source of the voice, P'Ko turned to run away, the voice interjected, "stop! Don't be afraid I'm not going to hurt you."

P'Ko tried to run but found that he couldn't move his feet. After a moment, P'Ko's fear drained away. He turned back towards the back of the shop and ventured wondrously deeper into the darkened shop. It was much darker than the near dusk outside and was filled with all kinds of weird memorabilia and stacks of who knows what, piled up leaving only a narrow path.

P'Ko, taking his time, letting his eyes adjust, found Mi'Ka seated at her Sooth Sayers table in a back corner. She directed his attention to her robotic pet and introduced "Ku'Ma[54]," a strange looking small matt black metallic four-legged creature with one green eye and one yellow eye, sitting at her side. Ku'Ma made a hissing sound. Mi'Ka remarked, "Give her (robopets are genderless. However Mi'Ka considers Ku'Ma female) time, she'll get used to you."

Stranger still was Mi'Ka, at first sight, P'Ko thought he was confronting an outcast and tried again to run but again couldn't move. Then he realized that he was in the presence of what could only be a Touch of God Survivor.

P'Ko looked at the lady seated before him, a Mi'Nr with long dark hair and smooth pale skin sitting slouched, as if exhausted, over a small rune covered table. Strangest and scariest of all, being her eyes, overly large glowing frosted orbs with electric looking arc flashes of light behind them.

---

[53] Sounds like Me-Kah.
[54] Sounds like Coo-Ma.

P'Ko had never met a Touch of God Survivor before and didn't know what to do or say, so he just stood there, dumbstruck. Finally, Mi'Ka said "P'Ko it's so good to see you. You must have some tea".

Ever since then P'Ko always made it a point to visit Mi'Ka whenever he came to Ol'Tn. He didn't visit as often as he is like, in spite of his parents trying to earn extra credits, were only able to schedule overtime once or twice a week, and since school and work were synchronized, he had trouble getting away unnoticed.

There's no need for libraries to study because everything is available on your multi-book. Of course, a bigger screen is available at your desk or an entire environment through VE (Virtual Environment), but the VE is used more for gaming than school. P'Ko usually got his fill of school in the classroom and wasn't interested extending the academic experience beyond the classroom.

The excuse of going to the park or the Memorial was difficult due to the TaC-B's ability to track, and the omnipresent surveillance system made available to parents for tracking of children, making it easy for parents to check up on the kids. To use going to church as an excuse for sneaking down to Ol'Tn felt sacrilegious, and P'Ko was much less inclined to challenge the Church than the CA. Even though the consequences from the Church, a verbal warning from an elder, seems trivial compared to what the CA could dole out. It boiled down to the Church being respected and the CA being feared.

The offer of tea was very special; Mi'Ka's tea is simply the best. When asked what recipe, flavor or brand it was, Mi'Ka only smiles and winks one of her large, frosted over, scorched glass, blind eyes and say only that it's a secret recipe and chuckle.

Blindness doesn't bother her in the least, the frosted orbs that are her eyes, at first appear dull and lifeless, but wait a moment and there's sparks deep within. Her actions and expressions show no hint of blindness, Mi'Ka seems to know, or sense more without sight than most people can see with perfect vision.

Mi'Ka is a Touch of God Survivor; the Touch of God took her eyes but gave her what she calls "Mind's Eyes" instead. And even though medical technology could restore her vision, she insists that she wouldn't change a thing, not for all the credits Dadr'Ba could carry.

She jokingly calls herself a witch and a soothsayer, and whenever P'Ko asked about what it was like, The Touch of God, Mi'Ka only replies, "be patient my child, be patient."

That first day they met and every time since Mi'Ka served up tea pouring it without sight and not spilling a drop and placing it on the table near P'Ko's hand. P'Ko felt her "Minds Eyes" turn towards him as she smiled and took a sip. P'Ko took a sip of the tea and savored the flavor.

Food and drink flavors and textures are critically important on Dadr'Ba. The food on Dadr'Ba is processed, refined, distilled, treated and manufactured, all in automated plants controlled by the CA. No one is allowed to know the whole process which is segmented and access controlled to only approved and cleared people. P'Ko knew because his father, a mechanic, can go just about anywhere and work on anything, but he's denied access to the food processing machinery.

Spices and flavors and food texturizers turn what many would think an unbearable existence into one pleasant and savory. The tea had a bitter initial taste which soon smoothed out and left sweetness after swallowing.

Today, setting and dipping tea, Mi'Ka asked "How is the training going," referring to his martial arts training, she had helped arrange, shortly after P'Ko's first visit.

P'Ko replied that it's going extremely well, then added: "every time I think I've got something mastered Lu'Gs[55] introduces something new." "The latest was going down to zone three; I was barely able to stand let alone jump kick." "I think when I come of age, I'll need to get strength mods."

Mi'Ka asked how things were going in school. P'Ko took a deep breath, my classmates and I get along fine. My grades are okay, but the upper-class kids still won't leave me alone, but I haven't used any of the moves that Lu'Gs has taught me on them. I've been tempted, but knowing that I could probably take them out makes it so I don't have to. It gives me a sort of peace in mind, and the concentration techniques help me to ignore the taunts. They still think I'm strange and slow and stupid, but I know inside that I'm not.

Mi'Ka reminded him that he mustn't forget how serious this is, martial arts are forbidden and if discovered, could result in clinical retraining, a euphemism for brainwashing, or even involuntarily retirement meaning he and Lu'Gs could be executed (retirement without passing).

Both of you could wind up in forced re-education another euphemism for forced labor in isolation for an undetermined period; it would be very long, though. No one P'Ko knew had any recollection of someone returning from forced re-education.

P'Ko felt the gravity of the consequences, risks to himself and the significant penalty that could be placed on Lu'Gs. It bothered P'Ko that his actions could bring about the CA's execution of Lu'Gs, never allowing him to pass on to his kids and have a legacy. It weighed on him and felt like what he imagined lower Zone Three or Zone Four to be like.

P'Ko replied yes, I know, I'm strong enough and mature enough not to risk an altercation. Lu'Gs has taught me to be as the Ether, to support while yielding, to influence without forcing and to be the foundation which all things draw support from and are measured.

After another sip, Mi'Ka asked "What do you have to say about your grades?" even coming from Mi'Ka P'Ko got a little defensive. It hinted of some of the taunts coming from Dan'Zu and even though P'Ko knew Mi'Ka was testing him. P'Ko was tempted to try a harsh reply psychically, without words, but instead held back, paused and said: "half of what they teach is too easy and

---

[55] Sounds like Lew-Gus.

the other a half is wrong or worse yet, CA propaganda." Concluding with "besides, if my grades are too high. I might not get the job that I want".

Mi'Ka had not been able to "see" it in P'Ko although job-related questions are common for a soothsayer, it had not matured or fermented enough in P'Ko's mind until just this moment. This was the first time P'Ko had mentioned the job he wanted. Mi'Ka had assumed, as most do, and is most often the case; the child follows in the parent's footsteps. P'Ko was already working under the table as a mechanic and was good at it, and he seemed to enjoy it.

Mi'Ka could see it now, but still asked, "What job is that?" Without hesitation, P'Ko replied, "a Mi'Nr." Mi'Ka paused a long moment studying P'Ko, then as if having come to a conclusion replied "Good choice, but a difficult path."

Chapter 13, Detection of Radio Signals from O'M

The alarm came; it was midday in sector three. The search for intelligent life had succeeded.

The search that began on our planet thousands of years ago, decades before the technology was developed to find habitable planets and many years before the discovery of O'M.

Potentially intelligent signals were picked up from around distant stars, most well over a thousand light years away, the closest ones were determined to be relatively low technology and at much too great a distance for an attempt at communication, the time delay was just too high, and for what purpose? Any useful dialogue would take decades, centuries or even millennia.

Our planet didn't have much time left, the people had outgrown, or more accurately, used up our planet and fate, the weakening magnetosphere and increasing solar flare activity was forcing our people to move, or risk dying as a species.

The existence of intelligent life in the universe was a certainty, but inconsequential because none was determined to be close enough to be of any consequence or help. Faster than light travel had proven to be impossible except for the theoretically possible imaginings of a few scientists and science fiction fans who assume some yet undiscovered technology can bend the laws of physics. We didn't have the time to wait.

The odds of *intelligent* life developing on any given planet, even in the Goldilocks zone, that zone where it's not too hot and not too cold, comfortable, capable of supporting life, had been estimated to be less than one in a hundred thousand. Those odds were based on the number of observed habitable planets plus an estimate of the number of yet to be discovered habitable planets divided by the few "suspicious" signals that could be attributed to intelligent life. Many put the odds at millions to one.

Our goal was to find a habitable world without intelligent life, because we needed a world to inhabit, to be our own and since there's plenty of habitable planets out there, pick one that's not already taken, or soiled. A clean new world, not polluted by someone else's industry or mistakes. Pure, with untapped natural resources that with our experience and care could sustain us into perpetuity.

The technology was available, to search for planets suitable to support life, many were discovered, and the best candidates monitored as potential destinations.

Final destination world selection was based on the best match, in the right place at the right time given the size and the trajectory of the long period comet that was to become the Starship Dadr'Ba and the positions of the

65

planets to be used for gravitational assists to achieve solar system escape velocity.

O'M was scrutinized for many years before the beginning of Dadr'Ba's journey. Or'Gn was already going into decline, the technology needed for the trip was refined and the resources invested in constructing what was to become Dadr'Ba.

Since its journey began, Dadr'Ba monitored O'M for signs of intelligent life, it didn't expect to find any, the experts calculated even higher odds against intelligent life developing on a world after being chosen.

Dadr'Ba's leadership was confident then there would never be intelligent life on O'M that they only allowed for monitoring O'M for a few minutes each day, on a "noninterference basis." The search antennas primary mission is to find obstacles in the path of Dadr'Ba with enough time to avoid a catastrophic collision or target and destroy the obstacle.

The deep space antennas look for medium to large objects, the near space antennas looking for medium to small objects; a spare, configurable for both missions is kept on line in case of problems, failure or during maintenace of one of the main antennas. And used for spare is also used for testing and research.

A small group on Dadr'Ba was tasked to monitor O'M and over the centuries the process had become routine. But now with this discovery, it was time to take it seriously. The SIL (Search for Intelligent Life) team on Dadr'Ba followed the established protocols to confirm the findings. They moved the antenna to a different star and watched the signal disappear then they coordinated access to another deep space antenna and verified the results.

The SIL team reported their findings to the CA. The CA didn't notify the SIL teams in the other sectors, but waited for independent verification from one or more of the other teams. In the meantime, the CA ordered the discovery team into a strict communications blackout.

Confirmation from the other sector teams took time; it seems the signals were intermittent but finally it was confirmed... there is intelligent life on O'M.

Chapter 14, Su'Zi's Boy Friend

Su'Zi began having second thoughts about having Pri'Api and Ti'Reso's as her mentors; their training had raised her expectations, and her experiences with Vas'Tu[56], the vehicle mechanic that supported her tunneling crew and a few other select individuals were not up to what she expected.

Vas'Tu, and the others, though good looking and nice enough were not very good in bed, she had found herself having to take charge of the experience, responsible for making it satisfying, for both of them. She's been able to reset regularly, but mostly due to her training, control and discipline which takes away from enjoying the experience herself, at least occasionally she would like to let herself go, not to be the one driving but enjoying the ride.

She quickly figured out that for many people being properly mentored is not high on the priority list, and picked mentors based on popularity rather than respect.

Some individuals fail to recognize the fact that there is someone else involved, thinking only for themselves and use the practice purely for entertainment or a quick reset after a frustrating day at work.

Vas'Tu was okay and had gotten better, being a Mi'Nr and having psychic ability he realized that their experiences together weren't up to Su'Zi's expectations.

Vas'Tu is at his core a simple basic guy and just didn't think of it the same way. It's not that he didn't care, he just expected his partners to feel the same way he did about it, he likes to eat a meal rather than dine. Occasionally Su'Zi felt like a meal, but more often she wanted to dine, a full-fledged experience, one that sends shivers all the way to your fingertips and toes, leaving you floating as if weightless, a truly existential experience. Su'Zi wanted something more out of a relationship; she would have to keep looking.

---

[56] Sounds like Vass-Two.

Chapter 15, Chn'Gi Reports to CA Council

Dr. Chn'Gi[57] dreaded giving these reports, since the initial discovery of Intelligent Life and its, confirmation, verification and security clampdown, Chn'Gi's life was turned inside out and upside down and having to face the CA Council and the Commander was torture.

What she thought would be her crowning achievement, a career maker, turned out to be a curse. In the immediate aftermath of the discovery of IL[58] on O'M her email account was locked, guards showed up at her door, and some of her coworkers disappeared[59]. She wasn't allowed to publish, at least not to the public, and all of her communications her email, text and voice became monitored.

The worst was her TaC-B was taken and replaced with an eTaC-M fused to her skull, and she was forced to move from her cozy little studio apartment into a large one bedroom with a small study. Her new place is equipped with the latest technology; automated access with intelligent lighting, integrated apartment wide sight and sound system with flat panels, and, surveillance cameras in nearly every room.

Chn'Gi prepared to report her latest findings to the Central Council. She hated it, the Council and in particular the Commander wanted information that just wasn't available yet, and no matter how hard she tried to explain that fact, they didn't seem to get it. They made her feel stupid, demanding more information when there wasn't any.

Before the discovery, there had been talk and speculation about what impact finding IL on O'M would have, but the statisticians made it sound that the odds were so astronomical, nobody paid any serious attention to the possibility of IL. After the discovery, Chn'Gi searched but couldn't find any record of any plans or contingencies, all traces of preplanning for IL, if there were any, simply disappeared.

Of all the hundreds of billions of stars in the universe and the tens of thousands of planets discovered and of the hundreds determined to have the potential for supporting life, doing statistical analysis in reverse made for impossible odds, on the order of trillions to one. Such probability calculations are fallacious and meaningless, because the fact is the fact, and no amount of calculations will change it, there's intelligent life on O'M.

We're only about a hundred years from Planetfall and passed the last chance to divert point centuries ago. There's no avoiding it; we're going to

---

[57] Sounds like Chin-Gee.

[58] Sounds like ill, stands for intelligent life.

[59] Later she learned that they weren't "qualified" for the new security protocol her program was now under, so they were 'moved' to different jobs but remained under surveillance.

need to learn as much as possible, as soon as possible to provide time to plan for how to deal with them. Chn'Gi can't blame the Commander and the Council for wanting to know, but why can't they be more patient.

The plan for monitoring the IL is evolving and needs to adapt as more information becomes available. The central council placed Chn'Gi, the lead scientist on duty during the discovery in charge of the IL research team. And to make matters more frustrating Chn'Gi and her team was given very restricted antenna time, not the full access she anticipated for such a vital mission.

Was it a miracle or a disaster? For life to develop at all, then evolve advanced intelligence, have the resources and then develop the technology needed for radio communications, for all that to happen was surely a miracle. But it means our O'M, our new world is tainted by some alien life form... our O'M is no longer pure.

Chn'Gi fears how the Central Council is reacting, approaching the only planet that they have detected so far to have confirmed and verified advanced intelligent life; and no other choice but to go there, could this be another act of God? The Church had not yet been informed and based on the rapidity and harshness of the security crackdown by the CA it's doubtful, the Church will find out anytime soon.

The CA's claim that the enhanced security is only precautionary didn't match up with the security level. The discovery of IL (intelligent life) was compartmented and given the highest level of control. All areas doing SIL (Search for Intelligent Life) work became controlled access; all people working the SIL crews were questioned, investigated, put under surveillance and made to swear not to communicate anything about IL to anyone outside the program.

The original group involved with this discovery and confirmation was whittled down to less than ten. Most of the purged radio astronomers and support crew were reassigned to navigation duties and told that the IL discovered was a short-lived natural phenomenon that stopped almost immediately. Even so, they were forbidden to mention it to anyone and placed under electronic surveillance.

Chn'Gi and her small crew were indoc'd into the new security program; their TaC-B's replaced with eTaC-M's, and moved to apartments "upgraded" with surveillance systems.

Chn'Gi as had nearly everyone aboard Dadr'Ba at one time or another contemplated what life might be like on O'M; some thought O'M might be devoid of life. Had that been the case, it would have introduced a set of problems about how suitable the planet's environment is and what terraforming would be required. Many had hoped that there would be life, just no IL. The probability that there is microscopic life that would be incompatible or a threat to their biology had been planned for. Protocols were prepared for ensuring compatibility between their species, down to the microscopic scale, careful introduction of Dadr'Ba's people to the new environment, then careful integration of the ecosystem of Or'Gn, which Dadr'Ba carried aboard her, frozen and preserved.

Dadr'Ba is an ark bringing a huge collection of the biology of Or'Gn, frozen in sealed containers nearly forgotten near the outer shell of Dadr'Ba, shielded from radiation by Dadr'Ba's artificial magnetic field, and tens of meters of compressed cometary material, kept almost as cold as interstellar space.

Or'Gn, whose real name the CA banned from Dadr'Ba's lexicon centuries ago is long forgotten, erased from the records and databases. It's another one of the CA's many secrets, that carries the threat of capital punishment, this particular one endorsed (though not the punishment) by the Church.

Dadr'Ba has always been focused on the future and forward motion, most notably since the Touch of God event. It was then that the instantaneous communications link with Or'Gn (as the old world, the old home world, became to be called) was lost.

The Touch of God corrupted and destroyed the QECS (Quantum Entanglement Communication System) that provided instantaneous communications with Or'Gn. At the time of the communications loss, it's said that the news from Or'Gn was the worst. The situation had gotten much worse in the thousand plus years since Dadr'Ba's departure. The predictions came true and all that remained of Or'Gn were survivors of an apocalypse living in bunkers buried beneath a charred landscape.

The loss of communications, aside from being viewed as a further act of God was the end of a continuous stream of bad news. Now without the QECS, it would take over a hundred years to get a reply from Or'Gn and any attempt was deemed worthless.

Now with the discovery of intelligent life, the microbiology has become of secondary importance. The timetable for working through the microbiology had always been considered to be relatively long, and they could stay in orbit indefinitely while the terraforming and biology issues are resolved. The problem of how to deal with IL raises a multitude of questions that have no answer yet and has much more severe implications for both the IL and the people of Dadr'Ba. Time is running out, Dadr'Ba's journey is nearly complete, having completed over ninety percent of the overall distance to reach O'M, with approximately a hundred years remaining.

Though Chn'Gi searched, she could find no record, speculative notes or discussions on what they would do if they found IL on O'M.

Chn'Gi had no idea how fast the aliens' technology might develop; she didn't even have any information based on their own history of development.

The CA prohibits anything to do with Pre-Touch of God history and knowledge of Or'Gn.

Chn'Gi and her team were told that they must work with the worst case. They are to report what the "O'Mi's[60]" as Chn'Gi and her team have come to call them, are expected to develop, in the hundred years remaining before their

---

[60] Sounds like Homies.

arrival. Will the O'Mi's develope advanced enough technology and multiply enough in numbers to pose a serious threat to Dadr'Ba and its people.

The CASC's (Central Authority Security Council)[61] precautionary security crackdown is probably warranted, to avoid rumor escalation and possible panic of the crew. But shouldn't the decision-making process involve more than the Commander, the four Sector Commanders, and the security chief?

Chn'Gi knew that the Council would grow tired of her first weekly then monthly, NSTR's (Nothing Significant to Report). She had hoped that the time distortion that often affects the crew, that loss of days that sometimes leaves the crew wondering where the last ten days, or years, or twenty-five or even fifty years have gone, would affect the Council.

But the Central Council is not like the regular crew. Their jobs keep them on guard, far from being a team they constantly compete among themselves for stature, status and position. Chn'Gi couldn't tell if it was friendly or belligerent, it didn't matter, it kept them sharp, on guard, always looking for an edge or a point to make.

These people, the Central Council, would never get lost in time, never be a cog, gear, or another component of the system of systems that makes up Dadr'Ba.

Dadr'Ba runs continuously. It's long work days divided equally and overlapped between the ships five sectors, ensured three sectors active at any given time, with the other two sectors on crew rest. No weekends to break up the routine and only three annual events and ceremonies; Graduation Day, Touch of God Day, and Memorial Day. These are Ceremonial Events only, not days off, nothing interferes with the carefully orchestrated operation of Dadr'Ba, never a day off to break up the continuous cycle. Nothing is allowed to interfere with the continuous mechanized clockwork cycle that marks the relentless progress of Dadr'Ba.

Chn'Gi looked again at the summons on the screen. This was to be a video teleconference from her office that would afford her the luxury of comfortable surroundings and easy familiar access to her data in case she needed it.

At the appointed time, Dr. Chn'Gi sat at her desk as the wall across from her desk disappeared, and she suddenly appeared to sit at a much larger conference table. Seated at the head of the table across from her, sat the Commander, to his right, the Vice, her new boss, (that used to be her boss's. boss). Since the IL discovery and security crackdown, the SIL program was moved from the navigation department to report directly to the Vice Commander.

At the time of discovery, Chn'Gi was only able to get intermittent slices of antenna time from the array of antennas arranged at the end of tethers attached to one of the observation rings that girded Dadr'Ba. In order not to put too much stress on the antennas, the ring the antennas are attached to

---

[61] actually just a name for one of the Central Councils roles, the members are the same.

rotates at a much slower rate than Dadr'Ba's gravitational rotation. Otherwise, the antennas on the end of the tethers kilometers away (to provide a large aperture) would be under so much stress that they would tear from the ship.

Additional antennas, operating together and opposite one another, had finally been constructed and connected to one of the other observation rings and had operating time allocated to Chn'Gi and her team.

The explanation provided to the rest of the crew is that these antennas were auxiliary antennas used to aid in navigation and object avoidance or eradication, whose frequency is expected to increase since they're beginning to enter O'M's Oort Cloud.

Everyone was sitting at what Chn'Gi assumed to be a virtual conference table. Most likely, no one actually sat next to each other, they were seated as she was, comfortably at their own desk.

Chn'Gi suddenly spotted and then, as nonchalantly as possible picked up several cartoonish alien figurines made of hardened modeling clay given to her by her staff, made by their children in art class. She placed the figurines in her desk drawer.

She went on acting as if she was straightening out her touch sensitive virtual desktop, flattening the heads up monitor into the table and looked up. All eyes were upon her.

She focused her attention on Commander Di'Zo. He sat at the head of the conference table across from her. She awkwardly said "Master Commander Sir" then remained silent, there was a hint of sarcasm in her comment. Chn'Gi inwardly kicked herself for not being better prepared. She reprimanded herself for allowing what she perceived as a scrap of contempt towards the Council show that she still resented the rough treatment she and her team received at first discovery.

The Commander, a thin man with fine dark hair, stony, expressionless face and cold piercing eyes. He wore a crisp military uniform with emblems that clearly showed his rank. He didn't seem to breathe as he glanced around the table at the other, equally stony, expressionless faced, uniformed officers around the table. Before speaking, he paused, then his eyes narrowed as he focused his attention on Chn'Gi.

Then in a cold flat voice, "Dr. Chn'Gi please tell us the latest status of the intelligent life you discovered on O'M and be as detailed as you can about these invaders" then after a slight pause added "and it had better not be, nothing significant to report."

Chn'Gi gulped, instantly recalculating her earlier decision to begin with "nothing significant" then go into what she deemed, "insignificant" but now trying to make it sound "significant." It's only been a week, or has it been a month since her last report to the Council? Oh my God! Am I getting lost in time? O'M technology doesn't seem to advance very fast, but if I say that, I'll get questioned: "fast compared to what?" I've got nothing to work with, nothing to compare or extrapolate against, what do they expect?

Then she decided, give them a thorough review of the latest findings and let them judge for themselves that nothing has significantly changed. Chn'Gi quickly rolled up a tally of the amount and kind of data collected, hoping to spit out some numbers that would fill the void and save her career from getting chewed up like official papers through an ancient document shredder.

She began with the antenna time used, the number of transmissions detected and the frequencies; then attempted a summation "the intelligent life shortly after the initial broadcasts have successfully started two-way communications, which was to be expected. The original signals were in quite broad bands, which made it easier for us to detect them. They've successfully begun to narrow the bandwidth of their transmissions, an indication of the advancement of their technology and the quality and quantity of transmissions has increased steadily."

"They have yet to begin to broadcast video, which is essential in breaking the language code. The signals have all been a series of long and short pulses, the combination of long and short pulse length along with the absence of a timing signal indicates it's not binary but rather a rudimentary code of approximately forty characters."

"Our analysis has not been able to detect a key or a pattern that we can identify. Without a key or pattern we cannot begin developing a translation of their language or languages. The IL doesn't seem to be aware that others, such as ourselves are picking up their signals and are not broadcasting a key, therefore, they are broadcasting for their internal use."

"As you should be able to see, they are pretty far from being able to transmit video or an image which, aside from sending a pattern or key that we can recognize is the only way we will be able to begin to understand their language."

"The advancements needed from where they are now to where they need to be to transmit images or video is substantial. My team and I have no anthropological data or comparables to work with or examples from even our own history of technological development. It would be helpful, may I ask, that my team and I be given access to our own history of technological development on Or'Gn?"

As Chn'Gi spoke the last sentence, that was later erased from the official meeting report, the room grew deathly quiet. The look on Commander Di'Zo's face hardened, and the others shrank back from the table almost as if anticipating an explosion. But instead, with an expression as cold as ice and a voice louder than normal speaking tone, but not shouting, sounding almost robotic, very controlled coming from someplace deep within him. He only said, "No, it's forbidden, and don't ever ask again unless you want to suffer the consequences."

It took the longest time for Chn'Gi to respond, but no one seemed to be in a hurry, the virtual room appeared to have been frozen, freeze-framed, it didn't even look like anyone, even the other officers around the table breathed.

Commander Di'Zo continued to stare directly at Chn'Gi. Finally, Chn'Gi managed a weak, distant but audible "yes, sir", then broke eye contact with the

Commander and glanced down at her notes, flustered beyond belief and trying to regain her composure.

Finally, she continued, haltingly at first, "Once they begin... transmitting video... we should be able... to decode, or develop a translation of the language or languages. That is the significant event that my team and I are waiting for because besides translating their language we will be able to see what the O'Mi's look like."

The assembled group seemed to go along with Chn'Gi's reasoning until the last, and looked at her in surprise; the Commander visibly stiffened and glared first at his vice then back to Chn'Gi, this time, level toned but shouting "What's an 'O'Mi?"

Chn'Gi couldn't bear to look at the Commander. She dropped her eyes and focused on the smart table in front of her. Sensing that she was on the edge of a precipice, summoning all her strength in a soft, meek apologetic tone replied: "that's what we've taken to calling IL on O'M."

The Commander responded this time in a calm even tone, almost as if making up for his earlier outburst "These things are not 'O'Mi's' they're invaders, they are a pestilence that has laid claim to our world and are undoubtedly poisoning it."

"Thousands of years ago, before they even had a brain to think with, we chose this world to be our home. They are invaders and robbers and will have to be dealt with. In your reports, refer to them as "IL" and I never want to hear the term O'Mi again, understood?" Chn'Gi, barely audible "understood."

"Now, you will be expected to keep me, and the council informed about how fast these invaders are developing and what we can expect concerning other forms of technology they may be developing. That's all." The meeting ended.

Chapter 16, P'Ko's Friend Tn'[62]

As P'Ko turned the corner on his way to school, He spotted Dan'Zu and his gang across the street in one of their regular hangout spots, where the surveillance cameras didn't have a very good view. Not unexpectedly, they were tormenting a new kid.

P'Ko could tell by the marking on the To'Ta's uniform that the victim was a fifteenth-year student. P'Ko was already in his eighteenth year and hadn't seen the kid before.

Must be a transfer P'Ko thought. P'Ko wasn't surprised that Dan'Zu would be up to his old pranks, P'Ko had learned how to avoid Dan'Zu over the years, and lately, he's done a pretty good job of it. For the most part, Dan'Zu and his crew moved on to younger weaker prey.

This poor kid must feel alone, afraid, new school and all, and looks weak willed and immature, not so much different than P'Ko was when Dan'Zu began picking on him. P'Ko thought back to the times that he fell victim to Dan'Zu and his gang.

Transfers don't happen very often; the kid's parents must have changed jobs or job locations to wind up here. P'Ko watched Dan'Zu and his gang laughing and shoving each other and the new kid. P'Ko knew that this roughhousing was experienced much differently by this kid, than for Dan'Zu's gang.

The kid was near the breaking point, hands shaking, arms brought up in a defensive posture, head down, staggering as the group shoved the kid around a rough circle.

P'Ko's blood boiled, he could imagine himself there. Years later yet still fresh in his memory this was P'Ko before he escaped and got so good at evasion that they left him alone. Now he's older, more mature and confident that if he needed to, he could take on the whole gang and this hidden corner would be the perfect place. He too could play this slaphappy game of theirs.

P'Ko went into action; he walked up to the group laughing and shoved one of the gang members out of the way catching the new kid just as he is about to fall and maneuvered the victim behind him, putting himself between the kid and the gang.

The bully that P'Ko shoved cursed, but the rest of the group laughed along with P'Ko. Then P'Ko swiftly started to work his way around the circle of bullies. The first he gave a friendly slap on the shoulder, followed by a couple of quick diversionary moves, then ending with a light, open-handed slap to the face that left the bully looking bewildered.

The second one got the same treatment but ended with an elbow to the midsection doubling him over. The others, including Dan'Zu, still laughed.

---

[62] Sounds like Ton, rhymes with Tom.

P'Ko was behaving comically, but when the last one crumpled to the deck, the laughing abruptly stopped. The mood instantly changed, and Dan'Zu yelled "Hey, knock it off" but when P'Ko continued, called the gang to the attack.

P'Ko ducked and dodged quickly and swept the legs out from under number three and shoved number one that had started to lunge into Dan'Zu. And turned to work on number four. Number four had been content to step back and watch began to back away. Dan'Zu yelled again "don't just stand there, get him!"

P'Ko lightly slapped number four across the face three times in quick succession while batting down his attempt's to block. Then grabbed him by the shoulders and spun him around, causing him to lose his footing and flop to the ground, he sat on the ground with a stupid look on his face.

Dan'Zu shoved the gang member that P'Ko sent his way to the deck and losing all restraint wildly tried, to P'Ko's surprise, a couple of rudimentary martial arts kicks and punches, forcing the rest of the bullies to step back in the process and watch with amazement.

P'Ko dogged Dan'Zu's failings easily, then stepped forward to Dan'Zu like nothing was happening and with one hand, took Dan'Zu's arm and twisted it in an awkward angle and with his free arm, P'Ko wrapped it around Dan'Zu's neck as if in an embrace pinning Dan'Zu so he couldn't move.

Then P'Ko said loudly "Dan'Zu, you're such a kidder, this is fun." Then, turning his head and whispering so that only Dan'Zu could hear "I'm going to let you keep your self-respect, but if you bother this kid or anyone else again, I'll embarrass you in front of your friends to the point that no one will ever respect you again."

Then P'Ko dropped his arm from around Dan'Zu's neck and shook loose Dan'Zu's twisted arm. Then stepped around, reached out and shook Dan'Zu's hand. With a sober, sincere tone, P'Ko thanked Dan'Zu for the fun, then saying, looking over at the new kid that they had been picking on, that it was "too much fun for little kids and that they should leave the younger ones alone. What d'ya say?"

Dan'Zu paused for a long moment, then responded "yes, I guess you're right" with that P'Ko stepped through the middle of the group, and passed over to the bullied kid that was watching it all. P'Ko said "let's go" to the kid, putting his arm on the kid's shoulder, and guided the kid away, once out of earshot P'Ko told the kid that these bullies shouldn't bother nim again.

The new kid's name was Tn', still a nor, ne was still undecided about what gender ne is most comfortable with. Rather effeminate, not prissy, more tomboyish, not at all uncommon for a fifteen. Tn' thanked P'Ko for the rescue, expressing amazement at how well P'Ko handled himself against five adversaries. P'Ko dismissed it as luck and by taking them by surprise, not wanting Tn' to guess about his martial arts training.

P'Ko told Tn' about how these bullies picked on him when he was younger and that he had run away, and eventually they got tired of chasing him, and that he had always wanted to stand up to them. Seeing Tn' getting picked on gave him that chance. P'Ko said that it was he that should be thanking Tn'.

P'Ko and Tn' became friends, Tn' was grateful and always looked for ways to repay P'Ko. Tn' would hang around P'Ko whenever ne got the chance. P'Ko could rely on Tn's company, and support. Tn' was pleasant to be around and always anxious to spend time with P'Ko.

P'Ko treated Tn' like a boy, an effeminate boy, but still a boy. One day after school, P'Ko and Tn' were hanging out sitting up in one of the best viewing places of Nu'Tn, talking, and as friends sometimes do the subject came round to gender, and rather matter-of-factly, in a conversational tone, Tn' asked P'Ko whether he liked boys or girls. P'Ko's response was "Girls, of course"; "Oh" was Tn's reply. P'Ko asked Tn' "what about you?" Tn' replied, "I haven't decided yet" paused, then "I guess I've got time enough to decide."

Chapter 17, Chn'Gi's Reports to CA Council Two

Chn'Gi reviewed her notes for the report; she still felt beat down and depressed. Since the discovery of the O'Mi's she's felt as if she's been sent to prison.

The eTaC-M fused to her skull seemed to produce a tiny ringing in her head. It was probably just her imagination, but it served as a constant reminder of how much things have changed. She longed for her little studio apartment, and wished that she'd never had the "privilege" to brief the Central Council on anything.

She'd gotten better with her reports, she learned at her original 'O'Mi' blunder not to try to decide for the Commander and the Council what was significant and what was not. But hasn't been able to purge O'Mi from her vocabulary and every time she reports she spends too much brain power trying to avoid another 'O'Mi' slip. According to her boss, she came dangerously close to getting herself mind wiped or forcibly retired.

The assembled Central Council in this week's virtual meeting were, as usual all focused on her, she could feel the pressure, but instead of nervous or excited, she felt deflated, like she was pancaked against the inside of the hull on zone four.

She began her report, as if starting a recording, "The transmissions have advanced to tighter frequencies, and we've been able to determine that the IL's are probably using more than one language, still with no key it's impossible to decipher. The IL's have recently begun analog type signals that we are reasonably sure is audio, but we can't be certain."

The Vice interrupted her and asked if they could hear a sample. Chn'Gi responded "certainly" and with a few strokes on her desktop, what sounded like someone trying to speak, garbled, sometimes muffled sounds, with frequent choking and retching, filled the room. After a few long moments of garble with pauses that could be interpreted as sentence breaks.

The Commander interrupted "Enough, we don't need to hear any more of that garbage." getting nods of agreement from everyone. "Continue with your report."

"We speculate that the IL is divided by language so there must be more than one set of populations separated by culture or geography. They must have a certain level of metal refining, manufacture, and technical capability in order to construct a radio. They most likely have manufacturing and a transportation system on a relatively large scale and be capable of supporting it. All of that would also necessitate population centers and the food production and infrastructure needed to support all of the above."

Someone that had been off camera, apparently monitoring the meeting suddenly appeared and the virtual conference table flickered as a new person joined next to the Commander, the person that had been sitting there shifted over a position, the virtual table compensating instantly. The new person was now at the Commander's right side while the Vice remained on the Commander's left.

Without introduction, the newcomer asked, "What weapons are they capable of producing?"

After a pause to reflect, Chn'Gi juggled the possibilities in her mind and responded: "that isn't my area of expertise, but with the metallurgy and manufacturing capabilities demonstrated, the ILs should be capable of producing explosives and projectile weapons."

The conference room went silent, and the view froze and frosted over, someone in the conference must have muted the conference as one or more meeting members had a private discussion.

Chn'Gi sat in silence. After several long moments that could have been seconds or minutes, the conference came back online. Her boss was now the only one visible across from her. "Good work, from now continue to report every development, and feel free to provide speculation on their weapons capabilities. We will have "appropriate" experts review your data and provide us specific detailed analysis and options. In the meantime, we want to continue to hear your interpretation".

The wall across from Chn'Gi's desk returned to being a wall, and Chn'Gi laid her head down on her desk and took a deep breath and exhaled, almost sobbing. What must these ancient cold, stoic people be thinking or planning?

The Council and especially the Commander most certainly must be Touch of God Survivors. There mustn't be any other way for them to attain such high positions. Dadr'Ba status and rank are based strictly on seniority; all the top people are Touch of God Survivors with perhaps only with minutes or seconds of travel time seniority separating them.

But more importantly, how does being a Touch of God Survivor change the way people think about things? These people have wealth beyond imagining, have lived for the greater part of a thousand years, what stories they could tell, and more importantly, they may have pre-Touch of God knowledge.

She wondered how it might affect one's mind to be on-the-job for centuries without any significant break, the competition for the top slots must be enormous and taking any time off must run the risk of losing your position. The Central Council must not be as central and cohesive as the name implies, it's clear to Chn'Gi it's a dictatorship.

The Commander's lieutenants, the Sector Commanders, and staff are free and ostensibly encouraged to give advice to the Commander, but the Commander has the final word. And although the Commander cannot force any of the staff to take time off, whereby ensuring his seniority advantage, he can influence their quality life by the tasks he assigns them and the freedom of action he allows.

It's a balance; he desperately needs his staff, therefore, must try to maintain their cooperation and obedience, if not loyalty.

Uncooperative staff members and even sector commanders given cause can be placed into a kind of internal exile and denied a say in the running of Dadr'Ba. They're allowed to live a life of quiet seclusion, given a mundane job inappropriate with their position, forever monitored by security. A recipe virtually guaranteed to turn all but the strongest person into a vegetable.

Chapter 18, Su'Zi Visits Mi'Ka

Su'Zi sat across from Mi'Ka and sipped the tea she had been offered. Su'Zi only lives one sector away in a Zone Two mining camp but this is the first time Su'Zi has visited Mi'Ka at her shop in Ol'Tn'Ka, zone three.

The CA makes a big deal of letting the crew know that they monitor cross-sector movement, the reason given being safety and environmental control to ensure efficient heat dissipation from the core. But cross-sector monitoring doesn't apply to Mi'Nr's, whose operations are now in the lower regions of zone three. Mi'Nr's know of sector crossings unknown or uncontrolled by the CA. Su'Zi used one of these uncontrolled cross points for this visit.

The CA prefers that people do all their recreational travel virtually. Virtual reality has gotten so good over the years that it matches the average person's senses, and unless close attention is paid, it can be mistaken for reality. With the ability to go virtually, anywhere and visit anyone on Dadr'Ba without leaving your apartment. Most people don't physically travel. Physical trips are viewed by most as unnecessary and time-consuming and are performed only for the novelty of the experience, most often for vacations.

Virtual reality mostly lacks the harder to quantify aspects of reality. There's something special about being physically in a place experiencing the visceral parts, the unique combination of sensations, smell, gravity, air pressure, vibrations, and especially, and the reason for Su'Zi's visit, the psychic environment.

For those with psychic ability, the feeling, and awareness created by interaction with an individual and the surrounding psychic community creates a unique experience. Feeling the psychic atmosphere of a spot can't be duplicated. Although psychic energy is dimensionless, the relative strengths and directions of the psychic matrix make every place unique.

To visit Mi'Ka for help with a personal problem required an actual visit to Mi'Ka's Curio Shop. To some Mi'Ka was a soothsayer to others, an oracle, to some a psychic medicine woman and to a few others a witch, whose concoctions can heal wounds of the soul.

One thing Mi'Ka steadfastly refuses to do or even attempt is to communicate with the dead. Su'Zi would like to have Mi'Ka help her get in touch with her father, but she knew Mi'Ka would refuse.

The dead are lost.

Most often in Dadr'Ba society the passed on or retired, live on through their contributions to their children and their grandchildren. They are not gone but are part of who we are and will always be with us. The lost ones, the dead, such as Ba, are thought to be in purgatory, a place full of emptiness and despair.

It's said that those who make contact with the lost go insane, and eventually become lost themselves because their insanity prevents them from retiring correctly.

Su'Zi was desperate for Mi'Ka to interpret her dreams and confident that if anyone could do it, Mi'Ka could.

If it weren't for Mi'Ka's absolute prohibition against contacting the dead, Su'Zi would have asked Mi'Ka about the nightmares Su'Zi had in the days and weeks following Ba's death.

Those recurring nightmares, reliving what she thought Ba must have gone through, being blasted out into space away from Dadr'Ba, the fear of being lost in interstellar space, only to be drawn into the engine intake. To be bashed, crushed, squeezed, ionized and obliterated in nuclear fire. Only to find herself lost in the black void, feeling panic similar to the Touch of God Ceremony. But in her nightmare never finding God or a star friend or a way out, or a way home, as a creeping hopelessness engulfs her.

Fortunately, that's when she wakes up and even more fortunate the nightmares subsided in frequency and intensity and over time stopped altogether.

Su'Zi told her mother who admitted similar dreams, but not as vivid; together they concluded that it was just the result of the trauma of the event. Su'Zi's brother never admitted to sharing these nightmares, but she sensed he did, and never questioned him about it.

These new dreams Su'Zi couldn't explain or attribute to anything she knew or experienced. She dreamt that she was on O'M, she knew it, felt it and wanted it to be O'M. The O'M in her dream felt good and more real than any virtual place or environment she's ever visited. It looked better than any of the artist conceptions of what O'M would be like.

She found herself on a beach on the shore of an ocean. The feeling was incredible, seeing the sky above adorned with a random pattern of rounded white puffy clouds that she'd seen tiny fragments of while going through airlocks, only gigantic scattered across the whole sky and taking various forms. Some seeming solid and slowly rolling and changing from shape to shape, some forming solid bodied creatures and inventions. These clouds could be the flesh covering the static points of light that form the skeletonous creatures that make up the constellations. But these creatures always move, now soft and cuddly then ever so slowly changing into a roaring monster, this living menagerie stretched from one horizon to the other, and the whole thing is slowly moving in mass across a blue sky.

The dream O'M was overwhelming, there was so much openness, it was like looking out through the secret observation port with her father that Su'Zi seen so much openness. But space was somehow fundamentally different, vast, open and awe-inspiring in its expanse, mostly black but with millions of bright points of light, some brighter than others, some a little hazy.

The mind arranging them in patterns that make outlines of familiar things and when one lets their imagination go, unfamiliar patterns can be created into new creatures or inventions.

But behind the clouds of stardust and the scattered diamond constellation creatures, space is cold and hostile. Appearing to be static it's full of high-speed particles and bursts of radiation that could kill you in an instant, or expose you to a death that takes weeks to zenith.

Space, cold and heartless, seems to Su'Zi's senses possess a soul, a very old soul, a very dark tired soul. A soul that pervades space, like the ether that provides the framework for the dimensions and whose existence lies between the infinitesimally small boundary between positiveness, negativeness, matter and antimatter. A boundary whose existence provides the foundation for the universe, and from what all matter and energies are formed.

All this, the soul of space, the vacuum, the ether, the energy, the matter, is hated by nothing. Nothing is the acid that seeks to torment and destroy the soul of space, it's no wonder space is so tired and feeble in places yet temperamental and violent in others.

Contrasting Space, in Su'Zi's dream she felt O'M, reaching as far as Su'Zi could perceive, reaching with her consciousness, her senses, her psyche, her very soul, and at that moment, Su'Zi felt the life, the soul of O'M, warm, friendly and inviting. She felt that if there is a heaven, then this must be it. She felt the warmth of the sun's rays as it penetrated her skin. She closed her eyes, stretched out her arms, and breathing deep, tasted the salt in the air. Then, using all of her senses, physical, psychic, and spiritual, soaked it all in letting her soul mingle with O'M.

Then, eyes still closed, feeling and sensing the world around her she felt a pain, a pain that, instead of originating from a particular location radiating out, it radiated in, from the outside, in waves, slowly growing, centering high in her chest and at the base of her neck between her shoulders, and penetrating deep down inside her.

She opens her eyes and to her astonishment finds herself still on the beach, still in pain. Then she returns, loosening her grip on her psychic senses and getting the feeling back in her bodies physical senses, and the pain recedes.

Su'Zi knows this has to be a dream, but like no dream she has ever had or heard of anyone ever having. She didn't know how long she's been here, hours it must be, the sun seems to be setting. Off in the distance very low on the horizon an immense display of gold's yellows and reds growing until it fills over half the sky. So much so that looking at it fills her entire field of view. It's beautiful, spectacular, but Su'Zi senses that this has something to do with the pain she was feeling, that there's something wrong, something she's missing.

Su'Zi gazes, taking in the scene, looking back and forth from side to side and high up, losing her balance, stumbled, but instead of falling seemed to float backward, preventing herself from falling.

Strange flying creatures soar past Su'Zi towards the trees behind her, and small alien creatures creep past in the sand and shallow dunes around her. The waves lap the water's edge in slow rhythmic patterns, receding slowly exposing even more strange alien creatures, none like she'd ever seen before, not even in artist conceptions.

Then just as she was looking closer at one of the tiny alien creatures, she became aware of a wailing like some gigantic creature dying. The sound is very loud, and Su'Zi can't tell where it's coming from. She tried focusing on the creature she was just looking at, thinking that the animal might be calling to her psychically. But even psychically, this tiny creature is far too small to make such a significant noise.

Then Su'Zi searches for the source of the wail psychically and feels the pain return. Then Su'Zi senses something and quickly looks down the beach, and some distance away, she sees someone standing, looking, at her. The person is too far away to recognize and seems to be also looking around trying to figure out where the painful wail is coming from, the intensity of the wail and the pain suddenly increases to a fever pitch and terrified she wakes up. She's had this dream every night for five nights straight.

After two nights Su'Zi told her mother, who had no explanation for it. The morning after the third night, they talked to a Church Elder; the Church Elder was at a loss for an explanation and hesitantly suggested she seek out Mi'Ka.

After hearing Su'Zi's story Mi'Ka sat back slowly. Ku'Ma, her pet folded up neatly on her lap and vibrated softly in a slow rhythm. Mi'Ka's blind eyes closed down to slits, everything in the little room in the back of Mi'Ka's shop became absolutely still, nothing moved, the air still, all sound disappeared.

Then in an instant Mi'Ka was leaning forward, speaking. Su'Zi, startled, caught by surprise, didn't even see Mi'Ka move. It was as if Mi'Ka had leaned back in thoughtful repose, then time stopped, or Su'Zi fell asleep, Su'Zi couldn't tell for how long, it couldn't have been longer than seconds, when Mi'Ka started talking.

Mi'Ka was looking intently at Su'Zi, an intense, compassionate expression on her face. Mi'Ka spoke, "my child, I'm sure you've realized that this is no ordinary dream, it isn't even a dream at all, you experienced an episode of spatial-temporal entanglement."

Su'Zi had never heard of such a thing, and even though Mi'Ka was blind, she could sense Su'Zi's puzzlement. Mi'Ka went on to explain "Su'Zi, do you remember the principle behind quantum entanglement? The basis for our QECS instantaneous communication that we had with Or'Gn?"

"When dealing with subatomic particles that are near enough to the core components of the universe. They cannot entirely be split, broken down or altered further, they are entangled. The entanglement occurs outside of our physical universe, in a dimensionless place. What happens to one can affect the other, no matter how far apart they are. It's like the psychic connection between family members, especially parents and children."

"What you have experienced is a connection across space and time. It's impossible to tell for sure where or when what you saw happened, it could've been yourself in the future or someone else in the future or the past. It's even possible that you weren't even connected to a body, but only in a place and time. Do you remember seeing yourself? I mean, did you look at and be able to see your hands or feet?"

Su'Zi thought for a moment and said no "I moved and looked around but never saw myself, only that other person in the distance and I'm pretty sure they saw me too."

Mi'Ka replied "You're not able to see yourself means that you were there psychically only, and not through a psychic connection through another person. The fact that you saw someone and they saw you meant that they were there psychically too, had it been someone there, in reality, they wouldn't have been able to see you; this is highly unusual. The odds against this happening randomly defy estimation, especially for it to happen now five nights in a row. The only explanation that could help explain it is that you have a strong psychic connection to that person you saw. Did your mother or brother have the dream too?"

"No," Su'Zi replied. "At least, I'm pretty sure not."

Mi'Ka "Well a possible explanation is that psychic wounds can make a person susceptible to these kinds of things, it's like a damaged area of your body where there is aggravated and exposed nerve endings causing them to be ultrasensitive.

I suspect that even after all these years. The psychic wound, the trauma of losing your father, has made you susceptible to this. It could've been random, but it being repeated portends otherwise. Psychic wounds are slow to heal and often require life events to occur to bring about healing.

You're young yet; I suspect that when you get older, and you find yourself a mate, someone that you want to bind with and, eventually have children, you'll finally feel whole."

"All of us have known, at one time or another, that feeling of something, some part of us, missing. We spent a good part of our lives trying to find that missing part, that person that makes us complete, and when we do we're content and happy."

"This dream won't last forever, and this dream may be the last, but there could be others. Rest assured though that as your psychic wound heals these dreams, these spatial-temporal entanglements will decrease, and they will reduce in frequency and intensity and eventually stop. It's impossible to predict where or when or how."

"Consider this a blessing of sorts. A miracle, a gift that very few people, perhaps one in every few generations get given. Most undoubtedly, mistake it for a mere dream. Tell me, how do you feel about this 'dream'?"

Su'Zi, not having to think about it, replied. "Most of it is so beautiful and pleasant that while it was happening and even now looking back, I'd want to be there and stay forever. It's only the last, the feeling of pain, the wailing coming from everywhere and nowhere that made it seem like a nightmare. Now that I think about it the pain may have been coming from the soul of O'M, because I first felt it when I reached out to feel, to connect with it. As I did, it was as if O'M's soul had been injured."

Mi'Ka paused a moment, then, "I've been given the gift of perception, you have a gift of vision. You see real things from some place, and some time, you will probably never be able to control it, but know this, it is as real as anything there is in the universe. What you saw was real in a different place and time."

Su'Zi thanked Mi'Ka and having finished her tea prepared to leave. Mi'Ka gave her a hug, telling her that she's welcome anytime, adding "if the dream doesn't stop by itself, she may be able to prepare a special tea that may help soothe her. But it would be better let this work out naturally, and that if she has any new dreams, that she'd be very curious to hear about them.

Finally, Mi'Ka cautioned, "The CA must never learn about these dreams. They know their nature and significance and would do terrible things to you to try to exploit your gift."

After Su'Zi left, Mi'Ka allowed herself to ponder... that other person, in Su'Zi's dream, for that person to be there they would have needed to share Su'Zi's psychic wound, and if it wasn't her mother or brother, who could have it been?...

Su'Zi made her way back home to the mining camp in sector two, feeling as if a weight had been lifted off her shoulders and wondering if she would relive the dream tonight. The next morning, she woke to feel happier than she had in a very long time, rested and refreshed.

The dream didn't return, but she still wondered about who she saw.

Chapter 19, P'Ko's Dream's

P'Ko stared up at the instructor, but his mind couldn't register what she was saying. Physics is his favorite class, but he can't take his mind off the woman in the dreams he's been having.

He can't complain or confide in anyone, his trouble learning in his first years, and the relentless teasing he received growing up made him want to blend in, not to stand out, to be quiet, reserved, okay, call it introverted. It would be impossible for him to share with anyone that a dream woman has been plaguing him.

Not long after the showdown defending Tn', Dan'Zu and his gang settled down and having failed using bullying and intimidation have been trying to be nice, but P'Ko never trusted him. Then at the end of the school year, Dan'Zu disappeared, P'Ko guessed that he had served his penance at public school and went back to his private school.

P'Ko hoped that he'd never see or interact with Dan'Zu again. There was something about Dan'Zu's actions, his demeanor, that didn't sit right with P'Ko, or maybe it was his imagination or paranoia stemming from being persecuted for so long.

P'Ko knew that from a certain perspective, he owed Dan'Zu thanks, Dan'Zu's continued assault pushed P'Ko to develop an inner strength and defenses and practically forced him to learn illegal martial arts. All things he wouldn't have attempted on his own.

His martial arts experience increased his self-esteem and self-confidence. Now some of the other kids have started to look up to P'Ko and admire him.

His problems growing up put enormous stresses on Ma and Ba back then. He doesn't want to put Ma and Ba through any more problems, after all, he's just a few years from graduation, and his new life will begin.

But these dreams and this growing unease about things he cannot touch or quantify, the uncontrolled strengthening of senses and feelings, though minor in comparison to his childhood. These latest dreams and power feelings are starting to cause problems. Like now, P'Ko still doesn't know what the instructor is talking about, how long has she been talking?

P'Ko can't focus. But is drawn back to the dream, such a strange dream, so vivid, so memorable, never had P'Ko been able to recall a dream so vividly. It was as if he had been awake and experienced it. The contents of the dream seemed to be written directly into long-term memory, and high refresh into short-term memory; he can't get it off his mind. So unlike other, ordinary dreams, usually forgotten seconds or minutes after waking.

P'Ko now awake, hours after waking P'Ko couldn't stop thinking about it, and about her, the most beautiful woman P'Ko had ever laid eyes on. Though in the dream, she was very far away, he could see her vividly. She wore a

Mi'Nr's uniform, the distinctive color was easy to see, and it was tailored and showed a shapely figure and though she was too far away to see her eyes he could tell that she was looking intently at him.

P'Ko found himself trying to dissect, and analyze this too vivid of a dream. His early childhood nightmares that plagued him as a Bo'Ba were as vivid but terrifying. P'Ko didn't want to remember them, he had experienced them before he learned to speak and sort out his thoughts. Making those first nightmares easy to forget because he had no language to catalog them with.

This latest dream having come to him five night in a row was pleasant, the beach, the sun, the waves, the breeze and especially the woman, too beautiful for words, he never wants to forget it. So many parts of this dream were so wonderful; P'Ko hoped that O'M was truly as beautiful and awe-inspiring as it appeared in the dream and that she would be there.

The only disturbing thing is the last part, not the spectacular sunset, but the feeling of pain and the wailing torturous sound coming from everywhere, it was then that she saw him too. Too far for eye contact but close enough for recognition, he knew that she saw him too, he felt her recognition; she had to be real. Then, a pang of despair or just part of the dream?

Despite Mi'Ka's encouragement P'Ko still hasn't tried to develop wholly or learn to trust in his psychic ability. He has trouble bringing himself to believe something that can't be seen, touched, analyzed or put into numbers. Why can't he just dismiss this dream woman?

P'Ko wondered if perhaps he should ask Mi'Ka about it, the dream had happened every night for five nights' straight. He resolved to visit Mi'Ka if it goes another night.

Upon this resolve, and to his surprise, he felt better, almost as if a weight had been lifted off his shoulders.

Ironically, as P'Ko's mind cleared and the distraction of his dream faded his focus returned to the classroom, the professor was talking about "nothing" P'Ko laughed to himself about the irony of this as the teacher very carefully and deliberately described nothing.

"Nothing" "is not empty space," she was saying "if you had nothing you wouldn't even have empty space. Empty space has dimensions and contains a flux of subatomic particles that are spontaneously created and just as rapidly disappear. Empty space is a very capable medium for the transmission of matter and energy. In contrast, pure nothingness is incapable of transmitting or allowing anything to pass through it. It's not that nothing is a solid or a barrier, it's just that pure nothingness is dimensionless, and as soon as dimensionless space is encountered, nothing can pass through it."

"Nothing exists outside our universe; Nothing exists beyond the three spatial dimensions supported by positive and negative space."

"And just as a reminder time is not a dimension, time is simply a method of keeping track of things in the present. Time can be thought of as the compilation of all the forces of the universe working in unison moving matter and energy, which in turn with our perceptions and our need to create order gives the notion of the passage of time."

"Our desire to arrange matter and energy to our liking and because we frequently prefer things a certain way or as they once were, creates the need for the concept of time and a wish to reverse time, which is impossible, except, of course, on the sub-atomic scale."

"When it comes to the sub-atomic environment, the laws of nature accommodate and even insist on the bi-directional action of forces, but that in no way translates to the macro scale in which we perceive our existence. To truly reverse time in the macro scale, that we experience life in, all the forces of nature all across the universe would need to be reversed."

"The impossibility of the reversal of time doesn't negate the need for our bi-directional perception of time, recognition of past and future is necessary to gain control of our environment. Without the perception of time, we'd be nothing more than very primitive animals that have no concept of the past more than a few minutes of seconds into the past or machines that operate strictly in the present. Because this perception is so ingrained in us, it is difficult for many to recognize time for what it is. We mistakenly believe that just because we can think ourselves into the past, we can go there."

"Now back to the subject of this lesson, nothing. Nothing must "really" be nothing. To ascribe nothing the basic ability to pass something, even light, or to provide it the ability to be measured, you provide it "something." so you see there is an immense difference between empty space and nothing."

"Continuing, it gets a little confusing because, although nothing cannot contain empty space, a little empty space can contain quite a lot of nothing. 'Nothing' in this sense is a kind of negative energy."

"Think about it, it takes matter and energy to create or introduce something into or out of nothing, and though the universe has for all eternity existed, the universe and all it contains has its origins from nothing. This creates a space/energy/mass deficit half of one kind of space/energy and mass and the other half another kind of space/energy and mass. That, if all things were brought together, would equal nothing, a zero-sum balance.

Matter and electromagnetic energy contain elements of both sides of this balance, though due to the effect of dimensional distortion created by their very existence remain stable.

"In normal space, the space around stars, and the space within solar systems contain little nothing. As a matter of fact, standard space contains the equivalent of a kind of "space pressure" or "ether" that may be devoid of gasses (that typically provide the source of pressure) but is packed full of electromagnetic and gravitational fields.

It's the level of intensity of these fields along with the spontaneous creation and annihilation of subatomic particles that provides the source of "space pressure," which in turn readily permits the transmission of matter and energy."

"Deep space, interstellar and especially intergalactic space contain the most nothing and perhaps at the edge of the universe, if there is one, there may exist nothing. But there would be no way of telling because as soon as we got there by definition, we would be finding or creating something in the process of discovery."

"The "nothingness" level of deep space creates a kind of negative energy that is responsible for the redshift, or the loss of energy from the light from distant stars and galaxies. That in the old days was attributed to the expansion of the universe. Rest assured the stars and galaxies are moving with respect to one another only they exist in an ocean of various levels of nothing, or negative energy, that some named dark energy. Deep space nothing extracts a tax or imposes a resistance on all things traversing it, affecting their movement and their energies, especially light."

"Right now we are leaving interstellar space, and there is still a good bit of nothing around us. This nothing, or negative space or dark energy was helping to slow Dadr'Ba robbing it of energy, but now as Dadr'Ba approaches O'M, the negative energy is working to push Dadr'Ba towards O'M just as O'M's gravitational field is starting to take effect. As a matter of fact, both negative energy and gravity are manifestations of the same force."

"If Dadr'Ba's engine wasn't active for the first half of the trip or O'M was further away the negative energy of interstellar space, interacting with Dadr'Ba's something-ness would slow and eventually force Dadr'Ba to a complete stop. This nothingness or negative, dark energy also affects our spin velocity that provides us our artificial gravity; we periodically have to add to our spin energy or our rotational velocity would also slow and eventually stop."

One of the other students caught the professor's attention and asked: "what happens then?"

The professor replied, "Then?"

Student, "you know, after everything stops?"

Professor "This process is still not thoroughly understood. Little data has been accumulated, and there is still much speculation. But research is ongoing; it's believed that all energy would be lost, escape and never replaced. Then slowly matter would eventually evaporate, the molecular movement would slow and cease in conjunction with atomic evaporation."

"Subatomic particles are not static; many are in a constant state of flux, energy from this subatomic flux will leak out similar to radioactive decay operating on seemly stable isotopes but in a hostile environment working on a time scale of billions of years. The negative energy of the nothing or dark energy would eventually consume the entire ship. But don't worry, according to our best estimates it would take many billions of years for even the deepest space to absorb all of Dadr'Ba."

The professor then went into the mathematics involved with nothingness, which P'Ko tracked along with on his desktop slate and before he realized it, the professor was completing her summary and dismissing the class. P'Ko felt good and for the moment forgot his dream.

P'Ko's O'M dream never returned, P'Ko still wondered about the woman on the beach, but dismissed it as only a dream, an unconscious manifestation of a conscious desire.

Chapter 20, P'Ko and Mi'Ka Discuss his Mentor

P'Ko sat on the cushion near the small table towards the back of Mi'Ka's shop that she sometimes uses for private readings, a larger table used for group readings lay propped up against the wall not far away.

He's nearing graduation, and he along with the rest of his class are making decisions and preparations. Excitement and curiosity are running high as everyone tries to find out as much as they can about everything involved.

P'Ko still hasn't picked a mentor, who for P'Ko is particularly challenging; he has trouble picking and even more trouble approaching and asking a date to accompany him to a sports or social event at school. There's no way he'd speak to Mi'Ka about such a personal subject. He was certain that she wouldn't be able to help on this account, and if he did, he was afraid to imagine what sort of recommendation she would come up with.

P'Ko's mission on this visit was to ply her for information, not so much about the Graduation Ceremony, but about the mysterious ToG Ceremony that follows graduation.

Mi'Ka answers the Graduation Ceremony questions as best she could, but everything about the Graduation ceremony is public knowledge, so she had little to add, adding that she rarely attends the Graduation ceremony in person. She prefers to watch online and avoid the stares and psychic comments that her looks bring from the residents of Nu'Tn.

P'Ko, deftly as he can, questions Mi'Ka about the ToG Ceremony, she steadfastly refuses to answer. He pressed her, and she got a little angry and flustered, anxious to change the subject Mi'Ka asks P'Ko about his bio-mods.

P'Ko is caught off guard and not realizing what exactly she meant, responds with what had been foremost on his mind and that of many of his classmates. Saying that he wants to be male, but hadn't decided on what mods he needed or who to pick for his mentor or mentors.

P'Ko sees Mi'Ka's surprised look and sensed her bewilderment, and assumes she wants more information. So he blurts out a list of names, some suggested by his parents, some he heard about from friends. Most he had never met, and a few were known to be regulars, willing to mentor anyone, strangers, and referrals alike. Then partially joking, P'Ko mentions La'Na and Fa'Na the two prostitutes that had offered him a good time.

Mi'Ka realizing P'Ko's predicament and reprimanding herself for not sensing it earlier, reading P'Ko's psychic signals, responds, acknowledges his poor joke with a short forced laugh, that sounded more like a cough.

Responding like she took P'Ko seriously, which in part he was, says "Fa'Na and La'Na are fine companions for recreation and would surely be able to recommend bio-mods and teach you how to use the equipment, but mentors must be chosen carefully and not left to chance." Mi'Ka paused, then continued

"A mentor and your choice of a mentor can impact you positively or negatively for the rest of your life, they can even ruin it."

P'Ko knew this to be true, at least from what his parents had tried to explain to him, and hidden behind some of the remarks by his friends, some of them, he knew even more seriously than he, were considering La'Na and Fa'Na as mentors.

Embarrassed by his attempt to make light something so serious and relieved that Mi'Ka didn't laugh at him outright or severely scold him, all he could muster in reply was "yes, I know… it's just that I don't know who or how to ask."

Mi'Ka seeing P'Ko's sincerity and feeling the edge of desperation behind it thought for a moment and replied "I think I know someone, she rarely mentors, but she's excellent. I can approach her, but you'll have to trust me on this, she's very selective. You'll be interviewed, at the end of that interview you'll know if she accepts you as a Lr'Lng.

If she accepts you and you agree, you're committed you can't back down. You are making one of the most important adult decisions of your life, one that could have consequences that could touch you virtually every day of your life." Then after a long pause, "Shall I ask her?" after another pause, P'Ko, trusting Mi'Ka and feeling relieved, "Yes, thank you."

The conversation moved to what Mi'Ka had intended earlier. She asked, even though she remembered his job choice comment a while back, she wanted to make sure he was still committed and cognizant of all the implications associated with the decision "Are you still certain about your chosen profession?" He said he was.

She said, "You need to consider how the bio-mods will mark you in Dadr'Ba society." This didn't faze P'Ko; he grew up 'strange'. As a child, he was kidded, teased and bullied, but when he got older and eventually overcame his persecutors, he grew privately proud of his uniqueness and independence, it inspired. Then, seeing more and more post graduates and adults embracing, and even striving for uniqueness in this world of clones, he took an even greater pride in his individuality and nonconformity, seeing it as a kind of strength and courage.

As an undergrad, P'Ko didn't go overboard with outlandish clothes, makeup, and temporary tattoos, but he knew plenty of people that did, and there are lots of people walking around Nu'Tn (Ol'Tn even more so) that look stranger than any Mi'Nr or combination Mi'Nr/U'Te he could ever imagine. P'Ko admired these people.

P'Ko replied, "I'm looking forward to it, if the CA doesn't ruin it by denying my job choice, I think that I'll be the only U'Te turned Mi'Nr ever, I'll be the first." P'Ko said with pride. "I've been teased, made fun of, harassed as a kid; I'm finally going to gain a little respect now and know with absolute certainty that I'm going to be a good Mi'Nr, one of the best!"

Mi'Ka thought for a moment, then "You're right to be worried that the CA might deny your job choice, we're going to have to take care not in any way to give the CA any cause for concern."

Mi'Ka "Have you spoke to anyone about your job choice?" P'Ko, "No, I'm sure my classmates would tease and ridicule me, and my parents would try to talk me out of it. It's not that I'm ashamed of the choice, it that they might take offense thinking I'm making a statement about their job choices, or that I'm turning my back on my race or that I'm better than them."

"I don't want to have to explain or justify it; it's just something I know I have to do. I don't have a simple answer, and I can't put it into words, it's just that deep down in my soul I've got this calling. I want to, I need to become a Mi'Nr, it's very personal I can't put words to it, and I don't want to have to by telling people too soon."

Mi'Ka used all her powers of perception to track, comprehend and validate what P'Ko was saying. "After my mods and I begin working they might see me as 'different' but inside I'll be the same. I'll be less different than lots of people out there with extreme body mods" and P'Ko couldn't help the thought crossing his mind that he'd look less 'different' than Mi'Ka. Who was truly unique. "I want to announce my job choice when I can walk away and get to work, limiting the exposure by limiting the time cynics and conformists have to challenge or influence my decision."

"I'm going to have the chance to be different and like so many others show it, step out of the norm, refuse to comply, refuse to be just another cog in the machine."

Mi'Ka cautioned, "The CA doesn't like non-conformists, they manage a population of clones, and they prefer them to behave that way, like machines. But they're faced with the fact that everyone strives for some level of individuality, of self-worth. The CA allows those that choose to, to have outlandish body mods knowing that it helps to pacify the masses desire for self-esteem."

"It's wise to delay the announcement of your job choice, aside from reducing your personal exposure to teasing and ridicule, it will limit the time the CA has to digest the situation; some could view this as politically sensitive. Remember from your history lessons there were protests and a threatened strike a few hundred years ago over this very subject. Your teachers say that it didn't come to a strike, that the CA tactfully and judiciously avoided it. I was there, I remember it, there was a strike and the CA finally did give in to the demands for freedom of job choice regardless of race. The guidelines they published for job choice made it practically impossible for cross race career choices, job movement or swapping."

"The concessions from the CA did make it easier for job moves within races which made it a relative success but hardly ever is anyone allowed to change vocations and never across the glass race barrier. To assure approval, the CA will need to see this as non-threatening; they need to see it as an example of extreme body mod and at the same time make themselves look good."

Chapter 21, P'Ko and Mi'Ka Discuss P'Ko's Mentor Part Two

P'Ko received a short call from Mi'Ka, Mi'Ka didn't like to talk on open lines, preferring psychic messaging instead, but because P'Ko's psychic messaging abilities are not fully developed, and she wasn't able to message P'Ko. Mi'Ka knows he has the ability, but P'Ko doesn't have enough confidence and trust, which in turn impacts his psychic sensitivity, precision, and accuracy.

P'Ko experienced an episode of Mi'Ka intruding on his thoughts, he wasn't able to get her off his mind and logically dismissed it as anxiousness about the whole mentoring situation, and he had begun contemplating how he might be able to back out of the deal he had made with Mi'Ka. His mind raced with images of what he thought Mi'Ka's idea of a mentor might be, and none of them appealed to him.

Mi'Ka's call tuned him to focus on her, and it didn't take much psychic energy to know she had tried to contact him psychically and to understand her frustration knowing that the CA was listening.

It's commonly known that the CA listens and uses automated keyword, pattern analysis, and call metrics to flag suspicious calls. Suspicious calls are scrutinized even further and may lead to the use of "other" surveillance methods and technologies.

Most people have grown numb to the monitoring; the CA has been doing it for as long as anyone can remember and for the majority of individuals it has zero impact. P'Ko had always been careful with his calls, but the feeling he got from Mi'Ka on this call stepped things up to a whole new level, a level that that P'Ko sensed could not be stepped down from.

She said that she had found the curio he had asked about, and she would set it aside for him on his next visit to her curio shop, then ended the call. She didn't give him enough time to speak, though he was juggling with the decision and some way of saying that he didn't want the curio after all.

P'Ko knew that Mi'Ka had arranged the appointment for the mentoring interview.

P'Ko's mind went into high gear worrying about who this person was that Mi'Ka knew or was friends with that would be a good mentor. His imagination ran a gamut of possibilities; he was aware that Mi'Ka knew a great many people.

Mi'Ka being a ToG survivor and influential in the Mi'Nr community he guessed that this person was probably a Mi'Nr, which was fine, he'd seen many Mi'Nr females that he found attractive, and he didn't share the negative prejudices that some Ute's have toward Mi'Nr's. He knew that they were people just like everyone else, with much the same hopes and dreams as he and his family, but due to their vocation they led a life of extremes that made them tougher and P'Ko thought stronger willed as a result. P'Ko didn't know what else to do but waited to be contacted.

The next day he was messaged an appointment reminder from a blocked id, the message provided instructions to go to a place and wait. To his utter amazement once he saved the appointment to his personal calendar the time and location changed, along with the security settings on his calendar and messaging system. Checking deeper he discovered that it created a hidden encrypted folder P'Ko could access but not decrypt. He avoided tampering with it, he guessed by the way it behaved that it was semi-autonomous and that it would detect any attempt at probing. He didn't know what it would do then; it could self-destruct, kinetically even and reached up and gently touched his TaC-B.

Chapter 22, P'Ko's Interview with Z'Shi[63]

At the appointed day and time, P'Ko's heart raced as he made his way to the designated place, then suddenly stopped. He turned a blind corner of a four-way intersection and found a white midsized car silently idling in his path, floating quietly on its maglev suspension, waiting for him. A car was the last thing he imagned.

A door opened from the car's glass smooth, seamless, featureless body, the door's edges forming as if melting from ice and a pleasant sounding female voice with a slight D'En accent said. "P'Ko, please get in."

Never in a million years would P'Ko have thought that he would be riding to this "interview" in a car. Out of the five thousand or so crewmembers of sector three, P'Ko heard of only a hand full of VIP's that had cars and didn't even know anyone that knew someone that owned one.

P'Ko stumbled almost falling on the deck of the car as he got in, and then catching himself and turning, sank back into a plush white cushioned divan bench seat. He had never ridden in a car before. The door automatically closed and instead of being plunged into darkness or enclosed in a wall panel lit tomb, P'Ko looked out through optically transparent windows that couldn't be detected from the outside. He looked closer and realized that they were flat panels only displaying the outside scene, the 3D capabilities of the system were superb.

The car's voice intoned in the same pleasant manner as when P'Ko first approached said as the car began to move, "We will arrive momentarily."

P'Ko marveled at the sophistication of this equipment, the son of a mechanic having apprenticed with his father and soon to graduate and begin training as a certified mechanic; P'Ko absorbed the environment around him.

In front of him, instead of any visible driving or steering mechanism, there was a small beverage compartment. Behind transparent sliding panels were a selection of sealed containers of liqueurs, cold drinks and hot and cold tea. All the drinks were smaller than those in the vending machines at school and in Nu'Tn. P'Ko figured that the small size would be appropriate for what would at most be a leasurely ten or fifteen-minute trip going from one side of sector three to the far opposite side.

P'Ko wondered if it were possible to go to another sector by car sector crossings were air locked and monitored by an automated system, it would be easy to restrict passage. Crossings and the transport systems are designed to allow movement of people and materials yet maintain the atmospheric isolation necessary for the efficient sector by sector heat dissipation from the core.

---

[63] Sounds like Zee-She.

On the few occasions when P'Ko had been to one of Dadr'Ba's observation platforms on vacation with his family, a school field trip or a sporting event in another sector, the trip was applied for and scheduled in advance. The justification was provided, and the passage was approved, and they traveled in a group using one of the transport tube modules.

P'Ko had never heard of people being denied travel authority, but the mere fact that the travel had to be requested and approved in advance made a few feel ill at ease. The explanation from the CA is that it's necessary to control and conserve valuable resources, but that explanation didn't quite make sense. One thing Dadr'Ba seems to have plenty of is energy. The Magneto Hydro Dynamic generated electrical power harvested off of the fusion engine was abundant.

The car slowed and turned sharply into a garage at the base of an apartment where only a moment before was a bare wall, the garage door opened and closed so quickly that it seemed to P'Ko the car should have hit it. The garage contained several other vehicles, but P'Ko saw no one. The car he was riding in pulled up adjacent to an open elevator door and stopped, the car opened its door and announced his arrival. After P'Ko had exited the car it thanked him, remarking that it would look forward to his return trip, the car door closed and noiselessly moved away parking itself.

P'Ko entered the elevator, which welcomed him in the same sweet voice as the car. P'Ko amazed at the level of sophistication of what he's seeing, or rather the hidden technology behind what he's not seeing. The car didn't a mark on it; the street had no name the building had no number, nothing at the ground level to distinguish it. There were no controls or indicators in the car and nothing inside the elevator.

Nothing indicated who he's visiting, or who the other inhabitants of this apartment building are. The elevator seemed to recognize him and know where he needed to go just like the car.

For a moment, P'Ko thought that since his chosen occupation is a mechanic how interesting it might be to work on systems like this. But as fast as he considered it, he dismissed it; he was certain he wanted to be a mining mechanic. Working on these systems would undoubtedly require a high-security clearance along with the extra scrutiny of the CASS. His father had been offered opportunities to work on special systems and so far, turned down every offer.

The back panel away from the door showed a virtual view looking out over Nu'Tn; the view changed as the elevator ascended, soon it was as high as the highest portions of the stadium and slowed to a stop, announcing that they had arrived. The elevator door opened not into a hallway as he expected, but opened directly into an apartment, or rather a suite.

There across the threshold stood a woman, small, petite and demure, the height of a Mi'Nr but slim, without the thicker skin, insulation and energy reserves, not the strong, stocky look of the Mi'Nr's, yet perfectly proportioned, as if she were born that way.

She could have been a perfectly scaled down version of a D'En her hair, delicate and dark, her skin, baby white, minimal makeup, and he could see no tattoos. But this woman was like no D'En P'Ko had ever seen. Of the D'En's P'Ko has seen or met most have been tall, height mods seeming to be a favorite bio-mod choice, none has ever been short. Height reduction bio-mods are rare, even among U'Te's, from this distance P'Ko guessed that she would only come up to his shoulder.

She was in a white ankle-length robe that covered her entire body with a broad dark red sash around her abdomen revealing gentle curves showing the proportions of her body. She wore house slippers and stood on a smooth polished floor; the walls glowed a pale gold.

P'Ko gazed at the floor, then slowly realized that the floor showed a beautiful intricate pattern of tiny red, gold, lavender, and green stones. P'Ko realized that it must have come from the asteroids that had been incorporated into Dadr'Ba's mass when Dadr'Ba first set out from Or'Gn. He had seen jewelry made from small pieces of these rocks, here was a whole floor made from them.

P'Ko's mind began to race, how could all this add up? This beautiful woman? A friend of rough and gruff Mi'Ka? All this wealth compared to Mi'Ka's grotto? The car? The garage behind the invisible door? An elevator with no controls? That opens directly into a luxury suite? How could this be real?

Could he be dreaming? How could this beautiful, unbelievably wealthy D'En even consider being a mentor for someone like "me?" A U'Te striving to become a Mi'Nr. Something these people must think of as going from low to lower?

The woman spoke, she introduced herself as "Z'Shi," it was the same voice from the car and the elevator, soft sweet with a slight D'En accent. All automated voices had a D'En accent so P'Ko didn't think that Z'Shi's car and the elevator would be anything other than the standard automated voice heard all over Dadr'Ba.

"It's a pleasure to meet you, come in and please, take off your street sandals and respect my home by using house slippers. My home is one of my companions; I'm sure you agree it's important to respect our companions?" P'Ko nodded agreement, not yet finding his voice and having more than once considered turning around and backing out of this venture. Z'Shi's words were soft, kind and pleasant, yet authoritative.

Just inside the apartment was a landing and off to the side was a pair of house slippers, obviously for him beside a small pair of sandals. P'Ko stared at the delicate demure sandals, amazed at the proportionality of Z'Shi's feet to her little frame.

P'Ko felt troubled, almost ashamed as he slipped off his dusty, rough-hewn mechanic's street sandals and placed them next to Z'Shi's pristine pair. He was a little relieved to note that the landing appeared to have a sort of air shower built in, feeling a breeze against his feet that slowly subsided. After putting on the house slippers, P'Ko nudged his street sandals a little further away from Z'Shi's.

Z'Shi had waited patiently and gave no indication that she paid any attention to P'Ko's actions. She invited P'Ko to follow her into the drawing room.

The gem quality floor felt smooth as P'Ko's house slippers glided across the floor, looking and feeling like walking on wet ice, but when weight was applied had the solid feel of walking on very dry ice.

Z'Shi flowed across the floor as if air carried her, and as she turned P'Ko saw that her dark hair had a reddish tint to it, and it draped all the way to the small of her back. Z'Shi motioned for P'Ko to sit on some cushions near a low table upon which sat a white teapot with two matching cups on a tray, the tea set decorated with an intricate design that resembled a snowflake made up of a combination of characters that P'Ko could make no sense of.

Arranged around them, sitting on stands, strange, intricate devices or instruments sat, some large some small. P'Ko couldn't recognize any of them, but he guessed that they were musical instruments. He studied them, some were horn-shaped showing some simple, some complex waveguides ending in flares, others had strings over a box that should serve to resonate and amplify. Yes, they are musical instruments, but nothing like any he had ever seen before.

Z'Shi sat down across from him, even sitting; she was shorter than P'Ko. Her bio-mods, what else could it be, had to be extensive, and he wondered why anyone would want to be shorter, smaller or petite.

Before P'Ko could muster the courage to speak Z'Shi began, "I am Z'Shi, Mi'Ka, and I have been friends since the beginning. I am an artist, a historian, and entertainer. Mi'Ka told me very little about you only that she considers you to be a very special person and is in need of mentoring."

"As for the rest, she prefers that I make my observations and come to my own conclusions. That said, the very fact that she referred you to me speaks volumes" – she continued talking as she began serving the tea, maintaining her gaze in P'Ko's direction with only occasional, friendly eye contact. She poured the tea perfectly, without spilling a drop.

"No one knows you're here; there was no need to use your tracking disabled TaC-B. Ever since you got into my car, the monitoring system would have you on a secluded walk." P'Ko sat dumbfounded, not knowing what to do or say. "You'd still have been able to send and receive messages, but our location is masked." Then she added, "My work requires the utmost of discretion."

"I can see by your movements, that you are martial arts practitioner, you need to speak to your sensei about how to mask your movements, you've been lucky. There are some among the CA security forces trained to spot the martial artist, and they would not hesitate to put you under arrest for suspicion of martial arts activities."

A flash of P'Ko's final altercation with Dan'Zu and rescue of Tn' raced through P'Ko's mind, followed immediately with imaginings of a CASS raid in the middle of the night. Thoughts of being stunned, apprehended and interrogated about his martial arts activities. Demands for information about who taught him and who knew about it.

P'Ko's throat froze, and he gagged spilling his tea. Z'Shi produced a napkin that had sat unnoticed upon the serving platter. P'Ko apologized profusely and offered to leave. Z'Shi, who had moved next to him placed her hand on his arm and gently refused his offer to leave.

Z'Shi returned to her original seat as P'Ko slowly regained his composure. P'Ko starting to think through things, reminding himself that the Dan'Zu Tn' incident was years ago and slowly put his CASS fears aside.
.

P'Ko apologized again "I'm so sorry, all this is overwhelming, I didn't know, you don't look like…" then "Do you know martial arts?" After a deliberate pause that said "I'm going to tell you something in trust and that trust must never be broken," regaining eye contact, Z'Shi replied, "It is one of my many skills."

The contrast in P'Ko's mind couldn't have been greater; it was almost as if they were opposite magnetic poles or ends of the universe. On one end, this petite, frail looking woman living in a luxury apartment and on the other end, his burly, gruff, tattooed sensei that lives in a converted cargo container in an Ol'Tn junk yard. Yet, both know, or seem to know martial arts.

Z'Shi appears to be extremely knowledgeable and possesses the observation skills needed to recognize the body language of a martial artist, despite her words maybe that's the limit of her skills. P'Ko couldn't believe it and made a conscious attempt to mask his disbelief.

P'Ko began to slowly realize that Z'Shi was carefully watching him, not obviously or directly, but like a martial artist watches their opponent. Not just focusing on this part or that, but watching in whole, assiduously, every move, and what's more, she wanted him to know it. Her eyes were attuned to his every movement, as sure as Mi'Ka could perceive psychically what most people were thinking, P'Ko realized that Z'Shi could see from visual clues, eye movements, trembles, muscle tensions, what someone is preparing to do, what they're feeling and maybe even thinking.

P'Ko realized that Z'Shi must know martial arts, and was ashamed that he doubted.

Z'Shi seeming to know what was going through P'Ko's mind. Having wordlessly confirmed to him one of her secret talents she relaxed her gaze. P'Ko felt his tension lessen but still felt small and insignificant setting across from Z'Shi.

He felt like he was in the presence of an advanced life form, someone from another dimension, then Z'Shi reached across the table to P'Ko's hand and gently squeezed it. The remaining tension that had built up drained away and she became the cute, petite, girlish figure that met him when he first entered.

With a wave of her hand, the adjacent wall turned to an ocean beach, the sound of waves against the shore filled the room. Neither one of them spoke for a while, only watched the seascape as they finished their tea. This sea scene was far different from the one in P'Ko's dream, and P'Ko knew from his first sight of Z'Shi that she wasn't the woman he had seen in his dream. But Z'Shi possessed a powerful quality that belied her stature and physical appearance, as profound and compelling and mysterious as the ocean in the scene before them.

Then in response to some hidden movement, the scene faded and returned to being a wall. Z'Shi broke the silence and said in a soft, sweet tone. "Now we must decide on the subject of mentorship; we shall leave it to the "dance" choose." She gracefully stood and walked up onto a low stage that rose, silently from the floor and the walls seemed to move further away, Z'Shi motioned for P'Ko to join her.

She took a stance and stood motionless, P'Ko realized that this was going to be similar to some of the exercises from his martial arts training and reflected her stance. Then, as if on cue music began to play.

It was probably from some stringed instrument, maybe even one of the instruments that had been arrayed against the walls, presumably even played by Z'Shi but P'Ko's focus was drawn towards Z'Shi.

She struck a pose and waited for P'Ko to mirror it. Then without another word she began to move, P'Ko followed, it was to be like one of his martial arts mirroring exercises. Slowly at first following along with the music, he became totally engulfed in the music and matching her movements. Though still in her robes, her actions hinted of a strong, lean body concealed beneath.

The gravity here, notably less than on the martial arts floor down in Ol'Tn made it difficult at first to follow Z'Shi's moves, yet his practice in Ol'Tn while living and going to school in the lower G Nu'Tn gave him some experience with adapting to changing G's.

P'Ko adjusted his speed and momentum to compensate for the altered gravity and followed Z'Shi's lead slowing and extending some movements more than what he was used to.

Soon he began to trust Z'Shi's lead; this was not martial arts, it was dancing, he became aware of the music and how the moves aligned with the sound. Their movements focused on grace, a moving art form, geometry in motion, physics, engineered to explore and highlight the limits of a bodies capabilities.

P'Ko had never danced like this before and began falling in love with the experience. The feeling of dancing, floating on the music and flying on air. He watched Z'Shi as she moved, not focusing on any one part of her body, but all of her body at once while letting the music whisper into his ears telling him what move is coming next.

Then, there was a short pause in the music. Quick eye contact, and nod. P'Ko took the lead and was spellbound as he watched Z'Shi mirroring his every move, he felt Z'Shi's focus upon him, not staring but observing him with all her senses and missing nothing. She mirrored his every move, his body and Z'Shi's linked.

P'Ko adjusted and shortened his movements because he felt the restriction in the robes that Z'Shi wore. The mind-bending experience made him dizzy, and he fell out of step with the music, and slowly sank to the floor to brace himself with his hands to keep from collapsing completely. P'Ko felt a wave of emotion flood over him, he failed.

The music had stopped, and Z'Shi was kneeling down beside him with her arm over his shoulders, cooing into his ear, "It's okay, everything is going to be all right. You did very well."

P'Ko hadn't seen Z'Shi since their first meeting but had been in touch with her; he had an awkward time telling his parents. P'Ko's parents have never heard of the alias Z'Shi had said to him to use. They were somewhat bewildered when he told them she was going to be his mentor. The official directory described her as a mid-level official working for the CA. P'Ko figured that Ma and Ba were probably relieved that he hadn't chosen La'Na and Fa'Na.

P'Ko had told them that he met Z'Shi through one of his teachers, which was often the case. People are wanting to find a mentor or are available to mentor frequently work through the teachers at school.

Teachers act as filters or referral agencies, and sometimes even mentor themselves. He thought of Mi'Ka as one of his teachers and an advisor of sorts; the thought crossed P'Ko's mind of Mi'Ka as a mentor, and he cringed, that would be bizarre, he'd have to guard that thought, he told himself; there's no telling how Mi'Ka would respond.

Using the strange message interface Z'Shi had used to contact him, P'Ko sent Z'Shi his modest sexual bio-mod preferences, avoiding some of the outlandish mod's some of his friends were toying with. He trusted in Z'Shi's role as his mentor to make any changes she thought necessary and she replied with some changes and suggestions that P'Ko wasn't even aware were available. P'Ko agreed to her recommendations, without modification.

He sought the advice of Mi'Ka on the work related mods since P'Ko had limited experience with what it takes to be a Mi'Nr. When it was all done P'Ko hoped that bio-mod requests have proper security controls, the thought of what Z'Shi and Mi'Ka had planned for him being made public made P'Ko want to go and hide.

Then he prayed that his bio-mod request would be approved, if they were rejected, he and possibly his parents would have to try to explain or justify them. P'Ko would rather retire.

P'Ko hoped that Z'Shi's involvement would help. He liked Z'Shi and was pretty sure she liked him, and she had influence and power that P'Ko couldn't fathom. P'Ko thought that Z'Shi almost has to have influence that goes all the way to the CA.

P'Ko's thoughts began to stray toward what the mentoring might be like. Z'Shi was subdued and mysterious, and P'Ko could only guess about what lay beneath the robes Z'Shi had been wearing. The way Z'Shi moved was provocative, it excited him, Z'Shi was confident but reserved and controlled. She could be kind and gentle and seemed to play at timidity while maintaining a comfortable, inviting atmosphere. Yet, she held an edge, could it be that all women are like this when you get close to them? It made P'Ko anxious.

Chapter 23, P'Ko's Bio-mod Approval

Zng"To[64] reviewed the bio-mod request before him and cross-matched it with the job qualification requirements, noted that the bio-mod cost exceeded the total authorized by the CA for graduation job placement. He was about to tag it rejected, which would send a "non-qual" message to the job placement office, and automatically queue up the alternate career choice. But this "P'Ko" character had selected Mi'Nr category jobs for his primary and all the alternates as well.

All of P'Ko's job choices required much the same level of modification. Ever since the Equal Job Rights Protests, the system was set to allow for only one non-qual job choice on a person's application. The system shouldn't have allowed all the alternate career selections to be the same non-qual category. There must be some glitch in the system, and this U'Te must be insane.

There's been U'Te's trying for Mi'Nr jobs in the past, especially since the Equal Job Rights Protests. The CA finally had to give in to a few but then managed to impose fiscal, safety and quality performance restrictions that made most U'Te's overqualified cognitively, underqualified physically and cost prohibitive financially.

It would be easier for a Mi'Nr to qualify for a U'Te job. The smarter ones would be plenty smart enough for many U'Te jobs, and Mi'Nr's are psychically superior to U'Te's, aside from height and reach, but it would be a waste of a valuable resource to have a Mi'Nr doing a U'Te's job.

Fortunately, in Zng"To's lifetime, he didn't know of, and never heard of a Mi'Nr ever applying for an U'Te job. There are certainly service sector U'Te jobs that a Mi'Nr would qualify for, but none ever had.

The database shows a few Mi'Nr's having been selected and placed in U'Te jobs shortly after the protests but a Mi'Nr has never been chosen for a D'En job.

After the protests few U'Te's were chosen for what had been D'En job's but the job descriptions were immediately changed and they were placed at the very lowest tier and never afforded the opportunity for advancement or promotion.

The few Mi'Nr's that had been put in U'Te service sector jobs didn't do well and winded up applying for early retirement.

Zng"To was just about to flag the bio-mod order as unresolvable and forward it to his supervisor, simultaneously sending a copy to the CASS when he spotted the fund site in the comments area. As soon as he linked the fund site to the order, the deficit was cleared with about twenty-five percent to spare. Zng"To reviewed the rest of the bio-mod request and marked it

---

[64] Sounds like Zing-Toe.

approved, clearing the job placement pending status and sent a copy of the approved and upgraded bio-mod order to the Med Group.

Chapter 24, Amazing Meeting

Su'Zi sat quietly on the secluded beach watching the waves roll in, and the clouds drift by. The programmers had done an excellent job of simulating O'M's weather. Su'Zi could see no discernable repetition in the clouds, all of them, even those of the same type are ever so slightly different and followed the weather pattern they were modeled after. Sector two's settlement was some distance away up the coast to the north on the south side of the bay across from settlement three.

The evolution of the virtual settlements was progressing rapidly. The developers managing the simulation, claim to use all the very latest, updated information about O'M. The sim-masters caution that many rapid and sometimes drastic changes will appear, like what is expected when they reach the real O'M and Dadr'Ba will have to adapt.

Su'Zi realized that this simulation is a teaser, the CA is using it to groom the way people are thinking. She looked around wondering what the next step might be?

Why does the CA overlook severe problems with O'M? Like, if O'M has plant life, it would also have microbiological life that may prove deadly to the people of Dadr'Ba. The sterile environment on the ship is safe. However, the GLC people of Dadr'Ba would be easy prey to a bacteria or virus.

Why isn't the simulation based on "most up to date and accurate data" not causing us to use biospheres and bio suits, at least at first? The CA is making O'M seem like a paradise, a dream come true.

O'M is going to be an alien world that Dadr'Ba's will have to learn to fit into and manage. The CAs prohibition against calling O'M alien doesn't make it less so. What's the CA's plan? It's up to something; Su'Zi just knows it. She closed her eyes and dug her bare toes into the sand and took a deep breath; no this doesn't feel right; she was certain that the dreams she had had were what the real O'M was like.

"It's just not right" Su'Zi heard next to her as if repeating aloud what she had just been thinking to herself. She responded, "no, it's not" then glancing up. Standing there, it was him, the man of her dreams. But no, looking again, this is a To'Ta, a teenager, he was far away in her dream and her Mi'Nr eyes, not naturally good at a far distance could have deceived her.

Yet, she knew psychically that this is the person she saw in her dream, beyond all doubt, this is the one, she was certain of it. An impulse came over her and without thinking and seemingly defying the capabilities of the virtual world's interface Su'Zi was up and had her arms around P'Ko while P'Ko stood there dumbfounded, wondering what had just happened.

During the repeating dreams, P'Ko had been curious, even anxious about the woman he saw; his dream vision was as good or better than his self-trained eyes in reality, and he thought the woman in his dream was more than beautiful, she was gorgeous, too beautiful to be real. Yet, he felt drawn, compelled to seek her out.

While the way the dream ended was disquieting, the woman in the dream captured his imagination, and P'Ko wondered many times what it would be like to meet her in real life.

P'Ko had finally talked himself out of believing it was anything more than a just an impossible dream, and dismissing it as something to do with natural tensions associated with the imminent coming of age ceremony and anxiousness in anticipation of the gender and bio-mod.

P'Ko was drawn to this out of the way virtual beach wondering and hoping the dream woman would be here. He spotted her from quite a way off, even though she was sitting instead of standing and was wearing a pastel colored, loose fitting shirt and shorts, he knew that this is the woman from the dream. His heart raced as he carefully approached, cautiously fearful that she'd disappear like a fog phantom that sometimes forms near opening and closing hatches in the lower levels.

He prayed that this wasn't just another dream that he'd wake up from, and she'd be gone. As he approached and the vision of her didn't vanish or fade away, self-doubts started to creep into his mind. Could she just be an avatar? In real life could this woman be clonely or a mishmash of poorly executed bio-mods? P'Ko was close now, approaching from a slight angle behind her. Then he froze, wait. He's walking up to perfection, while he, a To'Ta, as clonely as clones get, is going to walk up and strike up a conversation.

He doesn't even know what he was going to say; his mind went blank, speechless. She'll laugh at him. Okay, he's been using a little makeup, and he tries to dress well, but compared to her, he's nothing. "It's just not right," he said, without thinking, just as he was preparing to quit out of Vr'Chm[65].

P'Ko was stunned, frozen in time, mind racing, going nowhere. P'Ko had to shake his mind to bring himself back. If there was anything more troublesome to P'Ko, it's his tendency to over think. He can react quickly, but mostly for situations he had thought through in advance, and he wasn't at all comfortable with this virtual interface.

Now in a blink of an eye, he has a beautiful woman virtually wrapped around him. He's so flustered that he can't figure out how to use the virtual interface to respond. Had there been an automated embarrassed emote he would have surely maxed it out.

But now he doesn't even know how he wants to respond. This is the first time in his life that he's had a woman throw herself at him. And not just any woman, the most beautiful woman he has ever seen. The first thing that's coming to his mind is to quit out of Vr'Chm and disappear, but he resists the urge.

---

[65] Sound like Ver-Chome, rhymes with Birch-Home.

Finally, after what seems like an awkwardly long time, P'Ko, in response to her unrelenting hug, he haltingly and awkwardly put his virtual arms around her.

P'Ko always thought himself to be clumsy and shy in interpersonal relationships and not very open with his feelings, although the people and things he cared for he was committed to and felt he could lay down his life for. At this moment, he was lost.

In response to his touch, the woman gave a kind of soft grunt indicating, although not registering through the virtual interface that she just squeezed him tighter. Then slowly they backed away from each other and looked.

P'Ko, with a mechanic's background, normally had an excellent sense of time, but when it came to people and psychic things he was lost. He couldn't calculate how much time had passed, seconds, or minutes.

P'Ko didn't know how to react to having a distinctly beautiful, attractive woman, a Mi'Nr, shorter than he, with long dark hair, possessing sensuous curves with a little extra in all the right places, stand so close to him and to just have given him a long and clearly passionate hug.

Along with many of his friends P'Ko had dreamed of such an occurrence, often fantasying about it. But imagined it happening after they had the equipment to respond appropriately.

P'Ko didn't know what to do, or how to respond to this buxom and vivacious woman, a woman that exuded, even through the virtual interface a natural, comfortable, confident kind of beauty.

And P'Ko, not thinking in advance, still in his school uniform, translated, unaltered through the Vr'Chm access interface, stood bald, clonely, with no bio-mods, face to face with this beautiful woman. And she had just given him a passionate hug. It was impossible for P'Ko to feel smaller or more insignificant, he wanted to crawl under a virtual rock and disappear all he could muster was "I'm sorry."

Su'Zi stood looking at the To'Ta in front of her; he stood motionless, and his avatar image seemed to flicker as if his connection was failing, on the verge of disconnect. Su'Zi began to realize that her impulsive hug of a To'Ta, a young person, that could be half her age might have scared him out of his wits. Her psychic sense told her that he was a "he", and as she looked at him, his stammering voice slowly evoked an "I'm sorry" confirming her suspicion.

This To'Ta did nothing to be sorry for, and suddenly Su'Zi realized that the young man from her dream might at any instant drop out of Vr'Chm never to be seen or heard from again, and she doesn't even know his name.

She exclaimed in a Mi'Nr's accent, "No, no! Wait! I'm the one that ought to be sorry! It's me from the dream! Please stay!" "Tell me your name!"

P'Ko felt so bad and awkward, he wanted to be a hundred light years away; he felt like he was under water, starving for breath; he was a fraction of a second away from disconnecting and dropping out of Vr'Chm when he heard her plea for him to stay. This was the woman from the dream, and she wanted to know his name.

He paused, taking a deep breath and regaining a little composure, replied, "P'Ko." To which she replied, "Hi, my name is Su'Zi" her Mi'Nr's accent carried an air of feeling, sincerity, and compassion that went beyond the virtual selves they were interfacing through. P'Ko felt Su'Zi psychically reach out to him and comfort him.

P'Ko knew that he should be able to trust Su'Zi, but he was so far out of his element, so far out of his comfort zone. His first instinct was still to disappear or take off running, just like so many years ago running away from Dan'Zu and his gang. His second impulse, not even an instinct, to fight, never even attempted to surface. This woman could strike him dead, and he wouldn't have lifted a finger to prevent it.

He'd been training Martial arts for years, yet the more he learned about the techniques, the less he was inclined to deliberately use them. Unknowingly, he relied on his martial arts discipline and self-control now, it was the only thing keeping him from running or disappearing.

Most of all he didn't want to hurt by action or inaction the woman that had been for him the focus of his dream. The woman that he came here searching for. P'Ko was already afraid he had hurt her feelings by not responding more appropriately she obviously felt something for him. She hugged him, why hadn't he thought through that possibility?

He was attracted to her even in the dream and would have liked her to hug him, but had never actually expected it to happen. Why is he so stupid, so dumbstruck, it took a great strength of will not to abort the virtual connection and disappear from Vr'Chm.

Don't just stand here he told himself, say something, the longer it was taking, the worse he was feeling. Finally, after what seemed like an eternity the tumult of events and feelings were starting to settle.

Okay, deep breath, she cares for him, why else the hug? To this beautiful woman, he should be just another school age clonc you pass on the street without a second thought, no distinguishing marks except for school uniform, its Id markings, and maybe a little makeup.

P'Ko cursed the CA for insisting that your Vr'Chm avatar be based on your real self[66], created from your actual specifications and images. They claim that Vr'Chm is being used not only to introduce O'M to the people of Dadr'Ba but to be as realistic as possible, and assess how well the people of Dadr'Ba adapt to O'M.

Su'Zi recognized him from the dream, and she said so. She knew that he had had the dream too. psychically, it had to be psychically, of course, she's a Mi'Nr, and everyone knows that Mi'Nr's have stronger psychic abilities than the rest of the crew.

---

[66] Dadr'Ba has other online environments dedicated to entertainment that doesn't have the same rule, P'Ko had tried some of them, found them interesting and engaging for a while but wasn't able to maintain the interest.

He could recognize it now; it was a psychic feeling that brought him here, before he even saw her, he felt her and knew Su'Zi was the woman in the dream. P'Ko could feel her now, especially now that he's tuned, and she must sense him even more.

Thinking of the dream P'Ko remembered feeling drawn to Su'Zi. They would have probably approached, met in the dream if it weren't for the painful wailing that built to the crescendo that ended the dream.

But this was not the dream beach, the dream beach was more vivid more beautiful, it touched all the senses, there were different colors, grasses, trees and sea life, even the sand was different. This beach, although still under development was a cardboard replica of a generic beach.

P'Ko finally replied "This feels all wrong, this place" looking and gesturing around him, "how about we meet and get some tea, someplace real?"

Su'Zi's heart leaped, and she had to fight back the urge to give P'Ko another hug.

P'Ko said, "How does 'Ym'Cha's[67] in Nu'Tn'Ka sound?"

Su'Zi's heart sank, she knew of Ym'Cha's. Each sector has at least one, Ym'Cha tea shop, Mi'Nr's rarely go to them, not that the tea is bad but they are all in Nu'Tn's, and Ka is sector three, and she's in sector two. To go there would mean going from sector two to sector three, doable, she'd visited Mi'Ka, so she knows the way. But like most Mi'Nr's Su'Zi doesn't like going up to Nu'Tn, particularly when she would likely be the only Mi'Nr in the place, and get a questioning tone from the servers and sidelong glances from the other patrons. Then it's warmer in the Nu'Tn's than Mi'Nr's are accustomed to. She'd be hot and uncomfortable and to top everything off the blasted CA has its all-seeing surveillance system watching everyone and everything in Nu'Tn's. She felt deflated.

P'Ko sensed something wrong, as soon as he mentioned Ym'Cha's Su'Zi's expression changed and she projected a psychic pang of dismay. He quickly diagnosed his mistake and inwardly kicked himself for his stupidity. He knew Su'Zi was a Mi'Nr and had spent enough time in Ol'Tn among Mi'Nr's to know how they feel about Nu'Tn's.

P'Ko seeing his mistake interjected, "Wait! How about this?" and he walked over and squatted down next to Su'Zi and wrote the name of a place in the sand. Su'Zi enthusiastically nodded agreement, smiling and disappeared.

P'Ko looked around wondering where Su'Zi went; they hadn't set a time yet; he called her name, and then realized that she must already be on her way there. His heart started pounding, and he felt a tightening knot form in the pit in his stomach. He had expected to pick a time a day or so in the future, which would have given him time to organize his thoughts.

Taking a deep breath, he wiped out the name in the sand and exited Vr'Chm.

---

[67] Sounds like Yum-Cha it is a Tea House chain.

Chapter 25, Meeting at the Hn'Gri Bo'R[68]

Su'Zi got up quickly from the lounge chair she was reclining on and quickly changed out of the lounge clothes she had been wearing while she calculated the best method and route to get over and up to sector three Ol'Tn. She didn't have a very large selection of either clothes or routes to choose from. Most working miners that live in T'Bm's or one of the camps near the operations have little more than a foot locker for all their things.

Mi'Nr's live a nomadic life split between the T'Bm's, the migrant camps and the Ol'Tn's; the system works well and in spite of the separation, Mi'Nr's maintain a close-knit community. Mi'Nr's psychic powers are the strongest of all the races and the connection between family and friends is tight, unaffected by distance.

Living in the mining zone has its benefits, the greatest of which is that it's nearly impossible for the CA to exert much influence over the Mi'Nr's. All of the CA's attempts to exercise control in Zone Three have all but failed.

CA's control within Zone Three is limited to periodic inspections, establishing production quotas and getting copies of production and maintenance reports. The CA also administers the tests the children are required to pass, to qualify for graduation. The CA still has control of bio-mods. However, the Church maintains full control of the ToG ceremony, Birthing, and Retirements[69].

The CASS is constantly trying to insert or recruit spies and place monitoring or listening devices in the T'Bm's, the camps, and the Ol'Tn's. To little avail, the spies are soon exposed, due to the Mi'Nr's heightened psychic abilities. Monitoring or listening devices are sought out and covertly broken, disabled or, just disappear.

A few of the CA's devices are recovered in raids like the one that took Su'Zi's father. Which usually seals the fate of head of the household, if not the entire family.

Su'Zi had to hurry, she didn't want to keep P'Ko waiting, he's young and may be impatient and may surrender to the fear Su'Zi sensed just below the surface. The fear that he was inadequate, that they're incompatible, not meant or good for each other, was there and real. She tried to send him psychic reassurance but she wasn't sure of its impact.

---

[68] Sounds like Hungry Boar.

[69] Birthing and Retirement is a private affair especially in the Mi'Nr community which is handled in special chapel annexes beneath the Churches accessible from Ol'Tn.

Why did she leave Vr'Chm so quickly? Without getting his contact information. Who's the impatient one? Sometimes, she told herself, she needs to slow down and don't let her emotions and impulses take over.

Su'Zi didn't own any "go out" clothes or even "nice" casual clothes so she put on her best fitting work jumpsuit. The one she wore only once, it fits tight and restricts her movements a little, but she mostly doesn't wear it because all the guys and many of the girls look at her more than paying attention to their jobs.

Sometimes Su'Zi wondered whether her bio-mods were an asset or liability, she's proud of herself, and she considers herself as good or better a carpenter as any in sector two, probably as good as any aboard the whole ship. But knowing that she's better known for her looks than her job performance frustrates her.

As she slipped into her jumpsuit, she was glad that she didn't have the tailor loosen the fit. She looked at herself in the mirror and adjusted the fit, turning and passing her hand over her smooth, gentle curves and thought that her bio-mods aren't that much of a handicap, after all, she felt happy, confident and good.

Su'Zi stepped out the camp trailer she shared with Ro'Sa, who had left earlier to go to Ol'Tn'Ba with her boyfriend and spend some time together and maybe do some shopping.

The camp trailers, converted cargo units and fuel tanks on wheels, were lined up in two rows within the ten-meter-wide tunnel. A narrow pathway separated them that led up to an airlock of sorts that kept out the worst of the cryogenic environment.

Su'Zi wondered what P'Ko was doing at Vr'Chm; hes from sector three should've still been at school. He must be cutting class. But nearing graduation, he should have been studying for exams. The odds were against this happening by chance. She knew at her core that they shared the dream, then against all odds found each other in Vr'Chm. There's something powerful at work here. The thought pleased Su'Zi, as she trotted upslope in the heavy gravity towards the U'Tl[70] garage just inside the airlock.

There she found Vas'Tu tinkering on one of the various U'Tl's used to support the mining operation.

He noticed her trotting his way, stopped his work and focused his attention on her. They liked each other and for a while had a thing going, but it didn't work out, yet they remained good friends.

Su'Zi, almost out of breath said: "Vas'Tu I need to run a quick errand in Ol'Tn what do you have for me?" He responded with a smile, "What's your hurry? You got a date?" Eyeing her up and down in her almost skin tight jumpsuit. To which she replied, also smiling. "That's none of your business" after a pause Vas'Tu replied "oh-kay, take Jm'Pr[71], she's got a full charge."

---

[70] Sounds like you-till, short for utility.
[71] Sounds like Jumper.

Su'Zi thanked Vas'Tu, calling him a "gem" as she climbed into the small two seat maintenance U'Tl, it was the fastest U'Tl in the garage, designed to fetch parts or tools from Ol'Tn or Camp and get them to the T'Bm as quickly as possible to minimize downtime.

Having recovered from her run in the heavy gravity Su'Zi buckled in as the automated hatch closed. Su'Zi engaged the drive, and the machine sprang to life, all four wheels scratched the deck as Su'Zi mashed the accelerator, the double airlock doors used to protect the camp from the frigid cold barely had time to operate as Su'Zi raced through them clearing them with mere centimeters to spare as they opened.

Su'Zi is an excellent driver. She had competed in and constantly does well in the numerous "emergency supply" races that each sector "practices" on a regular basis, often inviting participation from other sectors.

A massive annual event is held to crown the champion driver of Dadr'Ba. The competition is fierce with competitors coming from Ol'Tn garages, T'Bm's and their supporting camps, and betting on the results is popular. Su'Zi even made the finals one year but had to drop out at the last moment due to a mechanical failure on her specially equipped U'Tl.

U'Tl racing is officially prohibited by the CA but treasured by the Mi'Nr's. The races are held in secret, and part of the preparation is clearing the course of CASS surveillance devices and screening the spectators.

Knowing Jm'Pr as well as she did, Su'Zi bypassed the safety controls programmed to provide a ten percent safety margin to protect the machine and its critical systems. Operating manually Su'Zi pushed Jm'Pr's safety margins down to nothing, and occasionally exceeded them, but was careful to back off afterward allowing the systems to recover.

She first crawled up from the lower levels of zone three. With each level, the gravity decreased, and Jm'Pr began to behave more like his name. Su'Zi chuckled to herself that Vas'Tu referred to Jm'Pr a "her," she always thought of Jm'Pr as a "him." wishful thinking on both of their parts, or so she guessed. She pushed Jm'Pr through a depression and felt the momentum press against her bottom, then as Jm'Pr surged out of the depression felt the shoulder straps securing her to the seat squeeze tightly against her body.

Su'Zi enjoyed driving Jm'Pr hard and felt exhilarated by the sensations she was in control of, she gunned Jm'Pr to the top of another rise feeling the momentary weightlessness, then the press of the landing that marked the point where the T'Bm that created the tunnel had angled down to the next level of borings.

Again and again, Su'Zi pushed through the levels getting a little more air with each until she had to back off to keep Jm'Pr's landings stable on the uneven tunnel floor and prevent hitting the tunnel roof. Making good time Su'Zi was soon at the unmonitored cross-sector utility airlock between sector two and three.

Jumping out of the U'Tl Su'Zi quickly disengaged the manually operated latch, and nudged Jm'Pr through the opening, the counterbalanced hatch swung closed behind her. Now it would only be minutes to get to sector three's Ol'Tn, where she'll meet P'Ko in person.

———————————————

P'Ko, uncertain if Su'Zi left Vr'Chm to get ready and go to the Hn'Gri Bo'R or not, got ready to go there himself. Going there and not finding her would be a small consequence opposed to not showing and standing her up. Perhaps there had been a malfunction or problem with her TaC-B connection or she got called away. He resolved to go Hn'Gri Bo'R and if she wasn't there wait a little while then leave.

P'Ko thought as he was getting ready to go that Su'Zi must know, or at least know of Mi'Ka. He would have to ask her.

He swapped out his TaC-B for his stealth TaC-B. P'Ko guessed that Ma and Ba must know about his stealth TaC-B, he's been sneaking out for years now, and there had even been a few close calls. But he'd never been caught outright or got into any trouble, successfully avoiding any run-ins or warnings from the CA. So his parents let him have his little secret.

P'Ko was supposed to be home studying for the final graduation exams but was so confident in his knowledge of the material that he'd been exploring Vr'Chm instead of studying. Now he was going to be off to Ol'Tn on a 'date' and not just an ordinary date, like the ones he'd had with other To'Ta's, but a date with a full grown, strikingly beautiful woman, one that he shared a mutual attraction with.

He put on his mechanic's coveralls and covered his bald head with the mechanic's cap and completed his disguise by shouldering his tool bag, then walked out the door, glancing at himself in the mirror as he passed. He thought he looked good, in spite of being a dressed up clone, and thought with a false sense of bravado, that maybe he could take Su'Zi by his side job at the D'Po, Lu'Gs would be so jealous.

———————————————

Jm'Pr lurched to a stop near the utility stair adjacent to the service elevator. Su'Zi jumped out and raced up the stair, though unlikely, given the distance she had to travel, she wanted to beat P'Ko to the Hn'Gri Bo'R.

Vas'Tu will be unhappy with the way she pushed Jm'Pr; he'll know when he checks Jm'Pr's trip computer how hard she drove, but it's worth it, it translates to more time she can spend at this critical first meeting with P'Ko. She'll just tell Vas'Tu that she wanted a practice run for the upcoming race though still months away. Vas'Tu should be impressed with her time, especially given the fact that she didn't break anything. All she need to do is remind Vas'Tu of the times she'd been out with Vas'Tu, and he broke something on the U'Tl he was driving trying to impress her.

She smiled and waved as she passed the broken security camera laying on the deck as she raced up the stair to Ol'Tn.

P'Ko was confident as he walked down the street toward the Hn'Gri Bo'R that he would beat Su'Zi there and would have a wait on his hands.

Su'Zi had to be coming from at least twenty levels down and even with his taking his time, it would be virtually impossible for Su'Zi to get there before he did.

As P'Ko got closer, his anxiety grew, and he found himself secretly hoping that he and Su'Zi had gotten their signals crossed and would have to reconnect somehow and reschedule, he needed the time to think this through.

As P'Ko walked up the steps of the Hn'Gri Bo'R, he contemplated having tea while he waited, but couldn't see himself sitting drinking a tea and have Su'Zi show up. He decided to wait half an hour maybe an hour, then if Su'Zi doesn't show, visit Mi'Ka or stop by the D'Po on his way home, then look for Su'Zi on the virtual beach tomorrow.

He walked in the small, crowded restaurant looking for a table and there she was! The sight of her was totally unexpected and as their eyes met, the expression on her face changed, as she sensed and saw through his disguise, her face brightened, and P'Ko felt a powerful wave of psychic energy focus on him. It felt like a blast of warm air flowed towards him. In an instant, she was giving him a real hug. Despite being better prepared this time, her powerful Mi'Nr arms squeezed him for a moment he thought she might break or strain something on him and for an instant, his vision began to close in.

After a long moment she relaxed her embrace, P'Ko recovered and was able to reciprocate, though not nearly as strong. This time, quite unexpectedly, he felt her equally powerful psychic embrace.

This was an instant friend, no, more than a friend, love maybe? P'Ko couldn't understand it; he didn't know what real love feels like, he felt powerful feelings from the instant he saw Su'Zi but couldn't allow himself to believe it was love at first sight.

Whatever this is, it marked the beginning of something profound. As all this sunk in, in just a few shallow breaths following the hug, his understanding, his intellect and his judgment began a war with his impulse, intuition, and perception.

P'Ko pushed all these thoughts aside, as he returned Su'Zi's embrace and allowed his psyche to shoulder up to hers, noting her unguarded welcoming energy. Although he sensed that she would not have minded and would have even welcomed a psychic embrace, P'Ko had never done so with anyone before, not even his ma or ba. His parents had cradled and caressed he and his brother physically when they were Bo'Ba's but had never shared a psychic embrace. He was raised believing that such things were for mates or couples looking for mates.

P'Ko, as he felt the embrace start to wain was the first to initiate the little extra squeeze to which Su'Zi joined in on, and he felt a sub-audible hum from Su'Zi deep in his chest. Parting they exchanged an up close glance, staring for a brief moment into each other's eyes, then walked over to the booth she had been sitting at. And sitting across from one another, ordered tea.

They discussed their shared dream, the genesis of their meeting, comparing details until they were both convinced that it was no fluke. They had been there together. P'Ko was astonished that Su'Zi had sought out Mi'Ka for advice and even more astonished to learn that Mi'Ka had diagnosed the event as a temporal entanglement. P'Ko had never heard of TE's before, but could think of no better explanation. After sharing with each other how they met Mi'Ka, P'Ko described his part-time job and his disguise.

They got on the subject of P'Ko's pending graduation. P'Ko was excited to share that his application to be a T'Bm Me'K (T'Bm Mechanic) had been approved, but his assignment had been listed as pending.

By this time Su'Zi knew the P'Ko was anything but an ordinary U'Te and though surprised at first, accepted the revelation about P'Ko's wanting to become a Mi'Nr and work in the mines as a T'Bm Me'K.

Su'Zi had reservations, how readily would the Bo'R clans accept P'Ko? As tactfully as she could, she shared her concern with P'Ko and asked P'Ko what Mi'Ka had said about his choice of professions. P'Ko stated that Mi'Ka's response to his job choice was strange, her response "good choice, but a difficult path." Neither of them knew quite know how to interpret Mi'Ka's statement. Both knew Mi'Ka well enough that she sometimes talked in riddles, and Su'Zi guessed out loud that, when Mi'Ka "see's" some things they appear to her as riddles, and that she's only telling it as she sees it.

P'Ko shared that his parents, especially his father had been disappointed and tried to talk him out of it. His ba had hoped to apprentice him. Apprentices being trainees are frequently exempt from the job placement process unless they are in a shortage field. Meaning, for example, that even if sector three didn't need a U'Te mechanic, P'Ko could apprentice with his ba and work with him until his apprenticeship was complete, only then would he compete for a job placement. The fact that P'Ko was accepted as a T'Bm Me'K meant that there was a shortage.

His parents had learned by experience that once P'Ko had his mind set that it was little use to try to talk him out of it. Instead of trying to talk him out of it, they supported him, telling P'Ko that if being a T'Bm Me'K didn't work out they'd stand behind him. They were confident that the CA would reassign him to a U'Te mechanic, and he would probably come home. P'Ko was already documented as having gone on many jobs with his ba, which would count favorably to be selected as a U'Te mechanic.

The impact on the family would be severe financially if he were chosen as a T'Bm Me'K and failed. P'Ko's bio-mods for being a Bo'R would be reclassified as cosmetic, and his family would either have to pay for their removal or pay for their install, either way, the cost would eat up years' worth of family savings.

P'Ko was determined though and said that he'd put up his meager savings and work to pay back his parents back if it came to that. With that level of determination and commitment, his parent's anxiety level lessened, they wanted P'Ko to be happy, and told him, that if it came to that payback wouldn't be necessary. P'Ko continued to insist that he'd pay them back, but at the same time insisting that it wouldn't be necessary.

Su'Zi explained, based on her experience, that as job openings appear, unless they are immediate critical fills, they are queued to be filled at the next graduation. Job opening announcements are released for applicants and candidate selection is based first on job qualification requirements on seniority.

Being an apprentice complicates things because an apprentice is not entirely qualified and therefore can't go right into a job. A master must accept the apprentice, and that is probably why his particular job location is pending. P'Ko will probably have to interview for the position; fortunately, the interview process should happen after the bio-mod. Like picking of players for a sports team, where he winds up will depend on how he stacks up against the competition, meaning that he will probably be the very last candidate selected for the last and least desirable position.

P'Ko asked if Su'Zi knew of any of the competition, he might be facing, which she did, mostly those from her sector. They were some of the younger underclassmen when she was in school, but many were already working alongside their mas' and bas', like P'Ko has been with his. She knew of no standouts and shared this info, which provided some relief to P'Ko's anxiety. To which P'Ko said, "wouldn't be great if we could wind up on the same crew." To which Su'Zi, realizing all possible implications remained silent.

The thought of being on the same crew as P'Ko at first made Su'Zi happy, then as she reflected she became concerned, she would have to deal with ex-boyfriends and friends on the crew that might not take well to P'Ko, some of which treated Up'Lndrs with contempt.

P'Ko is going to be in for a hard time. He will have to prove himself. If they ended up with the same crew, she knew she couldn't hide her feelings for him, and it would lead to problems. She could find herself in a position of standing up for or defending P'Ko, which could jeopardize or taint his acceptance and her own reputation.

As much as she wanted to be with P'Ko and work on the same crew with him, she couldn't allow herself to be put into that position.

Being on the same crew could ruin everything, so she hedged her response finally saying it might be better to stay in sector three, closer to home, at least at first. Then after he finishes his apprenticeship move to sector one or five where he might have a chance of doing some prestigious meteorite mining. It occurred to Su'Zi that she may then be able to transfer to his crew, leave behind old boyfriends and acquaintances and start anew. She had stayed in sector two to be near her ma and brother, everyone's getting along fine now.

Su'Zi has matured and gained confidence, and knows how to get around from sector to sector; they could see each other often. The more she thought about it, the more she liked the idea of being in neighboring sectors. She started thinking how she might influence the interview process for P'Ko and how she might obtain a transfer for herself later, maybe Mi'Ka could help, she'd have to ask her.

By this time, it was getting late, so they talked about how they should stay in touch, Su'Zi shared that she didn't like to use TaC-B's, she just didn't trust the CA and would explain more the next time they met.

Su'Zi said that short of meeting in person, meeting in Vr'Chm was best. Like today, they could set up a meeting schedule or perhaps leave signals or messages like what P'Ko wrote in the sand today on the beach, and that there may be a way to make meetings safe in Vr'Chm.

This peaked P'Ko's curiosity, this sense of mystery and intrigue. They winded up settling on, that it might be after graduation before they can meet in person again. P'Ko sharing that his mentor wanted to do the training all at once and that it would take ten days.

Su'Zi was surprised; her training was biweekly sessions over the course of several months. She asked P'Ko, who was going to be P'Ko's mentor. As soon as P'Ko replied with Z'Shi's alias, Su'Zi choked on her tea, she didn't know who this person was, but her name was clearly D'En, how could Mi'Ka have helped set this up?

Su'Zi suddenly grew exhausted, and she needed to go home. After another hug. This time, not quite as intense as the first, but was psychically trusting, warm and sincere. It helped dispel but not eliminate the dark cloud Su'Zi felt about Z'Shi, and after final promises to meet or leave word on the beach. They each went home.

––––––––––––––––––––

As P'Ko made his way home, this much he knew, he could trust Su'Zi, and felt that he would have feelings for her all his life. He felt that she helped fill a void in his life and that he's known her all his life but couldn't remember. He was stuck with the "I think I" feeling that's impossible to nail down.

P'Ko had felt out of place his whole life, his difficult birth, his slowness in learning to speak, his alienation throughout school. Does this have anything to do with who he is? Or was growing up to be? Or is it a coincidence, if not a coincidence is Su'Zi that perfect match? Is Su'Zi that one in a 1 billion chance? That complementary number that when combined with his, creates perfection, a perfect unity?

P'Ko's mind was working in overdrive evaluating these options, but without more information, he couldn't decide. For now, he was leaning towards three possible explanations; one being, it's all a fluke that he and Su'Zi were just two random people and are just strongly infatuated with each other. The other, that he and Su'Zi are soulmates and blessed to have found each other. The last explanation, the one P'Ko resisted but was inexplicably drawn to is; that he and Su'Zi are fated to be together.

P'Ko has heard the stories about fated couples, they've existed throughout the mystical history of Dadr'Ba, a history that exists outside of, but parallel to the documented and scientifically sound world they live in, near the outskirts and the shadows of the official religion of Dadr'Ba. Fated couples are doomed to extraordinary hardships and turmoils.

P'Ko forced the thought out of his mind; he knew that here, now, today, this instant, Su'Zi loved him. He felt an unyielding attraction to her, not just focused on her beauty as before, though he still found her to be beautiful and attractive, but a new feeling grew inside him. Is his psychic-self coming alive? His mind refused to release control to his impulse and emotion. He felt a conflict growing inside of himself a sense that a part of himself was damaged and probably responsible for the lack of true happiness he had dealt with all his life.

Chapter 26, P'Ko's Graduation

Gi'Ya[72] watched the graduation ceremony on the large display panel from her office in the administrative office structure adjacent the Church. Soon the initiates will be escorted over from the stadium.

There's plenty of time to walk the short distance to greet them and begin the Ceremony. She tried to remember how many Ceremonies she's conducted. It has to be close to eight-hundred, the figure made her head swim, that's a lot. It might actually be eight-hundred exactly, but in the early days, the ceremonies weren't nearly as organized as they are today. Their ceremonies were conducted on an as needed basis, often with small groups. Which made it almost impossible to put a number to the ceremonies she's performed.

She could probably come up with a number, but it would take more time accessing and processing the data than she had available right now. Besides, the number would be meaningless, the Church has, if not officially adopted, cooperated with the CA prohibition against backward looking. There's logic to it; the past is never actually recoverable and what impact would knowing exactly how many ceremonies she's conducted have on the present, none. Dwelling on the past wastes processing cycles, and power that could be spent on things that are more useful.

As a rule, each class of initiates has included a few interesting characters, and based on the CA's report and the Church's records this class is no exception. Gi'Ya scanned the reports; the CA report contained the medical and school records as well as psychiatric evals and notable surveillance summaries. She didn't trust the CA report, over the years, there are numerous occasions that she's found discrepancies in the report, various truncations, glaring omissions and deletions and not so frequent fabrications of information and all for no apparent rational purpose.

Gi'Ya supposed it wasn't much different than the "editing" routinely performed on the records the Church supplies to the CA. The Church's official report is comprised of the entire genealogy, including retirement records, birth records, church service attendance; notes, on the other hand, may or may not make it into the official report provided to the CA. There is an entire sub-database of information that's covered under the innocuous title "miscellaneous notes" that only select church officials can access.

For this Initiation/Coming-of-Age Ceremony, Gi'Ya's attention was alerted to be watchful of a certain individual by her old friend, Mi'Ka. Mi'Ka had sent Gi'Ya a psychic note to be watchful of P'Ko. He's not dangerous or threatening, not like some of the miscreant, spoiled D'En's, that take extra effort, pampering, coaching and coaxing to ensure they survive the ceremony.

---

[72] Sounds like Gee-Yah.

Gi'Ya manipulated the display and zoomed in on P'Ko sitting near but not among the top third of the class. She glanced down at her tabletop and scanned P'Ko's CA record. Slow learning to walk and talk, slightly above average academically, but comments indicate he didn't apply himself very hard, had some conflicts with some upperclassman as a Ko'Ka, and early his To'Ta years, but that passed, lately he seems to have gotten along with his peers. Introverted, average IQ, analytical, little psychic ability, but nearly all the evaluated areas have an abnormally wide probability of error.

Then she spotted within the report P'Ko's mentor, Z'Shi, using one of her aliases. It's odd that she's his mentor, she very rarely mentors men, preferring to mentor women in the art of satisfying a man and the even finer art of satisfying other women or themselves. Z'Shi had gathered a sort of posse of acolytes, some mated some not, but all practitioners of Z'Shi's art and doing quite well.

Gi'Ya knew Mi'Ka had to have something to do with Z'Shi being P'Ko's mentor; she would have to ask Mi'Ka about that the next rare occasion they were able to meet in person.

Most unusual was P'Ko's choice of profession, a T'Bm Me'K, (Tunnel Boring Machine Mechanic) a Mi'Nr's job. He must be only the second or third U'Te ever to volunteer and could be the only one actually accepted into a Mi'Nr's profession. Not just a Mi'Nr's profession but one that is the leading edge of Mi'Nr's professions, maintaining the T'Bm's.

This could be a first, in spite of the equal rights to occupation declaration the CA was forced into making centuries ago. So far the CA has successfully discouraged, arranged or pressured possible U'Te candidates against picking a Mi'Nr's job or selected them for an alternate career choice mandated not to be the same job class as your first choice, and from a job class of your native race.

Gi'Ya thought back to the protests, the work slowdowns, (forbidden to be called strikes), by mostly U'Te's (the numerical majority) but supported by the Bo'R's. Gi'Ya knew of no D'En that publicly supported the movement. The Church slowly, reluctantly, gave a passive endorsement to the equal rights to profession movement, mostly by staying neutral.

Gi'Ya glanced up at the screen on the wall and exploded into action simultaneously zooming back and panning away from P'Ko. He had been staring at her, or rather, at the camera, her heart pounding; she wondered how long P'Ko had been looking her direction. As she recovered her wits, she directed her screen back towards P'Ko, panning not too close and pausing on P'Ko for only for a moment.

This time, P'Ko was looking at, and seemed attentive to, the speaker's podium. The speaker was finishing, the graduates would soon be standing, going up and getting their personal recognition certificates and new name-profession access badges.

————————————

The eerie feeling that someone was watching him came over P'Ko, and he looked in the direction the feeling was coming from. At first, he thought that it was Su'Zi, Su'Zi, not liking to go to Nu'Tn; she was probably watching the broadcast from Ol'Tn. As close and emotionally tied to him as she was, she was still uncomfortable going to Nu'Tn.

P'Ko continued to look up in the direction he sensed the attention was coming from, and focused his attention there, trying to feel if it was Su'Zi and send her a psychic message. Almost immediately, he felt a wave of panic and glanced quickly around himself, looking for the threat, but as suddenly as it appeared the feeling passed.

He could tell it wasn't Su'Zi and tried casting his thoughts to her, he got a warm supporting feeling from Su'Zi. Su'Zi had been watching and waiting for his psychic reach.

P'Ko watched as the last of the speeches concluded and the graduates started to file up, each in turn after the announcement of their name and job and any significant awards. Each graduate proceeded on stage, shook hands with the officials and collected their new name-profession access badge then filed back to their seats.

When P'Ko's turn came, P'Ko had no significant awards; the announcer only announced his job. A dead calm passed over the crowd, and then slowly, starting with just a few or possibly only one, the applause grew and spread until nearly the whole stadium was applauding. The applause continued, causing a delay in the ceremony and only stopped when P'Ko returned to his seat.

After the last graduate had got back to their place and a final applause. P'Ko, and the rest the graduates filed out of the stadium. A small crowd had formed just outside the stadium as he and the other graduates came out.

He was surprised to spot Su'Zi in the gathering. Upon recognition, she placed her palm upon her chest, then raised her hand to her cheek acting as though she was wiping a tear from her face. She followed with her hand palm out toward him indicating that he didn't need to nor should respond in the same way.

P'Ko knew this was part of a special salutation between Mi'Nr's and also a special message to him. He felt flattered and honored to be recognized as a Mi'Nr and to be cared for by Su'Zi.

P'Ko did his best to send the psychic equivalent back to Su'Zi, and he wasn't sure he got it right. Whether he got it right or not, he didn't need to feel her psychic response, although he did, her broad smile said it all.

The graduates filed out to an open area just outside the stadium and were greeted by a Church Elder, as a group of soldiers formed a cordon around them. P'Ko couldn't tell whether the soldiers provided protection, an honor guard, or prisoners guard. They escorted the graduates the short distance to the Church; they followed the Church Elder into the Church accompanied by several Church Ushers that had been waiting for them outside the Church. None of the soldiers entered the Church.

Gi'Ya watched as the initiates filed into the ceremony chamber after the last had entered, relieved that Church grounds are off limits to Soldiers.

Gi'Ya doesn't like soldiers, these autonomous or semi-autonomous robots, exceedingly powerful, durable and deadly. There's no threat on all of Dadr'Ba that justifies such a creation, programmed for a function or a goal by the CASS and incapable of deviation. A single soldier run amok, unopposed by other soldiers could probably kill everyone aboard Dadr'Ba. Such things have no place here.

Soldiers have been known to "accidentally" kill people. Striking or crushing them either by reflex; (they've been programmed to take defensive action at the first hint of attack or feigned attack) or inadvertently activating a preprogrammed defensive posture with no regard to who or what is around them.

Young Ko'Ka's and naive To'Ta's were particularly vulnerable, the initiates here today are old enough to know better than to attempt a tease let alone a taunt of these mindless killing and maiming machines.

The CASS insisted on "supporting" the graduation and ToG ceremony by providing "escorts." They made it sound in the beginning like it would add to the grandeur and prestige of the moment. However, Gi'Ya had always thought that it had more to do with creating a visual reminder to all that the CA is everywhere and is in control of everything. Gi'Ya knew full well that everything within eye and earshot of these mindless brutes makes its way back to the CASS for analysis and exploitation.

The Church manages to restrict the presence of the soldiers; they are a distraction, and their presence interferes with the psychic aspects of church business. The psychic aspect is the core of retirement and procreation on Dadr'Ba, without which Dadr'Ba itself would die. Therefore, the Church successfully restricts soldiers from access to church grounds or offices.

The initiates filed into the old chapel, which was actually below the street level of the current Ol'Tn. This had been one of the original gathering places of the Touch of God survivors, and where many died.

Over the years, this ceremony has become well-coordinated and controlled. A room like this exists in all the sectors. This social and religious rite of passage must be identical for everyone.

The only ones to escape or avoid the ToG Ceremony, have either died, having no chance at an afterlife passing a part of themselves to their descendants. Or are outlaws or outcasts, they're the "unclean", who are who are supposed to be hunted by the CA and eliminated. To the Churches, disappointment many outlaws and outcasts hide out in the back alleys and outskirts of Ol'Tn's where the CA has little presence. There, unless they make trouble, they are ignored, avoided or reviled, perhaps for the better, a fate worse than death.

Since The Touch of God, the Chosen have built Nu'Tn's in each of the sectors with modern larger improved quarters and gathering places. Though, in a higher radiation area, the Touch of God survivors and their descendants have the gift of a much higher tolerance for radiation. The preserved the lower chapels, like this one as memorial's and modified them to serve the critical function of today's ceremony.

Gi'Ya spotted P'Ko immediately and watched him carefully as he took his seat. P'Ko didn't seem to pay too much attention to her, being more interested in, as most of the others were, the surroundings.

P'Ko listened attentively, as Gi'Ya gave her introductory speech, he and the others showed no indication they knew what was going to happen. At the appointed moment, Gi'Ya left and went behind the stage and watched on monitors as she got that all clear from the ushers, charged the system and pressed the switch.

The initiates jerked, muscles in contraction, then twisted, and doubled over, many vomited, despite the warning against eating or drinking, and then as the charge dissipated collapsed to the floor in convulsions.

Gi'Ya and the ushers strolled slowly back around the curtains within view of the stage. The sound of retching had stopped, replaced by slowly receding spasms, coughing and choking. Then all was quiet as the initiates entered coma, beginning their journeys, as the acrid smell of stomach contents, filled the room.

The waiting began, it will take several hours, perhaps longer for all the initiates to recover and based on Gi'Ya's evaluation, she expected one, not P'Ko but this other one near P'Ko, to die. This one, which had low cognitive scores and only average circulatory function, should pass quickly into oblivion.

Gi'Ya noticed that upon shock this one had gone immediately into the eyes wide and fluttering, arched back, stiff armed and legged, posture of pre-death strained-rigor-mortis. Symptoms, indicating a total cognitive break, instead of the cognitive arrhythmia and convulsions that the shock is designed to induce.

Once all of this one's energy is spent, it will go flaccid and limp, lifeless, voided, an empty container that once held the hope of everlasting life for its parents and grandparents. She could sense its pain, like a massive cognitive muscle cramp, but a thousand times worse. It took an effort to close her mind to this one's pain, but it should subside soon. As for the other initiates, they are lost in their universes, oblivious to this one's pain, and each other's struggles. It will take an hour or more for even the first of them to find their way.

Gi'Ya not willing to remain and watch the dying one, turned back around the curtain and closed her mind to wait out the last moments, the ushers clearly distraught by the scene followed suit.

It bothered Gi'Ya significantly. Waiting for death, death with no passing, saddening but not the mortal sin of the death of an adult member of Dadr'Ba society.

As with others in the past, the death of this youth is God's work, God's choice, viewed by the Church as the same choice that was made over eight-hundred years ago, when God choose who was worthy of survival and who wasn't.

Finally, Gi'Ya cautiously opened her mind and sensing the pain of the dying one was gone, she walked out around the corner of the curtains within sight of the initiates and froze. She couldn't believe her eyes, or her mind, she didn't know what to do, in all of her eight-hundred-plus years she had never seen this, there's no precedent and no protocol what to do.

P'Ko was awake and kneeling next to the initiate who should have died. The dying one lay relaxed, no longer in the pain arched pre-death strained-rigor-mortis, breathing even and regular, the posture of those seeking their way, P'Ko sat back as Gi'Ya rushed forward.

"What did you do?" Gi'Ya exclaimed in a harsh whisper straining to keep from screaming.

"Ne needed help, ne was dying." Said P'Ko emphatically.

"How did you know; how did you do this?" pressed Gi'Ya in the same harsh whisper but without the underlying scream.

P'Ko, uncertainly, "I've… I've been there; I've been lost before."

"Just now? But there wasn't time; you couldn't have!" said Gi'Ya trying to understand what had just happened, trying to figure out how P'Ko did the impossible.

"No, before."

"Get away!" Gi'Ya commanded, loud enough to startle the ushers standing nearby. None of the rest of the initiates had yet recovered, she pointed to a spot on the far corner of the stage, apart from the rest. P'Ko still on his knees scooted over to the place indicated, away from the one he had just helped.

Gi'Ya for an instant wished she there was a soldier nearby; her first impulse was to have it take this abomination away; she didn't know where but just away. She wasn't fearful of P'Ko, she sensed no threat or maliciousness from P'Ko, but she was scared, terrified of what this would lead to and what the consequences will be.

P'Ko had just unknowingly shattered one of the Churches commandments, and it was her fault.

"Sit there, face that way and don't move, don't do anything," Gi'Ya commanded. P'Ko puzzled, sat quietly, cold, hungry, wet with and smelling of vomit, gazed off in the direction indicated dejected and wondered.

P'Ko didn't know what he'd done wrong; he had, contrary to his nature acted on impulse when he saw the young initiate dying. P'Ko wasn't fully recovered from the shock himself, and hadn't yet regained all of his pre-touch (shock) memory. When he saw the dying one, he acted on impulse. He saw and felt the initiates excruciating pain and the underlying drift towards the abyss of death. The initiate only needed a little help to relax, thereby slowing down the spin just enough to recognize nir's center, a prerequisite necessary to spot the distant star that would guide their way out.

Slowly, Gi'Ya reclaimed her composure and began cautioning the initiates as they recovered against helping the others still finding their way, doing her best to ignore P'Ko.

Gi'Ya searched for a way out of this debacle; it may be that P'Ko had, technically, Gi'Ya hoped, not violated the prohibition against helping someone find their way, but only kept the initiate from dying, then let them find their way. The initiate, though more slowly than all the others, looked on the right path. Perhaps P'Ko had only prevented the initiate from dying outright. This is sure to create a stir within the Church. If condemned, what would the penalty be? Or if accepted how it would settle against all those like this one that the Church has let die in the past? Gi'Ya didn't know what the outcome would be.

There had been, thankfully, rarely, Touch of God Ceremony compromises, but due to the nature of the event, prior knowledge had little actual impact on the ceremony, the charge used to induce the experience far exceeded that necessary to cause temporary memory loss. Advance knowledge about what to expect did nothing to help initiates find their way because, theoretically, if the charge is calculated right, the knowledge is unavailable during the ceremony.

Could the charge P'Ko received have been wrong? Mitigated by clothing or something? P'Ko was made to stay in his corner stage isolation long after the ceremony while all these possibilities were investigated. The others waited as well, but were allowed to talk quietly among themselves; they had all been given cleaning cloths and something to eat and drink.

After what seemed like hours, and the video recordings and data were analyzed nothing abnormal was discovered, P'Ko had no explanation for what happened or why he recovered so fast, only that he had inexplicably experienced it before but couldn't recall when or where.

When questioned, he described the event precisely and with the same perceived time span, or lack thereof, like any other initiate. P'Ko experienced it the same as anyone else, but the external time was much, much shorter.

Review of surveillance video of the event showed that he seized and convulsed and fell exactly as all the others did. Spectral analysis of P'Ko as he was 'touched' showed conclusively that the charge, higher than the average and calculated precisely for P'Ko was correct and achieved the desired effect. Only P'Ko was down a little more than a minute before recovering, long enough for Gi'Ya and the Ushers to come out from behind the curtains, check on them and then return behind the curtains to avoid watching the dying one.

P'Ko along with the others were finally released and sent home to wait for their bio-mod. He went home feeling like he was being closely watched. Which prevented him from contacting Su'Zi, even in Vr'Chm. He tried her psychically, but with his current frustration and limited psychic abilities, all he got across was that he was alright, and he would contact her as soon as he could.

P'Ko spent the time listening to music, playing games and going on jobs with his ba. Perhaps impacted by what he experienced in the Touch of God ceremony, P'Ko grew closer to his ba, as the weeks passed, he gained more respect for his father and began to see him more as a real person and an equal more than ever before.

Chapter 27, P'Ko's Bio-Mod

Dr. Za'Ga sat at the small desk in the corner of her apartment, staring at the bio-mod order before her; this is going to be a complicated one. It's good that Z'Shi sent her the encrypted message, giving Za'Ga plenty of time to prepare.

Za'Ga remembered P'Ko; she had performed a side job on P'Ko when he was a young Ko'Ka. Unfortunately, her diagnosis proved false, and the illegal mod to improve P'Ko's cognitive capability didn't resolve his learning difficulty. The problem had to be emotional or psychological stemming from the birth trauma P'Ko's parents described. Unfortunately, Za'Ga didn't learn of the birth trauma till after the failure of the procedure, and she started investigating possible reasons why the procedure failed.

Za'Ga felt bad; she should have asked more questions before the procedure and possibly avoided the costly mistake. However, she did what she could to lessen the financial impact on P'Ko's parents. It proved cheaper to leave the mod in place and offer a partial refund to the family than to attempt to remove the mod.

Regarding P'Ko's prognosis and treatment, options are limited. The easiest and cheapest treatment for psychological problems is total reprogramming, which wipes out any trace of the parents and grandparents imprint partial reprogramming is accomplished through reprogramming sessions with a specialist and are very time-consuming and costly. Way beyond P'Ko's parents means to pay.

Dr. Za'Ga recommended the wait and see approach. It's possible that P'Ko's learning difficulties and possible emotional or psychological problems would resolve themselves and apparently they have.

Now, as Za'Ga reviewed P'Ko's records she was pleasantly surprised to discover that P'Ko looked very much like he had solved the problems that plagued him in his youth and was going to amount to something. Za'Ga knew that many, perhaps the majority of U'Te's become just another component, in the giant machine that is Dadr'Ba working all day. Only to go home to a small capsule flat to recharge, execute optimization utilities, return to work the following day, and perform their pre-determined functions

Upon reflection, Dr. Za'Ga realized that the mere fact that P'Ko's parents had risked everything to obtain the illegal cognitive enhancement for their son meant something. P'Ko was unique. Za'Ga remembered that day, the desperation, the hope and when the procedure failed the despair that P'Ko's parents felt. She felt the emotion too, the desire and the danger she put herself and all those involved in, the risk of performing the illegal procedure. But she had been taking risks as long as she could remember, quietly and discreetly supporting people in need whenever she got the chance.

Za'Ga didn't consider herself part of the resistance. But by performing P'Ko's side job, along with all those other mods that she's performed, and continues to perform, were then and are now, in direct violation of CA rules. By the CA's standards, she and all of her cohorts, as well as their families, are members of the resistance.

Without exception, all the people that Za'Ga helps are peaceful, hardworking contributors to Dadr'Ba and its mission, they only want a good happy life and wouldn't dream of doing anything in direct conflict with the CA and the mission of Dadr'Ba.

As it turned out, P'Ko grew up and stayed off CASS's radar screen. Za'Ga lived with the constant fear that one of her "unauthorized bio-mods" would be discovered. She was careful however to perform a fair number of illegal bio-mods for D'En's, as an insurance policy. She kept records, and if her activities were discovered, a good number of D'En's would be in as much trouble as the U'Te's and Mi'Nr's that she helped.

Za'Ga reviewed P'Ko's bio-mod order after P'Ko received a standing ovation at the graduation, she wasn't surprised that P'Ko's order included a CASS directed passive tracking and surveillance nanobot injection but, thankfully, no active tracking/surveillance or override implants.

When ordered to install active implants, on a suspect believed to be associated with the resistance, she would install substandard units, or install it in such a way that it wouldn't work properly, and she'd let the resistance know that the implants were there and who had them.

Then, the resistance would know what type of implant is installed and who has them. Then they can decide what to do, they usually inoculated them, but sometimes they used them to feed false or misleading information to the CASS.

Za'Ga had very quietly and carefully provided the resistance with a nano-bot vaccine that effectively disables the nano-bots and she assists the resistance in developing detection equipment for these and other bio-mod ordered surveillance devices.

This time, Za'Ga knew without contacting the resistance how to handle CASS's nanobot injection request. The message from Z'Shi would have been enough, but was doubled when she saw in the Bio-Mod order, the code indicating who P'Ko's mentor was going to be.

It was her friend, and own mentor, Z'Shi. The nanobot injection that P'Ko would get is from a specific lot, known only to a few people and reserved for Z'Shi's Lr'Lng's.

If tested they gave the appearance of working but didn't actually work. Za'Ga wasn't sure exactly how they're disabled, something with the sensory input or output, or it could be with the storage or retrieval mechanism. It could even be a combination of other factors. Za'Ga didn't know how, she just knows that she's used them for years, and they've never worked, and they've never been detected, yet.

But then, everyone that has them is in a trusted, prestigious position subject to additional scrutiny. If the CASS figured out the secret behind these defective nanobots a lot of high-level people would become suspect. If P'Ko's malfunctioning nanobots were detected they'd probably be dismissed as a one-off occurrence and not jeopardize Z'Shi's network.

Reviewing the Bio-mod order, Za'Ga saw that P'Ko's bio-mod will be very extensive. Taking a machine that was designed to operate at a normal temperature, gravity, and atmospheric environment. And configuring it to operate at temperatures approaching absolute zero, in gravity twice its design spec, and in atmospheric pressures ranging over several orders of magnitude, that are sometimes explosive and caustic will be no easy task.

Fortunately, there is a template to follow; the Mi'Nr's are designed for these environments.

The easiest way to achieve P'Ko's mods would be just to transfer P'Ko's cognitive components into a Bo'R chassis, which may have been what the CA intended her to do, but if she did that it would almost certainly change P'Ko's personality, destroying P'Ko and creating someone or something new.

The task facing Za'Ga will be to achieve the mods without making P'Ko unrecognizable as P'Ko, without breaking his mind/body link and change who he is.

Za'Ga knew of many instances of a personality change brought on by a bio-mod, most of the time she does nothing to avoid the change, bio-mods have been happening long enough that most people understand and expect the personality changes, this time, she knew she had to be careful.

To complicate things further Za'Ga needed to attempt to weigh in the personality change often brought on by graduation and, especially the Touch of God Ceremony. They've been known to alter a person's personality and sense of self, as much or more so than changes brought forth by biomods. It all depends on the person.

Za'Ga had seen something as simple as a tattoo change a person from meek to a confident outspoken individual. This time, since the bio-mods are so extensive, Za'Ga felt that not paying close attention to keeping P'Ko's outward appearance the same, would result in killing him.

P'Ko's order didn't list any tattoos, they are a waste of credits here, he will undoubtedly get those down in the mines. He will get new, tougher skin, including an enhanced touch/temp sensor map with subcutaneous fuel stores, his new skin will be unavoidably the darker Bo'R's tone due to the increased carbon fiber content, but Za'Ga picked the lightest tone available, a noticeable change but not strikingly so. She'll follow P'Ko's underlying facial features selection to a tee.

The worst part is going to be getting the new skin to fit P'Ko's frame; it's going to take a lot of work cutting, splicing and seaming P'Ko's skin and sensors, will cost a lot more than what was estimated in the Bio-Mod order, in just the time cost alone.

Za'Ga used computer modeling to optimize the changes necessary, maximized use of recycled components, and had her robotic micro-manipulator assistant make the critical sensor splices, triple checking the function of each splice.

P'Ko requested lighter hair color than the norm for a Bo'R, a color more closely matching his parents. It will make him feel more like himself, but will make him stand out in the mining camps. But his hair color and skin tone will be covered by his work uniform. But nothing can disguise his height. His height will cause him to stand out in the mining camps like a candle burning in a cave. Shortening him would solve some structural issues with dealing with a high gravity of Zone Three and especially zone four, but changing his height on top of all the other changes would create too great a risk to his personal identity.

P'Ko is very likely to meet with conflict and opposition. Extra height and reach will make it easier for him to defend himself and could save his life. Za'Ga ran some calculations and decided that if she keeps P'Ko slim, U'Te like, compared to the stockier Bo'R, it will offset the weight from his height.

Then adjusting the doping of the carbon fiber resin, increase the layers, his limbs should be strong and light enough to handle the higher gravity environments while keeping nearly the same height. Za'Ga ran the parameters through the design algorithm, then through the performance simulator. She made the necessary adjustments, checked the results, then sent the instructions to the three-dimensional printer/fabricator/kiln to begin work.

Physically, P'Ko will become a new person. Dr. Za'Ga crafted the changes to ensure that they are not readily apparent. P'Ko won't be notified or told about his new capabilities. It'll be better that he discovers and learns about them on his own, over time, which should lessen the impact on his personality. Za'Ga was proud of the work she just finished thinking that it will live up to the expectations of all the people that gave P'Ko a standing ovation at graduation.

Tso'Lo[73], Za'Ga's mate for over 100 years, interrupted "Za'Ga. You've been working on that bio-mod since I got home, you didn't even notice me when I came in."

"I'm sorry" Za'Ga responded, "I need a break, let's go for a walk."

Dr. Za'Ga and Tso'Lo started off on one of their regular routes, this one, chosen to stay distant from the CA surveillance system, allowing them to talk without being overheard. They talked about the meaning of life, hopes, dreams, and what it might be like on O'M. Never a word was told about each other's work. Za'Ga liked it that way, and she thought that Tso'Lo liked it too.

---

[73] Tso'Lo sounds like Solo.

Chapter 28, Chi'Yo Reviews P'Ko's Grad

Chi'Yo[74] stared at the screen reluctant to review the recorded graduation ceremony mentioned in his daily security brief as a notable, possible resistance related event. He'd much rather reflect on his situation and his plans.

He hates graduations; he even hated his own, the more he tried to forget his less than stellar placement at his graduation, the more he couldn't forget it and the closer to the top of his mind it remained. He barely managed to stay out of the bottom third of his D'En graduating class overall; his only saving grace was that he did well at security academics, consistently scoring in the top three percent.

Now he's the Director of CASS, the only real person in a position over him is the Commander. The fact that he purged and edited his academic records which may have helped him along the way doesn't matter. Results, the present, and the future are all that matters.

He only wished he could do something about the lingering doubts and fears that he could lose control of the security empire he created that relentlessly plagues him. He's tried to assuage his nagging insecurities by behaving like the pinnacle of military discipline and demanding the same from his subordinates.

His demands of zero-tolerance for transgressions and constantly reminding his underlings that he's in charge often by pointing out his subordinate's failings and errors (even insignificant ones) as frequently and publicly as possible, doesn't help his self-doubts or his self-esteem.

For those under him that he can't find fault with, he occasionally fabricates errors. After all, he's in charge, and nobody can question him, and he doesn't tolerate insubordination. Whenever a subordinate questions him, he ridicules them, demotes them or punishes them with menial disgraceful tasks, which teaches them discipline. He allows them to acknowledge their transgression and submit to his leadership. Then when he's satisfied that they've proven their loyalty and fealty, he may allow them back into his graces.

Chi'Yo wished his mate Me'Lng was more obedient and supportive. Despite being a Second Gn'R, the Central Council is all First Gn'R's and ToG survivors; he would fit in among the top echelon better if Me'Lng would attend all the functions wives are supposed to participate and treat him reverently, the way he deserves to be treated. Then the council would treat him more like an equal. Then, with the proper set of circumstances, he'd have a better chance at becoming Commander, in spite of his lack of rank.

Me'Lng can be made into not a problem. She's headstrong and smart, so smart that she's stupid. She doesn't see that it would have been better had she been more engaged and supportive during his career, instead of reluctantly

---

[74] Sounds like Chee-Yo.

following him and privately obstructing him. Considering the rank structure, it might not have made any real difference, but she will eventually pay for her impudence.

He mated with Me'Lng too early, and Chi'Yo's grand plan for pressuring Me'Lng's parents to retire early so they could birth early, and rear devoted accomplices to assist in the creation of his dynasty turned to disaster. Me'Lng's parents did retire early but gave the birthing rights to Me'Lng's brother.

When the time comes, Me'Lng will be in internal exile. Once he seizes control as Commander.

All ranks, including the top job of Commander, is based strictly on seniority. All the Sector Commanders are very close in rank to Commander Di'Zo most within a few days and over the centuries, the Commanders Position has sometimes changed over mere days' worth of seniority. As head of security, Chi'Yo knows the stats exactly.

The next rank assessment and realignment isn't until after they reach O'M and being a Second Gn'R Chi'Yo wouldn't even be in the top 100 in line for the top job. For Chi'Yo to become the Commander, the rank system would have to be changed from seniority to merit. Then, given his position as security chief, he could easily pull off a coup d'état.

Ah, the coup d'état, what an excellent concept, a shining example of why knowledge of the past should be controlled, banned completely from the masses, and reserved for the privileged elite like himself with the real need to know.

Even the central council and Commander don't "need" to know, (thanks to a little help from Chi'Yo) they don't have the time or the foundational knowledge necessary to access or understand it. It would only interfere with their duties. They need someone like himself to control and manage the information they receive.

Chi'Yo has done all the work for them, looking into the histories, and providing them only the information needed to support the decisions that Chi'Yo wants them to make. The first Security Director, the one that Chi'Yo successfully deposed was a genius for arranging for the council to enact the FOP (Forward Only Policy) with its prohibition against history and the waste of valuable resources. History taints us with past mistakes, degrades our noble cause, and carries with us the atrocities our ancestors performed against each other, and how we ruined our world and its environment. The FOP facilitated a bloodless information coup.

The council's decision to restrict access to the past enabled the first security director to put the controls in place to make him knowledge gatekeeper, and he restricted access to portions of the past from the Council itself.

Obtaining access to the forbidden information was one of the first things Chi'Yo did when promoted to Assistant Security Director. There he learned of historical precedents that gave him the confidence to arrange his ascension to top security job, and now his sights are set on Commander.

For his coup d'état to work, all he'd need to do is, fabricate a crisis, declare martial law, seize control of the council, and place himself in the top job, "temporarily." Then never relinquish command declaring Di'Zo incompetent for not foreseeing the crisis and put Di'Zo first into temporary then permanent internal exile. As the council did to Chi'Yo's father Cha'Bo[75], then isolate Di'Zo until he eventually loses the will to live.

By the time Chi'Yo's father, Cha'Bo, retired, he was virtually incapable of a proper retirement and Cha'Bo, probably prompted by Chi'Yo's mother Png'Yi[76] and sister Lu'Le[77] made it much worse by insisting that the birthright is split between Chi'Yo and his sister Lu'Le.

If it weren't for the help of the Church Elder that was called at the last moment to assist psychically, Chi'Yo's father and mother would have been totally lost. As it was, they were so far gone there wasn't a whole lot left of them to pass on. Just as well thought Chi'Yo, his father was a fool to allow himself to be trapped into exile; he wasn't strong or ruthless enough, and such softness shouldn't be passed to future generations.

Chi'Yo is proud of Dan'Zu, his only child, still young, and arrogant, but doing remarkably well at the private CASS Security Academy, that Chi'Yo as CA security chief has under his supervision and control.

Chi'Yo reflected back, on how Dan'Zu pleaded and begged not to be taken out of the D'En private school and sent to attend public U'Te school. The punishment Chi'Yo's chose for Dan'Zu after Dan'Zu lost his temper and struck another D'En because the other student caught Dan'Zu cheating on an exam and reporting him. It was a stupid mistake; Chi'Yo would have easily gotten Dan'Zu a copy of the exam for him had he only asked. But, Dan'Zu was too proud to admit he was having trouble and ask his Ba for help.

Chi'Yo was able to cover up the impropriety and made sure it wasn't documented, anywhere. To teach Dan'Zu a lesson, Chi'Yo sent Dan'Zu to public school (temporarily). To Chi'Yo's astonishment, after an initial rebellion Dan'Zu excelled and became top in the class (of course) academically and class leader before Chi'Yo pulled him back to private D'En school, (after making arrangements for Dan'Zu's success back at the new school). While Dan'Zu was in public school, he developed a welcome sense of superiority and contempt for U'Te's and the lower classes.

Now he's excelling as a cadet at the CASS Academy following in his father's footsteps. Dan'Zu's stubbornness, self-assertiveness, and guile should continue to grow. Facilitated by Chi'Yo's machinations, Dan'Zu will develop into a cunning, ruthless adult and a worthy lieutenant to Chi'Yo when he becomes Commander.

The greatest challenge will be keeping Dan'Zu loyal and obedient to Chi'Yo. Aside from imposing discipline on Dan'Zu from a young age, Chi'Yo

---

[75] Sounds like Cha-bow.

[76] Sounds like Ping-Yee.

[77] Sounds like Lew-Lee.

will withhold access to the past from Dan'Zu. Dan'Zu must never learn of all the historical occurrences of the princes deposing the King. First, Chi'Yo must take over the kingdom.

The aliens infecting O'M might be crisis enough to prompt his coup, especially if the aliens continue to progress at the rate they currently are. They've already provided justification for an increase in the soldiers' capabilities, their numbers, their weapons, and ammunition.

He still needs to work on softening the Council members, so they remain docile during and immediately after the coup, and he must line up suitable "replacements" because not one of them can be allowed to stay on the council. The replacements will need to be weak and obedient, but with proper credentials, either real or manufactured. Chi'Yo smiled to himself; his plan is coming along well; nobody knows what a coup d'état is, it's forbidden knowledge that he alone possesses.

Dadr'Ba's Commander Di'Zo doesn't suspect a thing, Chi'Yo keeps Dadr'Ba a well-functioning machine and keeps Di'Zo in power. For all practical purposes, at least as far as Chi'Yo is concerned Dadr'Ba practically belongs to him already. Nothing happens on the ship that Chi'Yo doesn't have his finger on, the problems with the surveillance systems, in Ol'Tn and below, notwithstanding.

The Bo'R's are a finicky lot, but they've proven they can be trusted to produce in spite of their grumbling and complaints. They had even met their minimums even during the Equal Job Rights Protests.

The Equal Job Rights Protests were mostly a product of U'Te boredom, and aside from the superficial concessions made by the CA, Chi'Yo has worked to ensure discipline is maintained.

Chi'Yo fast forwarded through the video of standing ovation given to a U'Te volunteering and getting a Bo'R job. It shouldn't have happened there are supposed to be controls in place to make sure that U'Te's don't get Bo'R jobs.

Someone goofed, no matter, all that this indicates is job boredom among a few of the U'Te's. He'll have a message sent out to tighten up job selection procedures.

Based on the, less than stellar cognitive scores and academics, there's little fear that this "P'Ko" is going to amount to anything other than an average Kr. Chi'Yo was confident that once sent down into the mines; this P'Ko would ever be heard from again.

He's not going to let it happen, but if tomorrow another U'Te were picked for a Bo'R job, Chi'Yo doubted that there is a ripple of applause let alone a standing ovation. The novelty is already gone.

What would be novel is a Bo'R applying for and getting selected for a U'Te job, but as a dumb as Bo'R's are they aren't that stupid, the level of job satisfaction between a production job versus a mindless service sector job is evident.

Chi'Yo will have someone keep an eye on P'Ko, and noted it on his console; this P'Ko might prove useful in infiltrating the resistance.

Chapter 29, Chn'Gi Seeks Out Information

Chn'Gi sat with her head down on her desk; the latest report displayed much larger than life on the wall panel across from her desk. In spite of the caution against and NSTR reports, her last several have been essentially that, the current collection numbers steadily increasing as well as the cumulative total, but without a language key the data she was collecting is little more than static noise.

The CA leadership, as inept as they appear in some of their comments and decisions, make up for it in their ruthlessness and total disregard for others. They operate on their own personal and corporate agenda, expecting everyone to behave like automatons, relying on imposed discipline. The CA treats everyone below them as if they're mindless, without independent thought, feelings or priorities of their own. They treat people like they have no family, religion, pride of workmanship or self-esteem.

Chn'Gi, a D'En, considered herself to be book smart, smarter than most, yet she knew herself not to be very psychic. She was nothing like the Kr's, especially the Dr'T's[78], Bo'R's or Mi'Nr's, who are naturally adept at it.

She didn't like the feelings she was experiencing, but couldn't help these emotional swings, these overwhelming feelings that made her light headed and made her stomach ache. These feelings began with the first detection of signals from O'M and had gotten steadily worse the more she's come to realize how little she knows about the O'Mi's.

She thought about stopping by that soothsayer's shop she'd seen in Ol'Tn and ask for help, but confiding in a stranger, especially something like this, knowing that she's being watched, that would wind her up in big trouble.

No, she can't speak to the soothsayer, that would end in disaster. The more she thought about it, the more she knew if she sent forward another report listing the number and types of signals they picked up from O'M, she'd face another confrontation with the Commander.

She'd face another reprimand, and probably get fired, or worse. She had to do something.

Chn'Gi and her staff were watching as O'M developed technology, she knew logically that other civilizations in the past must have developed technologies like those they see developing on O'M. By studying the development of the technology of past civilizations, she should be able to answer the Councils demand for more information.

But, how can she get around the CA's long-standing and strict "FOP or forward only policy" and its prohibition against A'Pa, (Anti-Progress activities, that carries capital punishment)? The research databases that she has access to are devoid of any historical information prior to the ToG event.

---

[78] Dr'T - a derogatory slang term for a Mi'Nr, sounds like dirty.

Any query or attempt to access older data results in a banner message "YOU HAVE CONDUCTED A PROHIBITED SEARCH - THIS EVENT HAS BEEN LOGGED AND A RECORD OF IT HAS BEEN SENT TO THE CASS FOR POSSIBLE DISCIPLINARY ACTION".

The relatively ancient history covering the times when Dadr'Ba's ancestors originally developed radio technology must have been purged, blocked, or perhaps destroyed or erased from the online memory system or system of systems that grid the core of Dadr'Ba.

But, thought Chn'Gi, there must be nonvolatile backups or archives, even if the CA chose not to load them. If she could get access to some of those offline nonvolatile backups and review some of the histories, it could help provide answers to the questions and increasingly threatening demands from the Council for information.

What kind of reaction would she get it if she asked the council for access to these archives? The Commanders earlier refusal and this banner warning, was answer enough. Contemplating the consequences of her searches gave her shivers, rumors abound about people caught and charged with A'Pa. "DISCIPLINARY ACTION" encompasses a broad range of penalties, none of which Chn'Gi wanted anything to do with.

The more she thought about it, the more Chn'Gi began to worry about her reports. Although she had stopped submitting NSTRs, reporting gradually increasing numbers of signals received, their types, magnitudes, frequencies, and frequency spread, she had a gnawing fear that she would soon be charged with FTP (failure to progress), or the most serious charge of HP (hampering progress).

She felt that she had two choices. One, she could continue on the present course and lose credits, mileage, position, privilege, and status by continuing on the current course by falling under charges of FTP or HP. Or two, risk the same by taking a chance and seek out Dadr'Ba's ancient history and coming up with the information the Council was demanding, keep and even improve her status, prestige, and reputation and as an afterthought, if caught, attribute her violations as attempts to satisfy the Council's demands.

Chn'Gi walked down the dimly lighted main street of Ol'Tn, slowly passing the street vendor stalls, occasionally stopping to purchase some spices and tea to complete her cover story. She paused momentarily in front of the curio/soothsayers shop but didn't go in.

It's not the first time she's gone to the street market, and although D'En's are infrequent visitors to Ol'Tn, it's not unusual for them to shop at the street market. Today, however, was going to be different, she walked on past "Mi'Ka's psychic readings and Curio's" then listed down one side of the door; "Aura's, Cleromancy, Numerology, Palmistry, Psychometry and Remote Viewing."

Despite her earlier contemplation of consulting Mi'Ka, Chn'Gi wondered how anyone could fall for such stuff. Sure, there's plenty of anecdotal evidence that precognition has merit, or at least couldn't be definitively disproven. Then there's Dadr'Ba's retirement and birthing process, which is absolute proof of psychic phenomena with every birth. Despite the CA's best efforts, their scientists can't figure out how it works, but it does. There's a religious explanation, but it relies on faith and not facts or anything measured with a scientific instrument.

But really, being able to predict the future defies the laws of physics. Being a scientist, Chn'Gi never placed any stock in fortune telling. She knew that the CA had conducted classified research into the subject, but rumor intelligence says there's nothing there that couldn't be explained probabilistically.

Chn'Gi passed a few more shops, taking notice of a tavern made from a passenger pod, she peeked in one of the oval viewing ports and saw a long bar that reached half of its length with booths along the opposite side. She passed a hotel that was made up of stacks of cargo containers, cut and welded together to form a haphazard pile of block-shaped "rooms" a walkway across the fronts with ramps and ladders. Doors with room numbers plainly visible. The office door stood open, covered with only a curtain blocking out the cold. A lighted sign, saying "Vacancy" on one side.

A few occupants leaned on the rails watching passersby. Chn'Gi cringed, she was sure that some of these "people" were watching her intently. She was afraid to look for fear of making eye contact and suddenly realized how cold it was, she wished that she had brought something to cover her thin, pale hair, which made her stand out in Ol'Tn as a D'En and an outsider as starkly as if she were carrying a strobe light. Next time, if she survives to return, she'll have to be better prepared.

Chn'Gi continued down the street, certain that she was followed. It was the middle of the workday, and not many people were around. She saw mostly Mi'Nr's and a few poorer looking U'Te's coming and going. She passed "homes" consisting of rows of carbon fiber nanotube cylinders sometimes stacked five deep and of varying lengths of five, ten or fifteen meters and about three meters in diameter insulated with foam, with doors cut in the ends that faced the street or the small alleys that provided access to the ones behind. Very few had windows adjacent the doors. Stairs and scaffolding provided access to the upper levels.

Chn'Gi walked past these original capsule flats, once serving as homes for everyone on Dadr'Ba but now home for the lowest ranking of Dadr'Ba. People who for whatever reason had not accumulated enough mileage or credits toward promotion to Nu'Tn. Or from some financial catastrophe lost their mileage credits and status.

Chn'Gi passed the common dining and bath facilities and wondered how it was possible that the people that lived and worked here managed for so long. Authorized History states that Nu'Tn wasn't constructed until after the ToG event, which means the original crew of Dadr'Ba lived in these quarters under these conditions for thousand years.

She couldn't get her mind around how people could live for generations under such sparse and harsh conditions and why the CA doesn't do something about the people forced to live here now. Tear down this, slum and remodel to modern standards, but then as she thought about it, she realized that the CA is so pragmatic, so waste-averse that they couldn't expend energy or resources "remodeling" these Ol'Tn shanty town tenements without there being a direct tie to forward progress.

Chn'Gi walked past the last rows of living modules and through a high gate into the junkyard. Marveling at all the various examples of old technology scattered around, shipping containers with doors open displaying all sorts of who knows what kinds of devices and machines, some of the machines so gigantic that Chn'Gi couldn't see all of it in the dim light.

The D'Po office was easy to spot, she walked toward a large structure, what may at one time (she guessed) part of a space station or huge cargo module or fuel tank. She noticed first, an enormous roll-up doorway, closed but large enough to drive a supply shuttle through. Painted on the door in big block letters with fluorescent paint and illuminated with black light "TRIED-N-TRUE CLASSIC STARSHIP PARTS EMPORIUM." Adjacent to the roll up door, stood an open personnel hatch with a neon OPEN sign directly above it.

She stepped through the hatch into a well-lit office space with a counter. Her eyes took a moment to adjust from dimness outside, then she approached the counter and saw the proprietor, a U'Te sitting behind an ancient terminal behind the counter, studying it.

Her hope increased. It was just the type of technology she hoped would possess, or provide access to, the ancient data she was looking for.

She stood for a moment at the counter waiting for the man to notice her. He was waving his arms and hands around frantically playing some game she didn't recognize. His eyes focused on the screen; it must use motion sensing hand controls and not the virtual reality mode that's been built into TaC-B's for as long as she could remember.

Finally, he noticed her, surprised and embarrassed by her presence, he made a sort of zigzag cross motion that closed the display, and probably saved his progress. He stood quickly and walked over to meet her across the counter, straightening his clothes along the way.

He appeared visibly flustered; he must not get many D'En's as customers. As he approached, he mumbled something about "Ah, I was just using an art program, uh, painting a picture… I get emotional with my art." Then continuing, slowly regaining his composure, straightened and said in a professional tone as he could muster. "Welcome to Tried-N-True Classic Starship Parts Emporium, where nothing goes to waste, and everything is waiting for a second chance to help bring us O'M. My name is Lu'Gs, what's your name and how can I assist you?"

At this point Chn'Gi was speechless. She hadn't thought beforehand what she was going to say once she got this far, and now Lu'Gs is asking her name. She didn't want to give him her real name, and she didn't know how to ask for something that's illegal from someone that might very well jump at the opportunity to burn a D'En by turning her into the CASS for illegal activities.

This person might just as easily think she's undercover CASS trying to trap him. She looked at Lu'Gs, and then towards the door, still open, then around the office, then back at Lu'Gs. Then she finally got out, "I…, I work for the department of science, ah, and technology; I'm doing some research on, ah, old technology, and I'm looking for some old da…" "You've come to the right place" interrupted Lu'Gs.

"Old technology we've got a lot of," said Lu'Gs as he came around the end of the counter motioning for silence and patted Chn'Gi lightly on the shoulder as he walked over and pulled the hatch closed, glancing around outside as he did. Then returned to his place behind the counter and flicked an old manual switch on the back wall. A strange bluish light in the middle of the ceiling sparked to life that a moment before looked as if it had burned out ages ago.

"I'm sure we can find what you need, ma'am, you can talk freely now, what are you looking for? My guess is, you're looking for something very old and very, unique." Chn'Gi nodded agreement. Lu'Gs continued in the same cordial tone as before, but it seemed clear that Chn'Gi's next response would determine what Lu'Gs would have or could find. Lu'Gs continued, "very old, very unique can be very expensive, how're you planning on paying?"

Chn'Gi's mind was telling her that Lu'Gs sensed or surmised the sensitivity of the situation and must trust her, or he wouldn't have taken actions to ensure their privacy. She was no longer at odds with Lu'Gs over the threat of turning each other into the CASS; it was now a business. Chn'Gi was more comfortable with business, she had bartered with the locals in Ol'Tn many times, so she allowed herself to relax, a little.

"If you don't mind, I'd rather not use credits," then after a slight pause Chn'Gi added, "they're too hard to come by these days." For most people on Dadr'Ba, this statement was all too true, but the real reason she didn't want to use credits is that they are much easier for the CASS to track. Chn'Gi knew, that Lu'Gs must know this, which prompted him to ask the question in the first place.

Lu'Gs played along, "yes, indeed," nodding agreement. Chn'Gi continued, this was more than negotiating a payment method, it was trust building between the two of them, passing a mutual test, "I can pay with, spices, tea, or liquor," not seeing or sensing a response, and not really expecting one, pausing for suspense Chn'Gi added. "I've even got a little paper," to which she noticed a flash of recognition that Lu'Gs immediately hid, he was hooked.

The mention of one of the rarest black market commodities on Dadr'Ba and the unchallenged king of barter items, valuable, easy to conceal and relatively easy to valuate, using a system of weight, size, finish and cleanliness that gives room to barter into an equivalent number of credits.

The suggestion of a paper transaction immediately put their deal into the realm of a Capital Punishment Black Market Crime, orders of magnitude more severe than spice, tea or liquor barter. Lu'Gs, his voice now hushed "clean or dirty." To which she coughed, then responded in an equally hushed voice, "clean," clean being the rarest and most valuable.

They had now cemented their commitments; both were now openly and mutually dealing in a Capital Black Market punishable transaction, which would wind them both in confinement and retraining, or worse, if discovered by the CASS.

Showing a marked change in tone and as if the earlier conversation never occurred, cocking his head and leaning forward Lu'Gs asked: "What specifically are you looking for?" Chn'Gi taking Lu'Gs' lead came closer, leaning forward and in an almost whisper, took the plunge and moved the whole transaction from years of hard labor or retraining to the distinct possibility of forced retirement. "I'm looking for pre-ToG historical information on the development of technology on Or'Gn."

Lu'Gs, martial arts enthusiast, (itself a capital offense), was unable to dodge the impact of her statement, he staggered back almost as if struck hard in the face. Then taking a deep breath, and shaking his head slowly recovered and stepping forward again said after a long pause, "Okay, that's something that doesn't get asked for a lot."

After a pause Lu'Gs continued, as if thinking out loud "If available, it'll probably be on nonstandard media. So you'll have to have a data retrieval device." Pause, "Standalone, it wouldn't do to have any of the stuff on the net." Pause again, "And the data may be buried or erased or overwritten and possibly or probably encrypted, so finding what you're looking for could be extremely time-consuming unless we get lucky, or can find a compatible search engine or someone that can program one for you to scan the media. I think I know where I can find some discarded pre-ToG media, but we're talking about tens, probably hundreds of petabytes that would have to be scanned or recovered and scanned. If you try to scan all that yourself, it could take thousands of years. I'll have to find someone that can help automate the process that won't ask questions. I know a place where we could set up the system, but all this is going to be expensive."

Chn'Gi, "How expensive?" After a long pause, "You say you've got clean, give me a square of clean heavy ultra-white, and we can get started. Give me a week and I'll give you a personal data retrieval system with some sample media that just 'might' have what you're looking for."

"You might get lucky and find it on the first media I give you. After you've had a chance to use it and look at it, let me know if you want me to set up an automated search system. It will search for exactly what you want, but it'll cost extra and increases the risk of detection by the CASS."

Chn'Gi's mind raced, that much paper, a square meter, clean, just to start. Her grandparents had secretly left a package of clean paper given to her in a sealed box by her parents when she graduated. She hated to tap into that treasure, as much for sentimental reasons as any, but almost as if her grandparents spoke to her from within; something told her to go for it.

"I don't carry a kind of paper with me, and I preferred to pay on delivery. How about I give you a decimeter clean and three deci's of dirty now, that's all I got on me. The rest clean when I get the reader and the media."

Lu'Gs paused only for a moment then responded with a double chest thump and a slight nod. Chn'Gi had seen this gesture before among Kr's[79] and not quite knowing the proper response, replied with a weak imitation, which by the expression on Lu'Gs' face sealed the deal.

Now, Lu'Gs just stood there waiting; Chn'Gi suddenly realized that she needed to produce the paper that she had carefully stashed under her clothes, more concerned about protecting it from the thugs, thieves and outcasts rumored to prowl Ol'Tn than to have it handy for a transaction.

Chn'Gi looked around for a restroom, uttering a subtle "Uhm." Lu'Gs seeing her instant discomfort smiled slightly and motioned Chn'Gi towards a door past the end of the counter, the need for occasional privacy appeared to be a not infrequent need for his customers.

Moments later Chn'Gi handed over the carefully folded paper. Lu'Gs still not asking Chn'Gi's name requested that she return in a week, on her next shopping trip, for her "merchandise." Lu'Gs suggested that they shouldn't try to contact each other, that she should just stop by, it's safer that way, no changes in personal behavior. If the merchandise is not ready, they would just have to wait another week and most importantly, if when she comes back, she thinks or feels she's being followed or monitored, just to walk away and come back when it feels right, but don't change her routine.

Chn'Gi left with a tumult of the feelings, satisfied that she made the deal, apprehension and excitement about what she would find out, and a terrible fear of what would happen if they were discovered by the CASS. She began composing in her mind what she might say to the Central Council in self-defense, about how she needed to do it to help satisfy their demand for information about the capabilities of the alien IL on O'M and what their reaction might be when Dadr'Ba arrives.

If she were able to convince the Council of her innocence, it would do nothing for Lu'Gs; Lu'Gs would be as good as dead. If she got caught, she'd have to try to warn Lu'Gs as quickly as possible. The thought crossed her mind that she may have to kill herself, but as soon as the thought entered her mind, she forced it out, vowing to stay positive and not to think about it again.

Lu'Gs tapped out a veiled message to P'Ko's unregistered TaC-B letting him know that he had a job for him. Lu'Gs was sure that the CASS knew P'Ko was working part time for him, there's nothing wrong with an apprentice mechanic like P'Ko doing this kind of work. Lu'Gs added a couple of non-display characters that would indicate to P'Ko that this was a "unique" job.

---

[79] Sounds like Kur, shortened form or worker, name used by D'En's for Mi'Nr's and U'Te's

Chapter 30, P'Ko Gets Chn'Gi's Reader

P'Ko had just arrived home from Graduation and the ToG Ceremony when he got the message from Lu'Gs on his unregistered TaC-B. He immediately wanted to go down to the D'Po to find out what the "unique" job was, but he resisted the impulse. A strong feeling that he was watched had come over him on his way home, and there was still no closure from what happened at the ToG Ceremony.

During the rest of the ceremony after being commanded to sit away from the rest, nothing happened. As the remainder of the initiates slowly recovered, and more intense questioning by Gi'Ya, followed by a long break where she ignored him, Gi'Ya began to act as if nothing was wrong. He was sure the incident had been reported but never saw her communicating with anyone about it. There's no denying, based on her questioning, tone, and emotion he felt from her that the incident was significant and that there must be some fallout as a result, but so far, nothing. A couple of days passed all the while P'Ko had a strong feeling that he was being watched.

He was notified to participate in a short notice job interview with the sector Maintenance Su'Pr[80]'s, hosted at the virtual meeting suite at his old school. They only gave him one days' notice and with the fear of surveillance, P'Ko didn't attempt to contact Su'Zi.

The 'Su'Pr's sat across from him at a virtual table; P'Ko sat facing them a couple of meters away. He was very nervous, they identified themselves, but all P'Ko could recall afterward was that Su'Zi's Su'Pr was one of the two friendly ones, two others were ambivalent acting like they had much better things to be doing at the time.

The last Su'Pr was openly hostile, making cutting and snide remarks about P'Ko's looks, knowledge, and intelligence. Openly stating at the end that P'Ko was totally, unqualified, physically and mentally incapable of doing the job. P'Ko was able to dismiss the hostile one, what he said made little sense, since he was applying for an apprenticeship and didn't have his bio-mods yet. In the end, he was hopeful that he would land a position on Su'Zi's crew.

A few more days passed with no outward indications, he was being watched, yet the feeling that he was being watched remained. He still had no word on his bio-mods, he had been staying close to home feeling claustrophobic and yearning to get out and about.

P'Ko missed Su'Zi, and wanted to talk to her about the job interview, but he wanted to wait until after his bio-mods to see her so that he could show off. However, he knew that as skittish as Su'Zi was about the CA that it would be catastrophic if he were under CASS surveillance and brought that spotlight onto her.

---

[80] Sounds like super, short for superintendent.

He needed to tell Su'Zi about the ToG Ceremony incident and wasn't sure how she would react, but it would be really, really bad if he led the CASS to her. He needed to play it safe; and didn't know how understanding Su'Zi would be.

He was sure she wouldn't want him to bring the CASS down on her; she would understand why he's delaying contact, but on the other hand, he wasn't sure, considering her tremendously strong feelings toward the CASS and the threat of surveillance how she would react to him? Would she turn on him? Would she lose trust in him?

Has what they felt toward each other been a fleeting thing? And is it now passing?

P'Ko stopped himself... he was over thinking, running around in mental circles, stepping on his own thoughts again. What he needed to do is stop thinking.

In an act of near desperation, P'Ko took a long moment and focused all of his attention on sending Su'Zi a psychic message of care, concern, and reassurance. After a moment he thought he heard Su'Zi speaking in his head, meaning without words, of love and reassurance. With that, he felt some of the tension drain away accompanied by a wave of warmth and relaxation.

P'Ko thought about what happened at the ToG Ceremony in detail and upon analysis began to doubt that CASS was watching him. The real watchers had to be, and he had never thought before they would do such a thing, must be the Church.

The Church is watching him because of what happened at the ToG ceremony. When it happened, Gi'Ya questioned him how he knew what to do, how to find the way out of the abyss. Gi'Ya didn't believe him, when he told her that he'd experienced it before, but had no memory or explanation for it. Which he had to admit was impossible. The Church if they think he's lying must suspect him of cheating. If they believe he's telling the truth, which they should with their psychic abilities and religious bent, think he's either a miracle or an abomination. They have him under surveillance while they decide what, if anything, to do.

The CASS if they found out would think that he's a freak of nature that needs to be investigated, tested and probably dissected in the process. If it were the CASS, he wouldn't be under surveillance he would be in custody.

P'Ko ran over the event in his mind, during the ToG ceremony, he had only reacted the way that felt natural, like muscle memory. The shock put him out of his wits; he had no memory of the past, there was only the present, and he just did what his impulses told him to do.

He wondered what the possible consequences were; he had never heard of the Church apprehending people, but that didn't mean it hasn't happened, it has had to have happened. After everyone had recovered, Gi'Ya told all the initiates about the prohibition against sharing knowledge of the ToG Ceremony, with the clear implication of severe consequences for violation.

So there must have been violations, some of the unexplained disappearances of people that everyone attributed to the CASS may have been church apprehensions. What with the CASS refusing to say one way or another and not seeming to care, the Church certainly could apprehend people and let them think it was the CASS' dirty work. He saw firsthand at the ToG Ceremony that the Church has actual soldiers at their disposal, and there's no telling what sharing arrangements the Church has with the CASS regarding surveillance systems and video or what methods of surveillance they have on their own.

After a few more anxious days all the while thinking about his new job, Su'Zi, his bio-mods, Z'Shi, the Church, the ToG Ceremony, the mysterious job Lu'Gs has for him, in other words, not being able to focus.

P'Ko managed to get out to help Ba on a few jobs and finally the feeling of being watched started to subside.

He longed for all this to be over, to be settled in his new job in the mines, in a T'Bm or mining camp far away from all this, he felt in his gut that he could find there a certain kind of solitude, of peace there. P'Ko could feel the high energy this close to Dadr'Ba's engine and hustle bustle press of the people that lived all around him and his family in capsule flats, and he wanted to get away from the sense of the watchers, and from the fear of the CASS.

P'Ko, feeling overwhelmed by everything he faced, decided to take each thought and feeling that was plaguing him and compartmentalize it, file it away, then process it bit by bit, a kind of meditation. He had done this, at first not even realizing he was doing it when he was a Ko'Ka dealing with the nightmares of his birth. Then again, as a To'Ta being picked on in school, his mental processing helped deal with his fears and foes.

He hadn't been meditating very long when he paused and sent Su'Zi a psychic message of reassurance and received an immediate reassuring response. Then he thought through and concluded that the Church isn't as pure as he grew up believing. Knowing this about the Church and not knowing what to do about it, made it difficult to set aside. He had to consciously force himself to set this problem, manhandle it into a memory location to work on later.

Now he focused on Z'Shi and his mentoring. Judging from his class ranking, he was probably a week or so away from getting his bio-mods and begin mentoring.

P'Ko was happy and a little apprehensive that Z'Shi, rather than stretching her mentoring out over the course of six to eight weeks, which would have been virtually impossible and incredibly awkward around his work on the T'Bm. To come up from the T'Bm or mining camp once or twice a week for mentoring for however many weeks would be extremely difficult at the very least.

Z'Shi arranged for ten days straight of one-on-one instruction in isolation. P'Ko's experience during his interview with Z'Shi was powerful and rewarding, but at the end he remembered the feeling of being overwhelmed and exhausted, having collapsed on the floor after what must have been maybe a couple of hours. He couldn't get his mind around the thought of ten days straight of such a powerful experience.

A fleeting thought of quitting crossed his mind, but he immediately eliminated it, refusing to even consider it. He found that he couldn't process his thoughts about his mentoring without ending up with the same anxious feeling that he might not be able to handle it or that he would somehow fail. Finally, he forced himself to file it away, to forget about it, as best he could, to wait for the actual moment to come and deal with it at the moment.

Next on his mental list to deal with was the job down at the D'Po. P'Ko was anxious to find out what the job was, he'd been itching to do something technical, that involved his hands. He always felt a sense of pride when he did something that produced tangible results. A D'Po side job would keep him occupied during this down time while he waited for his bio-mods.

The start of his "real" life, his "adult" life, his life as a "full-fledged" productive member of the crew depended on his bio-mods. This down time in which he was not progressing, not learning, not working, not earning distance credits, but being cargo made him feel lazy and guilty.

His parents were going off to work every day earning their way, supporting him. While this downtime was authorized, even directed by the CA, P'Ko couldn't get it out of his mind that, were he a "Full Adult" he could be charged with failure to progress and fined or arrested for wasting resources. He wasn't contributing to the ship's progress while at the same time consuming the ship's resources keeping himself alive.

P'Ko had avoided Ol'Tn since his graduation because of the fear he had of CA surveillance or being followed. But now enough time had passed, that his intuition or, so he told himself, his sleuthing determined that the Church, most likely, was beginning to lose interest in him. P'Ko psyched himself up to take a more clandestine than usual trip to Ol'Tn and while he was there he would pass a message to Su'Zi through, Mi'Ka, letting her know that he was okay and about his fear that he was being surveilled, and he'd contact her when he could.

P'Ko thinking through his visit to Mi'Ka decided that though she might sense it, he wouldn't mention his suspicion that the Church had him under surveillance. P'Ko sensed that Mi'Ka had some "relationship" with the Church. Mi'Ka didn't appear outwardly religious, she frequently offered, or seemed to offer, mystical rather than religious explanations for psychic events, the fact that they worked seemingly opposing sides of psychic phenomena to the same goal exhibited some cooperation, collusion, or at least mutual respect and restraint.

P'Ko entered Mi'Ka's shop as quietly as possible. Mi'Ka was in the back, as usual, tinkering with some brew or concoction in an attempt to discover, or create something new, an effect, capability or taste. Though she doesn't brag about it, Mi'Ka has many recipes to her credit and a few drug patents.

P'Ko had visited the CA's food and drug research labs while helping his Ba on maintenance and repair jobs, the contrast between those labs and Mi'Ka's "kitchen" is momentous. But P'Ko felt Mi'Ka, has had as much or more success than the CA's Labs.

Mi'Ka called out from the back. "P'Ko, when you are going to learn that to sneak up on anyone other than a D'En you are going to have to quiet your psyche! You barged in here like a soldier bot army wrecking crew!" P'Ko shouted back with his best psychic effort, "Sorry, I do better, next time!" To which Mi'Ka replied, this time physically, "You'd better!"

As soon as Mi'Ka broke the silence with her "You'd better!" shout towards the door where P'Ko was standing, Mi'Ka's robo-pet came scurrying towards him on the ceiling suspended by its retractable clawed magnetic feet. He looked up to see Mi'Ka's robo-pet "Ku'Ma."

Ku'Ma crouched, just out of P'Ko's reach and looked down at him, her one green eye and one yellow eye narrowed down to intense pin pricks.

Ku'Ma studied him, a low growling sound emanated from her. As the ancient robo-pet's complex mechanism of gyros and dynamo's spun up, building energy for action. Then, hissed as Ku'Ma, seemed to recognize him, and performed some kind of venting action, bleeding off energy she had built up for an attack.

Ku'Ma then moved down the side of the wall to eye level and stared at P'Ko, eye to eye, her lidless unblinking eyes returning to their normal soft wide glow, then seemed to flutter for an instant. Ku'Ma jumped down to the ground and rubbed up against P'Ko's leg. He'd, at least, had got the drop on Ku'Ma.

Mi'Ka came walking out of her kitchen. Naturally a little strange looking, but now even stranger looking. She was wearing a heavy apron and a respirator, taking off the respirator, she said, "I know you're in a hurry. A job waiting. You want to meet Su'Zi, same place, same time. I think she already knows. You'll come back again when you have more time."

Then, without pausing. "I've got some new tea I want to try out on you, I mean, 'see how you like it.'" Wearing thick gloves that covered her arms up past her elbows, she pushed a steaming cup of a surprisingly fragrant brew into his hands and stepped back to watch.

Not questioning the safety of the mixture for an instant, he sipped. Instantly, P'Ko felt as if Lu'Gs had just kicked him in the forehead; snapping his head back, P'Ko was just barely able to keep his footing. Mi'Ka stepped forward to grab the cup, keeping P'Ko from dropping it. Then continued, "I guess I made it a little too strong, how's the flavor?"

P'Ko, speechless, had to wait for the initial shock to wear off, then blinked a couple of times and smacked his lips. He felt wide awake, and the back of his neck tingled. "It tastes like burnt dielectric cooling fluid, but surprisingly good."

Mi'Ka nodded, as if in agreement, pausing before speaking as if making a mental note or calculation. Then said smiling "you'll get your bio-mods soon, I want to see them, all of them," then "look for this, but don't open it." And she sent him a mental image of some strange handheld device and some cartridges, and then said aloud, "I mean it, don't open it" "And one more thing, don't worry about the Church." Then she turned and headed back into the kitchen. P'Ko left wondering how many real words she had spoken.

P'Ko made it over to the D'Po and got his work assignment from Lu'Gs, who was happy to see him and congratulated him on his graduation. Then described the strange D'En and her more unusual, and dangerous, request.

P'Ko was up for the challenge and happy to be doing something productive. He went out into the seemingly random maze of modules, vans, cargo units, shipping and storage containers, racks, shelves. He passed piles, and heaps of used, broken, discarded, and outdated equipment parts and pieces tracking down an ancient handheld data reader and prehistoric data cartridges.

P'Ko had relatively little trouble finding what he was looking for. He had grown up poking around this yard and knew it well. As large as it was, covering almost half of Ol'Tn's zone, P'Ko had a mental map of its contents. The treasure was in a relatively uniformly organized section of the yard there were racks and racks of computer equipment and among them, cabinets containing cartridges like those Mi'Ka showed him.

Off to one side of the organized area of old storage cabinets, and racks were an actual pile of racks and cabinets, some partially buried. P'Ko had to use a portable mechanical hoist to uncover the semi-buried racks and cabinets but found what he was looking for.

Many of the data cartridges in the cabinets appeared to be wiped or had so been marked. But he knew that "sometimes" a tech tasked with the boring job of wiping a huge lot of data cartridges will sometimes "save resources" and just mark them wiped and put them in the reuse or recycle pile. The data recording process automatically wipes and overwrites the data on any cartridge it's using anyway, so why wipe them?

These older racks and cabinets appeared to have been just dumped haphazardly. P'Ko's excitement grew, as he noticed a lot of the equipment in the racks seemed scorched and P'Ko wondered if it was damaged from the ToG and the survivors chose to discard entire racks of equipment rather than attempt repairs.

The CA must have thought the ToG had done data wiping for them, which would have undoubtedly been true for all volatile data storage and probably true even for all on-line non-volatile storage, but offline data backups properly stored would be much harder to eradicate, and that was what he was looking for.

Knowing he was in the right spot and having decided what he wanted, it didn't take P'Ko much longer to find it. In a sealed and locked storage cabinet. P'Ko easily jimmied opened the lock, it was intended to prevent accidental or inadvertent access only. Inside, he found a well-organized and labeled container stacked and filled with data cartridges and along one side a now dead, power charging rack with a row of portable readers installed in a neat row.

P'Ko sorted through the cartridges from several of the containers until he found to his amazement data cartridges appeared to be backups of the school servers that predated the ToG by many years.

Realizing the incredible value, and danger associated with this stuff, P'Ko, took a few of the readers to work with, figuring he may have to use parts from several to get even one to work. Then, went through the data cartridges until he found some that looked like would contain Or'Gn history, and hopefully wasn't encrypted.

P'Ko closed the data storage cabinet and used the portable hoist to rebury it. He gathered the readers and the data cartridges and headed back home to his room and his desk/workbench to try to get these things working. The shoulder bag he carried felt hefty, he knew, that he was taking an enormous amount of data, perhaps the whole history of Or'Gn and along with a large part of its technical development and literature.

What he carried could be the entire history of their civilization like an entire civilization was draped over his shoulder. His civilization, his history, his ancestor's and ancestor's ancestor's history.

He felt himself get a little dizzy after he realized that he saw a name that on the cartridges. It must have been the true name of Or'Gn, a name he knew if repeated aloud and overheard by the CASS could result in a death sentence.

P'Ko resolved to deliver the goods to Lu'Gs and not mention that he had any knowledge of what they contained and put it out of his mind until he could discuss it with Mi'Ka, he wouldn't be able to hide it from her. Mi'Ka told him not to open them, but how else would he be able to tell which cartridge contained data and which didn't?

Mi'Ka should be able to help decide what to do, if anything, with his newfound knowledge. He shook his head to himself as he realized psychic ability didn't equivocate with technical expertise, this job was becoming incredibly deep, complicated, and dangerous.

Chapter 31, P'Ko and Su'Zi at the Beach

P'Ko spotted Su'Zi near the spot on the beach where they first met; she was as happy to see him as he was of her. She smiled, saying nothing but motioned to him to remain silent, and beckoned for him to follow her.

P'Ko followed Su'Zi down a path through the dry grass that sprouted through the sand along the beach. She pointed out to P'Ko an oddly shaped rock along the trail as they passed, then took two steps pivoted to the right and stepped off the path and disappeared.

At first, it appeared that Su'Zi dropped out of the virtual environment P'Ko hesitated, then followed, two steps passed the rock he pivoted right and stepped.

The room was plain, the walls a light gray, a smart table with a couple of chairs sat in the middle of the chamber. The room seemed to be lit from nowhere and everywhere, with no apparent entry or exit. The spot they entered from was not at the wall, but a meter or so from it and showed no visible sign of it still existing at all.

Su'Zi gave P'Ko a warm embrace, holding it for a moment as she whispered to him how much she missed him, he squeezed her tight telling her that he has missed her too, then they both settled next to each other into the chairs.

P'Ko sat next to Su'Zi, feeling good. Perhaps the good feeling was due to P'Ko's becoming more comfortable with the virtual environment or due to his growing his psychic abilities, or it could be the result of the bond they were creating together. But whatever the reason he didn't feel as awkward as the first times they met in Vr'Chm, the physical distance between them didn't seem as great now, and he could feel her next to him.

P'Ko and Su'Zi had grown closer than P'Ko could have imagined. Ever since they first became aware of each other, in the dream and even before the dream it seemed now thinking of the time before, like they hungered for the other but didn't know what they hungered for.

P'Ko couldn't understand why he felt the way he did, he didn't have his bio-mods yet, bio-mods brought biological and associated psychological baggage that might explain the way he felt, but he had none. He still couldn't understand that without bio-mods, what could Su'Zi be attracted to? His psyche? He didn't think his psyche was anything special. If anything he felt his mind was flawed; he possessed all kinds of doubts, thought himself damaged and couldn't even trust or use his weak psychic abilities very well.

Yet P'Ko felt the desire to be close to Su'Zi to hold and caress her, to be one with her and he sensed or hoped that she wanted the same with him, despite his lack of equipment. As much as he tried, he couldn't think through this conundrum and felt frustrated. P'Ko didn't have the experience, knowledge or equipment to process how becoming physical would impact their relationship and didn't want to risk altering or losing what they had together by introducing the physical element too soon or the wrong way.

There was no rush; they seemed to have a trust, a non-communicated, non-spoken, mutual understanding that they will eventually move to the next level of an intimate relationship, and there was no need to rush.

P'Ko soon found himself describing to Su'Zi the ToG Ceremony he experienced sharing it in as much detail as he could remember. It's rare to talk about the ToG Ceremony because it's such a personal experience, too personal to be shared and because it's a secret from the uninitiated, punishable by death many people avoid talking about it altogether or only speak of it in analogy or allegory.

Now so excited was P'Ko, sitting side-by-side with Su'Zi that they eagerly shared every intimate detail of their ToG experience. Su'Zi was surprised about the quickness of his ToG recovery, remarking that she too recovered quickly, but had no explanation for it. She wasn't surprised that he helped the one he did; she was tempted to help the others too, but the elder stopped her. Based on the elder needing warn off or stop people from helping each other it must not be that unusual. Su'Zi didn't think P'Ko needed to be as worried as he was.

Soon they were discussing bio-mods, Su'Zi's existing bio-mods and P'Ko's scheduled bio-mods. Then Su'Zi said what had been on her mind, something that had even crossed her mind when they first met on the beach but she was hesitant until now. "You know," she said, "I could be your mentor." "I know you've got that other person lined up, but she must be very busy." "She'd probably welcome the chance to free up her schedule, and her mentoring would probably be rushed, and not as good as it could be or should be." P'Ko immediately became uneasy, and Su'Zi, sensing it talked faster and more urgently "I could be your mentor, it would be easy to schedule and arrange." "Pri'Api and Ti'Reso were my mentors they're well known as excellent mentors, and they taught me very well. I know all the latest techniques" Su'Zi could sense turmoil in P'Ko, this was going very badly. Finally, she trailed off very softly "you won't be sorry." The psychic connection between Su'Zi and P'Ko was gone; P'Ko had withdrawn into himself, then still in turmoil, he tried to reach back out to Su'Zi, but she kept her distance.

P'Ko paused a long time before answering. He rolled over the options, and possible impacts. He was taking too long, feeling a stab of guilt, because he's analyzing the question that had come not from Su'Zi's intellect, but from her heart. Now his answer was coming from an analysis only slightly modified by his heart.

He truly cares for Su'Zi and is attracted to her. He gave his word to Z'Shi, made a commitment. Z'Shi didn't have to take him on as his mentor, she's totally out of his league. He thinks Z'Shi is very attractive and deep down the thought of being Z'Shi's Lr'Lng excited him. But his feelings for each is different, the feelings for Z'Shi, awe, and respect, for Su'Zi, inexplicably stronger and deeper along with a burning desire to impress her. How could he do that as a Lr'Lng?

Su'Zi is offering something very special and beyond all doubt, it would be. But if he took Su'Zi up on her offer, it would also shape their relationship forever.

P'Ko paused and swallowed. Even through the virtual interface he could see the pain in Su'Zi's eyes and felt her psychic anguish mixed with his own. He tried to choose his words carefully, but they came out feeling awkward and disingenuous.

P'Ko sought to explain that Z'Shi had already set aside the time for the mentoring and had helped with this bio-mod selections. If he were to cancel, it would be an affront to her. He just couldn't do that, if word got out, it could impact her reputation, and he didn't know how she would take it.

Z'Shi is a very wealthy and influential person; all these explanations felt empty, and P'Ko felt like the blood was draining out of his heart, and felt weak. He expressed how much he appreciated Su'Zi's offer, but he can't change his pick for a mentor, adding that it in no way changed his feelings about Su'Zi. All the while, trying his best to send psychic messages reinforcing his words.

Finally, he said what he should have said at first, and what was in his heart, "I want us to be equals."

Their psychic connection restored, P'Ko could feel the hurt in Su'Zi but also sensed her understanding and hope. He cursed the virtual interface; he wanted to embrace Su'Zi and feel her in his arms despite the conflicting messages it would send. He felt trapped, his mind felt heavy, and fog obscured his reasoning. He felt torn, like his insides were being drained and ripped from within him. Could this also be what Su'Zi was feeling? And he was responsible, why did she have to ask?

Su'Zi quietly, sadly, and very softly said, "it's okay, I understand, it was wrong of me to ask," then "when will I get to see you again?" And not mentioning that the mentoring immediately followed the bio-mods, "As soon as my bio-mods are complete. I want you to be the first to see me."

Chapter 32, P'Ko's Mentoring

As previously arranged, P'Ko woke from his bio-mods on a soft matt near the same practice platform where they had performed his interview. Soft music was playing in the background. It took P'Ko a moment to realize that he wasn't dreaming, he was at Z'Shi's apartment. He looked around to see the display panel ceiling of Z'Shi's apartment now a pale blue with random lighter colored shapes floating across it. It reminded him of the sky above the beach in Vr'Chm. Realizing that the ceiling too, not just the walls of her apartment could display virtually anything.

Refreshed and clear-minded, with no drowsiness whatsoever P'Ko got up on one elbow and looked around. He spotted Z'Shi at the same low table that they had first had tea as if on cue she motioned him to join her.

When he tried to get up it felt strange, a little dizzy; his limbs felt distant and slow to react, and the gravity changed. This was the first time he could remember not waking up in his room at his parent's apartment and its gravity level.

The last thing he remembered was he was in the Doctor's office in Nu'Tn. Now he was in Z'Shi's apartment high above Nu'Tn nearly the same height as the upper levels of Nu'Tn Stadium a substantial gravity change, not as drastic a change as in zone one, the power production and fusion drive zone. The workers there are in the microgravity near Dadr'Ba's center, siphoning off energy from and maintaining the nuclear fire coursing down Dadr'Ba's center line.

P'Ko visited there only one time with his ba when there was a project that needed extra bodies; it was exciting, but there were far too many D'En's working and in charge, the U'Te's were not allowed to do anything important, and P'Ko didn't like it.

P'Ko looked down and saw that he wore a loose fitting sleeved tunic, with long pants, and slippers not the knee length shorts of a To'Ta. He started to feel himself, his arms and legs were thicker, muscled, his head had hair, then, he checked his sexual mods, Z'Shi paid no attention.

The tea was a new flavor which didn't surprise P'Ko; Z'Shi undoubtedly had hundreds to choose from. As P'Ko drank the tea Z'Shi began to explain what was going to happen, as he listened, he started to feel a little strange, not knowing if it was due to bio-mod recovery or something else.

Z'Shi shared that the tea contained a mild relaxant that would help with what would come later. They would start with a repeat or continuation of his first interview. He needed first, to learn to control his new self, and the biomods he received required to work down in the mines. He was much stronger than he was before and it's important that he learn a new level of self-control and discipline.

152

They paired up on the stage and soon they were dancing, very slow at first. P'Ko struggled to maintain control under the influence of the tea and the uncertainty of his new physical capabilities and limitations. P'Ko soon realized that the tea was not just a relaxant, but must have also had some psychoactive/psychotropic properties.

Giddy from his bio-mods and new strength, influenced by the effects of the tea P'Ko tried to rush the training and tried to grab Z'Shi inappropriately. Her speed and agility combined with her martial arts skill left P'Ko embarrassed, incapacitated and in pain. Several times he found himself flat on the floor, Z'Shi standing over him, clearly disappointed.

P'Ko quickly learned his error, while still under the influence of the tea, P'Ko sobered up. Struggling under the effects of the tea, he fought to gain control over his mind and body. As the effects of the tea wore off, he found that he was better able to control his mind and body along with its new bio-modified capabilities without consciously trying.

The training went around the clock resting, eating, and hydrating as necessary. As the training progressed, he and Z'Shi became more comfortable with each other, over time, and after many hours, they moved to a new training site higher up in the building. The gravity was much lower and the temperature much higher, the practice continued in a large, dimly lit room, padded on all sides, with each of them wearing only tight-fitting, lightweight workout clothes.

Their practices grew in intensity. At first, P'Ko struggled to control his strength in the low gravity. Gradually he learned and became comfortable with his new strength and agility, now the training became more suggestive and erotic yet with a focus on form, self-control, and flow, they often spoke, but as practice continued and time passed, they developed a physical and mental language.

P'Ko began to wonder if he was falling in love, Z'Shi sensing his thoughts, replied with words that didn't register physically, only mentally. This took P'Ko by surprise because he hadn't vocalized his wonder about falling in love, or had he? Z'Shi tried to reassure P'Ko that what they were experiencing was wonderful and beautiful and should be focused on in the immediate, at the moment.

P'Ko's thoughts continued, has the connection he and Z'Shi built allowed her to read his mind? Or was it something else? As he wondered about it, he felt a poison seep into his mind, a poison he fought to suppress, but failed.

Had Z'Shi's "experience" with who knows how many other people, other men, developed in her an innate sense of what her partners are thinking and when they're thinking it? Was he jealous? Feeling inferior? The thought ate at him and gradually worsened. Then his mind flashed to Su'Zi and that this feeling was probably like what Su'Zi felt when he declined her offer for mentorship.

Suddenly Z'Shi slapped P'Ko, sending him spinning. As P'Ko came to his senses, he found himself on the floor in the dimly lit, low-G room, in an embrace with Z'Shi, he didn't know how they got there. But as he slowly regained his senses, guessed, that his mental self-interrogation, had once again been the root of the fall.

Z'Shi looked P'Ko straight into the eyes and said, very stern and serious, "P'Ko there are times to think and times to act, too often you spend too much time thinking and analyzing your actions before you act. So far you've been lucky, and there haven't been any serious consequences, but there will come times that thinking instead of acting could cost you your life."

"First and foremost you must make sure that the present is taken care of, only then worry about the past and the future; you'll find that you'll be happier and more alive if you do."

With that Z'Shi kissed P'Ko, and he allowed himself more than ever before in his entire life to be lost in the present.

The mentorship continued, and P'Ko learned techniques to control himself and to manipulate, to the extent Z'Shi permitted it, the sexual experience.

P'Ko learned the intimate dance on the edge of a precipice, the game of brinksmanship, the various degrees of pleasure, excitement and the feeling of two connected, becoming one. With practice and a little effort, P'Ko could imagine himself as Z'Shi and perform in ways that she would like, and she did the same for him.

P'Ko learned what it was like to be, with another, a single physical being. How to unite and became like neighboring organs within one body, functioning together to achieve a common goal. And that goal, after stripping away all the mechanizations was to become as one.

He imagined that it was like trying to embrace someone while standing tiptoe balancing atop a needle. At first, they never succeeded, then with practice they would come close to balance and for at time dance together as one upon the needle but would always fall in reset. Each time satisfied, but a little frustrated at never succeeding in prolonging the dance as long, or dance as deeply and unified as the longing and desire they felt called to them for.

In this way, P'Ko learned the art and discipline of working with his partner and mentor Z'Shi. He learned the art of reduction, reducing a person's existence to its simplest and purest forms. Focusing, creating, simplifying and maintaining a kind of bubble, one of nature's simplest, purest and most fragile forms. The pinnacle of physical pleasure that two people can attain, then, unable to keep it any longer, experience the flood of pleasure. Sometimes experienced as a feeling of falling, sometimes of draining away, at times soaring high, that accompanies some level of reset. Sometimes the reset would be partial and result in only a pause in activity, at times the reset would be total, causing a lapse into involuntary convulsions to varying degrees.

P'Ko knew and accepted that Z'Shi was always in control of her resets and only allowed him to witness them as part of their mentoring. This knowledge only drove him to try harder to satisfy her and feel legitimate pleasure in the knowledge that she shared, relinquished a part of herself to him. Just as he shared and abandoned part of himself to her. She couldn't hide that she liked what she did and was very, very good at it, and she liked what he did, and enjoyed it even more as P'Ko became more practiced and proficient, gaining confidence, the skill and muscle memory, that like many physical sports separates the novice from the expert.

Sometimes they would reset together, P'Ko liked those best, recovering in each other's arms, still coupled, then ever so slowly after the other woke, to begin the process again.

The mentoring included slow dances and massage sessions which served as both a break and a prelude.

They practiced pleasuring the other, which taught the technique of total focus on the other, without the distraction of self. How to sense and internalize the other's experience. Learning the pride and satisfaction of being able to, in a sense, play, interact, manipulate and control the most beautiful and complicated musical instrument ever, another being. P'Ko Learned how to make beautiful, satisfying and profound music, all the more meaningful because it can't be stored or recorded except in one's memory. It is the ultimate and most intimate performance art.

With Z'Shi's help, P'Ko mastered control of his bio-mods and the mentoring became more varied and began to include deep, serious, intense sessions as well as playful tricks and games. Z'Shi even played some of the musical instruments that adorned her apartment and demonstrated her deftness with each one.

P'Ko's psychic empathic abilities seemed to improve because, as Z'Shi played, he could feel his fingers touching and manipulating the instrument, much like he had learned during their sexual encounters, an ability that dramatically intensified the experience.

They had long discussions about right and wrong uses of sex, recreational sex, the importance of honesty and the distinctions between sex, love and procreation.

Once, as they were recovering from an unusually intense reset, Z'Shi waxed philosophical that long ago, before Dadr'Ba ever launched and left the Or'Gn world system, all people were bio-naturals. There were no radiation resistant, gene-locked, long-lived clones.

People's bodies grew and aged naturally, only rarely could people expect to live past one-hundred. Then, as today sex was used for recreation and satisfying self-esteem, along with the need and desire for a climaxing reset, pair bonding and sharing intimacy. Back then sex also had a biological function; it was the way most Bio-naturals exchanged genetic material to create a Bo'Ba. Few had psychic abilities and procreation was based solely on the physical sharing of genetic material and not on the psychic union used today to transition self to a Bo'Ba.

P'Ko was amazed to hear Z'Shi speak of this history, discussion physiology and pre-Touch of God history had been outlawed for hundreds of years. P'Ko wanted to learn more about how exactly people shared genetic material but was afraid to ask; he didn't want to spoil the moment. He decided instead to keep one the readers and data cartridges he had recovered in the junk yard and study them.

Z'Shi explained that while achieving ultimate unity of physical and psychic, that she and P'Ko danced around where a couple goes on the way to conceiving and bringing life to a Bo'Ba, it's a challenging and holy thing and should be reserved for and practiced only with your soul-mate, your true love.

P'Ko felt not a deepening of his relationship with Z'Shi but a maturation of it; he realized that they had reached the limit of the depth they would achieve and that knowledge brought along with it a level of trust and understanding. It carried a reminder of teacher, student, even during those times when Z'Shi allowed him the dominant role.

P'Ko learned that the martial arts that Z'Shi had mastered dealt with pressure points, speed, agility, manipulation of joints and exploiting the opponent's strength and momentum. When she wanted or needed to, she could move incredibly fast. More than once, Z'Shi demonstrated her speed and agility when P'Ko got too carried away or ignored the hints or signals Z'Shi gave him that he was going out of bounds.

Z'Shi never taught him her form of martial arts, saying he had no need, that his specialty should rely more on his own unique capabilities, concentrating on his strength, speed, and momentum. Still P'Ko learned the basic moves from having them used on him.

P'Ko began to sense that the mentoring was coming to an end, finally, Z'Shi announced that he was ready, but mentoring is not a one-time thing, it evolves. P'Ko should not likely need any more sexual mentoring, but there may come other "occasions" and should P'Ko feel the need, he should seek Z'Shi out and not hesitate when the need arises.

Z'Shi took P'Ko home to his parents' house in her car dropping him off on a blind corner, then after a warm embrace silently disappeared.

P'Ko's parents could hardly recognize the new P'Ko nearly everything about him had changed. But as he drew near first, his mother, then his father and brother made the psychic connection and anxiously embraced him welcoming him home.

Throughout his bio-mods and mentoring P'Ko didn't have his TaC-B and hadn't accessed electronic messaging, having left a non-availability notice (traditional during mentoring sessions). Once he got back online and checked his voice and text messages, labeled high importance among dozens of teases and congrats from his friends was his report to work notice from the CA.

P'Ko is to report to his new work site tomorrow; he found the package mentioned in the message, with his new work uniforms and two eSuits set to the side just inside his room by his parents. He immediately sent Su'Zi a coded message to meet, tonight.

Chapter 33, Chn'Gi Starts Using Reader

Chn'Gi spent several weeks contriving the cover for her access to the reader and data.

She began an exercise program, nothing in-depth, being clones without the power of natural regeneration and muscle building, the best a GLC (Gene-Locked-Clone) could hope for is to keep their systems working optimally and avoid atrophication.

A modicum of exercise several times a week is enough for most people who weren't practicing for a sport where improved kinesthetic sense or developing muscle memory is the goal. There are a few compulsive individuals that find exercise addicting, but Chn'Gi wasn't one of those.

Chn'Gi didn't feel much different after each workout; maybe she wasn't doing it right. But that wasn't the point; it was going home after working out and soaking in the bathtub behind a locked door that she longed for.

The bathroom was one spot in her house; that wasn't under CASS surveillance, (all people in critical positions are under home surveillance). Although the sound sensors in the adjacent rooms might be able to pick up something she always turns on music in the outer room loud enough to hear from the tub.

Chn'Gi was careful always to use the small reading light that Lu'Gs insisted on her taking and had stressed that she use it whenever she read. She keeps the light close by and always read out of view of the surveillance cameras.

The light fit rather comfortably in the palm of her hand when on it seemed to shimmer while looking directly at it, yet produced a soft light that was not unpleasant to read by.

Lu'Gs never explained in detail, but hinted that the "Reading Light" would somehow disable or interfere with the functions of some undescribed "other" forms of surveillance, but had to be used privately so that those surveilling didn't find out she was using it.

If discovered or questioned about the light her response should be something like she "just likes it", and the less she knows about its operation and function the better, she wouldn't have to hide or conceal what she didn't know.

Chapter 34, Su'Zi Meets P'Ko after Mentoring

Su'Zi walked into the Hn'Gri Bo'R, knowing that P'Ko would be there, she got the previously agreed to A-OK coded message to meet him that she'd been anticipating and tried to set a new speed record getting to sector three's Ol'Tn.

They decided to take turns visiting each other until they could arrange to get on the same crew. Su'Zi had hoped that they could get on the same crew someday. But privately hoped that P'Ko wouldn't get assigned to her crew. It would be awkward for P'Ko to show up on her crew. And after P'Ko's description of his interview, she realized that it was her Su'Pr that was super critical of P'Ko.

Her crew was also especially distrustful of the CA, D'En's and For'Nr[81]'s in general and in spite of P'Ko's friendship with Su'Zi or perhaps because of it, they would undoubtedly give P'Ko a hard time.

As soon as P'Ko gets assigned to a crew Su'Zi's plan will be to start working a job swap from her end. P'Ko wouldn't be able to swap jobs until he completed his apprenticeship and that would take, if they were lucky five or ten years. Many apprenticeships last as long as twenty-five years, it all depends on P'Ko and his trainer.

There was a one in five chance he would be assigned to her crew, but she knew already, he wasn't coming to her crew; Mi'Nr's are a close-knit community, and she used some of her contacts to learn which crew he was going to be assigned to. Mostly the Mi'Nr grads get assigned to the home sectors they grew up in, but since P'Ko was a U'Te/Mi'Nr transfer, it's uncertain what sector he would go.

She walked in and scanned the crowd, expecting P'Ko to play with her and try to hide. She scanned more with her psyche rather than with her eyes and spotted him right away. When she laid eyes on him she was surprised, he looked so much different, he barely fit into the used pair of his Ba's mechanic coveralls. And he had muscle's, muscle's that showed through the coveralls in his shoulders, arms, and legs, and he had an unruly mop of hair on top of his head instead of the mechanic's cap that used to cover his pre-grad baldness.

She couldn't help but stare, P'Ko looked good, exquisitely good. And though Su'Zi tried to restrain it, and P'Ko was still a relative novice with his psychic abilities, Su'Zi could tell P'Ko sensed her awe and basked in it. This, the first time since his bio-mods and mentoring. P'Ko's pride was overflowing, more so because this was their first meeting with the new, "P'Ko".

Su'Zi walked over to him and sat next to him at the bar. She held back the urge to wrap her arms around him and give him one of her best hugs. He smiled and said that he knew he couldn't hide and stood and did an amazingly

---

[81] Sounds like and means Foreigner.

158

dexterous pirouette, which didn't go unnoticed by the regulars who felt the Hn'Gri Bo'R was their second home.

P'Ko got an applause from all around, but unlike the old P'Ko, rather than shrink away P'Ko bowed in acknowledgment around the room and said: "Thank you, thank you." Su'Zi rewarded him with a big hug not holding back one iota and felt P'Ko's firm muscles beneath her own, as she squeezed him he responded in kind and Su'Zi found herself losing her breath and melting under his clutch.

They moved to the bar shoulder to shoulder. Su'Zi found herself strangely out of breath, fighting to recover, and trembling slightly hoping that P'Ko wouldn't notice. P'Ko didn't seem to notice and ordered two PCF's (Prompt Cold Fusions), powerful shots of liquor known for its instant effects. P'Ko sensed her surprise and seeing the surprised expression on Su'Zi's face, P'Ko smiled, explaining that it was a special occasion, and it was the first time that he would taste a PCF, and he hoped that it would be the first time for Su'Zi too.

Su'Zi shared that it was going to be her first taste of a PCF, (PCF is the most expensive drink the Hn'Gri Bo'R has to offer). Not that there weren't enough special occasions or reasons to imbibe in Su'Zi's life, but she could never bring herself to spend ten times the price of a cup of tea on a shot glass of liqueur. This was special, and she could tell that P'Ko was jubilant and wanted to impress her and wanted to have a special toast of something that she hadn't had before. P'Ko was going all out to make sure that he was providing her an experience she'd never had before, and she loved him for it, and couldn't help but show and act accordingly.

P'Ko acknowledged that it was going to make a dent in the gift credits he got from his family and friends for graduation, but it would be worth it. Sharing this first post-bio-mod, post-mentor meeting with Su'Zi and make it a special memory that they could reflect on the rest of their lives.

Su'Zi's response was that it would be special PCF or not. But, she added that she always wondered what a PCF tasted like. She thanked P'Ko and promised him that when he came to visit her in her camp that it would be her turn to impress, and she'd introduce P'Ko to Mi'Nr's HB (home brew). That Mi'Nr's, usually the mechanics, make a special drink from a contraption of broken and spare parts, using non-fuel grade substances found in the scree left from the mining operation. The drink is cooked and distilled then filtered through a barrel of the latest ore; it's then bottled and allowed to age. Each sector's HB is different, and each batch is different, and there is an annual contest between the sectors to determine which sectors HB is best. Su'Zi's added with pride that her sector has won the last few years in a row.

The bartender, a crippled Mi'Nr, who got seriously injured on the job and instead getting bio-mod repairs with the credits the CA gave for his repair. Took the bio-mod repair credits, paid off some officials and bought himself a share in the bar.

The barkeep has since been using the proceeds from the bar to slowly pay for his repairs. He had been listening down the bar while he was preparing the drinks and hobbled back with two shot glasses with a neon green glowing concoction that had sparkles of bright gold, with some frost around the rim.

He presented them the drinks saying that "no disrespect intended, T'Bm HB is very powerful, but my PCF is light years better than that rock gut they make in the T'Bm's." "T'Bm HB is a single stage rocket, and it might take several to get you to escape velocity. My custom made PCF is a full three stage rocket, guaranteed to get you to escape velocity in one shot."

A booth had opened up and upon the bartender's suggestion, they moved to it, and sat side by side and made a toast. "To New Beginnings" and took a sip of the powerful liquor, the liquid stung and burned causing them both to gasp and cough while trying not to laugh, but after a brief pause. They found themselves smacking their lips, enjoying the aftertaste as warm fire etched itself down their throats and smoldered into their stomachs. Then, gaining courage, they took another sip that turned into a downing of the shot, this time without coughing.

The fire started in their stomachs then slowly spread to their limbs making their skin tingle along the way. As soon as it reached their fingertips, they began to feel heavy, like they were descending to the lower levels. In spite of being Mi'Nr's and able to function in heavy gravity, they couldn't lift up their arms or move their legs, and they sat slumped in the booth. Their heads sank to their chest, making it difficult to talk. They spent a couple of minutes of rolling their heads to the side so that they could see each other, slurring their words laughing and joking. Then they began to feel weightless and giddy, though they didn't actually float they felt like they were floating. All the while still seated on the bench, but the feeling caused them to grab the corners of the table unconsciously.

The PCF lived up to the bartender's claims, and its reputation. The weightlessness soon wore off, allowing them to focus on the pleasant aftertaste, feeling relaxed and good with just a hint of lightheadedness.

P'Ko who just wanted to mark the occasion with something special and to toast, to christen, to mark his new status towards adulthood, and full crewmember status, felt like he achieved his goal and that cost of the liquor was well invested.

The magical draught had erased all anxiety laying hidden regarding who mentored who and humorous stories and experiences started to be shared about learning to use bio-mods. The bartender, overhearing the subject matter, turned up the music playing in the background, wondering what the likelihood would be that Su'Zi and P'Ko would remember their conversation tomorrow.

Su'Zi and P'Ko had opened a new area of their relationship and discussed it openly and friendly, they found themselves discussing their favorite sexual techniques and positions and though it aroused them, they understood without explaining, that this night would not be the night to put their discussion into practice.

Without being said, the night or day, whenever it would happen, it would be exceptional and exclusive in such a way as not to be influenced by intoxicating liquor, but the intoxication would be of an entirely different sort.

The subject finally got around to P'Ko's work orders; he is being sent to sector three. P'Ko told Su'Zi about the message and the package containing the new utility uniforms and eSuit, with instructions to wear them when he reports tomorrow. He is to report to the maintenance supervisor, T'Bm Sector Three, a supply shuttle is going to take supplies down from Nu'Tn the next morning, and P'Ko is to be on it.

Su'Zi was happy and excited, she could get to the sector three mining camp from the sector two mining camp easily, she knows exactly where the airlock is, and their shifts are little enough different to make visits easy.

The effects of the PCF was either wearing off or the less playful subject of work rather than recreational sex altered the tone of the evening. It was beginning to get late, and they both had to work the next day Su'Zi even earlier than P'Ko. But P'Ko is going to have a full day of seeing and experiencing new things and meeting new people; he'd need to be in top form, to make a good impression and be prepared to deal with people who will try to test him.

Su'Zi and P'Ko, sensing what each other was thinking, became sober. It might have been the effects of the PCF. Or a bit of overinflated ego from what must feel to P'Ko like Superman bio-mods. Or perhaps feeling rich from having spent the last ten days carousing with a millionaire D'En in her apartment. Su'Zi saw that P'Ko intended to strut into the mining camp like a celebrity, thinking everyone would be impressed.

Su'Zi found herself reacting hostilely towards P'Ko, she took a deep breath, calmed herself and said firmly. "Sit back and take a deep breath, you've got it all wrong. You need to know a few things about Mi'Nr's; I'd hoped to be able to tell you this over time and let it sink in slowly, that there'd be at least a few days before you report, but there's no time. You got home this morning, and you report to work tomorrow."

Su'Zi sent P'Ko mental reassurances so as not to belittle him. Then said "you're going to get there, and you're not going to be welcome or trusted. Sure they'll be "nice" but they're going to think you're a CASS spy. And may attempt to prove, you can't do the job or alienate you into quitting. You're going to have to use your personality, your wit, your intelligence and every ounce of psychic ability you have to win yourself over." "Mi'Nr's are not evil people, just cautious and guarded because of all the many hurts, snubs, persecutions, harassments, injustices and oppressions they've received and continue to receive from For'Nr's. They are going to see you as a For'Nr. Just about the only thing you've got going for you is your limited psychic ability and that you're an apprentice, free labor."

Su'Zi, now psychically, "you must be genuine, be yourself, don't put on airs, be humble, go into this thinking that you're starting off at the very bottom and that you know nothing. From their point of view, you don't. Pay attention to detail, once they've decided you're not a spy, they'll test you, at first, they might expect you to know what every Mi'Nr child should know and might act like you're stupid for not knowing. They'll tell you something once in passing and expect you to remember it later; you must bear this in mind, or they'll think you're stupid."

Then speaking once again, softly "You're going into a new environment; it's going to be like you're on another planet down there. Whoever set this up probably doesn't want you to succeed, it would work to the CA's advantage for you to fail, and then they would have justification not to allow cross class job selections."

"Even with your bio-mods, it will take you time to get used to the lower levels of zone three, go slow, if you fall and have to crawl it would look really bad." Then, with a sudden realization, like Su'Zi, almost forgot something, said: "don't wear any of the uniforms or eSuits the CA gave you, wear what you've got on now and be late for your ride." "It's getting late, there're some things I need to take care of before the morning, we gotta go."

They got up from the booth, after paying the barkeep, who gave them a hefty discount, they walked out to the street, the effects of the PCF was gone, it was much later than they thought and Su'Zi had a hazardous drive ahead of her, and she'd be at work in a few hours. Before that, she needed to talk to some people and make some arrangements before the start of her shift.

Su'Zi gave P'Ko a quick, passionate hug and an unexpected kiss and dashed off down the street.

Chapter 35, P'Ko's First Day at Work

With Su'Zi's last words to him the night before weighing heavy on his mind, P'Ko arrived at the lower-level warehouse of the fuel processing facility, only minutes before the supply shuttle that was to depart. He was thankful that the shuttle didn't leave early making him miss his first day, with who knows what consequences.

The supply shuttle operates autonomously, typically without passengers, this time, it had two, P'Ko and a D'En wearing an exoskeleton and eSuit (environmental suit).

This D'En that was going down to P'Ko's camp didn't possess the bio-mods needed. The D'En wore gear, though bulky, probably exceeded the strength and sustained endurance of the bio-mods of P'Ko and the Mi'Nr's. The D'En seemed almost like a person trussed up like a wannabe soldier and reminded P'Ko that occasionally soldiers accompanied high-level D'En's and other high-value assets at certain high visibility events.

The D'En scowled at P'Ko convinced that P'Ko was a slob and disregarded instructions and authority. Letting P'Ko know that he should have arrived properly prepared and on time.

P'Ko's sloppiness jeopardized his inspection schedule, and he cursed P'Ko for being late, mumbling something about Kr's being too stupid to follow simple instructions. P'Ko didn't think he was expected to hear. However, P'Ko had trained himself while working with his ba to listen attentively to machines to help diagnose problems, so P'Ko heard every word.

The D'En finally introduced himself as Sh'P'Po[82], an engineer being sent down to perform an inspection of the Mi'Nr's operations. Immediately, P'Ko didn't like the guy, and he didn't need to use psychic abilities to tell the feeling was mutual. But underneath it all, P'Ko could sense that this D'En was hiding something.

The supply shuttle was already loaded and ready to back into the freight elevator which would take them down to the beginning of Zone Three where they would exit the elevator[83] and ride the supply shuttle the rest of the way through tunnel passages to sector three's T'Bm in operation.

They'll pass through several airlocks which lay adjacent to circulation control baffles and pass condensers and pumps used to regulate the internal temperature of Dadr'Ba preventing it from overheating and melting.

P'Ko tossed his large duffel into the shuttle's cargo compartment under the rear deck with ease. It contains the new uniforms and eSuits Su'Zi asked him not to wear and most of the list of personal items that was attached to his

---

[82] Sounds like She-Pee-Poh.

[83] the lower elevators are not large enough to accommodate the supply shuttle

reporting instructions. Followed by, and handled carefully because it contains some delicate instruments (including diagnostic equipment and his micro repair station), his tool bag.

P'Ko carried his personal bag over his shoulder, it contained, among other things, an extra reader and data cartridges like the one he fixed up on his side job during his bio-mod wait. It was a match for the one he turned over to Lu'Gs for his un-named D'En client. Both readers are in excellent shape for being over a thousand years old, P'Ko upgraded the power supplies and RF shielding and disabled the wireless functions to eliminate any risk of stray emanations that the CASS might detect, (no sense inviting a visit from the CASS).

P'Ko was proud of the work he'd done on the readers, they possessed the bulk of the technological history of an entire civilization, in a package that you could hold in the palms of your hands. He couldn't help but keep one.

He had an unspoken agreement with Lu'Gs that he could take parts in partial payment for his labor. Lu'Gs never complained, and P'Ko never took advantage. It worked out well for Lu'Gs as the parts cost him practically nothing.

P'Ko and Sh'P'Po loaded into the shuttle as its D'En accented voice announced that passengers need to secure their gear and that it was going to depart in two minutes. They got to their seats just as the shuttles automatic doors were closing.

Once underway Sh'P'Po began to relax and soon began to make small talk, even apologizing for his earlier outbreak. P'Ko wasn't interested in conversation but relented after it became apparent that Sh'P'Po wasn't going to be ignored and persisted in earnest attempting to draw P'Ko into conversation.

Trapped, seated next to Sh'P'Po for the duration the trip P'Ko relented and began to respond. Though P'Ko still didn't trust him.

P'Ko soon deducted that though Sh'P'Po pretended to have no prior knowledge, Sh'P'Po showed indications that he knew a lot about him.

Based on the sequence and the phrasing of the questions Sh'P'Po asked, P'Ko began to feel like Sh'P'Po was digging for personal information. Sh'P'Po knew P'Ko was a new trainee on its way to his first assignment and asked about his family and how they felt about him becoming a Mi'Nr. Sh'P'Po gave away his advance knowledge when he asked about P'Ko's brother when P'Ko hadn't mentioned the gender of his sibling. P'Ko didn't let on that he noticed the slip.

It raised P'Ko's suspicion even more that Sh'P'Po seemed bothered that he wasn't wearing his CA issued work uniform and eSuit, hinting that P'Ko was violating some rule or regulation. The reporting instructions didn't explicitly state what clothes or uniform he was to report in, but the implication was clear. P'Ko was wearing a clean, pressed, used work coveralls given to him by his Ba, proudly displayed his id badge indicating his status as a sector three apprentice Mi'Nr.

P'Ko began to appreciate the advice he received from Su'Zi about not wearing one of the crisp new uniforms that were given to him by the CA; the more Sh'P'Po talked, the more P'Ko wanted to distance himself from the CA.

Nearly halfway to their destination, Sh'P'Po was still talking constantly, asking questions, acting more and more friendly. Sh'P'Po slowly needled information out of P'Ko, occasionally tipping off that he knew more than he should.

P'Ko found himself suckered into an overtly friendly, but with sharp undertones, verbal sparring match. At first, P'Ko thought he held his own in the verbal battle, but as it continued, P'Ko began to realize that Sh'P'Po was learning more about P'Ko than P'Ko had learned about Sh'P'Po, which was nothing.

Irritated P'Ko began to withdraw, sensing this, Sh'P'Po shifted gears and took on a noticeable change in attitude, bearing and behavior. Sh'P'Po's voice even changed, now smooth, and softer. Sh'P'Po leaned in towards P'Ko and reintroduced himself, saying that he liked P'Ko and wanted to be friends. Sh'P'Po went on to say that he was in a position to help P'Ko and offered P'Ko his non-D'En nickname, "Lo'Ri."[84]

This new name and attitude was friendlier on the surface, but P'Ko's psychic senses alarmed with deception, and P'Ko had to force the tension in his muscles to relax to prevent them showing on his face or posture and tip off to "Lo'Ri", Sh'P'Po's failed deception.

P'Ko realized that Sh'P'Po/Lo'Ri was good at getting information out of people, better than P'Ko was at preventing it. P'Ko tried to divert the conversation and move the topic from P'Ko to Lo'Ri. P'Ko asked if Lo'Ri wasn't a girl's name? To which Lo'Ri replied, and patted P'Ko on the thigh, "yeah, but it was given to me a long time ago, and I've grown attached to it." Sending P'Ko a clear signal verbally, physically and psychically, that Lo'Ri was moving his conversational dominance into a whole new realm.

P'Ko did his best to ignore Lo'Ri's advance, but it didn't stop Lo'Ri. Lo'Ri went on to talk about how "I" could "really" use a friend among the Mi'Nr's and how "we" would make a "great" team. Lo'Ri and P'Ko would need to keep their friendship private "just between the two of us" and that Lo'Ri knew of some "ways" to help keep their relationship secret. So that the "others" who wouldn't understand, wouldn't find out.

With P'Ko's help, Lo'Ri could help P'Ko, his family, and even his Mi'Nr friends. Lo'Ri asked what P'Ko wanted out of life? Credits, nice clothes, bio-mods, vacations, perhaps a better apartment for his family in Nu'Tn.

Lo'Ri went on to say that aside from making "good" things happen that a friend with connections to the CA could help prevent "bad" things from happening too. The threat underlying the statement was clear, that if P'Ko didn't agree that bad things were in store for himself and everyone around him.

---

[84] Sounds like Lori

All this was too much for P'Ko and P'Ko went silent, he stared out the window. But this didn't stop Lo'Ri, who seemed to sense that he'd achieved a goal. Putting his hand on P'Ko's shoulder said very softly "I know it's difficult, but you don't have to worry, we can be very discreet."

Then after a long pause, watching P'Ko carefully as P'Ko stared out the window, "I understand, you need to let this all soak in, but don't worry, you're my friend, and I'm going to look out for you."

P'Ko could sense the deception oozing out of Lo'Ri and had to practice one of his martial arts mind-clearing meditation techniques to control a sudden feeling of nausea, and to keep from striking out at Lo'Ri.

Lo'Ri must have been successful with his technique, or he wouldn't be as practiced and confident with it as he projected psychically. Lo'Ri's method must work most of the time against U'Te's, which would explain why Lo'Ri used it against P'Ko, but P'Ko couldn't imagine it working against a Mi'Nr, a Mi'Nr would sense right through the deception.

P'Ko sensed Lo'Ri setting next to him gloating in self-satisfaction thinking that he had turned or trapped P'Ko into becoming some pawn or instrument to be used at his or the CASS's bidding.

They descended the mining tunnel to the lower levels, passing through the atmospheric control locks, the gravity increasing substantially and the temperature decreased significantly. P'Ko could feel the growing pressure on his joints and his muscle tension firm up in reaction. He also felt a difference in his breathing and wasn't sure it was due to the gravity or to the change in the atmosphere.

The environment outside the shuttle was becoming increasingly hostile, the puddles the shuttle was splashing through were ammonia or possibly methane, by the time they arrive at the mining camp the puddles will likely be nitrogen or oxygen.

Even with his bio-mods survival without an eSuit would be measured in minutes. P'Ko began to doubt the wisdom of not wearing the eSuit the CA provided, what would happen if the shuttle broke down and its environmental system failed, how fast could P'Ko get to his duffel and dig out the eSuit and put it on?

The supply shuttles AI (Artificial Intelligence) performed flawlessly, and the machine seemed to run quieter and smoother the deeper they got. There was no hint of the biting cold outside; the shuttles evacuated carbon foam insulation and its unique tri-layer windows, developed, tested and used over hundreds of years, tuned to perfection performed flawlessly.

The driver optional, optionally remotely operated, autonomous shuttle, guided itself smoothly and without hesitation, fed by hundreds of sensors, the system learning the peculiarities of the route from many supply runs over centuries of operation.

P'Ko distracted himself from his fellow passenger by watching the AI deftly negotiate a switchback. He wished that he could drive, it's got to be very different than driving the VR (virtual reality) vehicles that are available online.

There's no way to simulate the continuous changes in the environment and those effects on the driver; that vary depending on what zone and level they're on and its resultant gravity. Track conditions are not constant, or predictable, but vary depending on the length of the tunnel and the location of circulation vents or condensing stations.

Ever since he heard Su'Zi describe what it's like driving Jm'Pr, he's been anxious to try. Even though this supply shuttle is a massive brick of a vehicle and the AI running it is optimized a hundred different ways, P'Ko had the urge to reach over and press the manual override, which would bring up the manual controls allowing him full and total control and subjugate the AI to advisory mode only. Then, he would try to better the AI's performance.

P'Ko's imaginings were interrupted as the shuttle pulled up to and slowly through the portal airlock to the active portion of sector three's T'Bm loading bay. They were now inside the far end of the T'Bm, moving slowly down the freshly made tunnel.

A light frost flashed across the shuttle's windows as moisture of the climate controlled air from inside condensed, froze, then disappeared as the window system adjusted to the new environment. Some frost remained on the edges of the exterior panels of the shuttle as P'Ko and Sh'P'Po exited the cargo laden shuttle now setting significantly lower on its suspension.

P'Ko wobbled a little as he stepped down to the deck. It was his first experience at this G, around twice that of Nu'Tn, he felt a little top-heavy, and he felt like his feet were stuck in mud, it would take some getting used to. Sh'P'Po hopped out with relative ease, his exoskeleton suit automatically compensating, pre-calibrated to Sh'P'Po and the G load. He landed with a noticeable thud, his suit's systems, an intricate system of sensors, gyro-stabilizers, pumps and contraction panels kept Sh'P'Po upright without the slightest hint of wobble.

P'Ko noted that Sh'P'Po while unable to walk or even crawl without the suit probably couldn't fall while wearing the suit, even if he tried. P'Ko thought of martial arts, never far from his conscious mind and noted that the exoskeleton and eSuit, inability to fall would be a handicap in a fight.

Although Sh'P'Po seem to move with ease, P'Ko could see and hear that Sh'P'Po's breathing was labored, his blood pressure and breathing assisted by the exoskeleton and eSuit.

The thought of fighting Sh'P'Po helped P'Ko gain back some control of his thoughts and emotions and feel less subordinate to Sh'P'Po, the D'En, the CASS spy.

The shuttle had entered the loading bay through a single ramp and door, which then opened up to a loading dock that could accommodate two supply shuttles side by side, one side a loading dock which the shuttle was marrying up to and the other was a dual function loading dock/vehicle maintenance bay.

P'Ko found himself on the far side of the bay from the vehicle maintenance area. P'Ko could see some movement underneath behind one of the oversized ATV's (all-terrain vehicles) used by the Mi'Nr's. He his gaze drawn toward the vehicles DU's (drive units), noting the DU's used up in Zone Two are puny in comparison.

P'Ko's focus was pulled away by some alarm sounding on the loading dock ahead of him, and his curiosity about the tools and lifts in the maintenance bay would have to wait there would be plenty of time for that later.

P'Ko turned to find up on the dock, a large, stout four-legged security bot sounding off fiercely. It bounced lightly back and forth on its front legs in spite of the heavy gravity, its long sharp metal teeth glaring.

P'Ko turned to find Sh'P'Po, who didn't seem to show any concern for the bot already pulling his gear from the shuttle's storage locker beneath the rear deck. Reluctantly P'Ko followed suit. They walked over to the stairs at the far end of the loading dock.

The shuttle had already docked, and the robo-lift had already started to offload the shuttle's cargo.

P'Ko, though at first fearful of the vicious security bot, noticed that it was clearly focused on Sh'P'Po as it stood its ground at the top the stairs as they approached. P'Ko began to relax a little, yet wondered how this approaching face-off between Sh'P'Po and the security bot would end.

A loading dock door opened, and three Mi'Nr's strode onto the dock, two in front and one trailing far behind. P'Ko stopped and pretended to adjust his gear and fumbled with some of the straps, creating as much distance between himself and Sh'P'Po as possible.

Sh'P'Po stopped at the bottom of the stair looking up at the security bot, his hand resting on a pouch attached to his belt, was his hand quivering? P'Ko couldn't tell for sure.

The three Mi'Nr's didn't call off the bot until they were beside it and Sh'P'Po started up the stairs. They clearly didn't like Sh'P'Po. P'Ko shouldered his bag and walked over to the stair.

Sh'P'Po was speaking with the three as P'Ko approached. The apparent senior of the three addressed P'Ko "Welcome. I'm Ve'Ln[85] the Su'Pr (Superintendent) here at Bo'R three; you can call me Su'Pr Ve'Ln. You must be P'Ko, we've heard a lot about you, you got here at a good time for training, things are running smoothly." P'Ko sensed that the statement was for Sh'P'Po's benefit as much as his.

Su'Pr Ve'Ln turned and introduced the other two. "This is An'Ja[86] the chief mechanic who will be your section supervisor and T'Mo, who is your sponsor and the cleanup crew lead." "T'Mo, why don't you take P'Ko and start his in processing? An'Ja and I will help Sh'P'Po with his inspection."

P'Ko followed T'Mo through the door the three had just come through and down the central corridor past the lobby and a conference room to the crew's quarters.

T'Mo showed P'Ko to his quarters and asked for the uniforms and eSuits that the CA had issued to him. Saying they needed to be "inspected" that the

---

[85] Sounds like Vee-Lynn or Vee-Lin.
[86] Sounds like Ann-Jah.

"quality control" from the CA is not on par with that of the mining community.

T'Mo pointed towards a cleaned and pressed used eSuit neatly folded on one of the two chairs of his new home. Asking him to get settled and change, that he'd return in half hour and take him on a tour of the T'Bm.

P'Ko handed T'Mo the crisp new uniforms and eSuits still in their wrapper, and picked up the eSuit setting on the chair and looked at it carefully. It was worn thin in a few places but had been patched and reinforced. The fresh seals around where the arms and legs had been lengthened stood out against the rest of the suit, giving it a striped look.

P'Ko looked closer at the eSuit he held, and saw that someone had spent some serious time and care making it for him. All the seams were done by hand using a unique stitch that was stronger and more flexible than a machine stitch. He thought of his mother as he scrutinized it, recognized and understood how much thought had to go into it and how difficult making this eSuit must have been. He knew how hard his mother worked as a tailor, and how hard she worked and how little she was appreciated.

T'Mo nor the other Mi'Nr's that greeted P'Ko had reached out to him psychically.

Now T'Mo, seeing P'Ko's actions, guessing disappointment added: "the tailor and her assistant did their best estimating your measurements. It should work well enough in the cold areas in and around the T'Bm. I wouldn't recommend it for continuous use or venturing very far from shelter. After your CA supplied eSuits are checked out, they'll be returned to you, and you'll need to go to the tailor and have them properly fitted."

T'Mo turned to leave.

P'Ko stopped T'Mo, saying and feeling his words. "Wait, I know quality when I see it, this was made with outstanding care and workmanship. Please thank the tailor and her assistant for me." T'Mo, psychically surprised, with a startled look on his face. Paused a fraction of a second smiled and replied as he left, "No, you'll meet her soon enough, and you can thank her yourself, she'd appreciate it more coming from you direct."

P'Ko's quarters consisted of a single room on the T'Bm's upper deck. It is slightly larger than his room at his parent's apartment, but with an arched ceiling. He had a small bathroom and a small sitting area large enough to host one or two visitors. He, or rather his parents would be allowed to keep his room in their apartment for him while he is in apprentice status. Once he completes his apprenticeship, his parents will have to give up the extra bedroom and move or have their apartment reconfigured.

P'Ko took the opportunity to message Su'Zi, his parents, and Mi'Ka that he had arrived, and he'd send more info about his first day later. He then began familiarizing himself with the controls for the room and syncing them with his TaC-B.

Then he put on the eSuit that had been altered, the arms and legs were a little too short. Thankfully the body length was right, and it fit well across the chest and shoulders, but was loose in the middle and around the arms and the thighs.

T'Mo returned and took P'Ko on a tour of the T'Bm; their first stop was the medical bay. T'Mo introduced P'Ko to the resident med-tech who showed P'Ko some of the equipment in the bay, most of which necessitated remote doctoring, by a doctor zones and sectors away, with the MedTech only performing what they are instructed to do by the remote physician. The MedTech had P'Ko lay on an exam table while he demonstrated how the diagnosis and scanning equipment operated. Then gave P'Ko's a "sample" body scan and a vaccination, described as something that would help him adjust to his environment.

What followed this was a very thorough tour of the T'Bm. P'Ko was introduced to all the crew, with only a few laughs and jokes about how he looked in the ill-fitting eSuit. That was quenched when T'Mo cautioned them not to get on the wrong side of Dr'Zi[87], the tailor that made P'Ko's eSuit, she has a way of getting back at anyone that offends her.

Then they had lunch in the T'Bm's small mess deck with that part of the crew that was rotating out[88]. P'Ko was famished; he soon realized that just existing in this zone took more energy, and it was compounded by the fact that he skipped breakfast, and was too embarrassed to mention it to T'Mo.

They continued the tour and near quitting time met in the conference room with Dr'Zi, Bo'R three's tailor, who came over from the camp to take P'Ko's measurements to make the necessary alterations to P'Ko's CA issued eSuits. She offered P'Ko a fifty percent discount on his first order, which he gladly accepted. The significant alterations would take almost all of his remaining graduation credits, but P'Ko was glad that his savings would remain intact. He wasn't concerned, as he didn't plan on spending any credits down here in a T'Bm.

They finished up back in the dining area, this time with the whole crew present; P'Ko was introduced once again and received a guarded warm, but not enthusiastic welcoming.

After dinner P'Ko was exhausted, he had spent his first full day in gravity that was roughly twice what he had spent his entire life in, and it was a concerted effort the whole day, not to let it show. He had aches and pains but was confident that those along with his fatigue would slowly go away as his systems adjusted to the new baseline.

P'Ko hadn't seen Sh'P'Po since they parted that morning, and was glad for it. He settled into his room, barely taking the time to unpack and slept like a rock in his new home.

---

[87] Sounds like Darcy or Dar'Zee.

[88] T'Bm's don't stop for lunch, but rather the crew splits up, allowing for part of the crew to eat while the other part keeps the T'Bm running.

Chapter 36, Chn'Gi Reads Or'Gn's History

Chn'Gi lay naked, soaking in the warm tub, away from the prying eyes of the surveillance cameras scattered through the rest of her quarters, the scented bath emollient making her skin feel smooth and slick against it.

Under the eerie glow of her "reading light," Chn'Gi figured out how to use the reader and found that the data cartridge was part of a sequential backup of Dadr'Ba's historical archive.

The reader, being a data storage diagnostic device, was designed for verifying and viewing samples of the data that had already been indexed and sorted during the recording process, so it was slow. The thing lacked the processing speed and bandwidth for data mining of bulk media, the high density, highly compressed data cartridge held a petabyte. It was like trying to find a particular star in a far away galaxy using the naked eye.

Just when it was beginning to seem an impossible undertaking and Chn'Gi began worrying that she might have to go back to Lu'Gs and part with more of her precious paper to get help finding what she was looking for, she got a break through. She found the cartridge's metadata index. Using the metadata index, she was able to manually scan the entries and hyperlink to the raw data.

However, even with the index, the search was time-consuming, there were thousands of metadata sets, each containing hundreds of elements. The puny device couldn't even sort and she dare not risk exporting it to a real computer, the CASS with its data crawling search routines would surely detect her activity. But the way was clear, given time she'd have her answers.

With the deliberate focus of a scientist on the path to discovery, Chn'Gi dove into the task of tedious organization and study. Soon she gathered data points linking them together in a far scattered mesh, as she amassed ever more data points and matrixed them into her data set, she was able to outline the history of her people. The more she learned the more she came to understand why the CA might want to eliminate the past, to outlaw it, to forget the past.

The CA council, especially the Commander and the CASS Director, should already know this history. Even without psychic abilities Chn'Gi sensed that they telegraphed their suspicions plainly enough. If what she suspects is true, it's no wonder the CA is so concerned about O'M and she wondered if all ToG survivors knew.

Then, Chn'Gi cursed herself; she's stuck, how's she going to produce an unbiased result. How's she going to hide what she's learned and the powerful feelings festering inside her?

Chn'Gi decided that the safest way forward is to dumb up and resolved, in spite of the fact that the Commander asked her to, not to make any predictions. She could safely make deductions and conclusions based on the facts, but she would base her reports on what she and her team had detected and confirmed.

It's unavoidable now, and will be agonizing to continue to allow the council to treat her like she's stupid and incompetent. Chn'Gi will continue her analysis of the Or'Gn's history. She paid a dear price for the reader and data cartridge and always believed that knowledge was power, and as a scientist realized that knowledge was necessary to solve complicated, protracted problems. Hopefully if she learns enough she'll discover a way out of her predicament.

In the end, Chn'Gi might be able to show everyone that she's not what people have made her out to be. Chn'Gi spent most of her life with people treating her childishly, and she hated it.

She grew up never tiring of toys and dolls, even after graduation, she liked having her imaginary friends and playmates around. They were always there, good listeners and hardly ever contradicted or disagreed with her.

Chn'Gi reflected further and forced herself to acknowledge, that at least in part her being treated subordinately is due to her not having found a mate in the one hundred plus years since her graduation.

She can't help that she hasn't found a mate; she hasn't met and fallen in love with that special someone yet. Now, Chn'Gi, approaching midcareer can see that her peers, her supervisor and now even the Central Council treated her as a tween (someone "between" graduation and an established career) and not a full-fledged career person. Someone that is granted the respect that a person of Chn'Gi's education, position and age would typically possess.

Chn'Gi set the reader aside and splashed warm water against her face and ran her fingers through her hair and down her face, then across her body, forcing herself to relax. She caressed herself, tensing her muscles hard, then relaxed, feeling the little pleasure flow up her body.

She's still comfortable with her female gender, sometimes questioning the choice she made so long ago. And still not settled on her sexual preference. She'd experimented over the years with both sexes as partners and though she tended to prefer female partners was attracted mostly by personality.

Chn'Gi was not comfortable with the idea of pre-mated[89] sex, making it hard find someone. In spite of its social acceptance, CA's endorsement and the Church's ambivalence towards the subject. Chn'Gi's relationships often ended when the potential partner wanted sex, and Chn'Gi wanted to wait.

Despite the negative impact on the social aspects of her career, Chn'Gi reassured herself that she would remain resolute in her decision to wait for a committed relationship before having sexual relations and not go out of her way searching, she's not desperate. Thankfully Chn'Gi told herself, she's still decades away from being labeled a "leftover[90]." Until then she could take care of herself.

---

[89] Sexual relations outside the bounds of that recorded and documented in official Church and CA records.

[90] The label used to name a person unable to find a mate and therefore fated not to have children.

Chapter 37, Prep for Run with the Se'Ro'Bs

P'Ko started work on the cleaning crew; his apprenticeship would have him work thru all the functional areas of the T'Bm starting with the cleaning crew, and there he would become familiar with the location, functions, and hazards of the T'Bm from one end to the other. Once he had become proficient on the cleaning crew, he would transition to maintenance and work through proficiency training, learning to maintain and repair all of the machinery that makes up the T'Bm. It will take years to attain Journeyman Mechanic status and become a full-fledged T'Bm mechanic and years more to become a Master Mechanic.

P'Ko was assigned to the cleaning crew of ten, led by a crusty old crew chief, Ni'To[91]. The team worked a staggered shift from the production crew, starting before the end of the production shift, then working past the production crew end of shift all the way till the production crew came back online for their prechecks. Most of the cleaning and much of the maintenance needed to occur while the machinery was offline. This schedule bit into the time available to spend with Su'Zi, but he and Su'Zi were determined not to let it interfere with their relationship and worked around it.

There was another apprentice on the cleaning crew, An'Gi[92]; that had started the previous year, and although she and P'Ko worked on different teams, they became friends.

P'Ko learned from the rest of the crew that he got there just in time for the Run with the Se'Ro'Bs. The run is conducted annually shortly after graduation and is an indoctrination/rite of passage for new Mi'Nr's.

One combined run is carried out for the five sectors and is hosted on a rotating basis between the sectors. This year is Bo'R three's turn to host and even though P'Ko had just arrived, he will be expected to participate like all the other new apprentices, unless he refused.

Without hesitation P'Ko agreed, then the first chance he got he called Su'Zi and asked what he had just gotten himself into. Su'Zi grew silent, when P'Ko asked, and P'Ko could feel a tumult of emotions emanate from her, despite the fact that they were talking over a Comms Link and had a kilometer or more of Dadr'Ba between them.

Finally, with an enormous effort to maintain self-control, she said that it was probably a mistake for him to agree, even though he would have had to face some shame and humility. He would've been able to run next year. When P'Ko asked why, she said, gravely "sometimes people die."

---

[91] Sounds like Knee-Tow
[92] Sounds like Angie, Ann-Gee

Su'Zi went on to do her best to explain what a Se'Ro'Bs is. It's a skittish creature that lurks in the dark shadows and is practically invisible. When hit with a light it appears to be a black shadow, not reflecting any light. The stories say that it's soundless and swift and that there might be more than one. There have been reports of encounters near the same time in different sectors, and sometimes it seems at first, to be following, then inexplicably it appears ahead or to one side instead of behind. But no one has ever encountered more than one at a time or if they have, didn't live to tell about it.

A few people have said that if they listen very carefully that they could hear them walking or running on padded feet, especially if they splash across a puddle on the tunnel floor, but they have claws, evidenced on some of the remains that were found so the claws must be retractable.

The few survivors that have lived to tell about a brush or close encounter, say they must be sensed more than seen. But not sensed psychically, they seem to be psychically invisible. They need to be detected by the combination of all a Mi'Nr's senses and then by the lack sensory detection, by not getting back the indication of something that should be there.

Su'Zi was pretty sure P'Ko's Mi'Nr's' senses weren't developed enough to detect and evade a Se'Ro'Bs. And the runners must work together, and share their senses, something that P'Ko had little practice with.

The Se'Ro'Bs is said not to be "alive" which makes it psychically invisible; it's like a living black hole, all energy goes in but nothing comes out.

It seems to live to feed, but is rarely encountered, it remains hidden, perhaps dormant until someone vulnerable, usually alone stumbles across its path. Then the Se'Ro'Bs will stalk its victim until the perfect moment and then strike.

The victims' bodies are rarely found. The few that have been found have been crushed and sucked dry of all fluids, desiccated somehow by the cold, dry environment, or by the Se'Ro'Bs. The remains become difficult to recognize, often appearing only as a discolored patch of frozen tunnel wall or floor.

Su'Zi explained that the number of runners in the run is limited, it starts at the host sectors Ol'Tn and ends at a survival station down in Zone Four at the edge of Dadr'Ba's hull. The survival station is small being made only to hold ten comfortably, but the number of runners is restricted to twenty-five, so at the end, they'll be packed in.

Everyone must make it to the survival station. They'll be running not as a large group, but smaller separate teams or packs. It's not a race. The challenge and thrill is to get a Se'Ro'Bs to start chasing a pack. Then the packs must work together, mostly psychically, to evade the Se'Ro'Bs. The packs must cut each other off, before the chased pack gets too tired, and draw off the Se'Ro'Bs before they're caught.

They've been lucky, it's been many years since anyone was lost, but many are saying that their luck is due to run out.

After the run, everyone packs into a single Supply Shuttle and they ride together, back up to a celebration and award ceremony in Ol'Tn.

P'Ko can't back out; it would make permanent his label as a For'Nr, a U'Te attempting to join the elite corps of Mi'Nr's. If he backed out, he'd lose face in this proud, highly competitive, tight-knit community of Mi'Nr's. He'd always remain a wannabe forever, never fully accepted into the community, excluded from the main group. He'd be given menial jobs, and eventually, perhaps, sent back Up'Ln and forced by the CA to spend the rest of his life working off the cost of removing his unauthorized Bio-Mods. There's no way P'Ko would allow that to happen, even though it would be a mortal sin, he'd rather die first.

The run was only a week away, and there was just barely enough time for Su'Zi to put her name in the lottery to be one of the returning runners, the odds are not good, there being less than a one in twenty-five chance of your name being drawn.

Despite the danger nearly all the younger Mi'Nr's, especially those un-mated wanting to prove themselves mate-worthy, and a few old ones wanting to take back youth by challenging life, participate.

Su'Zi managed to make it over to Bo'R three every night for the week before the race and do short practice runs with P'Ko. Su'Zi's attention helped P'Ko get accepted by the rest of the Bo'R three crew. After only a couple of days, Su'Zi and P'Ko had company from Bo'R three on their practice runs. They managed to run sections of each of the zones that the course covered, the whole time there was no sign of the Se'Ro'Bs. Su'Zi cautioned P'Ko that the Run with the Se'Ro'Bs has never failed to find one and have it engage in the chase.

P'Ko had the most trouble transitioning to all fours near the bottom of zone three, approaching zone four, most of the native-born Mi'Nr's spent a part of their Bo'Ba years scampering around on all fours and trips to "The Edge" are a popular field trip for Mi'Nr families. P'Ko found Zone Four barely walkable, more like stagger-able, and most comfortable on all fours. Thankfully the Se'Ro'Bs is forced to slow down in the lower levels too.

There was too little practice time for P'Ko to get accustomed to Zone Four before they realized it, it was the day before the race, and the lottery announcements were published. Su'Zi didn't make it.

Su'Zi realized that the odds of her getting in weren't good, but she was still hurt, almost devastated. She knew people and had a couple of friends that made it; they offered to let her take their slots. But the rules were clear, the lottery is the hand of fate and tampering with fate invited disaster, no substitutions are allowed.

Su'Zi tried to reassure P'Ko that he was ready, but there was no hiding the fact that they were both scared.

Chapter 38, Chn'Gi's Turmoil

Chn'Gi was finding it more and more difficult to control her emotions the knowledge she was gaining from reading Dadr'Ba's pre-ToG history was challenging and awkward. The people spoke and wrote differently back then; they used a different vernacular and syntax, but with practice, it got easier for Chn'Gi to understand.

Over time, the language got easier to read, and Chn'Gi learned how the data was organized. The disparate data elements that had at first seemed like random pixels of a loosely woven matrix slowly began to form an image. As the picture became clearer, Chn'Gi's mind grew full and heavy. It was like a whole new universe was opening up to her, she felt cheated and betrayed by the CA for keeping this knowledge from the people.

The end of our world was not what we were told, at least not entirely. The actual part of the story was that it was caused, as forecast by our scientists, by an increase in solar storm activity in conjunction with a reversal of Or'Gn's magnetic field. Either event survivable had they not occurred simultaneously.

The end finally came after Dadr'Ba had left and a massive Solar Flare Coronal Mass Ejection struck the planet. The planet with its weak magnetic field had its atmosphere decimated and its surface irradiated, huge fire storms irrupted that quickly consumed what little oxygen was left in the dwindling, fleeing atmosphere. The disaster killed most, if not all life on the surface and left the planet virtually uninhabitable, according to the best estimates by the few survivors that escaped the holocaust in underground bunkers. What we were not told was that our ancestors had used up and poisoned our world long before.

It was a slow process, at least at first, gradually, over the course of thousands of years, people moved from hunter-gatherer to agrarian societies and formed into towns and villages. People continued to gather, technology evolved and as individuals and groups became empowered, they formed governments and states. These states became able to impose their State's multiself will upon others. Some becoming hegemonies.

But then, from within these nation-states, individuals and groups coalesced and gained power through the use of mass media and instantaneous communications, and gaining the power of numbers made demands of their governments, more and more frequently with the threat of violence. People and groups demanded a voice and a say in the decisions the government made. Demands not just their own government but other governments as well.

In a world where malcontents, disenfranchised and radical militant groups can communicate freely, and media makes news of their complaints, small groups can organize and grow to be a force to be reckoned with and force concessions from nation states using protest and the use of violence by exploiting the ready availability and easy manufacture of weapons of mass destruction.

Violent extremist and terrorist groups formed, some supported by nation states seeking to undermine rival countries. The terrorists feed off of and hide among the masses. With access to high volumes of high power, high capacity weapons, explosives and weapons of mass destruction, even lone actors can kill hundreds or even thousands, threatening and intimidating whole countries along with its people.

Complicating things further, governments, handicapped by the precedent set by their willingness to go into debt to pay off demands of their constituents, go into further debt to pay new demands. Declining budgets are the inevitable result and the already anemic efforts to properly steward the planet, and its recourses become hardly more than stuff for white papers and documentaries.

With no strong world leadership, different factions in control of various parts of the world refused to cooperate on what was best for the planet. They placed their own constituent's wants and needs above others and the health of the world.

As mismanagement and misuse exasperated the planets already limited resources, wars broke out, both conventional and nuclear. Critical sectors of the world's ecosystem became unbalanced and poisoned, leaving vast areas of the planet virtually uninhabitable.

The people cancer that was plaguing the planet left the world unable to do much of anything to cure itself. Billions of people were already suffering, and their suffering made them more desperate and less willing to make further sacrifices that would remedy the planet's sickness.

The planet's natural balance became unstable. Terrible droughts and storms developed. It was as if the world was attempting to fight off the cancer that had taken over and that now impacted the planet's health overall. Famines resulted in the deaths of many millions of people and left more millions to live on death's doorstep, weakened by malnourishment and suffering from disease.

The survivors in the war-ravaged and environmentally decimated, nearly uninhabitable areas attempted to take vengeance against the ones they felt responsible and new waves of terrorist attacks spread the globe.

When the end came, the world was, according to some in temporary stagnation, while according to others in decline. There wasn't enough food, drinking water, sanitation, and health care for the planets billions of poor disenfranchised souls.

Most of the world's population had been surviving on subsistence rations in megacities. While the rest, diseased, starving, or dying of thirst or poisoned by polluted water, attempted to scratch out an existence trying to grow crops in putrefying, arid lands or poisoned swamps. Those really unfortunate survived by digging through contaminated putrifying wastes piling up around the mega cities.

As the sureness of the impending natural disaster coalesced into certitude, some realized that had the planet been healthier and the central governments stronger, and wealthier the outcome could be much different. As it was any attempt to save the world or mitigate, the planet-wide effects would be futile.

That left few options; technology was advanced enough that a few of the saner groups banded together to build Dadr'Ba and a couple of other ships like it, and allow a few to escape the devastation. We had reduced our world to a massive rubbish heap. It was time to leave.

The universe that had opened up before her weighed down on Chn'Gi. If O'M follows the same development path as Or'Gn, based on the rapid decline of what happened on Or'Gn, there might only be a poisoned, cancerous hulk of a planet left by the time Dadr'Ba arrives.

It had already become increasingly difficult to keep her reports to the CA benign. Chn'Gi knows that despite all her practice that she's not a good actress. These latest revelations will be impossible to conceal.

Just the other day Chn'Gi's comfort turned to fear when she got a confused look from one of her technicians when she accidentally used phraseology she picked up from the histories. The language of the history she was reading had infected her. She grew terrified that she would slip in one of her reports or in front of the Council and tip them off that she had gained knowledge of forbidden history.

She compensated by standardizing her reports even more than before, tightening the controls on the automatic checks done by her word processor. Surprisingly the Council didn't seem to mind, just as long as the general content changed and new information was presented, delivery and format didn't seem to matter.

Her regularly scheduled reports became mechanical and autonomic but inside she was terrified. The insight provided by her study of their history created in her mind an unavoidable collision between O'M and Dadr'Ba. Knowing how we or rather our ancestors destroyed Or'Gn and how the O'Mi's seem to be following down the same path made her sick to her stomach, making her mind feel as if it were melting down.

After her reports, she would break down, weak, panting, heart pounding soon followed by a feeling of intense pressure in her mind. She would be forced to stop everything and focus on mind clearing exercises, meditating on nothing until the episode past, but it was beginning to take longer and longer to recover.

If only she had someone to share this information with, to help carry this burden, to collaborate with in deciding what to do. She began to appreciate why the CA had banned this information, this study, if she were a religious person she would have described this information as the knowledge of the gods, with the power to destroy Dadr'Ba society and cause the failure of their mission.

Chn'Gi had estimated the population of O'M to be in the billions, based on solid number extrapolation from the figures she'd been accumulating.

Then finally, her team detected TV (Television) signals, and finally were able to start deciphering the O'Mi's language, or rather languages, the O'Mi's were still too primitive to have a unified world government or a common language. And she discovered that they had fought many wars, hundreds even, that on several occasions spanned the entire globe. The parallels between O'M and Or'Gn are unmistakable and terrifying; it is certain that O'M like Or'Gn had so many years ago would soon develop nuclear weapons.

But why should she pre-judge or predict that the technical developments and actions of the IL on O'M would parallel that of Or'Gn? What right do we have to assume that these people will make the same bad choices that we did?

She contemplated confessing to the Central Council, she's a D'En and has clearances for sensitive information; they may not punish her, but may welcome her into the fold of people "in the know." It would be hypocritical to punish her for possessing knowledge that they possess. As soon as the thought flashed through Chn'Gi consciousness, she dismissed it. The CA is built on double standard, elitist hypocrisy and in their view she was nothing.

Even if she were allowed to live, what would become of Lu'Gs and Lu'Gs' helper "P'Ko"? They would probably be apprehended, imprisoned and, possibly, probably, even forcibly retired.

Chn'Gi felt herself weakening under the stress of it all. Her around the clock act is only relieved by occasional exhaustion induced sleep with an increased desire for the assistance of liquor. The only other relief is when she's soaking in the tub "reading" engulfed in another world, a former world, her favorite being the industrial age, when science was king, without bounds and anything and everything was believed possible.

After every one of these escapes upon return to the present and the private perdition, that she'd created for herself, a flood of guilt and remorse surrounded her.

She's already made mistakes, like her use of old language, to one of her technicians. When she slipped, using an old phase the tech gave her a very funny look. She, of course, corrected herself, but for hours, even days afterward she feared that, at any moment, soldiers would bust in and take her away.

Sadly, she found herself welcoming the event.

Other times, the worst of times, Chn'Gi contemplated voluntary retirement. She saw the real possibility of a catastrophe when Dadr'Ba arrived at O'M. In many respects her personal life was a failure, she was unable to find a mate, though admittedly she hadn't tried very hard, preferring to devote her time, including away from work, to her job, her career, and her studies. Something must be wrong with her; she felt she must be defective.

Now that she had stumbled, or sought out and discovered what was far and beyond the most significant discoveries since the Touch of God event, she was unable to act on it or to announce any hint of what she's discovered. She doubted, yet hoped that that boy P'Ko had read it, then she wouldn't be alone. Then she took back her hope, had P'Ko looked at it, he, she was confident, would be destroyed the same as it was destroying her.

In her desperation, she considered all of the options she could think of, just publishing it and letting things sort themselves out, but that would create anarchy and destroy all order on Dadr'Ba. She could confess to the CA, but that would lead to isolation, imprisonment and probably forced retirement. She could turn it over to the resistance, but what would they do? Use it against the CA? To what end?

All these choices she felt would lead to disaster, or nowhere. There was one hope, one possibility, one group, that might be able to help and they possibly already knew this "God's knowledge", and that's the Church. The Church would be able to help, but how can she contact them, privately, without raising any alarms?

Chapter 39, Run with the Se'Ro'Bs

The day of the race was exciting, all working T'Bm's were minimally manned, and it seemed like Ol'Tn'Ka couldn't hold any more people, the narrow streets and alleyways were packed. It was early mid-morning for sector three, everyone in Nu'Tn was either at work or school and the few surveillance sensors operating in Ol'Tn, as poorly maintained as they were, finally failed completely.

Portable displays of many varied types and sizes appeared all over Ol'Tn. Though virtually everyone could view the run through their TaC-B's, watching the run on a conventional screen as a group, enhanced the group aspect for the psychically connected spectators. There was hardly a direction to look that didn't have a blank space or bare wall containing some display with some portion of the event on it.

People stood next to mats, folding and inflatable chairs and couches that lined the street that served as the beginning of the course and by the way which the finishers would return. Once the run started and the runner had passed, the spectators would overflow into the middle of the street, with the viewers settling into a comfortable position to watch on the multitude of screens viewable from nearly every spot along Ol'Tn's main street.

The staging area for the runners was at the far end of the street from the access ramp and airlock to zone three. The runners' check-in at a table where race officials verify their id and assign them their run number and give them a set of closely fitting goggles, a compact respirator and a sealable bag to put their things in with their name and number on it.

From check-in, the runners go to one out of a row of tents, each clearly identified outside to indicate the artist within. There they take off their clothes and are given a coat of cryo-reactive exothermic body paint; the paint amounts to a self-destructing eSuit that slowly burns away during the run.

The runners choose in advance their artist as well as the design and thickness of their "suit". The thickness is based on how much they think they'll need. The paint is cumbersome and inhibits freedom of movement. The goal is to have just enough to get the runner through to the finish, but not too much that it will weigh the runner down when they need to be fastest but still sufficient to keep the runner from freezing in the cryogenic temperatures of Zone four.

The goal is to gauge just the right amount of paint against the external temperature factoring in the runner's internal heat generated by exertion and to end the race alive, naked, and un-frostbitten.

P'Ko chose a light coat; his practice runs with Su'Zi had been in leotards for all the zones except for zone four. For Zone Four during the run, he as most of the others expected to be at maximum exertion and maximum internal heat generation and not to need as much thermal protection. Mostly, his decision was based on Su'Zi's recommendation, plus another factor, avoided in most conversation, that being the level of terror from having a Se'Ro'Bs chasing you.

P'Ko, naked, covered with only a thin coat of cryo-reactive exothermic body paint found himself near the center of the group of other similarly clad runners. A head taller than the rest, he could see just about all of them.

The runners, clones all, scream through their appearance, their personal individuality and uniqueness. Each runner is attempting to be more outlandish and distinct than the runner next to them. They mill around behind the starting line, each painted in a wide variety of bright fluorescent colors and designs creating a psychedelic chorus line of grandiose and visually striking displays.

The runners as a whole stood out from the much larger crowd surrounding them and lining the street. As the starting time neared, the runners start to coalesce, riding on the force of the will of the runners as a whole and backed by the psychic essence pouring from the surrounding community of Mi'Nr's. What had started as a visual cacophony and a collection of discordant individuals melded together, become synchronized with a common goal on a common mission.

They all face the starting line and the stage set up adjacent to it.

P'Ko wished he had his TaC-B, but none of the runners were allowed their personal communication devices. He was made to remove it and put it in his personal effects bag. Su'Zi had told him about this, but it made him feel even more naked without it. He would have no way of communicating and without its positioning function, he wouldn't know where he was. Su'Zi just told him to play it safe, stay in the middle of the pack, follow the rest and that he'd be okay.

Once it was confirmed all the runners were prepped in the starting area, a race official got everyone's attention. After the crowd quieted, the chaplain, gave a prayer, asking God to protect and guide the runners. The race director came back and reviewed the rules, then introduced the M'Vr[93] from the previous year, who said a few words of encouragement.

The race director returned, then after slowly raising his hand above his head quickly brought down on a switch that was at the corner of the podium near where he was standing.

A bright flash erupted from a large strobe light that had been suspended over the runners. P'Ko's vision was blanked for a moment when he recovered; he found himself moving across the starting line in pace with the rest of the runners.

The psychic energy around him was high; everyone was as excited as he was but nobody was running, this was more like a trot, wasn't this about running? But immediately the answer came to him from all those around him,

---

[93] The "Most Valuable Runner" Sounds like Emm-Ver rhymes with Denver.

no, it's about running, it's about "the run", the course, the experience, challenging death and bonding with your teammates.

P'Ko was experiencing a whole new level of psychic experience; the answer he received didn't come from a single individual but the group. He got a little dizzy as he began to comprehend it. He didn't fully realize it before, but this was a run for the group, not the individual.

To survive without losing one of its members, the group must act as one. P'Ko realized that this answer to the question he thought to himself was the first step in being accepted.

As P'Ko thought about the team and what they are setting out to do he realized that if he's going to finish this run successfully the itty-bitt of acceptance he has now must grow substantially. He didn't get any reassurance from his neighbors as this thought crossed his mind, they seemed not to be paying him much attention.

When he focused on it, he sensed his running mates were congealing; this wasn't a group of "individuals" but a "team" and forming up as one as they trotted down the street. The crowd, psychically aware, connecting with the runners, endorsed their mission, were excited, and shouted encouragement to their runner(s). Many among the crowd displayed banners, some even painted themselves naked in the same design as their runners.

Psychic energy grew, and the runners trot became faster, and their strides stretched out. Then as one they broke out into a run and picked up speed. P'Ko found this transition difficult; he hadn't practiced it, his height made his stride much longer than the rest, making him feel disconnected from the group.

As they reached the ramp, the pace had increased enough for P'Ko to feel more comfortable. They ran down the ramp, through the air lock, forced open for the event, and found themselves entering the maze of tunnels as the air lock closed behind them.

P'Ko sensed their first goal was to scatter and find a Se'Ro'Bs his long comfortable stride took him to the lead position; it felt good, but he sensed only skeptical acceptance and some resentment from the group as he did this. He tried to reassure them that he wasn't out for the glory of the lead, that it was his comfortable pace, but he also couldn't hide the thrill he got from being in front.

Then he remembered Su'Zi's advice to "stay in the middle of the pack" he slowed a little, and let someone else take the lead, he sensed it was one of the more experienced runners. P'Ko decided to try to stay with him even as they passed the first split, a group of runners at the tail of the leading group split off and took that path. The main group staying with P'Ko and the leader.

They passed more tunnel splits and at each, another group split off until the number of runners was reduced to five. The tunnels grew darker until an inky darkness prevailed. The darkness was interrupted only occasionally by automated lighting at the tunnel intersection as it branched off to lower levels.

As they descended each level, it got colder; dim light started to glow as the group's body paint began to activate. P'Ko hadn't realized before that one of his bodymods included infrared vision.

He began to feel part of the group he was with as he adjusted his stride to match his pack mates, and with practice became accustomed to it. He exercised his full stride as he bounded over obstacles that appeared as they came across partial tunnel collapses and sags, caused by accidental overheating of that part of the tunnel or a weak reinforcement, that could have occurred centuries ago.

They sometimes climbed ladders or slid down a hole to the next level. The five packs they had separated into were combing the entire sector, trying to find a Se'Ro'Bs, something that down to the very fiber of its being wants to catch and consume them.

P'Ko in the middle of his group began to hear clicks, he didn't know what it was coming from and thought it could be coming from a Se'Ro'Bs, but it was coming from somewhere within his group. Without speaking his group said back to him, "listen and see."

P'Ko didn't quite know what that meant, but did as he was asked and focusing on listening and seeing at the same time, his mind opened to the rest of the group, and he began to see the tunnel around him lighted in still frame with each of the clicks he heard.

At first, it was distracting trying to run using still frame flashes of vision, but he soon began to focus on the distant parts of the images and running from the memory of what's in between. Using the dim body paint glow to help fill in the near gaps.

P'Ko tried and discovered that he too could click, he didn't know what part of his body, it emanated from but he could do it, and he soon developed a timing joining, like joining in with a song, with the pack to form a jagged picture of their progress.

Why, hadn't Su'Zi mentioned this? But he dismissed the question rapidly. The practice tunnels were relatively well lit, and Su'Zi might not have realized that P'Ko could see echo click, so neglected to mention it. She told him just to play it safe and stay in the middle of the group.

P'Ko soon realized that staying in the midst of the pack wasn't going to work. Su'Zi must have thought that the pack would accommodate P'Ko, leaving him in the middle of the pack rotating around him. However, they weren't, and P'Ko's psychic queries on the subject were resoundingly rebuffed.

After a little while the runner that had been trailing last surged forward and took over the lead, soon he'd be trailing last, then he will have to move into the lead.

He liked the idea, to be in the lead during those first moments of the run, but he still had no idea where they were. He could tell by the weight he felt; they've descended but had no idea how much or how much further they had to go.

He felt that it was a long way yet because they hadn't yet, as far as P'Ko knew found a Se'Ro'Bs. Once they found the Se'Ro'Bs, the run would turn into a race against the Se'Ro'Bs.

P'Ko's group crossed paths a couple of times with other groups, all seeming to operate at the same steady pace that P'Ko's pack was running.

Then, with P'Ko trailing and just as they passed down another level they just knew that one of the other groups had found a Se'Ro'Bs. The Se'Ro'Bs was fresh and fast, the pack it was chasing was already beginning to tire, the group was in trouble.

All of the groups of runners began to converge on the Se'Ro'Bs and the group in trouble. The pace picked up dramatically, and though P'Ko was able to handle it, he knew it wasn't a pace he or the rest of his group could maintain. But people were in danger, and they needed their help, needed P'Ko's help, so they pushed on. Along with the feeling of urgency, P'Ko began to feel like he knew where they were and where they were going. He was aware that where the pack with the Se'Ro'Bs chasing it was, how to get there, and how to intercept them.

They neared the predator and the prey, P'Ko's pack had been closest, and it was P'Ko's turn to take the lead, without thinking much about it, he surged forward into the lead. Then realized that he didn't know what he was supposed to do when his pack made the interception. It was just ahead, P'Ko overcome with excitement, and a surge of a kind of panic was running all out as he saw the glow of the pack ahead and the trailing body painted runner partially obscured by a blackness bounding too close behind it. P'Ko and his pack were coming up fast. P'Ko had put some distance between himself and his pack, echo clicking in rapid succession. The echo clicking showed nothing of the creature, but a large dark cloud with what could have been arms caught in freeze frame sweeping forward, trying to trip up the runner just out of its arms reach.

P'Ko felt his pack trying to caution him, to hold him back, but it was too late. The dark shadow somehow sensed that P'Ko was there, too close to stop at the speed he was running and quickly stopped turning to face P'Ko.

All P'Ko could see was a dark shape in front of him, and dark, thick appendages stretched wide to greet him. P'Ko lunged up and over, hearing and feeling the pressure of the atmosphere as it was pressed against him by the creature clawing up against him, millimeters separating him from almost certain death.

P'Ko tumbled to the tunnel floor, on the far side, and using his martial arts practice rolled to his feet and continued running at nearly the same pace as before. The creature, startled, off balance, fell on its back, then rolled to its side, and tried to get back on its feet. Just as the rest of P'Ko's pack running at full tilt rushed past it on both sides.

They soon caught up to P'Ko with the Se'Ro'Bs on their trail as P'Ko turned down another tunnel taking the Se'Ro'Bs off the chase from the pack that it almost caught.

From then on it became a practiced routine of a pack intercepting the tiring pack just ahead of the Se'Ro'Bs, drawing off the Se'Ro'Bs before it got too close. The fresh pack would continue, down through the levels. Then be relieved by a fresh pack taking over the task of leading the Se'Ro'Bs on its chase. Allowing the other packs to rest while taking short cuts at a relaxed pace to the new intercept point. All the while the runners stayed in psychic contact, having a mental map of exactly where they are and where they need to be.

P'Ko began to experience trouble as they descended the levels, his long frame, and stride, an asset at the upper level where he leaped over the Se'Ro'Bs became a liability at the higher G of the lower levels. He found himself feeling the urge to go down on all fours while the rest of his shorter, stouter pack mates continued to trot along, seemingly unfazed by their increased weight.

He had to slow his pace even more, despite knowing that it slowed his pack mates, but after the miracle of surviving his first encounter with a Se'Ro'Bs they didn't seem to mind. When it was their turn to take the Se'Ro'Bs, they couldn't stay ahead of it for as long as the rest of the packs and the other packs had to accommodate their handicap, and sometimes skipped P'Ko and his pack in the rotation.

There were a few more close calls, but nothing as close as P'Ko's first encounter, finally all the packs were on all fours, scampering ahead of the Se'Ro'Bs, who had also slowed and was forced closer to the deck.

The Se'Ro'Bs seemed as if it was growing fatigued. The packs, although scrambling on all fours at these lower levels had a relatively easy time staying ahead of it. Finally, the run was nearing the end.

P'Ko found himself tail scampering ahead of the Se'Ro'Bs. Another chase lead change or two and they would all be safely in the survival shelter. But there was a problem, at first nobody noticed it, not until P'Ko glanced back and saw that the Se'Ro'Bs was closing on him. The Se'Ro'Bs had held back and waited until P'Ko, the weakest scrambler of the all the runners was the prey.

The Se'Ro'Bs was too close to P'Ko's pack for a safe intercept, and it would do no good for one of P'Ko's pack mates to fall back and act the prey, P'Ko was still the weak link ahead of the prey. P'Ko would have to push, and hopefully, create a safe intercept distance.

The other packs attempted intercepts drawing dangerously close to the Se'Ro'Bs at several intercept points, but nothing could draw the Se'Ro'Bs' attention away from the weakest member, P'Ko, who was growing weaker.

P'Ko let the rest of his pack know what needed to be done, and they all began to feed him as much psychic energy as they could spare. Though the psychic capabilities they have is not in any way psychokinetic, the effort helped P'Ko reach down inside and bring forth increased strength and agility.

But he/they were still unable to increase the gap between P'Ko and the Se'Ro'Bs, as a matter of fact the Se'Ro'Bs continued to close the distance between them. Ever so slowly, every so many steps, the Se'Ro'Bs got millimeters closer. The packs giving up on an intercept made a direct path toward the survival shelter. It was their only chance.

P'Ko knowing that the Se'Ro'Bs was close behind him, so close in fact, that had this been at a higher level, it could catch him with one leap, focused on his scramble. The deck hit him through his arms and legs like a sledgehammer. He tried to numb himself to the pounding and concentrate on the forward motion, and on the bright glow of body paint ahead of him of his fellow pack mates urging him along.

P'Ko consciously refused to think about how far it was to the survival shelter or the time it's taking to get there. P'Ko felt only the rumble in his limbs, as he crawled along he tried to will the rumble faster. He could no longer feel the parts of his body coming into contact with the deck; he had no awareness of if the protective body paint was thicker there or not, or whether it was totally worn away and he was crawling on frozen stumps.

P'Ko lost himself to time, isolating himself to a place in his mind where time and the present didn't exist, he knew what was going on; he just didn't pay any attention, almost a day sleep. He thought about God and about what the afterlife might be like.

He thought of living on through his descendants, if he would have any self-awareness once he'd passed those essential parts of himself on through his children to his grandchildren.

Then, when one of the glowing figures in front of him disappeared, he realized that they had just passed through the gel curtain into the survival chamber.

He snapped back to the present. P'Ko thought he could feel the Se'Ro'Bs chasing him bump against his feet as he crawled. The psychic energy of all the rest of the runners and even the spectators watching on live video feeds fed to him, telling him that the Se'Ro'Bs had been just one long reach away. With every last bit of energy he could muster, he surged forward.

A long claw swept at him. The swipe cost the Se'Ro'Bs some speed as the last of P'Ko's pack disappeared through the gel curtain. P'Ko sprang forward, pushing through the gel curtain as the Se'Ro'Bs made a second swipe catching P'Ko on the side of the leg, knocking him off balance and tearing flesh as his pack mates pulled him the rest of the way through the gel curtain.

The Se'Ro'Bs', blackness and cold lunged against the gel curtain, but the gel curtain strong and elastic, made only to allow warm things through refused to let the liquid gas cold Se'Ro'Bs through.

Whoops and howls of victory erupted from the twenty-five runners stacked two deep in the survival shelter made for ten. A bandage was hastily slapped on P'Ko's leg as the dark shadow outside nibbled up the scattered frosty pebbles of P'Ko's blood. It had frozen before it hit the deck as it poured from the gash the Se'Ro'Bs put into P'Ko's leg as he was being pulled through the curtain.

After sniffing around to make sure it didn't miss any of P'Ko's blood, the Se'Ro'Bs slowly, tiredly skulked away.

Once the Se'Ro'Bs left the area, and the runners felt sure it was safe to venture out the runners sent for the supply shuttle that had been staged not far away. They crawled and staggered out of the cramped emergency shelter they had piled into and piled into the back of the supply shuttle. This time only half on top of each other. Adjusting to stay warm from shared body heat, fortified by the joy of accomplishment. They had faced down death, and passed around a flask of a special "athletic" concoction Mi'Ka designed especially for this event and had placed in the shuttle for them.

They soon felt no pain or even twinge of the cold, despite the fact they left the cargo doors of the shuttle wide open and everyone's exothermic body paint was nearly gone, worn bare, or in tatters.

The shuttle took the fastest, most direct route back to Ol'Tn and in no time, perhaps feeling the effects of Mi'Ka's drink, they arrived at Ol'Tn's cargo access ramp.

The shuttle backed up the ramp through the air lock, and the runners exited the cargo bay and paraded back up the same street they had come down many hours before. Passing cheering crowds.

The spectators had seen it all. The run organizers had stationed camera-mounted robots at strategic locations over the anticipated course. The robots were mobile, able to scamper from place to place to intercept the runners and get a good camera angle.

Some of the experienced runners accepted the opportunity to wear a forward and rear looking personal camera built into the tight fitting goggles that all the runners wore to protect their eyes from the intense cold.

P'Ko, as well as many of the other runners limped, they would have left bloody footprints had they not been given medicated tight fitting constriction slipper socks, knee pads, and gloves when they got off the shuttle.

P'Ko felt no pain; he was riding high on the thrill of accomplishment, acceptance, camaraderie, and, Mi'Ka's athletic drink. The runners passed a receiving area of sorts near the stage and starting, now finishing line, and were each given a medal of achievement. The medal had each finisher's name and race number on one side, along with "800th Run with the Se'Ro'Bs" around the edge. On the medal's front, an intricate color profile diagram of a runner in full stride closely followed by a dark shape with two massive arms reaching out towards the runner.

After receiving their finishers medal, the runners loitered around the staging area, now turned triage area, where they waited to be checked out and repaired by one of several doctors that had set up treatment tables near where the body paint tents had been and were making repairs on the runners.

As soon as all the finishers received their Medals of Achievement, the presentation of the group and individual awards were made.

There were individual awards for oldest and youngest and most times run, along with pack awards, which included the fastest pursuit and longest distance pursued. There was the M'Vr (most valuable runner), an award which went to the runner that discovered the Se'Ro'Bs. Her pack also won the longest time pursued by the Se'Ro'Bs over the course of the run award, P'Ko's pack a close second[94].

---

[94] P'Ko's pack lost this title despite the lengthy pursuit of P'Ko and his pack at the end the race, because they had lost too much pursuit time earlier in the race when P'Ko was having trouble transitioning from running to scampering on all fours and the other teams skipped P'Ko's team several times

On what should have been the end of the presentations, there was an unexpected pause. The race official presiding on stage excused himself and disappeared from the podium; he was gone some time. Then returned, smiling, and began an impromptu speech, announcing that the run organizers and the monitors had, after much deliberation, agreed to the presentation of a first, a one of a kind, special award.

Adding that each year after this, injecting, that it will be based on different criteria unique to that year's event.

Continuing, this year, he cautioned, is one that the run organizers never want to see repeated or even attempt to be repeated, and in fact, if the run organizers and monitors suspect that if someone tries to repeat it; the runner will be penalized and sanctioned.

"The reward for the longest single pursuit ever recorded, it bests the previous record by a factor of three and God willing will never be repeated or exceeded. It goes to Pack Two, the second pack to be pursued by the Se'Ro'Bs." P'Ko's team filed up onto the stage in the same order as they were during the final pursuit. They received a specially designed medal similar in size to the medal of achievement.

The longest pursuit medal, still warm from coming out of the fabricator, was rimmed by the words "Longest Se'Ro'Bs Pursuit 3 h 28 m 8 s". It showed a front on view of five runners scrambling against a field of black with jagged edges in the shape of a fang-lined maw, the back inscribed with the Runner's name, Race number 800, and 1 of 5, 2 of 5… P'Ko's was 5 of 5, indicating that he was the last, the one the Se'Ro'Bs was closest to catching and nearest to death.

After the Longest Pursuit Awards had been handed out, pack two started to file off, but the race official asked that P'Ko remain behind. Then the race official requested that the rest of the Ti'Ro's[95] come up on stage. Out of the crowd, three other runners came forward and up onto the stage with P'Ko.

The race official announced, "Now is the moment many of you have been waiting for, the Crystal Tear Ceremony." The official paused, and the crowd grew silent.

"The Chrystal Tear Ceremony traces its origins to before Dadr'Ba's official recorded history, before the ToG. It allows us to acknowledge publicly, the sacrifices our ancestors made for the more than one million hours over the course of their lives that each spent working to produce the fuel that is taking us O'M.

Our predecessors worked every day of their life's with no relief or reward other than barely enough credits to buy spices to make energy cake palatable and too short, and too long in between, vacations. Only to become so fatigued with life that retirement begins to look good. Retirement that means passing

---

in the rotation. Their sacrifice allowed P'Ko the time and practice to get used to the new environment and awkward pace.

[95] Sounds like Tea-Row, meaning beginner, novice.

from this existence, sending a part of you to join your grandchildren, but never, ever, meeting them in person.

The Run with the Se'Ro'Bs began by accident shortly after the ToG, when the Se'Ro'Bs was first discovered. Or, more properly, when we were discovered by the Se'Ro'Bs and Mi'Nr's had to be watchful and wary if they didn't want to fall prey.

Since then Run with the Se'Ro'Bs has come to exemplify in a matter of hours the life of a Mi'Nr, the struggles, the hardships, the pain, the Spector of death. It also represents the teamwork, cooperation, and self-sacrifice that are cornerstones to a Mi'Nr's existence.

Many years ago we combined the two, beginning with the Run with the Se'Ro'Bs and concluding with the Crystal Tear Ceremony. The Crystal Tear displays on the face of all Mi'Nr's a sign that we respect our ancestors, ourselves and our profession, by wearing this sign it says to all that we are Mi'Nr's, and we're proud of it.

Many Mi'Nr's have worked their entire lives knowing that they will never see O'M themselves. They sacrificed their lives so that their children or their children's children might one day look out over the vast open expanse of O'M and see the horizon, walk upright, light of step and breath warm clean pure air where liquid water flows freely.

The life on O'M will have a retirement without passing, and we'll be able to meet, in person, our grandchildren and perhaps even our great-grandchildren, we work for that goal" a loud and prolonged applause followed.

"Now, bring forth the Crystal Tear Stylus," a long, slender rod, tapered to a fine point on one end and blunt at the end was brought forward. With a striker, the speaker struck the blunt end of the stylus, and it erupted in flame.

"This represents the extremes of our environment; the flame represents the fusion fire of the engine we mine the fuel for. The flame draws the heat from the opposite end of this stylus, making it as cold if not colder than the temperatures of Zone four, at the edge of space."

"It's time to recognize the Ti'Ro's, who with their escorts have retraced many of the tunnels that our parents and their parents have carved through Dadr'Ba. They've experienced the full spectrum of G's, from a comfortable walk to an onerous crawl. They've run from an environment where ammonia and methane are gaseous, past where these gasses turn to liquid, then solid. Where oxygen and nitrogen become liquid and further still to where they turn solid. They've sought out and faced the feared Se'Ro'Bs and have learned that survival depends on teamwork and looking out for each other as one looks out for one's self."

"Now the Ti'Ro's receive their Crystal Tear, marking them as members of the Mi'Nr community, that symbolizes the bond between Mi'Nr's, representing the pain and sacrifice that Mi'Nr's have shared and endured together."

With that, he walked up to the first Ti'Ro and raising the stylus up high blew lightly on the sharp end, the flame flared at the other. He walked up to the first Ti'Ro, an attractive young woman P'Ko recognized as being the trailing runner from pack number one. The pack, his pack, first intercepted, saving them from behind rather than the norm of cutting in between them and the Se'Ro'Bs.

The race official slowly lowered the stylus to her cheek and as it touched, the flame on the far end of the stylus became blindingly bright "Welcome, Sa'Di, this name means Lucky". He did the same for each of the other Ti'Ro's, giving each of them a new name, a Mi'Nr's name, a nickname or handle of sorts, used within the Mi'Nr community.

Finally, he came to P'Ko, who was awestruck by all that was going on. P'Ko had noticed the snowflake design on the cheeks of just about every Mi'Nr he had come in contact with and thought they were tattooed. He had meant to ask Su'Zi about them but had never gotten around to it. P'Ko thought Su'Zi had a particularly nice looking one and even complimented her on it, but she never elaborated on it, and P'Ko never pursued the subject.

P'Ko now wanted to know more about Su'Zi's Run with the Se'Ro'Bs and what her "handle" is.

The stylus was raised above P'Ko's head and slowly came down to touch his cheek. The instant it touched. P'Ko was blinded by the brightness of the light, even though he had instinctively closed his eyes tight against the glare. The light seemed to come from inside his head as well as outside; he heard the sound too; it didn't appear to come from his ears, but from inside his head.

"Welcome, Lele'Kolo this name means Leap-Crawl." He had some trouble maintaining his balance and struggled to stay on his feet. As his senses returned, he was back on the stage with the race official and the rest of the Ti'Ro's receiving a loud applause. After the applause had subsided, they filed off the stage to be mauled by the crowd with congratulations, handshakes, and pats on the back.

Su'Zi managed to find P'Ko and helped guide him through the congratulatory crowd to the Doctors station. P'Ko had not yet been patched up and was limping more than before, though he claimed not to feel any pain. By the time they got there, the repairs on the last of the runners were just finishing. P'Ko was once again the last of the runners.

This gave P'Ko and Su'Zi a few moments before the Doctor got to work on him. Su'Zi was drawn to P'Ko's Crystal tear frost burn. P'Ko couldn't see his own, but now appreciated their significance and took notice of the finely etched six-sided Stellar Dendrite on Su'Zi's cheek near her eye. It shimmered faintly and seemed to change colors in the light.

P'Ko never actually paid Su'Zi's crystal tear much attention, he had thought it only an elaborate Mi'Nr's tattoo, a decoration. Now he appreciated it and looked at it like never before. A sudden realization came over him, and he glanced around, noticing that, he had assumed they were all the same. But now on closer examination the six-sided crystals varied, some were Stellar Dendrites like Su'Zi's, but others were Sectored Plates or stellar plates, still others were Stars or triangular Crystals, they all were unique, like real snowflakes.

He mentioned it to Su'Zi, while she still intently studied P'Ko's own Crystal Tear, she confirmed all Crystal Tears were different, just like natural snowflakes.

"I can't remember ever seeing one," Su'Zi said softly to herself. About that time Mi'Ka appeared making like she was pushing through the crowd, though the crowd gave way readily, showing their deference. She mumbled something about people needing to pay respect to their elders, as she put on her best good-humored crotchety show.

Su'Zi turned to Mi'Ka, "Mi'Ka, P'Ko's Crystal Tear is twelve sided not six sided, have you ever heard of such a thing? A twelve-sided Stellar Dendrite?" Mi'Ka came over and pulled P'Ko down for a closer examination and ran her fingers lightly over P'Ko's cheek, then pulled very close as if she could see something through her blind eyes if it were close enough.

"Hum," Mi'Ka went on, "I've heard of them before, they're rare, but not unheard of, it might be due to his made over U'Te skin, but nothing about this one is ordinary. Did you see him jump over the Se'Ro'Bs? He should be half digested by now. Then he had to torment the poor thing by groveling away from it at the end, only leaving it a taste."

Then, changing the subject, Mi'Ka continued, "enough of that, I just wanted to congratulate our P'Ko Lele'Kolo on completing the run." Then directed towards P'Ko, "stop by my shop later, it doesn't have to be today, I have something for you, and she winked a blind eye at P'Ko." "Now go get patched up." The doctor's station was now available, "and get some clothes on, show off!" and she walked away.

P'Ko, suddenly self-conscious, realizing that he was now the only one in all the crowd wearing nothing but threadbare and tattered body paint, all the rest of the runners had donned finishers jumpsuits upon completion of their repairs at the doctor's station. P'Ko walked over and hopped on the exam table, gladly accepting the sheet that was offered to him, and sat back letting the Doctor and his Med Teck do their work.

P'Ko's exothermic paint had nearly completely burnt off, leaving him mostly bare, with a few thin patches and tatters hanging. The carbon reinforced patches were gone and blood seeped through abraded and cracked skin, saturating the bandage and compression slipper socks and gloves P'Ko and the other runners, that needed them, received immediately after the run.

The Med Tech, an attractive U'Te started to work removing the left over exothermic paint and residue from P'Ko's. She was soon assisted by Su'Zi.

The doctor allowed the Med Tech, with Su'Zi close by to work on P'Ko's frost burns using special applicator to apply a high strength nanobot lotion. The body painter had done a good job. The one recommended by Su'Zi that P'Ko used had over a century of practice and knew just where and how thick to apply the multiple layers of exothermic paint and where to add carbon fiber reinforcement patches.

The doctor applied a topical anesthetic to the abrasions and cracks and a local anesthetic near the gash on his leg. Then began cleaning the wounds using a powerful smelling solution that washed away the damaged flesh. He then laid new skin over it and using a strange looking tool, the doctor sort'a welded it in place around the edges. Then covered the area with a shaded lamp which he turned on and let sit for a minute or two as if to bake, while he worked on the next area. Moving from one blood soaked area to the next.

The gash in his leg took a bit longer, and the doctor did most of the work under a drape that covered the gash and obscured what the doctor did inside the wound.

While the Doctor worked, P'Ko was saddened as he realized and that his Nu'Tn friends weren't here to participate in the festivities. Only yesterday life seemed simpler but now, as he contemplated the future that lay ahead, he realized that when he chose this profession that he'd to begin to lead a sort of double life. He had won acceptance here among the Mi'Nr's, but all of his U'Te friends would feel out of place here. Just as all these new friends would feel out of place up in Nu'Tn.

He knew that if he tried to use what little influence he had with his new Mi'Nr friends to force acceptance of his U'Te friends it wouldn't work, at least not now. Maybe someday.

The Doctor completed his repairs, and they were on their way.

P'Ko for the moment was something of a celebrity. Su'Zi pulled P'Ko to the side, and giving him a hug and kiss, whispered teasingly that there would be girls showing up all over the place, after him, worse even than the Se'Ro'Bs. But not to worry, she would help him through the gauntlet.

She was right, P'Ko noticed girls, attractive girls, looking amorously at him, a few in spite of his being with Su'Zi sent him psychic invites. P'Ko didn't rebuff the psychic overtures, doing his best to stay aloof and focused on Su'Zi. Who he knew was proud to be with him.

Su'Zi didn't mind the looks and signals they got, let them have their dreams. She sensed P'Ko was flattered by the unexpected attention, but she knew he was proud to be with her. She soaked in the attention she got from the guys and the girls, envious of her, as she strutted proudly snuggling next to P'Ko.

P'Ko and Su'Zi wandered around the run celebration turned street party, sampling food, drinking lightly, mostly celebratory toasts. P'Ko met lots of new people, and Su'Zi introduced him to many of her friends. He got lots of compliments from people that had bet he would escape the Se'Ro'Bs, and good humored gibes from those that bet he wouldn't.

There were lots of food vendors, drinking, music, and dancing on impromptu dance floors. They milled about the street party into the early evening then retired to an Ol'Tn town rental apartment Mi'Ka had helped Su'Zi secure for the occasion. P'Ko and Su'Zi spent hours talking; lounging together, sitting on a love seat, feet up before a bay window overlooking the main street of Ol'Tn.

The one-way glass showed the crowds still jostling about, the street below. The many display screens are showing various run highlights with commentary. They shared their experiences and feelings about Running with the Se'Ro'Bs and discussed the details of each other's race.

Su'Zi told of her first race and chided, P'Ko that she finished fastest among the Ti'Ro's. They talked philosophically and wondered why they couldn't sense the Se'Ro'Bs and whether Se'Ro'Bs even lived.

They talked about life, what the meaning of life is or might be and what they wanted out of life and how they were lucky to have found each other. The whole time, they shared and exchanged unspoken feelings psychically.

They talked about how they first met and how P'Ko was so attracted to Su'Zi and how beautiful she was. Su'Zi spoke of how she was first attracted to P'Ko on a psychic level, even in her dream. Then she confessed that since laying eyes on him after his bio-mods, a passion had started to kindle in her and was magnified a thousand times when she saw him in nothing but body paint. Then topped by watching the slow motion replays of some of the most energetic portions of the run, especially his great leap.

Su'Zi had longed for this night. The visceral attraction she felt for P'Ko piled on top of the psychic and emotional feelings was unlike anything she had ever experienced before. She felt her inhibitions drain away.

As they spoke, laying in each other's arms the passion that each felt for the other grew, and they began to caress. Losing themselves in time and space, existing in the here and now they made love.

It was passionate and intense. Neither one of them could hold back, and they quickly and simultaneously reset, and fell into a little death so intense it was minutes before their hearts started again. Then made love again, and again, each time softer and slower, seeking to prolong the experience as long as possible.

The next morning, they both had the day off, P'Ko going negative to get the time off, but feeling it was well worth the debt.

They woke wrapped in each other's arms, cheek to cheek, feeling as if they were one body, refreshed and satisfied. Slowly, as their senses returned, with sadness, they recognized their bodies as their own. The sadness was offset by the realization that this wasn't the last and out of the separation grew a greater appreciation of what they had shared. They knew without speaking, that nothing in each other's experience could match what they just had.

Slowly, taking several playful false attempts to separate, they untangled from each other. Su'Zi got up first and stood for a moment, each admiring the other's naked body. Then Su'Zi walked over and started brewing tea.

As the tea brewed P'Ko went to the bathroom and returned with a warm, damp cloth and they laid back down and P'Ko gave Su'Zi a sponge bath. Afterward Su'Zi did the same for P'Ko, finishing up with a light coating of scented lotion for both.

They slipped on robes that Su'Zi had prepped in advance, and sat once again before the bay window watching the street vendors below and drank freshly brewed tea and ate breakfast wafers, given to Su'Zi by Mi'Ka for this particular occasion.

They talked about how good it was the night before, and how happy they were to be with each other, how they couldn't imagine it being any better. The unspoken implication being the question of if they had crossed the rarely discussed line between sex; the recreational stress reliever, the psychic reset, exercise and fulfillment of gender identity, and love; the deep pair bonding prequel to procreation, the joining that usually begins to occur between mated couples twice their age.

P'Ko's next thought, he couldn't tell if he spoke or just thought "are we in love?" Su'Zi responded in kind, P'Ko still not sure if he heard it with his ears "of course we are. I have loved you since the moment I first saw you." Then Su'Zi, speaking, aloud, "I believe we've been somehow connected since long before we met, that there exist soul mates that are timeless, that we are meant to be together."

Then, after a pause, "What is love?" answering herself "Love is the sense of belonging, the sharing of yourself, sharing of your self-control, your knowledge, your very awareness, sharing that part of you that makes, you, "you." When two people love each other, they lose themselves, give up thinking about themselves as individuals, unconditionally accepting each other for who they are and begin to think of themselves as a couple, as connected with the person they love."

"People who love each other create a new, multiself, a virtual person that is a combination of the two individuals; the individuals disappear, and the couple remains. Separation or anything that threatens separation hurts as much a physical cut or injury, even more so because it's painful to the heart, to the soul. People in love are never the same as before, everything they do has the touch or imprint of their loved one. Lacking the knowledge of the other, like we were before we found each other, creates a longing for the seed of true love, the want to belong to another."

"When I first saw you in my dream, I didn't see a To'Ta, I felt something deeper, I saw something deeper like there was an aura around you. Then when I saw you again in Vr'Chm the aura was missing, but it was like tunnel vision, I could see through the virtual interface, see you directly, like looking through a portal. I sensed it was you and longed to be with you, to be part of your life. It was love at first sight, but I could tell that at first you didn't feel the same way, and it hurt and terrified me."

P'Ko replied, "I was terrified too. I knew that I was attracted to you, but I couldn't tell it if it was physical attraction or true love. I had to get to know you on a deeper, more personal level to decern if it was a physical longing, or more, a longing for the real you, underneath that beautiful body. I had to get to know the deeper you, your personality, your wants, your goals, your values and desires, the more profound you, before I knew if I actually loved you."

"I didn't know then what real love was. Now, and it's not just because of last night. I know that you have forever changed my life and whether together or apart "we" will always influence my life, my decisions, I can't think of myself without including you. "I do love you." And they touched psychically and embraced.

After more tea and wafers, Su'Zi produced P'Ko's utility overalls that he had worn to report into the run, freshly laundered, he had forgotten them completely; Su'Zi had thought of everything and P'Ko lavished the attention.

They spent the rest of the day together exploring Ol'Tn and even paid a visit to Mi'Ka, who gave P'Ko a neck charm of sorts, a tiny, sturdy little bottle containing a clear liquid appearing to have sparkling snowflakes drifting through it. She said that it was a powerful first aid kit and to be only used in dire emergencies, and in the meantime, it was nice to look at, and it was; P'Ko found himself momentarily transfixed watching the sparkling snowflakes drift on the tiny currents in the bottle. He broke himself away and thanked Mi'Ka profusely; he had never seen or heard of anything like it before.

P'Ko and Su'Zi became a couple, unusual for people so young, but not unheard of. They settled into something of a routine, seeing each other as often as their schedule permits, sometimes P'Ko visits Su'Zi more often Su'Zi visiting P'Ko, due to her access to a vehicle and her more advanced driving skills. P'Ko didn't mind because they would often go for rides and Su'Zi would teach P'Ko how to drive like a pro.

P'Ko's apprenticeship was slow and methodical. He needed to complete his apprenticeship and get a permanent job assignment before they could try to get into the same camp. Between learning his job and spending time with Su'Zi, P'Ko's life was happy and contented, He had all but forgot about the reader neatly stowed in the sack safe fused to the bottom of his locker. He stayed friends with his U'Te classmates mostly on social media and online, but over time grew more and more distant. Until an old friend asked a favor.

Chapter 40, A Favor for Tn'

As P'Ko rode the supply shuttle up to Ol'Tn, he reflected on the message from Tn', it felt and sounded urgent. P'Ko knew that Tn' was getting ready to graduate and thought that Tn' might be wanting P'Ko's advice on Job selection and bio-mods, but why the sense of urgency? P'Ko thought back to Tn's question so long ago up in the stadium overlooking Nu'Tn. They had been asking each other about their likes and dislikes. When Tn' asked P'Ko if he liked "boys or girls." Tn' was back then and might now still be undecided about gender and wanting advice.

Everyone stresses over bio-mod and job selection as they near graduation. But back then Tn' seemed even more undecided than most. Could Tn' be debating over gender identity? P'Ko suddenly wished Su'Zi were here, she would be able to give a female's point of view.

If Tn' is undecided, perhaps it would be best to stay U'Ne ne wouldn't have been the first and it's the right choice for some. P'Ko was frightened of suggesting any particular gender identity to Tn' because it's such an important decision, one that will impact you for the rest of your life. While gender reassignment is technically possible if a mistake is made, the cost of sex reassignment, an unfunded elective mod according to the CA, could cost twenty-five to fifty years of savings. P'Ko didn't want to be responsible in any way for such an important decision.

P'Ko had always known and felt comfortable with Tn' as a U'Ne. Tn' was three years younger than P'Ko and they were best friends growing up and maybe not best friends now, still good friends. Knowing Tn' as well as he did, P'Ko's choice for Tn' would be between U'Ne and male, probably U'Ne.

P'Ko made it to Ym'Cha's and found Tn' already there waiting. After a warm welcome, they bought tea, sat at a table talking superficially about P'Ko's job, transitioning to the core topic of school, graduation, job selection and bio-mods.

P'Ko was flabbergasted when Tn' finally told him that ne decided that ne was going to be female; Tn' was going to become Tn'Ya.

Tn's disclosure knocked P'Ko off balance, and it took a while for him to come back to his senses and sort out what he just heard. He reflected back on what he knew of Tn'. Tn' had been a little effeminate growing up, but that wasn't unusual for a To'Ta. But then P'Ko recalled getting subtle hints that Tn' desired to be physically intimate with P'Ko. Remembering occasional comments, touches and edging inside the standard male/male comfort zone of interpersonal space and more often than necessary choosing to come close to whisper something when it didn't warrant secrecy. It didn't threaten P'Ko; he just didn't pay it any attention.

P'Ko knew Tn' was still grateful to P'Ko and indebted to P'Ko for that time long ago when P'Ko rescued Tn' from Dan'Zu and his gang. Tn' couldn't seem to let go of it, in spite of P'Ko's attempts to minimize it. P'Ko felt more than repaid by Tn' staying a trusted and loyal friend, pleasant and fun to be around.

P'Ko had no idea, that Tn' might be thinking anything more than friendship. P'Ko's psychic perception wasn't as developed or trusted then and even now P'Ko had trouble accepting the idea that Tn's friendship might have been turning into something more.

What's more, "Tn'Ya" wanted P'Ko to be her mentor. P'Ko's initial reaction was to refuse; he had no physical attraction or emotion deeper than a friend to Tn'Ya. Tn' was and is a good friend and now P'Ko knew Tn'Ya felt strongly toward P'Ko.

This shouldn't have been a surprise; P'Ko should have seen it coming. P'Ko looked into Tn'Ya's eyes and saw, enforced with his psychic sense, love. P'Ko sensed trouble; Mentors are not supposed to be too emotionally attached to their Lr'Lng.

That's going to be a problem. P'Ko remembered Z'Shi's lecture to him on the distinction between recreational sex and love and P'Ko didn't know what to do about it.

P'Ko could refuse, but to do so, would be cruel and go against the social mores and honor associated with being asked to be a mentor. There's an etiquette involved with the selection process and accepting or rejecting the honor of being asked to be a mentor is no trivial matter.

P'Ko's mind raced, how would Su'Zi react? P'Ko thought back to when Su'Zi broke protocol and asked, not offered to be his mentor. Grasping at a possible solution to get around the problem, maybe Su'Zi could be part of the "Mentoring Team". After all, Su'Zi was mentored by a couple.

As P'Ko thought about it more, he began to calm down. Mentors have complete say over the mentoring process, which would help in handling it. He could use his authority as Mentor to set rules and calm the situation.

If he and Su'Zi did this together, it could be a positive experience for everyone, or so P'Ko hoped, and a way to accept while at the same time defuse this feeling of love P'Ko was getting from Tn'Ya.

P'Ko politely told Tn' that this was unexpected and that he needed time to consider it. When they parted Tn' gave P'Ko a friendly hug. Which P'Ko responded to in a "guy" way. Tn' was a caring friend and deserved compassion.

P'Ko had told Su'Zi all about Tn' previously, and Su'Zi had never met Tn' and thought of Tn' as just a U'Ne friend of P'Ko. Now when P'Ko told her about Tn's choice and request, Su'Zi, sensing a rival, questioned "Tn'Ya's" motives.

Su'Zi echoed P'Ko's concern contrary to the noblest aspects of mentoring, that Tn' might be attempting to use mentoring as a way to get close to P'Ko. Which should have provided grounds to turn down the request.

The situation was significant enough to warrant the advice of someone more mature and unbiased Su'Zi and P'Ko agreed that before any decisions were made that they'd get Mi'Ka's advice.

A few short messages later and a date and time were set for Su'Zi and P'Ko to meet with Tn' together, for a mentoring interview. After the interview P'Ko, Su'Zi and Mi'Ka decided, on Mi'Ka's advice, that P'Ko and Tn' would meet with Mi'Ka and have a psychic reading without Su'Zi present.

Mi'Ka thought it would be better to minimize participants, especially since Mi'Ka intended to evaluate Tn's motives towards P'Ko while advising Tn' on Tn's future. Suspecting how Tn' feels towards P'Ko, the presence of Su'Zi might make Tn' jealous and distort the results of the reading.

Chapter 41, Tn's Psychic Reading

The intent of the reading was intentionally vague, had Mi'Ka explained too much about what was going to happen; it would have tainted the results. Psychic readings are fluid and dynamic and can take twists and turns depending on the reactions of the people involved and what is revealed or discovered along the way.

It would have been better if P'Ko wasn't there, but Tn' refused to come without P'Ko. Any third parties, cooperative, are not, complicates, and changes the energy balance and perspectives of the reading, limiting or mollifying it so that the information gathered is less authentic, more restricted limited to a more specific set of circumstances. It might take additional readings with Tn' alone to provide a better insight.

Mi'Ka conducts a reading by psychically observing the person and their reactions while Mi'Ka introduces objects, which can be almost anything, a word, phrase, feeling, emotion, image, vision or even an event, past, present or possible future.

The strength or the substance of the object is impacted by the psychic power of the person she's doing the reading on and on their cooperation level and expectations. It's impossible to predict what the reading will reveal.

All psychic interactions have a balance; the balance is between openness and sharing, the willingness to cooperate on one side and the power, strength and agility on the other side. The most efficient way to achieve a balance between what amounts to giving up strength and maintaining power is with a common goal, realized or not.

During sex, it's giving and taking pleasure with each other and achieving reset. For birthing it goes beyond a give and take, it's a complete merging of psychic energies with the goal of initiating the psychic and cognitive processes of the Bo'Ba.

For a reading, the objective is to create an experience like a guided conversation, but designed to feel like ordinary, free thought. It's most successful if the subject believes they are simply free thinking and react and respond to thoughts and ideas that they think are their own, but in reality have been very carefully crafted and suggested by the reader.

Mi'Ka's readings of P'Ko had been "interesting" she's never given him a formal one; all of her readings of P'Ko had been surreptitious and opportune. Although Mi'Ka thought P'Ko would accept a reading by Mi'Ka if she asked, his awareness of it would color the results. But that wasn't the biggest problem with reading P'Ko. Mi'Ka could tell that P'Ko has the same psychic capabilities as many of the better psychic Mi'Nr's, but he doesn't trust them and without realizing it he's natively on guard. This guardedness would probably plunge the reading into a psychic sparing match. Which Mi'Ka was

200

confident she could win, but not without altering their relationship negatively forever.

Because P'Ko's doesn't trust his native psychic ability, it cripples it. His mistrust of his psychic abilities prevents him from bringing to bear his more sensitive psychic abilities towards others and what it's telling him about the psychic activity around him. He's unable to reach very far or discern very much detail.

Mi'Ka has noticed a gradual improvement in P'Ko psychic abilities. Since she met him, he improved a little on his own; there was a notable improvement after his mentoring with Z'Shi and, most recently, the Run with the Se'Ro'Bs.

Mi'Ka's best readings of P'Ko have been when he wasn't expecting or even aware of it, like when he's walking down the street in front of her shop. However, he's learned to expect something psychic from her as soon as he crosses her threshold. But lately he's been prepping earlier, putting himself on the alert, and on guard further and further down the street.

This interaction is good for both of them; Mi'Ka has enjoyed the challenge. It's been a long while since she's felt challenged. To think that it crossed P'Ko's mind of Mi'Ka as his mentor, ha! He wouldn't be able to handle it! She's been P'Ko's psychic guide since they first met and in a way have been having psychic foreplay since then too, as for the other, maybe after a few hundred years, when he's mature enough?... Mi'Ka chuckled to herself.

As P'Ko and Tn' approached Mi'Ka's shop, Tn'Ya, not having visited Ol'Tn very often, was nervous, but she was with P'Ko and P'Ko exuded familiarity and confidence which comforted Tn'Ya. Her nervousness and anxious apprehension began to turn to excitement as they neared Mi'Ka's shop. She was on an adventure with P'Ko.

They had gone on some explorations and adventures before, but those had been in Nu'Tn, Ol'Tn was... Old it's almost like walking through a museum. But rather than being an organized museum, it was a haphazard conglomeration of nearly two-thousand-year-old trusses and modules. There were some structure and organization of the larger structures but the smaller things were a mishmash. Ol'Tn consisted of everything too worn, used or damaged to warrant a place in the D'Po. From one end of Ol'Tn to the other lay the remnants of fuel tanks, cargo transports, habitats. Littered with bits and pieces of old broken or worn out, life supports, controls, research equipment, maintenance or manufacturing equipment and occasional command module junk.

P'Ko told Tn' about Mi'Ka in advance and cautioned Tn' that Mi'Ka's appearances can be deceiving, she looks, sort of, rough, but she's a very sweet person.

By the time P'Ko and Tn' approached Mi'Ka's shop Tn' was feeling comfortable, but when Tn' finally met Mi'Ka face-to-face Tn' was shocked. Tn's shock was short-lived, Mi'Ka anticipated her reaction and used her charm and psychic abilities to make sure Tn'Ya was comfortable, it would be essential for an accurate reading,

Even Ku'Ma, Mi'Ka's pet, was well behaved. Tn'Ya didn't even notice Ku'Ma hiding in the shadows; P'Ko spotted Ku'Ma though, and playfully feigned a motion toward Ku'Ma and got a silent hunchbacked snarl in response. P'Ko sent the robotic creature a psychic pat, not expecting a reply from the robotic animal and was astonished to see Ku'Ma take the arch out of its back and swoosh its tail, then settling down crossing its paws in front of it. P'Ko was dumbfounded; robots shouldn't be able to communicate psychically. But then, how does Mi'Ka interact with it? He never really thought about it before and didn't have time to now.

The three of them gathered around Mi'Ka's little reading table. They sat on mats, a teapot with three cups was already there. Mi'Ka with her usual tea pouring dexterity poured perfectly placing the cups directly in front of her guests.

P'Ko sipped the tea and tried his best to detect if Mi'Ka had added any "special" ingredients, he could discern none. The tea was one of her usual's, a sweet, smooth slightly sour blend with a sweet aftertaste. They made small talk while they calmly drank the tea, what tension and anxiety there was, slowly disappeared.

Mi'Ka asked Tn'Ya how she had met P'Ko and got a somewhat inflated (from P'Ko's perspective) description of P'Ko's single-handed defeat of Dan'Zu's gang of five. Mi'Ka noted almost humorously the accidental reuse of the term "gang of five" the private term of reference the resistance uses for the CA Central Council.

Mi'Ka was tuned psychically to the story as well; Tn'Ya was very open, open to a fault. Openness that Su'Zi had noticed and shared with Mi'Ka from Su'Zi's meeting with Tn' earlier. It was readily apparent to Mi'Ka that Tn'Ya wasn't hiding anything, there was no deception or underlying motives driving Tn'Ya, but that didn't mean there weren't concerns.

Tn'Ya had absolute trust and devotion to P'Ko and P'Ko felt it. When he thought about it too much, he felt tied down, obligated, and a little smothered by it. He cared for Tn' but not nearly as much as Tn' cared for him. Tn's feelings were what was to be expected between a much more mature couple, and Tn' was way too young to have as strong as feelings as this.

Mi'Ka realized right away that this triad, this small group, was dangerously off balance, the risk of emotional pain and devastation is all too real a possibility. To avoid pain to one or more lives and relationships, and to avoid ruin or disaster, expectations would need to be worked out, some give and take needs to take place. These young people need time to mature.

Mi'Ka knew P'Ko and Su'Zi individually were developing properly, but they had a strong attraction for each other, and their relationship was progressing too rapidly. P'Ko and Su'Zi were pushing their relationship too fast, which made Mi'Ka uneasy about their relationship. Mi'Ka sensed that P'Ko and Su'Zi, are going to face some tremendous hardships.

Tn'Ya might be able to help. She could be just the thing to help slow P'Ko and Su'Zi down, and at the same time, P'Ko and Su'Zi could help Tn'Ya get her emotions under control. If she could get the three of them to work together, they'll mature and work through their desires, and be equipped with the tools to understand life, and find their soul mates.

If the give-and-take needed for a healthy two-person relationship can be achieved for these three, it would become a tremendously positive thing. The three of them together could achieve things otherwise impossible, something hundreds of years from now, they'll be proud of. Then somehow, coming from somewhere deep in Mi'Ka's gut, something told her that the fate of all of Dadr'Ba is linked to these three.

The hardest thing for Tn'Ya to get used upon meeting Mi'Ka, where Mi'Ka's large frosted over eyes, Tn'Ya thought she could see twinkling behind the frost, infrequently, unexpectedly and erratic, sometimes blue, sometimes white, contrasted against Mi'Ka's actions which were as smooth and controlled as a gymnast or dancer.

Tn'Ya sipped the tea; it's the best she can remember tasting, soothing with a light sweet aftertaste leaving her mouth feeling clean and fresh. Her fear and apprehension, already buffered by the presence of P'Ko subsided further. This small, dark, scary blind eyed woman, was no threat, and underneath a gruff looking exterior was a very gentle, compassionate soul, that would be hard-pressed to hurt anyone.

When P'Ko and Tn'Ya arrived, Mi'Ka sensed right away that Tn'Ya was psychically linked to P'Ko, and hiding in his shadow, only peeking out occasionally, cautiously and out of curiosity. Mi'Ka could sense that Tn'Ya felt P'Ko's psychic attention towards her and is comforted by it. Although P'Ko trusts Mi'Ka and understands what she's doing his naturally guarded psyche, focused on Tn'Ya, might cause a problem. Mi'Ka will have to be very subtle.

They must help her make the right bio-mod and job selection decision and learn what Tn'Ya's motives are and if Tn'Ya is trustworthy.

Mi'Ka found herself reading not just Tn'Ya but the multiself consisting of Tn'Ya and P'Ko. Tn'Ya is already bonded to P'Ko and P'Ko to Tn'Ya, though at a much lesser level and not fully conscious of it.

All couples, friends, groups, and communities are bonded, they're not actual individuals. People think of themselves as alone in their existence, but they behave and react to external influences with the others they're bonded to in mind.

Once the other member or members a couple, family or group accept a new individual as a member, they become a part of a virtual being, participating, to various extents, in the thoughts, motivations, personality and psyche of the group and each of the constituent individuals.

The virtual person is a matrix the individual at its core. Branching off from this core is their mate, families, and friends. Which branches off further to groups and groups of groups, encompassing whole communities or categories the person identifies with and has loyalty to. Every individual becomes a matrix of matrixes with many, sometimes hundreds of inputs from the many connections to other individuals and groups.

Tn'Ya had become part of P'Ko, as much a part of P'Ko as Su'Zi, and Mi'Ka, and the mining community. Just as the mining community now includes P'Ko, especially after the Run with the Se'Ro'Bs and the Crystal Tear Ceremony. Now even though P'Ko is not aware of it, he's become part of the resistance. And now, Tn'Ya is part of them all, connected by only a few degrees of separation.

Mi'Ka, in order not to cause alarm, will need to make this reading seem superficial, focusing on safe yet pertinent subjects facing Tn', like the choice of professions and bio-mods. Then carefully Mi'Ka will be able to cozy up for a glimpse Tn's core motivation, Tn's source code.

It wasn't hard, the stated goal of the reading was job choice and bio-mods, all that was necessary was to create the right atmosphere, eliminate external distractions, light, sound, vibration, breezes, smells, and psychic noise. Then gently and imperceptibly introduce objects into the calm, observe and guide.

As they finished their tea, Mi'Ka got up from the tea-table and cleared the teapot and cups. Her tea table also doubles as a small group reading table.

Though they hadn't noticed it before, soothing music was playing in the background. The music gradually became more noticeable as specific systems built into the room gradually eliminated external stimuli. Sights and sounds from the street outside disappeared as the windows facing the street changed to an opaque black.

The lights dimmed and noise canceling systems eliminated the last of the external sound. The music itself became imperceptible and the slow breathing of Tn'Ya, P'Ko and Mi'Ka seemed to amplify.

The noise canceling systems of the room switched modes, and even the sound of breathing disappeared. It became so quiet that the internal rhythm of their hearts pumping, their gut processing their last meals and even the blood coursing through their veins seemed to creep forward to their perception.

Then Mi'Ka began, though the others were not aware that she did anything, the internal sounds disappeared and time appeared to lose meaning. Their internal systems appeared to slow; bodily awareness faded from perception.

A feeling of aloneness crept over them. As the feeling came over Tn'Ya, she instinctively sought out P'Ko and gathered comfort from him. P'Ko wasn't supposed to be an active participant. Mi'Ka had cautioned both P'Ko and Tn'Ya to stay center focused. This told Mi'Ka the extent that Tn'Ya needed P'Ko, even when P'Ko and Tn'Ya had no psychic connection Tn'Ya created P'Ko within herself, and Mi'Ka assessed that Tn'Ya did an excellent job.

Tn'Ya has a unyielding and unique psychic ability when it comes to P'Ko, Tn'Ya had, acting on Tn'Ya's own, and only passively on P'Ko's part permanently implanted P'Ko with herself.

This is rare among the young and usually only happens with mated couples that have birthed children. Tn'Ya isn't trying to be P'Ko, but Tn'Ya's so enamored, so devoted, so in love, that Tn'Ya's more than willing to make changes to herself to fit P'Ko's into herself as firmly and entirely as possible.

Tn'Ya is no threat to P'Ko or P'Ko's extended self, including Su'Zi, Mi'Ka, or the resistance. Now Tn'Ya is part of them even though they hadn't been aware of it. Mi'Ka noted to herself that Tn's connection with P'Ko wouldn't go unnoticed by the CA.

Today Tn'Ya's safe, Ku'Ma's been programmed to detect nano-bots, and would have alerted if Tn'Ya were infected. But it's impossible to prevent the CA from infecting Tn' with surveillance nano-bots without setting off alarms. And if the CASS is going to use her as a spy, they'll want her in close contact with P'Ko yet still maintain as much control of her as possible making it easier to harvest the nano-bot data.

If they're very careful, it could work to their advantage. Once Tn'Ya is infected, the CA will believe that Tn'Ya is a walking, talking recording and playback machine, they'll authorize almost anything that Tn'Ya asks, believing that it'll help get closer to P'Ko and through P'Ko learn about the activities of the resistance.

The resistance could use Tn'Ya as an unwitting double agent, and feed the CA false information. It would be risky, and they shouldn't let P'Ko know, not yet. He's not fully aware of the resistance and its activities. There's still the chance that the CASS might not infect her, they'll have to wait and see.

Tn'Ya's job choice, though at first glance should be a stand-alone decision, independent of everything else. However, to make their interactions smoother in the future, her job choice should complement P'Ko's and to be self-satisfied her bio-mods needed to be aesthetically pleasing to P'Ko.

Mi'Ka proceeded with the reading, Tn'Ya is not suited to be a mechanic. Mi'Ka used her connections to review her job aptitude and assessment test results and though she qualified for most jobs, what stood out was, computer system or network administrator, which would probably be too sensitive a position to be comfortable for the CA, which left tailor, chef, and fabricator. A fabricator would complement a mechanic well, and although the mining camps have their own fabricators, there are certain parts that the mechanics have to have made in Nu'Tn due to the materials involved and the complexity of the part. Mi'Ka floated the fabricator thought toward Tn'Ya and both Tn'Ya and P'Ko received it warmly.

Now for the bio-mods, Nu'Tn fabricators need little by way of bio-mods. Their jobs need little biological tweaking, nearsighted visual acuity, hand-eye coordination, attention to detail, and short term memory speed along with bandwidth. Attention to detail could make it difficult, to try to hide certain things from Tn'Ya and feed other things to her. Mi'Ka considered attempting to change the job choice, and float another option, but it was too late.

While she was second guessing the job choice, Tn'Ya and P'Ko had been solidifying the job choice and getting excited about the prospects of working together. She'd should have been more careful.

It was time to guide Tn'Ya and P'Ko as an observer toward thoughts concerning gender mods. The subject was a bit more conflicted. Tn'Ya wants anything that makes her more attractive to P'Ko. Mi'Ka detected from Tn'Ya thoughts of exaggerated gender-mods, more pronounced than Su'Zi's.

Her thoughts being that she could win over some of the physical attraction P'Ko displays for Su'Zi. But Tn'Ya was missing, at least in part, some of the most important driving or motivating factors behind P'Ko's attention to Su'Zi, those that have nothing to do with physical attributes. In thinking this Tn'Ya, completely missed many of the intricacies of interpersonal relationships and love that have nothing to do with physical attributes. Mi'Ka needed to help Tn'Ya decide what gender mods she would be happy and satisfied with.

What was left out of this scenario was that with most sex mods the mentor, or mentors, advise their pupils on what should make them happy. Tn'Ya wants what will make P'Ko happy, not what P'Ko and Su'Zi think will be good for Tn'Ya.

For this to work Mi'Ka needed to discover what would make Tn'Ya attractive to P'Ko, without P'Ko realizing it. Then, hopefully at the same time, let Tn'Ya experience or consider the mod, from her perspective and decide if she likes it or not. Were it not for P'Ko, Mi'Ka sensed that Tn'Ya would have leaned towards the male gender instead of female or could have even become U'Ne.

Once Mi'Ka nudged Tn'Ya into mentally trying on various bio-mods, Tn'Ya soon began to relish the experience. Especially when Mi'Ka allowed Tn'Ya the privilege of sensing P'Ko's participation.

It was essential that P'Ko participate in this exercise. However, Mi'Ka crafted the presentation of the thought so that P'Ko was unaware that he was viewing Tn'Ya. From P'Ko's perspective, he only rolled over various female gender mods to himself.

Tn'Ya's comfort and confidence level grew as the exercise progressed and she became more adept at mentally changing her gender mods shapes and sizes. She was getting genuine pleasure, getting a little excited as if it was a preliminary of things Tn'Ya hoped to come later.

P'Ko knew that the psychic reading was intended to include gender-mod selection, but was Mi'Ka successfully kept him unaware that his mental wanderings while he thought he was waiting for that portion of the psychic reading to begin, about the attractiveness of various gender mods, were being used to help guide Tn'Ya's selection.

In the timeless reading environment, unaware of what was going on. P'Ko started to enjoy the exercise, surprising himself when he became mentally aroused as he visualized his U'Ne friend becoming a tall, slim, attractive female, with gentle curves, undulating with desire.

He began to think that mentoring Tn'Ya wouldn't be such a difficult task after all. Tn'Ya not shielded from P'Ko's thoughts swelled with pride, excitement, and anticipation and though Mi'Ka attempted to prevent it, fell deeper in love with P'Ko.

Tn'Ya's gender mods were much different than Su'Zi's which would succeed in reducing some of the tension between her and Su'Zi. Since they wouldn't be competing physical attribute, to physical attribute, one would be exquisite and the other gorgeous. Tn'Ya would be taller, being a U'Te, slimmer, leaner with lighter, suppler, smoother skin, not nearly as strong as Su'Zi but with heightened touch sensitivity, dexterity, and flexibility, the outward displays of her femininity less pronounced. Tn'Ya's passion for P'Ko is stronger, but Su'Zi's love for P'Ko deeper and more mature.

Mi'Ka thought that Tn'Ya could benefit from martial arts training, but with her near guarantee of surveillance nano-bots, Martial Arts would be out of the question. Nonetheless, her absolute devotion to P'Ko appears hardcoded into her, and it will make her a force to be reckoned with. Making her a true asset to their virtual being. If, they manage to overcome the fears, jealousies, suspicions, possessiveness and distrust that will stand in their way.

Having achieved the goals of the reading, Mi'Ka slowly brought the participants back, reversing the process; they had started with at the beginning, except that now they felt more refreshed and clear minded with no haunting or underlying questions, all the issues they brought with them in their minds had been resolved.

P'Ko hadn't at the time thought that he was participating in Tn'Ya's decision-making process. He only thought that he had been mulling over the possibilities to himself independent of Tn'Ya and Mi'Ka. It was only afterward that he realized that he must have been participating when what he had concluded, supposedly to himself, was also what Tn'Ya and Mi'Ka came up with. Had he considered it more carefully, he would've realized that the process was atypical for him; there were none of his usual rounds of second-guessing and doubts.

Tn'Ya was happy and relieved. She had harbored anxiety and apprehension about her supposed necessity to surpass Su'Zi's gender mods, the thought of life with what she anticipated was needed to best Su'Zi's artful voluptuousness, had left her feeling overwhelmed and fearful that she could ever get used to them.

She was elated when, and for the first time P'Ko showed an aroused attraction to her and the slim, gently curving almost boyish look she was most comfortable with.

Mi'Ka activated the smart table before them, and the three of them reviewed the job selection and the bio and gender mods. It was settled. They celebrated with a small glass of sparkling punch and P'Ko escorted Tn'Ya home, Tn'Ya, utterly euphoric, strutted at P'Ko's side.

Chapter 42, Mi'Ka's Counselling of P'Ko and Su'Zi

This turned out to be a difficult time for P'Ko and Su'Zi. P'Ko still had some apprehensions about being Tn'Ya's mentor, particularly about Su'Zi. Su'Zi, on the other hand, viewed Tn'Ya as a rival for P'Ko's attentions, and Tn'Ya for her part had no malevolent intent or subterfuge, she just wanted to be part of P'Ko's life, not necessarily to the exclusion of others.

During the initial meeting between Mi'Ka, P'Ko and Su'Zi to review Tn'Ya's job choice and bio-mods. Su'Zi became belligerent, she challenged Tn'Ya's request to be P'Ko's Lr'Lng. Despite P'Ko's assurance that they would keep it a Mentor Lr'Lng relationship and emotionally detached.

Mi'Ka was forced to step in to mediate; she began counseling both P'Ko and Su'Zi. Mi'Ka soon realized that P'Ko and Su'Zi had bonded too strongly, too rapidly for a healthy relationship. Unlike Tn'Ya's open unconditional love for P'Ko; Su'Zi had developed a possessive kind of love, and forced them into the problem they now faced.

Tn'Ya's job selection and bio-mod requests were submitted, it was good that she had started her plans early, as recommended by the CA. They had nearly a year to work through things. It was trying for P'Ko and Su'Zi and entertaining for Mi'Ka. Who would have guessed that so much had to be done that had nothing to do with Tn'Ya directly? Mi'Ka in her eight hundred plus years of experience could only cite a few examples.

The counseling sessions lasted over many weeks, and included several periods when P'Ko and Su'Zi didn't see or contact each other. During those breaks Su'Zi and P'Ko returned to their mentors for refresher training on the recreational aspects of sex, and its distinction from love, pair bonding, and birthing.

Mi'Ka's counseling focused on dealing with Su'Zi and P'Ko's wants, desires and expectations about each other and their relationship.

It resulted in a cooling and maturing of their relationship, is was hard to accept and very painful at times. But in the end, left them more at ease, comfortable and more confident in themselves and each other. They had weathered a storm that threatened to wreak havoc on their relationship, surviving left them feeling better, stronger, and well balanced in the end.

By the time her counseling with P'Ko and Su'Zi concluded, Mi'Ka felt comfortable that the adjustments made to the virtual being that made up P'Ko and Su'Zi together were healthier and in better shape to handle whatever they may face in the future, including mentoring Tn'Ya and that Tn'Ya would become a valuable addition. The three of them together will have a very broad knowledge and capability background that combined will provide them the wherewithal to achieve things impossible, for each to achieve individually.

The question left is how to ensure the resistances continued secrecy. Mi'Ka was confident of Su'Zi's ability to guard the resistances secrets psychically, but P'Ko on the other hand, younger, natively U'Te and doubtful of his psychic abilities, he might have more trouble keeping the resistances secrets psychically.

This isn't a problem yet; P'Ko hasn't been introduced or even fully indoctrinated yet. There's no pressing need for P'Ko's involvement with the resistance, there's time for P'Ko to mature and train his psychic abilities.

Chapter 43, Tn'Ya's Mentoring

Tn'Ya arrived early at the Nu'Tn apartment that had been requested in the mentoring plan and authorized by the CA. The mentoring sessions P'Ko and Su'Zi had devised had been going well, after a slow, awkward start, they progressed quickly to an advanced academic explanation and familiarization process, then they evolved to the methodology they had now practiced for the last several weeks and were practicing again today.

There was a lot of talk in the beginning about the different aspects of sex, the difference between sex and love, different kinds of love, pair bonding even birthing. Tn'Ya wasn't too interested in these academic issues, feeling that they should come later, after she had some experience about what was being discussed.

Tn'Ya wasn't very psychic but got the distinct impression that P'Ko and Su'Zi had a particular interest in these academic parts and wanted to make sure that she knew all about these dry academic topics. With no psychic indicators, she wondered if maybe they were stalling and weren't sure how to proceed.

Tn'Ya knew when she asked P'Ko that he'd never mentored before and found out later that Su'Zi hadn't mentored either. So that may explain their uncertainty and delay. She could be patient; she had been waiting and looking forward to this for years.

At first, Su'Zi led the sessions, supported by P'Ko, which then evolved slowly and comfortably into some hands-on that resulted in turn to, playing doctor, learning and discovering how to give and achieve different types of stimulation. Then finally reset, then on to the role-playing that they're currently practicing.

Each session hosted by one of them, taking turns. The host gets to plan and design the activities of that particular session. The sessions progressed naturally geared to their level of comfort and confidence. As the mentoring sessions improved, the level of satisfaction and fulfillment increased.

Tn'Ya was able to ensure that her first reset was with P'Ko, it wasn't as private and intimate as she hoped, but she would cherish the moment for the rest of her life.

They had just started turn taking and depending on what was being practiced during the session; it allowed a certain level of physical and psychic privacy. She saw her chance and took it. It wasn't hard, she had come close to reset many times before, but held back. Then when she had the opportunity and the private moment, she couldn't hold back, she let herself go; the reset took over her entire being. She lost all sense of herself as the waves of pleasure rippled through her body, and she melted. Then, she felt herself fluid, letting herself engulf P'Ko, holding him with every fiber of her being, P'Ko didn't

211

resist but allowed himself to be cradled and caressed by her bodiless form until she finally returned to her senses and her body.

There was no possible way she could hide it. P'Ko had to know. He was gentle and kind, and never mentioned it or reprimanded her for going too far. Psychically, P'Ko let her know that he liked it too and that it was to be a cherished memory for both of them and never shared.

If it were possible Tn'Ya's love, respect, and admiration for P'Ko grew even more.

Su'Zi was apprehensive at first about mentoring Tn'Ya suspecting that Tn'Ya was only interested in further establishing and tightening her grip on P'Ko. Her fears were alleviated a little after she met Tn'Ya in person and diminished even more after the mentoring sessions started and progressed.

Tn'Ya wore her emotions and intentions openly; she was plainly in love with P'Ko, love, which in Su'Zi's estimation was innocent and immature. Su'Zi almost found herself worrying about P'Ko's ability to deal with such a devotee; he could easily, accidentally really hurt Tn'Ya's feelings.

It was evident that Tn'Ya's was entirely devoted to P'Ko. However, Su'Zi doubted it would stand the test of time; such a young, early love won't have much chance to survive.

Su'Zi's sessions, having been mentored by a couple herself; were well-versed on different threesome variations, two on one, one on one assist, one on two, the Y, Delta and others.

All this P'Ko was unfamiliar with, and Su'Zi quietly reveled in the knowledge that she was able to teach P'Ko something new and P'Ko seemed to enjoy every minute of it. She relished being in control and the center of attention.

All too often Su'Zi's sexual partners insisted or assumed that they were the ones that needed to be in constant control. P'Ko's preferred style, on the other hand, seemed to be more equal, give-and-take, more like a dance, frequently changing leads often during a single session.

Su'Zi's fears of Tn'Ya as a future mate rival slowly diminished, and Su'Zi began to take a liking to Tn'Ya. Tn'Ya emotionally very young, totally honest, naïve, innocently and unknowingly seemed susceptible to manipulation and coercion. Contrastingly, Tn'Ya's strength is her devotion to P'Ko, it is her foundation, she'd self-retire before allowing any harm to come to P'Ko. Su'Zi worried that that love could become a tool or lever the CASS could use to turn Tn'Ya into a weapon against the resistance, especially if the CASS could convince Tn'Ya the resistance meant to harm or intended to use P'Ko in a bad way.

Su'Zi would be sure to add these insights into Tn'Ya's record, initiated by Mi'Ka, who asked for Su'Zi's input shortly after Tn'Ya's reading with P'Ko. Tn'Ya's attitude toward the CA and the CASS is naïve, as with many other U'Te's, she has a favorable or at worst ambivalent attitude toward the ship's command and its enforcement arm. She's not concerned about being deprived of the knowledge of their intent, or knowing answers to secrets, that if revealed, in her mind, wouldn't change anything.

Tn'Ya doesn't realize that secrets in a totalitarian society allow for the exploitation of the people, turns them into mindless tools, devices, little more than machines carrying out the regime's grand plan... a grand plan that's not what they say it is.

The point of view of the resistance is that the secrets they're keeping don't support the stated goal of delivering Dadr'Ba, its crew, and cargo safely O'M. The resistance suspects something evil and malicious, why else would they be willing to kill to keep the secrets.

Mi'Ka's concern about P'Ko's ability to compartmentalize himself satisfactorily and be trusted with keeping Resistance secrets, a critically important matter, seems to be unfounded. More than once a partner in the throes of sexual intercourse has let slip private thoughts with disastrous consequences. P'Ko has demonstrated that he has a particular innate control even under the throes of passion.

It's no easy task to hide things when together, as one, exploring, understanding, giving and taking of each other's pleasures, searching for, finding, and sometimes even creating a stress or frustration, only to later satisfy it, letting go of inhibitions, then finally losing oneself in a final reset.

Even during their most intense mentoring sessions P'Ko displayed an instinctive ability to, without deceit, keep private that which needs to keep secret and share that which needs to be shared. He possesses a kind of natural psychic modesty that many naturally psychically adept Mi'Nr's take decades to develop and some never do.

P'Ko doesn't hide many of these things from Mi'Ka, a trusted, impartial third party; this shows an almost incredible level of psychic control Mi'Ka hadn't expected. Z'Shi may deserve credit for some of this; Mi'Ka will need to discuss it with her to help figure this puzzle out.

Tonight it was Tn'Ya's turn to lead the session, and she was to take a risk and do something she had fantasized about for a long time. It was risky and if it didn't go well could end their relationship. If successful, it would take them to an entirely new level of trust.

P'Ko and Su'Zi, her mentors, arrived together as was their custom, the three of them sat and drank a cup of tea; Tn'Ya had sought out a special tea, which wasn't psychoactive but was known to create a mood of calmness yet heightened awareness.

At the appropriate time, she revealed the lesson plan for the session. It involved her blindfolding and tying restraints to P'Ko and Su'Zi; then she would be the sole actor during the session.

Tn′Ya explained that her whole life she felt that she had never been in control, never trusted to be in control and that she had been pushed around and taken advantage of all her life. When she met P′Ko that first time and every time since, while she was with P′Ko she felt protected and didn't fear being taken advantage of.

This session would put her in control of others for the first time in her life. She made it clear that she cared deeply for P′Ko and Su′Zi and that she wouldn't dream of hurting them, they needed to trust her. She introduced a code word "Tff Ni"[96] but that they would be expected to remain silent, and keep their thoughts to themselves, but if for any reason; if they felt they had to end the session to end all they need to do is to recite "Tff Ni."

P′Ko and Su′Zi apprehensively agreed, Tn′Ya dimmed the lights, and while all were still fully dressed, she restrained their arms and legs and blindfolded them. Then waited while the tension built, guarding her mind as strongly as she could to prevent P′Ko and Su′Zi from reading what she intended to do next. She then touched both of them. First one, then the other trying to stay unexpected, heightening the tension, working deliberately to tease, increase their senses and raise their levels of arousal, slowly increasing the amount of contact, eventually rubbing her whole body against theirs.

The feeling of power and control she felt was exhilarating, she began to feel intoxicated, she then undressed them, slowly and carefully, untying an arm or leg as needed to accomplish the task. If one of them tried to reach out, she took hold of them gently and waiting until they relaxed the urge to move or reach.

At this stage, she took the blindfold off P′Ko and Su′Zi having placed a pillow between them so they couldn't tell that the other could see and then she began to undress, occasionally touching, P′Ko and Su′Zi with a part of her body or clothing she just removed or unveiled.

Once completely naked, she blindfolded P′Ko and moved the pillow to allow Su′Zi to watch as Tn′Ya worked on P′Ko. Nobody called the code word as Tn′Ya slowly and deliberately bought herself and P′Ko to a reset that sent spasms radiating through their bodies, Tn′Ya collapsing on top of P′Ko.

Oblivious to Tn′Ya, Su′Zi also reset, although much milder, just by watching and sensing the psychic energy. Tn′Ya then blindfolded Su′Zi and un-blindfolded P′Ko, allowing P′Ko to watch as Tn′Ya performed on Su′Zi with the same results.

When finished Tn′Ya got a basin of warm water, scented it with a perfume and bathed first P′Ko, then Su′Zi and finally herself. She then unbound them, satisfied and exhausted she lay down between P′Ko and Su′Zi and they all slept.

The session had lasted many hours, which meant it wasn't long before Su′Zi had to go to work. Tn′Ya and P′Ko got up and saw her off.

Everyone was in an excellent mood. They drank strong tea while discussing the night's session, ending with a toast. It was an entirely new

---

[96] Sounds like "Tiffany"

experience for them all, allowing each to experience and recognize new aspects of themselves, challenging and opening in certain real ways capabilities of trust and relinquishment within themselves that they had never experienced or exercised before.

As Su'Zi left for work, her parting comment was "don't do anything I wouldn't do." And not long after Tn'Ya and P'Ko were having for the first time, their own session. Yet, they both could feel Su'Zi's presence psychically.

Chapter 44, Chn'Gi Gets Religion

Chn'Gi entered the chapel late at night; she was troubled and desperate. What she was doing could result in forced retirement, she could be terminated, or just disappear, like so many others, to be declared never to have existed.

She knew of one person that she had personally known to have disappeared. A young person, younger than herself, a friend, single. He was living on his own. He just disappeared, his apartment turned up empty, entirely vacant. An available for occupancy, notice suddenly appeared, that had supposedly been posted for weeks.

All evidence that he ever existed was gone, photos and documents that had been stored in online storage disappeared. As well as, all government records. No one within the CA acknowledged he ever existed, and offline photos and documents were declared fakes.

Family and friends investigating were accused of psychiatric illness. The CA' response, was "That person, doesn't exist." Followed by a not-so-subtle hint, "I recommend you don't pursue this fantasy. It shows possible instability and may result in your psychiatric evaluation and treatment".

Alternatively, they were accused of contriving a prank, which prompted the CA response of "Stop wasting our time and attempting to file false complaints. This wastes CA resources and is A'Pa[97].

Chn'Gi had even heard of family members living together in an apartment who have disappeared. The family member's bedroom door would just vanish, replaced with a seamless wall. Any contact with the CA, met with, the same as before, "That person, doesn't exist" along with the same threats of psychiatric treatment, retraining or arrest. Most people painfully leave it at that and quietly mourn.

Those that don't, actually do get psychic evaluation and treatment. When they return, they've lost all joy of life, barely recognize their family or friends, and perform the functions of life robotically, having lost the spark, the joy of life.

Psychiatric treatment mostly happens to U'Te's, due to sheer numbers and the jobs involved. U'Te's can undergo psychiatric treatment without significant impact to maintaining their work quotas. The times it's been done among the Mi'Nr's, the victims of the treatment have met with "accidents" after their return in the mines.

The mines are a dangerous place; it doesn't take much impairment to turn a worker into a danger to themselves or their co-workers. The loss of a fully qualified Mi'Nr takes away a valuable resource that takes fifty to seventy-five years or longer to replace.

---

[97] Anti-progress activities and its violation carries the penalty of retraining or early retirement. One of the many charges leveled against the resistance.

Most Mi'Nr's that are condemned to psychiatric treatment, instead go into isolation at a forced labor cell. After fifty or a hundred years of forced isolation, made to perform tedious, hazardous or robotic tasks for extended periods of time, without contact with family and friends, come back changed. Not the vacant shells that are the fate of the treated U'Te's, They're altered, changed, they know what being forcibly retired is like. They have had much of their adult life taken away, bleeped out of existence and live a half-life, a part of their lives is a void, not unlike those that have had a loved one disappear.

Chn'Gi felt terribly alone; she had started having nightmares, terrible dreams. Foggy and out of focus, her dreams are of O'M, polluted with industrial waste, the atmosphere corrosive, the waters and oceans poisoned and diseased, and every major city devastated.

In her dreams of O'M, death abounds, so much death. Billions lay un-retired in the devastation that had once been cities, littered across countryside's and along shorelines. Millions float bloated, mixed among the debris of massive destruction carried to sea by some gigantic apocalypse.

Images that she saw of Or'Gn in the histories she was reading, she saw applied to O'M, but magnified manifold.

She dreamed too of Dadr'Ba, dead, broken, dirty, strewn with debris and most troubling, littered with bodies.

She thought of P'Ko, and Lu'Gs, she wants to trust them, but what if they are discovered and forced to tell, she could be found. She should warn them against reading this knowledge, but it might be too late.

She knows she's monitored; is she being followed? What do the people watching her know? She looked around and saw a few people nearby, was one or more of them following her? Are P'Ko and Lu'Gs suffering her same fate? She closed her eyes and practiced slow breathing, calming herself not very efficiently, wishing she had drunk just a little more liquor, just to calm herself down, reprimanding herself for being paranoid, is she going insane?

She shook herself back to the present, and reached into her pocket and felt the note she created during her last reading under the strange glow of the reading lamp Lu'Gs gave her and remembered his instructions always to use it whenever she studied the histories contained in the reader. Was it the lamp? Could it be doing something to her mind, it had become her habit to take long baths away from the surveillance cameras alone in her bathroom with only by the reading lamp for company.

She made it a point not to even look at the note she made after its creation. Palming the note and passing it to the usher, who shows just a hint of surprise, recovers quickly and welcomes her into the Church, directing her to a seat in one of the pews near the back. There were no services in progress, other worshipers were there, and others arrived, some appeared to be already praying, others meditating, some repeating a mantra, song like, not unpleasant, providing a tranquil aura.

At the front of the Church on one side was a podium, the other side stood several rows of seats for the choir. Behind the podium and the choir, a broad

arch that reached up to the top of the building and near the apex, a bright star
that lit the podium and choir area. It was strangely pleasant to look at, despite
its intense light. It illuminated the podium and choir area in a bright halo.

Along the back against a black backdrop, were racks upon which sat rows
of small translucent bowls, some containing a light, small and bright. The
unlit bowls, almost disappearing into the dark background.

At the near end of the racks, closest to the door, sat a credit reader for
donations and a dispenser for the light tabs. A simple gesture authorizes a
debit of your choice buying you a small tab that ignites when placed in one of
the clear bowls. The tab reacting with a catalyst in the bottom of the clear
bowl becomes a small bright pinpoint of light; the symbol of the Church and
the Touch of God.

Chn'Gi wanted to purchase a light, but had trouble moving, trouble
translating what she wanted to do in her mind into action.

The peace and serenity of this place were in such sharp contrast to her
visions that she found herself blinking and with each blink seeing flashes of
Dadr'Ba, this place, devastated. She saw flashes of O'M devastated, strange
dead faces sprawled before her eyes, flashed before her eyes, fueled by the
forbidden knowledge she was harboring. She became dizzy and started to have
trouble breathing. She felt flushed; her hands were shaking, and her spine and
legs lost all energy, and she slumped to the floor between the pews.

Chn'Gi was engulfed in a miasma; she could make out people speaking
words of encouragement. In the fog, she became aware that the usher and
some other person helped move Chn'Gi quickly along the side of the Church
through a door behind the podium into a hallway, then into an office. She was
laid on a couch with her legs raised, someone offering her something to drink,
then a brief examination, she was asked questions but didn't know if she even
answered, then followed an injection, it was all very dreamy, she closed her
eyes.

When she opened her eyes again, everything seemed different; she couldn't
tell how much time had passed. She couldn't afford to raise the attention of the
CASS following her and tried to get up mouthing "how long?" but was
interrupted. "It hasn't been long" and someone helped her sit up, it must have
been the other person that had appeared with the usher; the usher was gone.
The room's lighting had a strange tint to it. She recognized it as the same as
the light given off by her reading lamp.

A woman's voice said, "it's safe to speak, Chn'Gi." Chn'Gi forced out, not
caring anymore about the consequences, needing to get the poison out of her
mind and share her pain, desperate for help "I know, I mean, I've learned,
about Or'Gn." The woman, "How? Where did you get it?" Chn'Gi, "An old
reader, and backups from before the Touch."

The woman gave Chn'Gi something more to drink, saying that she had
become dehydrated and hadn't been eating properly. The drink will help make
her feel better and clear her mind.

As Chn'Gi's mind cleared, the woman told her that what she had done was very dangerous, but that she had made it to the right place to get help. Adding, that she could have died.

Whether it was the drink or the peaceful, safe and secure place she was in or the injection.

Chn'Gi began to feel better. Not knowing if it was the drink, it was cool going down and soothing to her stomach, or the woman's calm, confident, comforting words.

The woman identified herself as Gi'Ya. She explained to help properly; she must know more about what forbidden knowledge she was exposed to and if anyone else was exposed. Gi'Ya reminded Chn'Gi that "we're not the CA, and the CASS has no power in our spaces, though they try." "We must act quickly, though, if you are here too long. It will raise their suspicions; they'll send someone to check up on you."

Chn'Gi thankful to Gi'Ya for saving her life and feeling that a great weight was lifted off her shoulders, confessed all the forbidden knowledge she discovered. She talked "around" P'Ko's and Lu'Gs's involvement, not naming their names, but realized later that she gave enough info about them that the Church wouldn't have any difficulty figuring out who they were. But she trusted Gi'Ya and knew that the Church was at odds with the CA and especially the CASS, and hoped that Lu'Gs and P'Ko would be safe.

Not much time was spent on explaining the content of the forbidden knowledge; Gi'Ya seemed to know already and didn't ask any questions. She just let Chn'Gi perform her data dump.

Gi'Ya showed little outward emotion when Chn'Gi reported her discovery of IL on O'M and her reports to the Central Council. But by this time, Chn'Gi was feeling much better and starting to get her wits back. She detected hesitation in the woman's questions and responses and guessed that Chn'Gi's latest revelation was probably new information. She began to cut short her answers.

Gi'Ya with a sudden sense of urgency told Chn'Gi that she was going to be alright for tonight. The injection she was given will calm her, and it will last through tomorrow, adding that she should go to Mi'Ka's in Ol'Tn tomorrow, and get some tea. Mi'Ka will know what is needed and have it ready for her, and she should follow Mi'Ka's instructions.

Gi'Ya told Chn'Gi that the CASS has been dispatched to check on her, and she needs to go back out to the chapel and kneel and pray or at least pretend to pray before the CASS operatives arrive. Gi'Ya cautioned Chn'Gi to avoid liquor and not to read any more from the reader, but to "continue to use the reading lamp for privacy and come back immediately anytime, day or night, if you feel another attack coming on or whenever she feels the need." Adding "This is a peaceful calming place, even if you're feeling better come back in a week, or sooner if you feel the need, enjoy the peacefulness here and we'll talk more. Try not to worry; we'll help you."

Chapter 45, P'Ko's Quarters Broken into

P'Ko listened to the girl's voice singing through his TaC-B, she was accompanied by a band and had a steady beat. It was a Mi'Nr's song, made for working. It was the perfect accompaniment for performing routine cleaning and servicing of the bore head. None of the cutting disks had been identified as needing replacement, which would have made it at least a two-person job, so he was working alone. He had done this many times since the start of his apprenticeship and was trusted to accomplish the task alone. This work was considered routine, and all the critical components of the T'Bm and his work will be inspected before the start of the next day's bore.

P'Ko reflected on all that has happened since the beginning of his apprenticeship, the Run with the Se'Ro'Bs, Tn'Ya's mentoring, and P'Ko's father assigned a new job. P'Ko knew little about his Ba's new job, only that it was supposed to be a promotion. Then after he accepted discovered that it's in a secure area, tightly controlled by the CASS, he's forbidden to say anything about it.

The junkyard where P'Ko used to work was placed under CA control. Lu'Gs is making the best of it, is still there but was shuffled into a liaison position, saved from a total job reassignment by his in depth knowledge of the junkyard.

P'Ko put the bore head cleaning and servicing on autopilot as he frequently did with repetitive tasks and waxed philosophically. P'Ko thought how much of a double standard it is, the CA strictly forbids philosophy, but both the CA and the Church use philosophical arguments to bolster their positions.

It doesn't seem fair; the CA asserts that it's the CA's (and the Church's) right to decide on philosophical matters such as destiny and right and wrong. Individuals, on the other hand, are forbidden to raise a counter argument or self-derived philosophical concept. The people are expected to accept the tenants and dogma provided to them without question and never to contradict authority.

P'Ko knows that the CA and the Church can't stop people from thinking, the people that get into trouble are the ones that come out and begin debates or proselytize their views, views the CA, and the Church might have trouble defending against.

The Church is relatively immune from philosophical attack; it simply falls back on faith. A religious concept once accepted as an article of faith is impossible to argue against or logically defeat. How can you argue against something that doesn't exist in the physical world and is backed by doctrine?

The psychic ability that all the people of Dadr'Ba are conceived and born with is molded and reinforced during the ToG Ceremony, which serves as the basis of its religion. The workings of it remain an unexplained mystery and provides a solid platform for the Church, where science fails faith prevails.

The Church and the CA work together, though they wouldn't openly admit it.

The Church cares about the people, their feelings, and emotions, their hopes, and cares. Its role is to supply a peaceable stable, productive and reproductive workforce for the CA.

The CA's role is the running of the ship, and its multitude of interacting pieces, parts, mechanisms, structure, and infrastructure, guiding it to O'M. The CA, unlike the Church, abuses its authority by many orders of magnitude. Using its role as the governing command and control of the ship as its power base, the elite in control of the ship have disenfranchised the people and strives with its multitude of secrets, indiscriminate punishments, restrictions on speech, to turn the ship into a massive machine.

Are the people so dangerous that they can't be trusted to gather and talk about things, anything, without presenting a danger? P'Ko didn't think so.

P'Ko moved to a different section and continued his work. The trouble with doing this particular maintenance routine is that most of the work must be done while the equipment is shut down, cutting into the time he could be spending was Su'Zi. It even cuts into the time he could spend with Tn'Ya, but not as bad.

Being Tn'Ya's mentor gave P'Ko a sort of respected teacher status, which has helped keep Tn'Ya at a safe distance, yet comfortably cordial.

P'Ko had doubts that Su'Zi would accept the situation with Tn'Ya but after her initial anxious, hostile rejection followed by their counseling with Mi'Ka, she accepted it. As a matter of fact, they seemed to hit it off. The three of them have become friends, even maintaining a physical relationship, sometimes two's and sometimes three's, but, thanks to Mi'Ka's counseling, staying within the bounds of a continued mentoring relationship.

Tn'Ya's devotion to P'Ko remained undaunted, she's been slow to make other friends at her apprenticeship in sector three's fabrication shop, but progress has been achieved.

All in all, P'Ko was satisfied and comfortable with the P'Ko, Su'Zi, Tn'Ya multiself they've created. As far as P'Ko could envision they seem destined to continue to be best friends. P'Ko could foresee after some years the Mentor respected teacher relationship toward Tn'Ya will fade. It could be possible for Tn'Ya to pursue a more romantic relationship with P'Ko and he wondered if he would be against it and how that might work out and what kind of couple they would make.

He and Su'Zi aren't mated and haven't even discussed it yet; they're decades away from that discussion. Both are still each other's best boyfriend and girlfriend. P'Ko put the thought of future mates out of his mind, there will be plenty of time for that later, and if Su'Zi sensed these thoughts it could cause unnecessary and meaningless hurt feelings. P'Ko instead focused on the good things, here and now.

Instead of creating frustration and drifting apart, the differences in jobs, locations, and work schedules, only seemed to heighten the anticipation for their meetings and gave each plenty to share with the rest when their schedules allow them to meet.

Messaging technology helps, but Su'Zi always mistrusted messaging, and P'Ko has grown reluctant to trust it too. The messaging system is operated and maintained by the CA, and they have grown to prefer, if not in person, mutual visits to virtual worlds, harder to monitor. Their favorite virtual meeting place is Vr'Chm, P'Ko and Su'Zi introduced Tn'Ya to "their beach" and Tn'Ya loved it. Unbeknownst to Tn'Ya, they also had her occasionally visit their private room, Tn'Ya never recognizing the protections in place. P'Ko and Su'Zi furnished it, and instead of being bare, decorated it similar to an apartment that one would find in Capsule Flats, complete with personal touches.

P'Ko thought of people who go through their entire lives without establishing multiselves[98]. He, Su'Zi and Tn'Ya make a trio multiself. There are community multiselves, U'Te's aren't a good example, they're not a close knit community, but Mi'Nr's are, and P'Ko had to admit D'En's even without much psychic ability are an excellent example of a community multiself.

P'Ko replayed in his mind the feeling he had during the Run with the Se'Ro'Bs. Running down dark tunnels, not as an individual, but as a group, seeing and sensing not only from his senses but the whole group's senses. It was awe-inspiring; he actually felt connected; he felt larger and stronger than any one person could ever feel. Even toward the end, when at times he thought it was just he and the Se'Ro'Bs, he knew that his pack was with him, sharing his experience of the chase.

P'Ko thought of the Mi'Nr multiself-community; he had become comfortable and felt accepted, but he still didn't have the full feeling of oneship with the Mi'Nr community as a whole. Not like he felt on the run.

He still had so much to learn about the job and Mi'Nr life; he hadn't yet visited the community school in the Mining Camp or visited many Mi'Nr homes. He had so many things he needed to learn to have the core, base knowledge needed to be one with the Mi'Nr community.

P'Ko wondered how long it would take him to learn the core Mi'Nr knowledge necessary to really, truly become "one" or how he would even gain the more esoteric knowledge. He didn't know if he would ever achieve it completely, Mi'Nr's are born a Mi'Nr, they live a Mi'Nr's life from Bo'Ba's and know no other. Will he ever really be a Mi'Nr or will he always be on the edge?

There are many multiselves, they're not exclusive, a person can be part of a Mi'Nr multiself and part of a gender multiself, and family multiself. Sports fans are multiselves, some multiselves are short lived, a sports team fan multiself's might only last the length of a game. But P'Ko felt that he would have a

---

[98] The bond with family and friends and people you identify with that creates a virtual being capable of independent action, influenced but not totally controlled by any single member.

special bond with his pack from the Run with the Se'Ro'Bs for the rest of his life.

P'Ko expanded his thought and wondered about the Church, the CA, and even the Dadr'Ba multiself. He was a minuscule part of their multiself's. Did that make him in some small way responsible for the atrocities that the CASS was conducting? Then he thought, no, the complacent ones were passively complicit, he wasn't complacent, but he wasn't exactly actively trying to make things better either.

How did the Dadr'Ba multiself go so wrong and allow the CA to take control? And turn Dadr'Ba into a victim, keeping so many secrets, using, and persecuting its people?

The root of the problem had to be the military origin of Dadr'Ba's command structure and the creation of the Central Council to manage and run things. The Central Council had become too strong, and too independent, too disconnected from the people.

People had gotten too wrapped up in their personal lives and ignored what was going on around them, thereby relinquished any say they may have once had regarding the management of Dadr'Ba.

The Central Council forgot who they owe their existence to. Instead of serving the Dadr'Ba community the CA is making the Dadr'Ba community serve them. To make matters worse, it's an unchallenged rumored that the Central Council is virtually powerless, that it is dominated by the Commander and his henchmen that use rank, bribes, intimidation, threats and blackmail to neuter the other members of the council, gutting the council of its authority. Leaving control of the ship practically to one person, alone, not even a multiself.

That instant P'Ko got the TaC-B alarm from the sack safe in the bottom of his footlocker, he knew that somebody was in his quarters, had found and was attempting to probe or open his sack safe. P'Ko dropped his tools and scrambled through the hatch at the T'Bm bore head and within seconds was racing toward his quarters near the other end of the T'Bm. As P'Ko got to the crew quarters hallway, he spotted someone outside the door to his quarters.

What happened next occurred so fast, P'Ko had time only to react, not to think. Only afterward would he have a chance to replay the events in his mind and try to make some sense of it. At first, the intruder didn't see him, P'Ko saw him but didn't sense him. Then an alarm began sounding from above the intruder. P'Ko glanced up and saw something move, it was the size and roughly the same shape as Mi'Ka's Ku'Ma. As soon as it stopped moving, it seemed to disappear.

The intruder turned away from the door and looked directly at P'Ko. They made eye contact, but P'Ko still didn't sense him psychically… the intruder was invisible. The person P'Ko looked at is clearly a Mi'Nr and wore a data helmet similar to one that he'd worn during training.

P'Ko couldn't get over the fact that he couldn't sense him, especially, considering the expression on the intruder's face. The expression of shock, apprehension and something P'Ko had trouble isolating without psychic clues, maybe pain, or longing.

The thief shouted something over the alarm coming from the bot on the ceiling; it may have been "let's get out of here." There must have been someone inside P'Ko's quarters. Then, with one hand the intruder pulled open the front of his overalls with one hand and reached in with the other. Strangely the intruder awkwardly turned more than necessary giving P'Ko a glimpse inside his overalls.

P'Ko for a split second saw the glint of metal where the intruder's inner clothes should have been. Then the thief withdrew something from an inside pocket and threw a small object towards P'Ko. Though P'Ko's first impulse was to catch it, which would have been easy, an impulse warned him otherwise. Instead of snagging the thing out of the air as it passed his shoulder, he dodged it.

It detonated with a blinding flash, the overpressure, like a tunnel collapse, forced him forward pinning him to the floor. They must have been thieves, but what would they be stealing? Theft is a serious crime, with serious punishments. The multitude of surveillance systems scattered throughout Dadr'Ba ensured nearly all thieves get caught, making theft rare. But if it's not theft, what was it?

It took a few moments for P'Ko to recover and as the tunnel vision caused by the force of the explosion began to fade, and his eyes focused, P'Ko saw two Mi'Nr's in work coveralls exit the hallway leading to the stair down to the lower level. P'Ko crawled forward his equilibrium slowly returning.

Some of the rest of the crew that stayed, electing not to go to the Camp or Ol'Tn began to arrive on the scene from their quarters and the recreation room. They helped P'Ko up, questioning what had happened. P'Ko quickly explained but didn't go into detail about what these intruders or thieves may have been after.

By this time, P'Ko realized that the only thing of real value, in his sack safe, the only thing that would be worth killing or being killed for must have been the reader and the data cartridge it contained.

A search ensued, and it was soon discovered that the culprits entered through the processed fuel transport tube. They cut into it a couple of levels up and descended into the T'Bm, in their haste to leave, they left where they broke into the delivery tube open. The tool marks that remained made it apparent that they had planned on sealing it, but their being discovered spoiled their plans.

An investigation ensued, the intruder's showed on no security cameras. P'Ko identified them as Mi'Nr's. No Mi'Nr's had ever been turned and worked for the CASS. The psychic ability of the Mi'Nr's would have quickly discovered it.

It was possible that the CASS could have taken one of their detainees, perhaps, thought dead by the community, and not expecting to get caught, they could have coerced them into doing the job.

It was evident that reporting it to the Up'Lndrs, in spite of their advanced forensic tools, was a waste of time. There's no way this is going to be reported outside the mining community, and it's equally obvious that this wasn't an ordinary theft.

P'Ko's sack safe that had alerted him was an old model that P'Ko upgraded with a scan alarm. By looking at the sack safe there was no way to tell that the sack safe had a scan alarm, that was the intruders mistake. When the thieves tampered with the sack safe and scanned it to discover its contents and access code it alarmed.

There was something about the intruder that he saw, something about the way he acted. It was like the intruder was trying to tell him something, the intruders could have killed P'Ko.

As near as P'Ko could tell nothing was touched in his quarters, but later when the Mi'Nr investigator arrived with specialized equipment, equipment that P'Ko was surprised that the Mi'Nr's possessed, and performed a scan, a surveillance device was detected and carefully removed.

Chapter 46, P'Ko's Burglary Investigation

Su'Pr Ve'Ln led the investigation, Mi'Ka assisted, and more surveillance devices were discovered, not just in P'Ko's quarters, but elsewhere as well, which initiated a thorough search of other T'Bm's, mining camps and key locations in Ol'Tn's.

Analysis of the devices provided emission signatures that made it easier to discover others but yielded no clues to who was responsible. The CASS was the prime suspect, though the Church, as noble as they strive to be, is known to have its intelligence requirements, and motivations for keeping tabs on the Mi'Nr's.

The suspicion of the Church increased when P'Ko shared his experience from the Touch of God ceremony followed by the not so discreet surveillance he was subjected to afterward.

Mi'Ka conceded that the Church probably surveilled P'Ko but had nothing to do with the break in. Based on these few data points, using her psychic ability and centuries of experience living under CA control, Mi'Ka became convinced that the Mi'Nr's involved were Prz'Nr's forced to help the CASS.

The metal glint P'Ko saw beneath the coveralls must have been a shield device preventing psychic communication. The CASS has been working for centuries studying psychic abilities and how to understand control and exploit them. The vest probably included a remotely controlled explosive, known to be used by the CASS in the past to control Prz'Nr's.

The data helmet communication device the perpetrator wore was probably used to direct the actions of the Mi'Nr from a control center somewhere.

A course of action evolved. First, they needed to find out more about the intruders and who's behind them.

226

Chapter 47, CASS Report on Failed Burglary

CASS Director Chi'Yo sat at his desk staring at the report, his anger and frustration surging, not so much, by what the report contained but by what it didn't.

This idiot Sh'P'Po standing before him should be retired immediately. He's being forced to risk his career, his hard-earned status, his life... on this clumsy buffoon. He was sorely tempted to reach for the weapon in his desk drawer and retire this idiot, now.

Chi'Yo continued to stare at the report and ironically found himself practicing the mental calming techniques that his surveillance agents had discovered Chn'Gi beginning to practice.

Sh'P'Po stood at attention, facing Chi'Yo across the desk that separated them, and watched.

Chi'Yo stared at his report, thinking through the disaster. Okay, the operation failed, that's one of the risks in this business.

But based on their analysis and profile of P'Ko and his financials, he shouldn't have been able to afford a scan alarm model, and the records show that he purchased a non-scan alarm model. There's no way the team could have known that that Dr'T loving U'Te P'Ko upgraded it himself. EXCEPT, for the fact, plain in his record, that P'Ko is a mechanic and a good one too, and had access to the components and tools to do the sack safe upgrade himself.

They should have suspected and came prepared, but to get that level of expertise down in a T'Bm would have meant using a D'En agent in an exoskeleton equipped eSuit instead of those stupid Prz'Nr's[99]. He and his advisors should have known they would eventually get caught; there had been close calls before.

But an exoskeleton equipped D'En's sneaking into an operating T'Bm even off shift is a recipe for disaster. It's like sounding off with loud speakers "Hey, everyone, we're not supposed to be here! And we're up to no good!"

Studying the report, Chi'Yo saw that they got sloppy, they deviated from the plan, and took too long. They were directed to plant the surveillance devices and look around for and investigate anything that could be linked to the resistance, including the cheap budget model sack safe purchase records indicated P'Ko had.

They failed to check the sack safe for an alarm and failed to detect the silent alarm when it went off. Had they aborted as soon as the alarm went off they would have been free and clear. This stupid P'Ko that discovered them would have come running to an empty room and would have thought it a false alarm.

---

[99] Prz'Nr – sounds like and means prisoner.

Using the Prz'Nr's was the right choice; they had been used many times before, though there had been close calls, they should have been prepared. Now on one of the few times he wasn't in the Op Center the Op'Cm (Operation Commander) and operators panicked and aborted. And they failed to have an adequate abort plan in place.

It's good they didn't get captured, but they did have time in Chi'Yo's estimation to nab P'Ko and have him "disappear." P'Ko would've made an excellent addition to the Prz'Nr team. There are a couple of members showing signs they're overdue for retirement, well not retirement, there would be no passing, we should call it "tech refresh."

Word of this episode with P'Ko has undoubtedly made it back to the rest of the Prz'Nr's. He might have to increase the drugs being fed to the Prz'Nr's to keep them complacent, but that slows them down and can even be hazardous in a mining environment.

Using one of his provocation techniques on them to keep mindful of the "rules" might be appropriate. Blame this episode on the Prz'Nr's and withhold spices and take away their food texturizer for a month or so. Make them eat tasteless mush. Or better yet, it's been a decade or more since the last mock-E (mock execution) and probably a century since the last real one. Each time it's successfully motivated/subdued the Prz'Nr's. Mock-E's have even energized ones he has been considering for a tech refresh. Chi'Yo made a mental note to implement a mock-E, soon, that should head off some of the trouble that this fiasco may cause and keep the Prz'Nr's good for another decade or so.

Chi'Yo looked up at Sh'P'Po, as stupid and incompetent as Sh'P'Po is, he still the best he's got for dealing with the Mi'Nr's. This episode has been an enormous setback, but this lousy excuse for a Chief of Mpr'ISR[100].

To Sh'P'Po's credit, and Chi'Yo's dismay, Sh'P'Po has successfully eliminated or undermined his competition, securing his position, and populated his staff with people even more incompetent than himself, guaranteeing that there's no one qualified, and has the specialized knowledge and experience to promote over him or replace him.

Bringing a replacement in from the outside, would take time and placing someone from the outside in charge Sh'P'Po's staff of hand-picked and groomed nincompoops, who are totally dependent on Sh'P'Po for intelligent action, is as good as not having a Mpr'ISR program at all.

But, right now something is better than nothing, and Chi'Yo, with practically no psychic ability, knows that Sh'P'Po knows it.

"There better not be any more mistakes, I'm putting you on notice, you can be replaced" Chi'Yo lied, Sh'P'Po held back a smile. Chi'Yo continued "it would have been better if there had been an unexplained fire or an explosion, destroying all the evidence, including that P'Ko character, rather than tipping off those, godforsaken, Dr'T's" to our operations.

---

[100] Mining Personnel Intelligence Surveillance and Reconnaissance sounds like mipper-eye-ess-are rhymes with sipper-I-S-R.

"You left out of your report that since this mission failed, most of the surveillance nodes in the T'Bm's and mining camps have dropped offline. Even our Ol'Tn sensor network took a hit; the remaining modes are practically worthless. It's going to take us decades to recover. Thanks to your mistake; we're nearly blind and deaf to what's going on with the resistance. We could have a repeat of the equal job rights protests and a general strike." Sh'P'Po's held back his smile.

Sh'P'Po wanted to say 'Calm down, there's no risk of a protest or strike, the resistance isn't that powerful. We have enough soldiers now to crush them', but instead quoted another report that he'd read once before. "The Mi'Nr's are volatile but disciplined; our modeling shows that they won't strike as long as we don't press them too far. There's a small percentage of hotheads, which we could take out with a minimal loss of production, but the models show that if we do, the rest of the Mi'Nr's will strike. There's been no open obstruction to our activities so what's there to worry about?"

Sh'P'Po continued, "As for the U'Te's they're so stuck in their day-to-day routine, most can be treated like machines, nothing short of a total collapse of security and public release of our secrets would rile them up."

Chi'Yo stared at Sh'P'Po as he talked, he felt himself getting hot. He wasn't breathing, even though Sh'P'Po spoke the truth, he couldn't let this challenge to his authority go unpunished. Chi'Yo let Sh'P'Po finish and waited, then taking a deep breath, as if he was preparing to leap across the desk and rip Sh'P'Po to pieces.

Chi'Yo glared at Sh'P'Po, waited for the gravity of the situation to sink in. Finally, after a long silence Sh'P'Po fidgeted and Chi'Yo said "I don't like not knowing what my enemy is up to, it's not a risk that we can take, it jeopardizes the success of our mission. Do you want to leave reaching O'M to chance, after almost two thousand years? I'm placing you on restriction. You're excused." Stunned, Sh'P'Po turned sharply and left Chi'Yo's office.

Chi'Yo sat back in his chair, Sh'P'Po shouldn't have been so arrogant; he forgot the situation, and who he was speaking to. The fool should have taken what was going to be a verbal reprimand and let it go, instead, he attempted to minimize the magnitude of his mistake and lecture "Me."

Let Sh'P'Po stay on restriction for a while and see who steps up from within Sh'P'Po's organization to fill in the gaps just created by Sh'P'Po's restriction. A restriction that will last as long as it takes for Sh'P'Po to apologize and show due deference and respect to his superiors.

Chi'Yo couldn't help but think that this episode will remain in both of their memories as a sign of Chi'Yo's weakness, he should have had Sh'P'Po executed but given the situation he couldn't. Chi'Yo will have to break Sh'P'Po or find a replacement.

The report will need to be edited before going to the Commander and Central Council. To avoid blame towards himself, the new report will have to minimize the impact of the failed mission and somehow have a positive twist.

I could say that it was planned to provide the resistance a false sense of confidence and make them open to exploitation.

Chi'Yo wished he could leave the report unedited, place all the blame on Sh'P'Po and execute him, but without a replacement he couldn't. If he did Chi'Yo would have to step in and perform Sh'P'Po's role. But this would send a message to the Commander and the Council that his organization is flawed.

Better to do it this way, restricting Sh'P'Po's is right, Chi'Yo decided to give a few of Sh'P'Po's responsibilities to an aspiring lieutenant, that would put more pressure on Sh'P'Po and begin prepping a potential replacement.

Chi'Yo's mistake was not having replacements lined up for all his key people; he resolved not to make this mistake again.

As they been nearing O'M the attitude on Dadr'Ba has changed, it's improved, but he can't afford to take any chances. In the long run, they'll get their surveillance nodes back online, but it shouldn't matter, they will reach O'M soon.

But he can't stand not knowing; his desire to be in total control was overpowering, even now the lack of inside knowledge about the resistance was beginning to eat at him.

Chi'Yo called Ol'Tn and made arrangements for a massage and some private entertainment to be discretely delivered to his secret flat in lower Nu'Tn, then got up and left through the back entrance to his office.

Chapter 48, Meeting of the Resistance

Despite the insulation of the eSuit, P'Ko could feel Su'Zi's warmth as he sat close behind her with his arms around her on the quad, of course, it could have been psychic warmth, P'Ko still had trouble distinguishing his physical senses with his psychic sense.

They weren't going slowly; P'Ko didn't think Su'Zi knew how to go slow, she placed in the top three in the quad category in the last race, excellent for her first race using a quad.

So far P'Ko hadn't managed to make the winners bracket in any of the races he's entered so far. He still has trouble adjusting to the higher G's at, the lower levels even while operating a vehicle. The G's seem to do something to his senses that he hasn't yet been able to master, to program himself around. But he's not going to give up; it can't be much harder than the self-programing, he accomplished when he enhanced his low light vision.

Su'Zi was taking him down to the outer edge of Dadr'Ba. His intellect told him that he's never been here before, but his psyche was trying to tell him otherwise. It was maddening; he must be confusing it with one of the passages he'd been down during the Run with the Se'Ro'Bs or was he picking up something psychically from Su'Zi?

P'Ko cursed to himself; he hates when he gets like this, all psychically upside down. As if on cue, Su'Zi sent him a reassuring thought. P'Ko took a deep breath, calmed his mind and allowed the G's to press himself closer to Su'Zi, and she wiggled closer to him and sped the quad down through a dip, squeezing them together even more. Su'Zi interrupted P'Ko's thought, "Don't get any ideas for a detour, save that for another time, we're almost there and the meeting is getting ready to start."

They rounded a bend taking a dip, then reversed through a narrow opening that opened up into a wider passage that had an assortment of vehicles aligned down one side. Su'Zi parallel parked the quad and P'Ko dismounted followed by Su'Zi.

They were at the very edge of Dadr'Ba now. P'Ko felt like he was made of lead, especially his arms and legs, he was tempted to go down on all fours, but seeing Su'Zi standing upright, P'Ko fought the impulse. He followed Su'Zi over to a hatch that was smooth against the side of the passage. Su'Zi accessed the hatch; it belonged to an old derelict ship.

P'Ko recognized the model, there were some at Lu'Gs's yard, it was a transport used to ferry the crew, materials and supplies from Or'Gn's spaceport to Dadr'Ba. It had to have been one of the last to provide Dadr'Ba and instead of returning to Or'Gn was intentionally impacted into Dadr'Ba. The transports awkward orientation meant that Dadr'Ba was probably rotating, and it must have been traveling at a pretty high velocity at impact and would have had to shoot anchors into Dadr'Ba to prevent it from being flung back out into space.

P'Ko wondered what sort of act of desperation would cause someone to make such a risky maneuver. The hull of the transport would have almost certainly have damaged.

P'Ko didn't have much time to wonder because, once inside, he was surprised to see a group of people that he hadn't sensed before entering. He was welcomed by Mi'Ka, who hobbled around much like she did in Ol'Tn at the end of the Run with the Se'Ro'Bs despite the G's.

Mi'Ka introduced him in a conventional way to the others; it was dark, but P'Ko made out their features well enough. As Mi'Ka introduced them, she told him psychically that the names she was using were not their real names but their codenames. It was very rare for a meeting such as this to occur; the cells within the resistance, as a rule, never met directly. P'Ko sensed that he was the reason the group gathered, this was an interview, an interview that had to be in person.

After the introductions, P'Ko realized that while Mi'Ka was introducing him and distracting him, by providing unspoken psychic commentary. The people he was meeting were examining him, psychically and physically. They were very discreet, and he didn't realize it was happening until the end of the introductions. When he began receiving psychic thank you's and congratulations on having passed the "interview."

P'Ko's original sense of trickery and violation was soon replaced with awe, operating here at the edge of his capability in the presence of the top echelon of the mining community. P'Ko was surprised to see past the assembled group a telecommunications system set up against the back wall the communications system display was divided into four quadrants, each connected to another location within Dadr'Ba, undoubtedly linked by a PST (Phase Synched Transmission) impossible to tap or monitor without detection.

The gravity of the situation was matched by the G's of the environment; every step at four G's was a deliberate effort. P'Ko had never before stood and walked so much in it. As much as he wanted to he couldn't crawl, not while everyone else stood. After a while, he began to discover subtle tricks to make it easier. He started to like it; he felt like he was on a plateau of solid rock, his muscles straining, were forced into a new calibration, he felt a new strength and stability, feeling like his legs and backbone were solidifying, thickening, becoming carbon-fiber columns.

Taking it all in P'Ko took a deep breath and settled his weight onto a sturdy shipping container near one side, next to Su'Zi as Mi'Ka made her way to the front at the other end of the one-time passenger/cargo hold of the derelict ship.

The group led by Mi'Ka began a heated discussion about what to do about the Prz'Nr's. P'Ko didn't at first know what they were talking about, but soon figured out that two of the intruders that had attempted to search his quarters, were Prz'Nr's held by the CASS, and there were others. His encounter with them led to the discovery that the CASS was secretly holding Mi'Nr's Prz'Nr and using them for forced labor.

Shortly after the break-in, clued to their existence, the resistance asked the right questions to the right people, who in turn investigated and at great risk to themselves confirmed their suspicions. Secret Prz'Nr's are being held in specially designed cells that the CA had been able to seal off from psychic detection with specially energized seals and alloys.

Outside their cells the Prz'Nr's are made to wear a special gear that blocks psychic transmissions, vests fitted with a destruct mechanism and head gear with communications gear turning the Prz'Nr's into a living, breathing robot made to follow the CASS's orders or be killed along with anybody in the vicinity.

To infiltrate the prison, the resistance needed someone that with little in the way of disguises could pass for D'En, has expertise as a mechanic and has psychic abilities, which narrowed the candidates down to a few trusted U'Te's and P'Ko. P'Ko's strength and martial art knowledge would allow him to beat any hostile D'En's or U'Te's, so P'Ko was the logical choice.

What worried everyone, are the soldiers guarding the Prz'Nrs.

Chapter 49, Prison Routine

It was a slow process; using their network of informants, the resistance gathered information and began analyzing the pattern of life of the Prz'Nr's and guards. They studied the outside of the box that held the Prz'Nr's and what went in and what came out, unable to penetrate inside the prison cells where only the Prz'Nr's and the soldiers guarding them are allowed. Gradually and deliberately the resistance assembled and analyzed every detail, working up a hypothesis about what lay inside. There are five Prz'Nr's; they're kept in an isolated area of Zone One separate from ordinary Prz'Nr's serving fixed sentences. These five Prz'Nr's had been supposedly executed, but now make up a team forced to mine Dadr'Ba's asteroids for "special" materials while under constant monitoring by the CASS.

The "special" materials mined by the Prz'Nr's don't appear to go into the regular production cycle for any of Dadr'Ba's standard functions; they go to a secret D'En fabrication shop for processing from there it seems to disappear. All the resistance could determine was that when fab shop finished it work, the finished "special" material bypassed Dadr'Ba's inventory of energy, food, infrastructure, or consumer products. The special material goes directly to a customer, without any accounting or documentation. The variety of special materials going into the Fab shop indicates a wide range of products must be being produced.

Based on information gathered from informants and P'Ko's description of the break-in, they know the crew is made to wear surveillance equipment and kill-vests, and the CASS has discovered a way to block psychic communication.

After careful mapping, the resistance found a dedicated series of passageways and elevators blocked from all other traffic and monitored round the clock with cameras and motion sensors. Since there have been no reports of sightings, these must provide the passages between the confinement area and the worksite.

The blocked off areas change over time depending on which asteroid is being mined, which is determined by what special material is needed. Access to the blocked off passageways is through an entry control point guarded by a soldier.

The mining operation is all old-style. Acoustic and seismic monitoring of the area shows that no T'Bm's are in use, only small blasts, picks, and shovels, undoubtedly to ensure that the special materials recovered are undamaged.

They need to be careful it's taken months to get to this point, a mistake now would jeopardize everything and bring soldiers down into the mines and probably cost the lives of the forced mining labor crew being held, Prz'Nr.

P'Ko, Tn'Ya and Su'Zi have practiced for weeks the resistance's newest weapon, they took an ordinary pocket sized inspection tool, and transformed it into an enhanced microbot, the pocket-sized robot that he and most other mechanics carry that enable them to send eyes and ears into a troublesome machine to discover what's wrong before tearing the thing apart.

Working with the resistances' engineers P'Ko and Tn'Ya had created something virtually undetectable. Equipping with translucent legs, with a layer of radar absorbing adaptive camouflage covering its body, low power systems utilizing a tiny shielded source of energy, that keeps electromagnetic emissions low during operation and virtually nonexistent at rest.

P'Ko's tricked out pocket knife sized diagnostic tool was now stealth rover with enough power to run for hundreds of hours, but at a low power draw consequentially forcing draconian TTP's (Tactics Techniques and Procedures) regarding power usage and levels. Never being able to do more than one thing at a time well, constantly prioritizing and scheduling all activities.

P'Ko, Su'Zi, and Tn'Ya learned to make the microbot a virtual extension of themselves, becoming nearly as comfortable with its controls and sensors as their bodies. Its sensors are not the most powerful or long range. They're made to operate close up, almost touching the thing to be analyzed are designed to be sensitive and accurate. A jammer using technologically related to the reading lights sometimes used to cover covert activities. Simple, efficient and challenging to develop counter-countermeasures for topped off the microbot's defensive suite.

Tn'Ya's expertise, knowledge of the latest fabricating techniques, and a deft hand in using micromanipulators was instrumental in designing, miniaturizing, fabricating and integrating the new features into P'Ko's pocket microtool transforming it into a stealthy remotely operated roving observation platform and science laboratory.

The CASS uses surveillance bots too; CASS minibots are general purpose, a mobile version of their fixed site video surveillance network. Elaborate stealth is necessary for these bots since the CASS uses them as a deterrent, for real stealth they use other methods like the nanobot blood implants.

Minibots are huge in comparison to the resistance microbot and hundreds of times heavier; they are equipped with EO (Electro-Optical), IR (Infrared), low light and radar capabilities. It lacks the hyper-spectral, x-ray diffraction and neutron sensor; the resistance managed to build into its microbot. The minibots size and power draw forces it to use a more traditional robot power supply rather than the trickle feed antimatter power supply utilized in the resistances microbot.

The minibot's stealth capability is limited to its relatively small size, its mobility and its ability to change surface color to match their background which has no effect on radar. Using radar, the CASS minibot stands out like a beacon. The resistance microbot counters radar detection with a radar absorbent coating, but it has frequency and exposure limitations. Fortunately, the resistances intelligence has determined that the CASS minibot's radar mode is rarely used unless in near total darkness, preferring the more natural and aesthetically pleasing images from its EO/IR sensors.

CASS minibots do have a significant advantage that P'Ko and Tn'Ya's bot entirely lack. They have offensive capabilities: a laser system capable of dazzling a potential enemy, or with sustained exposure, burn through many materials; a claw capable of crushing or even severing a limb. And spiked legs that can easily puncture skin and light ballistics fiber; its legs are connected to a stun capability powerful enough to paralyze and kill, through the disruption of heart and brain function.

The CASS minibots are deadly.

Despite the many advantages, the CASS minibot has over the resistances microbot, the resistances choice to use a QECS (Quantum Entanglement Communications System), gives it an edge. It provides secure, instantaneous, un-jam-able communications that impact all of the microbot's functions. A capability and expense that the CASS, to the best of the resistances knowledge, have been unwilling to commit. The CASS's considers their minibots to be expendable and carry a self-destruct charge programmed to explode in the event of compromise or loss.

The willingness of the resistance to turn over a QECS to P'Ko and Tn'Ya spoke volumes about how important this mission is to them. A QECS pair is worth millions of credits; even the CASS restricts their use to only the most critical systems, rare, even among the soldiers. Especially now with the numbers of soldiers multiplying, only the lead soldier within a squad or sometimes a whole company gets a QECS.

The vast majority of soldiers is chained to the QECS possessing leader or rely on relatively easy to intercept or jammable conventional communication systems, using autonomous programming to fill in the gaps.

The resistance, after watching the entrance to the passageways leading to the prison cells and charting out and studying the closed passageways, had a pretty good idea where the special mining area lay and knew when the soldiers guarding the Prz'Nr's rotated and the paths taken.

P'Ko, disguised, walked past the surveillance system monitored guard station just as the soldiers were entering through the entry control point door. The microbot that he and Tn'Ya customized clung to P'Ko's pant leg, just as the door opened the microbot launched. With Su'Zi at the controls and Tn'Ya monitoring power levels and watching for hazards, the microbot scampered through the door, at an angle calculated, so P'Ko and the soldiers blocked the view of the cameras. The soldier's three hundred sixty-degree vision was blocked by its body as the microbot ran perilously under its feet.

Even with all non-essential sensors, and systems powered down, except for camouflage and EO Su'Zi was just barely able to keep up with the soldiers coming on duty as they made their way towards the prison cell. The soldiers entered a doorway which led into a staging area just outside the Prz'Nr's cell. Su'Zi raced the microbot in just as the door shut and Su'Zi and Tn'Ya put the microbot in protect mode.

The microbot lay huddled in a corner with its active camouflage turned on and its transparent legs folded up underneath it as its severely depleted systems recovered.

The next day the team was ready, they knew precisely when the mining team would be returning to their cells and were prepared. They were relatively safe in what appeared to be an airlock like vestibule used for kill-vest donning and doffing.

P'Ko sat in the pilot's seat, Tn'Ya filled the role of systems engineer, monitoring power levels and the sensors, while Su'Zi was in charge of the defense team. She had people watching the soldiers, the Prz'Nr's and the environment for any hint of danger. Part of her team monitored CASS's communications. Although most of CASS's communications were encrypted, the resistance had studied and analyzed CASS's communications for long enough that they knew what types of signals and on what channels meant something was wrong.

As the Prz'Nr's accompanied by the soldiers entered the vestibule, P'Ko gave the command to begin overcharging the maneuvering systems needed for the massive jump to access the kill-vest.

Not far from a soldier, P'Ko looked up; it was like standing near and looking up at a hundred story building that was moving. P'Ko got dizzy; and though sitting he felt like he was going to fall. He had never experienced vertigo like this before. Not even while standing on ledges near the top of the stadium. The area he was looking up at was so big and flat it invited the senses to presume that it's a new floor, and upset his equilibrium. Some of the others experienced it too. He felt himself teetering back; it was a little like the first time he experienced weightlessness. P'Ko reached back into his memories of weightlessness and the compensation techniques he used then, and he soon recovered.

The perspective was very strange, and it took a long while for P'Ko recognize the Mi'Nr that invaded his quarters. Not knowing his name P'Ko decided just to call him Number One, appropriate since he also seemed to be the one in charge. There were four others in this group; all their work uniforms still showed impacted dirt but dust free. The Prz'Nr's must have gone through an air shower and blown clean of loose material. There will still be plenty of microscopic material embedded in the kill-vest for data to be collected and analyzed. They should be able to determine where they're working by matching the dirt to known mining locations in the Mi'Nr's database.

As the microbots power levels gradually crept up, the Prz'Nr's took off their work overalls. The kill-vests were clearly visible, a glistening vest a few millimeters thick, looking almost like flexible metal, but when zoomed in was composed of a very tightly woven fabric of metallic and optical filaments. It will be a challenge to hop onto it and cling to it as the soldiers place it the locker. P'Ko ordered the programmed application of the special adhesive to the microbot's legs as it makes its jump. The adhesive, having been prepositioned on the underbelly of the microbot, in anticipation of this need.

The team watched as the kill-vests, sealed in place by what looks like a zipper up the back of the kill-vest, were unzipped, the zipper was activated by a soldier pressing a sensor near the center of the back of the kill-vest a few centimeters to one side.

By the time the third Prz'Nr had doffed his kill-vest the microbots power levels were ready, they could only stay overcharged for seconds before damage to the circuits occurred, the team prepared for the jump/grab ride onto the kill-vest as it was placed into the storage locker/charging station.

P'Ko had to get the microbot into just the right position at just the right time, all non-essential systems were powered off, the energy capacitors of the microbot's systems were redlined, and the system temps were redlined when P'Ko initiated the jump-grab sequence. It was over in less than a second, and they rode the kill-vest into its storage/charging cabinet.

Once safely inside the locked kill-vest cabinet Tn'Ya ran her system checks and began a battery of tests, including the use of insect-sized beetlebot probes to explore the kill-vests harder to access recesses. She focused on collecting the data, the analysis would take longer. She collected data first on the kill-vest, its destructive power, its control mechanism and the locking system that holds it in place.

There was one close call during the kill-vest analysis mission, as safe as it sounded inside the locked storage cabinet did have a close call. A doffed kill-vest passive tamper detect system, tied directly into the destruct circuit was discovered almost at the point of tripping the destruct sequence. It was found that the kill-vests internal communication channels ran a continuously running self-diagnostic hashing sequence. Tn'Ya had to call in programmers and engineers to help with the data collection to ensure their sensor probes didn't affect the self-diagnostic hashing system and set off an instant destruct sequence.

 The data would be compiled and analyzed immediately, but it could be hours before the final results, including a possible way to disable or defeat these cruel, despicable devices would be available. Then with the little time remaining Tn'Ya collected data on the residual dirt that was left on the kill-vest to get an idea where the worksite might be located and what special materials might be that they are mining.

The team knew going in that the microbot wouldn't be able to follow the Prz'Nr's all the way to the mining site. It was just barely fast enough to keep up with a walking soldier or Prz'Nr for short distance. Keeping it up for very long risked disaster. Su'Zi confessed that she was lucky to keep up with the soldiers and keep from being stepped on during the initial entry into the Prz'Nr Vestibule. She didn't want to risk a second, longer attempt.

The microbot is tough and could survive getting stepped on by a Prz'Nr, but the Prz'Nr would surely react and give away its presence. If stepped on by a soldier the microbot would be severely damaged or crushed, and its antimatter power source could catastrophically fail, destroying the microbot, along with all of its equipment, including the irreplaceable QECD. The fact that it would probably take a portion of the soldier's foot along with it would be little consolation.

It had first been considered riding the kill-vest onto the Prz'Nr and then to the work site. That was decided as too risky; it would be virtually impossible to ride out the day without being noticed and discovered. Even though knowing the routes to the mining area and knowing about the mining area itself was important, and even prove critical to the resistances developing plans. They had no way of knowing how the Prz'Nr would react if they discovered the microbot inside their kill-vest or in a fold of their clothing. The surveillance system was tuned to monitor every move of the Prz'Nr's and detect any telltale indications that something was amiss.

So instead of riding the kill-vest onto the Prz'Nr it was decided to sneak into the Prz'Nr's' cell unobserved by the soldiers and surveillance cameras. Then after lights out, establish contact with one of the Prz'Nr's, once in communication, accompany them on their workday and complete the pattern of life data collection and analysis, tracing and timing routes, locations, and duties, then devise an escape plan.

All they had to do was get out of the kill-vest cabinet and to some safe hiding spot then sneak into the Prz'Nr's cell.

There was a lot of anxiety about jumping to the floor. The engineers assured P'Ko, Su'Zi, and Tn'Ya that the microbot could handle the G's from what amounted to a fall of a relative distance of several hundred meters, but the first person experience from the operator's perspective was scary. The door opened and with others focusing on where the soldiers and the Prz'Nr's were looking P'Ko focused on the leap.

As soon as he got the all clear. P'Ko launched the microbot out of the cabinet and for a moment there was the sensation of falling. When they hit, everyone could have sworn that they felt it physically. The microbot bounced, and P'Ko luckily managed to hit the deck running after the first bounce. Once safe in the corner and in protect mode, the team in the control room cheered and wanted to do it again.

Everything that they did now ran an even higher risk of detection. In spite of high the level of confidence among the resistances analysts that the soldiers and other surveillance systems were operating in a mode intended to monitor the Prz'Nr's and not look for microbot infiltrators. The detection and loss of the microbot, with its QECS would be a devastating blow to the resistance. If captured, they were prepared to short the antimatter power supply and self-destruct the microbot, but it would be a loss that the resistance could hardly afford and wanted to avoid at all costs.

With last night's mission was a success, the kill-vest analysis determined that its lock transmits an unlock code generated and stored in the locking mechanism each time the kill-vest is worn. The unlock code is passed to a control point using a phase locked communications method whose communications encryption is relatively weak, but is very secure in that any tampering or attempts to intercept or monitor would be instantly detected, setting off an alarm and security response. There's no nonvolatile RAM in the kill-vest, only volatile RAM storage tied to a detect tamper system linked directly to the destruct mechanism. The kill-vest is not fail-safe, it's fail destruct, once the destruct sequence begins it will destruct unless phase locked communications from the command post is resumed and an abort destruct signal with the unlock code is received from the command post.

Tonight's mission will be the most dangerous yet; it will leave the microbot exposed without cover longer and presumably there will be more surveillance devices where they will be going. P'Ko knew that it cost a significant portion of the resistance's budget to build this first machine, building a second machine may be impossible.

P'Ko didn't know if the resistance even possessed a second QECS. And a mistake would add months to the rescue attempt and likely result in the execution of the Prz'Nr's. Failure was not an option. If successful, the resistance for the first time will have a system that can sneak into the CA's most secretive meetings and find out what the CA and the CASS are up to. They could lift the veil of secrecy that surrounds so many of the doings of the CA and CASS, and finally, answer some of the most plaguing questions about Dadr'Ba.

P'Ko will be "driving" again with Su'Zi operating the defensive sensors and, hopefully, establish contact with one of the Prz'Nr's. Tn'Ya was told that she'd have to sit tonight's mission out, as much as she wanted to be there, she was under CASS surveillance, and they couldn't risk raising the suspicion of the CASS by being "off their grid" too many nights in a row. She would be needed for later missions and can review the recording of tonight's mission during the post-mission debrief and analysis later.

Having practiced on a virtual simulation, P'Ko ran along the floor under the soldier's feet. It's fortunate that soldier's steps are predictable, and they don't need to see their feet walking, otherwise, it would have been hard to miss the microbot as it scampered back and forth between its feet, its adaptive camouflage fluctuating from the ebbing energy expenditure taxing its systems.

If P'Ko ran too fast, for too long, while sensors were running, he would lose too much energy and systems would quickly fail. Thankfully the failures are programmable, priority was given to motion, adaptive camouflage, and motion detect warning. Radar, EO (electro-optical)/IR (infrared) and HS (hyperspectral) had already been shut down. X-ray diffraction and neutron imaging/spectroscopy systems have been fully powered off and secured. They use too much power to allow movement and need a stable, static platform to operate optimally.

Now all those sensors were just dead weight, with the power running low P'Ko felt like he was operating at 4 G's at Dadr'Ba's lower levels with a Se'Ro'Bs on his heels. He dodged back and forth between giant feet, first of the soldiers and then of the Prz'Nr's as he worked his way into the cell.

As difficult as it was to keep from getting stepped on by the soldier it was more difficult staying between the footfalls of the last Prz'Nr as he entered the cell following his four comrades. The Prz'Nrs must have been tired; his steps were labored and halting, unpredictable, which forced P'Ko to accelerate more quickly, more often and force the depletion of the microbots energy reserves more quickly.

P'Ko wished suddenly that Su'Zi was "driving" she was a better driver than he, but it was too late, there was no time to switch positions. Luckily P'Ko only needed to avoid a few steps.

The Prz'Nr was watching the back of his cell mate in front of him and not his own feet as they entered the cell. Had the Prz'Nr looked down and saw the microbot scampering underfoot and showed any notice or surprise the surveillance cameras looking down on the scene would have surely detected it. The resistance's analysts had assured them that the surveillance systems monitoring the Prz'Nr's are tuned to watch the Prz'Nr's and their actions, not tuned to detect a micro-robotic intruder, and so far their assurances held true.

After a couple of harrowing steps, P'Ko was inside, and he guided the weakening microbot out of harm's way. He slowed the microbot attempting to conserve enough power to find and reach safety. The team shifted into high gear in their search, a broad beam EO/IR scan was executed. LIDAR would have been more useful, but it consumed too much power and was incredibly easy to detect, so it wasn't installed on the microbot. P'Ko had ducked the microbot to the left just inside the door staying near the wall using for cover, the commotion of the Prz'Nr's entering, their movement around the room, and the shutting and sealing of the door. Some of the Prz'Nr's exited what appeared to be a day room and headed down a hallway across from the entry door.

P'Ko crept the microbot along the wall edging around the room towards safety behind a couch that he spotted just after entering the room, the microbots power reserves nearly depleted, but slowly starting to build again.

Su'Zi, psychic alarm startled P'Ko and he impulsively attempted to jump, but found she had engaged the freeze function available at her terminal, it then settled in, she had also sent a psychic alarm to freeze. P'Ko worried that they had been detected. But Su'Zi was saying wait, wait... now! P'Ko jumped, using every joule of energy available, launched the microbot toward the place Su'Zi indicated, a narrow crack between the sofa and the wall.

The microbot lay dead, crumpled on its side, in total system shutdown, it's power supply slowly built power back up and as the communication system connected to the QECS on board the microbot rebooted and came back online the microbot team nursed the precious little warrior back to life.

Su'Zi slowly increased power to the passive sensors and the displays started to return to life. Su'Zi thought to the microbot crew, 'this is going to take some time,' an alert was sent psychically for experts to gather to analyze the new threat, Su'Zi already had a clip, and passed a high-resolution snap to the team's displays.

As they moved into the Prz'Nr's quarters from the kill-vest airlock the microbot executed an EO/IR scan; its sensors picked up a CASS minibot. It was electro-optically camouflaged to blend into the wall and ceiling color but wasn't actively camouflaged from IR detection. It was on alert indicated by its heat signature and its sensors focused on the Prz'Nr's as they entered their quarters.

The initial reports from the experts, many of them at remote locations, began filtering in.

The preliminary analysis is that it is a conventional general purpose CASS minibot built and designed like most other CASS other surveillance systems to monitor people and are not adequately equipped or programmed for the detection of something like the resistance microbot.

The report cautioned against being too bold within line of sight of the CASS bots, whether soldier robots or minibots, their senses are adaptive and will take notice if exposed to an anomaly, even a minor one, too frequently.

Once discovered the minibot's laser system could make short work of the resistance microbot. The laser could easily damage the microbots trickle feed antimatter power source causing it to lose the magnetic integrity holding it's antimatter core in place. Although it's incredibly small, the systems failure would cause a good-sized explosion.

Respecting the analysts caution not to repeatedly expose themselves to the minibot and cause notice, the team waited. After a while the rest of the Prz'Nr's headed down the hallway to what must have been the kitchen/dining area. The team deployed a pair of its single sensor beetlebots one EO and one IR. The microbot team watched as the beetlebot probes slowly scuttled out from the microbots hiding place and surveyed the scene.

The beetlebots were made for close work, designed to operate inside tiny crevices, not out in the open. Exposed as they were for this mission the beetlebots found themselves virtually blind, suffering extreme tunnel vision, the technician supporting the mission began scrambling to adjust the operating parameters and software to compensate for the probe sensors myopic limitations.

Slowly the view began to come into focus; it took some maneuvering to scan a view of the whole room and determine its layout. The room must be their day room; it held a couple of divans and a couple of lounge chairs facing a free standing flat-panel display adjacent to the entry door whose edges glowed green from some energized seal. Opposite from the entrance, a hallway, and upon adjusting the sound controls, came the noises of conversation and food preparation. On the ceiling, the beetlebots detected a second minibot on the ceiling above divan where the microbot lay hid. The other minibot still in the room positioned to watch the activity down the hall

So there's least two CASS minibots, each staying within direct line of sight of the other leading the analysts to suggest that at least one form of their communication is line of sight. The room also possessed two EO/IR/lowlight surveillance cameras positioned so they can't be physically approached without observation by itself or the other camera. The cameras are high-resolution wide-angle able to zoom in with no need to pan or tilt, a much smaller version of the wide area surveillance system that is used to monitor Nu'Tn.

Finally, the decision was made for the microbot to come out of hiding and use its more advanced sensors to evaluate the threat. P'Ko, having charged up the microbot during the wait carefully guided the microbot out from its hiding spot and recovered its beetlebots.

Once positioned so that its sensors could operate, prepared to retreat at any moment, operating in stealth, low emanation mode. The team performed a remote analysis of the CASS minibots; they didn't appear to be emanating, leading them to conclude that they must be operating in autonomous or semi-autonomous mode. Which made sense, because the room is entirely sealed off. There's no way for the minibots to communicate with the outside. Proven by the fact that communications traffic from the cell area stopped once the soldiers sealed the Prz'Nr's inside.

The microbot was unable to detect the method or means behind the door seal. Somehow CASS succeeded in preventing psychic penetration into the cell and adapt it to the kill-vests the Prz'Nr's wear outside the cell. But the microbot's QECS still functioned.

What happened next took only a few seconds, suddenly all activity and conversation fell silent, and the CASS minibot on the ceiling went on full alert and started to move down the hallway. At the same instant, P'Ko felt it, and Su'Zi exclaimed, P'Ko unable to distinguish whether spoken or psychic, I can feel them! P'Ko's eyes and attention fixed on the CASS minibot stalking down the hallway, toward the Prz'Nr's.

Warning! And almost instantly, the conversation started again, and the noises from the kitchen area resumed, the CASS minibot stopped, paused and reversed its movement a few steps, without turning, not having a real front or back then settled down still on the ceiling in a resting position and remained on alert.

Chapter 50, SMT MOC

The geo-positional alarm went off again; it had been happening intermittently and got worse over several weeks. Somethings wrong with the position tracking system monitoring the SMT (Special Mining Team).

The technicians have checked out the Comms link and the SMT's headsets but haven't been able to reproduce the problem. They've thoroughly checked and even replaced the headsets. But the problem keeps coming back. There must be some stray interference from something in the area, they're almost finished getting the "special materials" needed from this asteroid, they'll see if the problem follows them to the next job site.

The good thing is that the problem doesn't seem to affect the video feeds as much, only a few glitches here and there. Between the five feeds from the Prz'Nr's headsets and the remote surveillance cameras, there's enough data to identify the location and ensure the security of the operation. Otherwise, they may need to halt operations until the technicians can iron out the problem. The other good thing is that the kill-vest links, using triple redundant PST (Phase Synched Transmission) security has never lost a link or showed any indications of a problem.

The MOC (Mission Operations Commander) silenced the alarm like he did the night before and reminded the surveillance analysts to pay close attention to the video feeds and watch for any anomalies.

The SMT exited the freight elevator at the predetermined level and down the passage to the entrance to the work site. They passed single file through a portable air shower, and across a sensitive scale used to ensure they don't attempt to take anything from the mining site. They appeared to march as they made their way in the massive gravity down a smaller tunnel the rest of the way to the work site.

The MOC stared in amazement as he watched on his multiple monitors the SMT enter the worksite, a cavern, covered floor to ceiling with precious minerals metals and gems. The MOC never got tired of the sight and wished he could see it in person, but it would never be, the asteroid they mined was deep within level four, and the gravity at that level would probably break his legs.

The SMT paused to take in the view, then slowly entered. Their work order today was to finish extracting a pair of extremely large crystals, for use in some classified high-tech experiment or make a couple of exquisite, million plus credit lamp bases for end tables or nightstands. The work order on the MOC's console didn't specify. However, he suspected that these would wind up decorating some high-level official's private quarters.

The work was slow and meticulous; the SMT seems to be taking extra precautions, first one and then the other crystal was freed from its mineral encasement.

Then disaster struck, the SMT all five of them started to leave, two of them straining to carry the work order crystals. The rest picked up tools and jammed their pockets and the inside of their coveralls with gems. Then all of them began making their way to the exit in a tightly packed group. The MOC initiated the alarm that would instant message Chi'Yo and dispatched soldiers to the site.

In voice contact with the SMT, the MOC ordered them to stop, not once, but twice, then initiated the stun function built into the kill-vests, by this time, Chi'Yo was in video communication. The MOC shared his screen over the video interface with Chi'Yo; showing him that the stun had no effect. A surveillance technician reported that the single elevator to the site had been left at the mining level and doesn't seem to respond, adding that technicians were already working on it. It would be some minutes before the soldiers would be at the site.

Chi'Yo knew that with the tools that the SMT carried, they could make it to the access tunnel or elevator shaft and possibly escape. Chi'Yo and the MOC didn't know how or why the stun function of the kill-vest didn't work; the Mi'Nr's must be betting that Chi'Yo wouldn't blow the kill-vests fearing to damage the crystals. Well, Chi'Yo's wife would just have to get over it, "Blow them," he ordered, "Blow them, now!"

The MOC keyed the destruct sequence, adding the authorization code from Chi'Yo and all the video feeds in the area, including the stationary cameras in the immediate vicinity went blank.

Chapter 51, Heroes' Celebration

P'Ko didn't like being a hero, sure he first suggested using a modified version of his pocket sized diagnostic tool, but Tn'Ya was the one that went crazy with the mods making it into something he'd never dream of. And yes, it was his idea to hack the video systems and switch the crews, he'd been evading and fooling video systems as long as he could remember, but it was the team that made it all come together.

Then Su'Zi and Tn'Ya together came up with the brilliant idea of using a kind of Crystal Tear Stylus absolute zero freeze strip to defeat tamper system seal on the kill-vests.

Su'Zi and Mi'Ka prepped the SMT psychically, and Su'Zi even insisted on being one of the five volunteer replacements for the SMT padding herself in places and strapping herself down in other locations she replaced number one after the switch. They pulled off the switch in less than three and one-half seconds under, the cover of a carefully created splice of video fed into the SMT monitoring system, which was incredible since they never had a full dress rehearsal.

P'Ko had wanted to be one of the SMT volunteers, but with his height, he'd never been able to masquerade as one of the SMT's. He helped with the hacks of the elevator and the video surveillance systems, but the most dangerous thing and arguably the bravest, was that he carried the activated, could explode at any second, partially frozen kill-vests to the blast zone, using another part of the rough-hewn passage a safe distance from the fake SMT. Which turned out to be even more dangerous because the CASS detonated them sooner than anticipated. Everyone, expected the CASS to detonate the kill-vests sometime after they planned to cut the video feed to help cover their escape. The unexpected blast wounded P'Ko and some of the volunteers on the fake SMT nearby. But they all managed to escape through the elevator shaft down to the next level and out through another tunnel, the surveillance camera's having been spoofed, covering their tracks.

Maybe next time the CASS won't use so much explosive, the blast of all five kill-vests in such close proximity obliterated the whole area, but to be sure the escape team added a little extra explosive to make doubly sure no evidence of their mission remained. The CASS engineers and technicians that made the kill-vests will have some explaining to do.

Mi'Ka is taking charge of the rehabilitation of the SMT; they had all been drugged and infected with surveillance nanobots, and at least partially mind wiped or had been in captivity so long it affected their minds. For most of them, their past remains a mystery, one or two could even be Touch of God Survivors, there's no way to tell. The important thing is that they're free and happy to be back among their people and were adapting quickly back to Mi'Nr society and the best part, CASS is none the wiser

To P'Ko's relief, the celebration wasn't really a celebration, and he wasn't the star, at least not the only one. The rescue was weeks past, and this event turned out to be more a recognition ceremony. It was held at the resistance safe house at the edge of Dadr'Ba, and P'Ko was thankful to find that no individuals were recognized, but the whole team was, including Tn'Ya wearing an exoskeleton equipped eSuit that included a surveillance nanobot suppression system.

Several people came up making short speeches citing the accomplishments of the team, even some of the team got up to say a few words thanking their teammates. There were no awards presented. Presentation of an award would risk its discovery by a CASS spy or raid and wasn't worth the risk.

There were handshakes and toasts, then everyone headed up to Ol'Tn'Ga, because the ceremony had been carefully planned to be on the same day as the annual Run with the Se'Ro'Bs and Ol'Tn'Ga was just beginning to liven up. P'Ko and Su'Zi had wanted to run, but neither of them got picked, but that didn't dampen the mood any.

Chapter 52, Detection of Nuclear Detonations on O'M

Chn'Gi could feel her throat constrict, and her chest tighten, she began to have difficulty breathing. The data she was reading was unequivocal; the O'Mi's had developed fission based nuclear weapons and almost immediately used them on each other and then in short order progressed to fusion based devices.

The TV signals and deciphered language provided proof that the O'Mi's have a propensity for death and destruction. Decades ago, they developed high volume automatic projectile weapons and increasingly large chemical-based bombs and deadly gasses. With these weapons they devastated and destroyed not just military targets and battlefields, but entire cities, population centers and the infrastructures necessary to keep the residents alive.

Chn'Gi began to realize that if the O'Mi's continue to improve and develop weapons at this pace, reinforced by correlating data regarding the rate of weapons development on Or'Gn, the O'Mi's will have weapons capable of threatening Dadr'Ba by the time they arrive.

Chn'Gi felt an ache behind her eyes that slowly spread to the back of her head as she reviewed the latest population projections. In spite of the O'Mi's propensity towards killing each other, their population has doubled in just the last hundred years. If the population continues to increase unchecked, the population could be nearing ten billion by the time they arrive. They will be facing severe shortages of food, water, medicine, energy and other vital resources. They've shown little concern for protecting the environment and controlling pollution. Or'Gn's history showed a similar pattern, never completely gaining control over the population, regional rivalries, resource management or stewardship of the environment.

There's no chance now of Dadr'Ba's arriving at O'M as clean and pure as they envisioned. O'M will be a poisoned resource depleted rock covered with a starving, diseased population choking on its own waste. Perhaps our only hope is that the O'Mi's will self-annihilate, or face a worldwide pandemic or collapse of vital infrastructure causing a mass extinction before they arrive. The statisticians put the odds of O'Mi self-annihilation at close to fifty-fifty, but Chn'Gi doubted these numbers. Based on her study of Dadr'Ba's ancestors during the same period in their history, Chn'Gi's educated guess placed the odds more like only twenty to twenty-five percent. She kept her numbers to herself and dared not brief it to the Council, and used the statisticians fifty-fifty number instead.

Given the even odds the Council started to hedge their bets for finding O'M free from the pestilence and began an aggressive weapons development program.

Before the latest set of predictions, the council planned a protected settlement and "working" with the local population on better stewardship of

O'M. They had increased the numbers of soldiers, enhanced their capabilities and weaponry, but after these new revelations realized that there was no way they could produce enough soldiers to conquer the planet. So they began developing advanced weapons of their own in preparation for a battle with the O'Mi's on a (potentially) near peer level.

Chn'Gi closed her eyes and began the deep breathing exercises that Gi'Ya had taught her, forcing back the constriction that made it difficult for her to breathe, and attempt to drain the energy from the pain in her head while willing the tension that had crept into her shoulders and upper neck to relax.

Chapter 53, CASS Meeting Regarding O'Mi's

Chi'Yo, grim-faced, listened intently to the briefing, it would have to be carefully edited before presentation to the Central Council, and he may have to brief it himself. The briefer, Zhu'Ro[101] is the quintessential scientist; totally absorbed in the science behind solving the problem and oblivious to any of the moral or ethical implications, with no leadership potential, or aspirations, and prone to ramble.

It's going to take the time to get through all three potential COA's (courses of action), "Theoretically it's possible to set the atmosphere on fire, utilizing the techniques we use in fusing the heavier elements in our fusion engine and create a chain reaction." Zhu'Ro paused as if running calculations in his head, then continued. "If started in one spot, it would be tricky to prevent it from expanding too fast and push out into space and fizzling out. It'd need to start as a cluster of smaller devices rather than one huge one; the more minor explosions would then merge into a much larger self-sustaining size that would then grow to envelope the whole planet." Then, almost as an afterthought added "but that option would burn away not just the atmosphere but the oceans and a significant portion of the topsoil stopping only when the iron content got too high. Then it would burn itself out, the surface probably to a depth of kilometers would consist nearly entirely of extremely radioactive ash and slag composed of iron and heavier elements."

Du'Shi[102] cut in, "Our perfect world for habitation would become nothing more than a giant asteroid, devoid of all life-sustaining elements, an enormous spherical cinder, devoid of all atmosphere and water. Life would be impossible."

Chi'Yo had assigned Du'Shi to run an OPT (Operational Planning Team) to come up with these COA's, and her enthusiasm was showing. She wanted to be in charge of executing whichever option gets chosen. She's stating the obvious, Chi'Yo thought; she's going to have to step up her game if I'm going to pick her to run this operation.

COA two was briefed and would have been ideal, using asteroids to pummel the aliens into submission, but the timing just didn't work.

COA three was a more conventional approach and would need more time to prepare, and more resources, which we have. It will also give Chi'Yo more power, so Chi'Yo decided on COA three. The COA brief to the Central Council will make it obvious which COA to take, it will have the most favorable data supporting it.

Chi'Yo looked around the room and asked, not expecting a response, if there was anything else from those present that they wanted to bring up.

---

[101] Sounds similar to Zoo-Row.
[102] Sounds like Dew-She.

To his surprise Zhu'Ro raised his hand, Chi'Yo looked toward Zhu'Ro, "yes?"

Hesitantly at first then building up steam Zhu'Ro said "Sir, although not timely for dealing with the O'Mi's (referring to COA two). We could set in place the injection of a comet into orbit around O'M which would provide a wealth of resources that we may need later." Then cautiously ,"but easier to do than that we could initiate a Dadr'Ka, a next generation Dadr'Ba, crewed with volunteers.

A suitable cometary mass from the outer solar system could be nudged out of its orbit and with gravity assists along the way pass through the heart of this solar system out the other side toward a new home. Like our ancestors did with Dadr'Ba. These volunteers could help us colonize the galaxy."

Chi'Yo liked the idea, and knew that the CA would like it too, the resource comet might also become useful in case COA three fails. Shutting Zhu'Ro down Chi'Yo responded "That's not our concern, our job is the safety and security of Dadr'Ba and our successful landing and colonization of O'M. Everyone is dismissed." but he resolved to mention the idea of a Dadr'Ka to the Commander.

Chapter 54, Vr'Chm Ambush

P'Ko, Su'Zi, and Tn'Ya crawled through the thick scrub bushes near the forest not far from the beach. They narrowly escaped the O'Mi's that had been watching the landing zone and had waited until the three of them had begun to feel comfortable, then ambushed them as they started to move down the beach to their hideout. Fortunately, one of the O'Mi's got trigger-happy and tried to take a shot from too far off and missed. The three of them ran for the cover near the trees, as other O'Mi's opened up shooting wildly and fortunately missed.

P'Ko, Su'Zi, and Tn'Ya dove into the brush cover and tried to be as quiet and still as possible, holding their breath as the O'Mi's passed through and around them shouting and beating the bushes with their weapons trying to force them to give away their hiding spots.

The CASS' reports painted the O'Mi's as a pestilence, a mistake of nature, genetically flawed but prolific enough to overwhelm all other strains of intelligent life.

At first, there was debate among some experts whether the O'Mi species is truly genetically defective. But as time went on, and the CA's propaganda and public information "filtering" campaign progressed, O'Mi defenders "disappeared." The O'Mi genetic story evolved into one of an intelligent cancer bent on self-destruction and destined to ruin a wonderful, near-perfect world that doesn't deserve the treatment it's getting.

If they had some positive genetic traits, must have died off during one of the many conflicts the creatures brought upon themselves. The reports went on to posit that the O'Mi's would be centuries more advanced had not so many of their kind fallen victim to their own genetically innate, selfish, violent nature. It was only the planets abundant natural resources, and resilience, that prevented the O'Mi's from already killing the planet, on the way towards killing themselves.

The whole intent behind Dadr'Ba was to discover, colonize and husband a magnificent, peaceful oasis, but the world they found had a cancer. Evil and disease had infected a good and pure world, exploited the fair benevolent nature of the planet. The cancer worked its poison, turning a thing of beauty into what will become, unless something is done to intervene, dead rotting flesh. The propaganda the CASS began to churn out was that good doctor or a decent gardener upon finding a diseased limb on a patient or plant would treat it or cut it away. And soon anyone that voiced sentiment otherwise fell silent.

Chn'Gi and her team, couldn't argue with the data. Their analysis, models, and predictions came to approximately the same, though not as extreme, results. Chn'Gi couldn't help but see and reflect on their own history, her ancestors and how very much like these O'Mi's her people were, or are but she dare not reveal it.

On the contrary, to make the situation a thousand times worse was that most of the reports, even the greatly exaggerated CASS reports were attributed to Chn'Gi and her team and their passive collection of signals collected from O'M. The CASS signals specialists were hidden, protected, a CASS secret, unknown to everyone but a few within the CASS and Chn'Gi. She saw and read reports attributed to her, and suffered.

She began to feel that the fate of the entire O'Mi civilization, the whole species, come to rest on her shoulders. She began to spend more and more time practicing, mind clearing exercises and drinking more of Mi'Ka's tea, forcing herself, more and more often unsuccessfully to avoid liquor, and she attended more church services.

As the three of them huddled in the tall weeds and brush, fear and loathing dominated their emotions, as they waited for the O'Mi's to pass by so they could make their escape, and get to their safe room hideout.

P'Ko couldn't help but recall the similarities to their early history. P'Ko had viewed some of the historical archives using the reader and data cartridge he held on to when he had scavenged the same device for that D'En woman.

It was a good thing that he kept a reader and a set of data cartridges, not long after he got the thing and around the time of the T'Bm break in, the CA had seized control of the D'Po. Now there exists a copy of at least part of the previous history the CA has been withholding. Luckily Lu'Gs wasn't arrested, but he was placed into a sort of caretaker status, and not allowed to roam the yard unaccompanied.

The explanation was, and P'Ko believed it, at least in part, was because of the need to safeguard materials for the CA's weapon development program. Though, he didn't trust the CA and guessed that there might have been more to the D'Po take over than what the CA revealed.

What sorts of weapons they are developing has remained secret, but it is clear that the manufacture of soldiers increased, before rarely seen, soldiers have become more and more visible. They've even started patrols, not too frequent, on a set schedule and path, and programmed to ignore just about everything except an attack or perceived attack, but of tremendous concern to the resistance.

There were a lot of complaints at first, but after a while, most of Nu'Tn hardly notices them anymore, but for the people of Ol'Tn, the patrolling soldiers are a festering wound. The experts within the resistance say that the soldiers have been modified and improved, and are placed in the general population on patrol during the later stages of software checkout to assure their ability to function safely and reliably and distinguish between friend and foe.

Since the start of the patrols, there had been some "accidental", injuries but so far no deaths. Sometimes somebody intentionally or accidentally makes a hostile movement near a soldier, which results in an instantaneous, violent response. Some of these "hostile" actions are rumored to be only a show or gesture of disrespect, often when the provocateurs thought the soldiers couldn't see, even when behind cover, the soldier's sensors have somehow picked it up.

The injured are cited and made to pay for their own medical treatment, then threatened with more severe consequences for a repeat offense.

P'Ko felt it hypocritical that the CA imposed a double standard on the O'Mi's, our ancestors lived through and survived a very similar sordid past, an ignoble past that is now forbidden knowledge. At first, P'Ko didn't know what to make of the history; it bored him. His respect for the knowledge ban and penalties kept him from sharing with anyone yet, but now P'Ko began to see the twisted rationale behind the knowledge ban.

The CA was attempting to rewrite history by abolishing it, by abolishing anything that may detract from the CA's holier than thou stance, that we are great, powerful, flawless, and perfect. The CA is not dealing with reality, but a reality of their own making, history is written by the victors, the ones in control.

P'Ko began to realize more so than ever before that people; all people have flaws. We're not perfect, and we have no right to come to an alien planet and sanitize it, expunge or cure the O'Mi cancer, but that is exactly what the CASS seems to be preparing for.

These thoughts and emotions began to crystallize within P'Ko in spite of the fact he and his friends were now being hunted by (from all appearances, an accurate representation) O'Mi's he was thinking might be worth saving.

The O'Mi's, are rather weak and slow, noisy, dirty, cannibalistic, often diseased, and it's rumored that they stink. If the wind is blowing in the right direction, their putrid odor can be detected from far away. Here on the coast, the breeze was predominately from the ocean, and the three of them didn't pick up the O'Mi smell.

They did hear them speak; it's difficult to describe, but it sounded like what P'Ko would imagine a microphone and amplifier very close to someone eating in a hurry, interspersed with yaks or gagging like they were belching or spitting out a large swallow of something nasty, on the verge of vomiting.

The CA started publishing a series of information bulletins by CA experts on how these O'Mi's came to be the dominant species. The focus on how a vermin genetically lazy, seek out and exploit the weaknesses of the other species on the planet. Like a virus infiltrates, exploits and takes over a host cell, forcing it to the diseases' purposes, ultimately destroying the cell and eventually by their sheer numbers, excessive consumption and waste products kill the host.

In this case, the entire planet is at risk. The "experts" claim that the O'Mi's are incapable of any higher-level thought patterns, that they don't recognize or comprehend what they are doing to the planet and can only focus on the satisfaction of biological, animal needs, self-satisfaction, and greed. Otherwise, they wouldn't have destroyed the world's ecosystems, exterminated many of its species and killed so many of their own kind.

All was quiet. Su'Zi motioned that they should make their way out and try to double back to their hideout. P'Ko and Tn'Ya nodded agreement. The tight quarters and the chosen direction dictated that Su'Zi take the lead, followed by P'Ko then Tn'Ya. They made their way out of the brush, crouching low, followed a path through tall grasses and down the beach.

They got to an area where there was a break in the shore grass and stopped. The rest of the way was exposed to the beach, but their hideout wasn't far, running they would make it to their hideout in seconds. Hunched low, with the O'Mi's out of sight, they started to skip down the beach. Skipping allowed them to move quickly and stay closer to the ground (in the light gravity) rather than running.

They were almost to the hideout. Su'Zi began to enter it when several shots rang out. P'Ko turned to see Tn'Ya fall, a large bloody, ragged hole clearly visible through her chest. P'Ko sprang to her, making it in one small leap. He crouched beside her when a burst of weapons fire ripped through P'Ko in multiple places, and he fell beside Tn'Ya. O'Mi yells of apparent joy, rang through P'Ko's ears, then fading as the world went dark.

P'Ko recovered in his quarters with a mixed feeling of hate for the O'Mi's and the CA; he cursed the CA for ruining Vr'Chm by populating it with so many armed and hostile O'Mi's. His feelings are not unique, there have been many other visitors to Vr'Chm that have also complained, but the CA's claims that Vr'Chm is an accurate representation based on what they've learned about the planet and its dominant species.

P'Ko quickly messaged Su'Zi and Tn'Ya making sure they were okay and passed the code phrase that they would have to meet in person at the regular place and time in Ol'Tn.

They should've known better than to attempt making it to their virtual hideout in broad daylight, the CA set up an O'Mi city nearby. The O'Mi's soon discovered the people of Dadr'Ba's visiting them, and the O'Mi's automatically started to hunt them setting up watch posts and patrols.

It wasn't clear whether it was the CA's programming within Vr'Chm or the O'Mi's own maturing artificial intelligence, but the O'Mi's haven't yet taken any prisoners, not even those wanting to surrender. They simply kill first, and it's said that they attempt to perform autopsies on them to learn how to better kill them and try to capture and exploit their technology.

So far the O'Mi's have been frustrated because shortly after the murder of a visitor from Dadr'Ba the virtual body disappears. The O'Mi's latest tactic is for the hunters to carry ice chests and have been trying to cut off a piece of the body, usually the head and ice it down. Hoping that it will prevent the body from disappearing.

P'Ko wondered how his ancestors would have reacted to off world visitors at the same point in their history.

Chapter 55, Tu'Tan's Problem

Tu'Tan, P'Ko's father, used to like his job, but not anymore. Ever since Gn'Da[103] was assigned to his team, despite his continued rejections she keeps trying to come on to him. Now he dreads coming to work, and be subjected to her smiles, winks, and veiled sexual innuendo laced comments.

In the beginning he tried to remain cordial and friendly and ignore her advances, but when no one was present she'd come on to him, he'd refuse she'd feign hurt feelings.

Then she began taking credit for his work reporting his accomplishments as her own or by claiming that she had directed him to do the tasks as if she were his supervisor and then came on to him even more.

Tu'Tan didn't know what to make of the situation, was she attempting to repay him for letting her take credit for his work with sexual favors? Or was she retaliating for his refusal to notice her in that way?

She wasn't his supervisor, if anything Tu'Tan should have been her supervisor, he had more time on the job, was older and had more training and certifications. He was told by their supervisor they were supposed to be equal coworkers.

When Tu'Tan reported her inappropriate advances it to their boss, he was told to not to worry about who gets credit for the work getting done. His boss went as far as to suggest that if Gn'Da wanted sex, to just give it to her; that should make them both happy, and she'll probably treat him better.

There's no way Tu'Tan would do that; Gn'Da had already been playing the lead role with work, if Tu'Tan had sex with her it would only exasperate things and cement the dominance Gn'Da was attempting to establish. He would be submitting to her in the workplace and sexually.

Driven by the reaction from his supervisor, Tu'Tan knew that he needed to get out. He needed to move out of this work section completely.

Tu'Tan began biding his time, seeking a way out. After a few weeks Tu'Tan came to realize what Gn'Da is doing; she joined his group and made friends with him creating a multiself. Multiselves occur all the time and are a natural, healthy, good thing, a virtual being or person made up of the shared awareness, knowledge, influence and control of her and her (victim Tu'Tan). But, instead of sharing the awareness, knowledge influence and control of a healthy multiself, she's trying to take over and dominate the relationship.

Tu'Tan asked around and discovered that she's tried this on others. She seeks out and preys on nice guys, makes friends, then twists and exploits that friendship into a virtual multiself enslaved to her will.

Tu'Tan saw this as a particularly heinous kind of evil. Taking a friend, or mate, or group, and stripping them of their self-determination and self-control.

---

[103] Sounds like Jin-Da rhymes with Linda

The evil person attracts others to form a virtual being bond, perhaps at first sharing but then takes over offering little if any, awareness knowledge influence or control to their victim(s). Like a biological cancer or virus, that infiltrates the cell, and seizes control, using their victim's resources to proliferate and spread.

The worst of these evil ones, if they can't have or take what they want from their victim(s) try to destroy them.

Tu'Tan wondered, then decided that in other places in the universe, or the past or future, there must exist these heinously evil multiselves on larger scales. They might be, communities, societies, nations, governments, even religions, that come into being and gets twisted by powerful individuals or power drunk and take control of others without sharing control. These virtual evil beings once established, will seek out new individuals for membership. If a person sought for membership refuses and can't be taken by force, the evil will kill or destroy them. The same fate goes to an existing member that renounces membership in the evil multiself. That which the evil multiself cannot possess and exploit it destroys.

The thought that such entities exist out in the universe was scary, and it occurred to Tu'Tan that the O'Mi's might very well be one of these evil, malignant beings, or have fallen victim to such a one. It made Tu'Tan shudder and thankful that the CA was stepping up weapons production. And it helped put his situation in perspective; Gn'Da is a temporary problem; he'll eventually be able to escape, either by avoidance or transfer, and he wouldn't miss this job.

Tu'Tan hoped that he could last out the rest of the year and apply back to Field Service Repair, back in the general population working on escalators one day and changing lighting modules the next. He loved the freedom of getting around, working on a broad range of things, talking to people, feeling their appreciation when he fixed something for them or built something that made someone's life easier.

Chapter 56, Dadr'Ka

The launch preparations, and simultaneous launches of Dadr'Ka and the special mission vessel, code-named An'Su[104] executed flawlessly.

With great fanfare, Dadr'Ba sent part of itself, its people and resources on a mission to build a new Dadr. Its mission, to pick an object from O'Ms Oort Cloud and to craft it into a ship as they nudge it out of position to fall towards the sun, carefully planning gravity assists from the planets along the way to get thrown out of the solar system on the path to another O'M.

This new ship will embark on a journey, a trip that could take, like Dadr'Ba's, thousands of years. This brave group of people will never see the O'M that they've spent their lives working toward but will ensure that Or'Gn's great gamble almost two thousand years ago will continue beyond O'M. Their descendants and Or'Gn's descendants will, through their efforts and sacrifices, live on into perpetuity and, God willing, spread across the universe.

This is the proudest moment of the Di'Zo's life, not since the launch of the original seed vessel launched from a captured asteroid space station orbiting Or'Gn has there been such a historic undertaking. That seed vessel like the one they were launching now had the mission of taming a long period comet and turning it into and interstellar spacecraft and ark.

But what they're doing now has the potential shifting Or'Gn's desperate leap of a dying species from a collapsing world to safety on a habitable neighboring planet, into colonization of the galaxy.

The excitement and morale on Dadr'Ba are at an all-time high, and there have been no signs of activity from the resistance. Dadr'Ka will be taking nearly one-fifth of the crew of Dadr'Ba and almost as much of its equipment and resources. But now that they are so near O'M they don't need to hold as many resources in reserve and everyone is excited and willing to pick up the slack for those that are leaving for the short time left till they reach O'M.

Dadr'Ka takes with it everything that it will need to craft and shape a long period or proto-comet into a starship, much like Dadr'Ba was originally. Like Dadr'Ba but even better, taking advantage of Dadr'Ba's centuries of interstellar technical evolution. Candidate destinations have been identified, but the final selection won't occur until after initial shaping and start of Dadr'Ka's fusion engine and de-orbit maneuver.

Following what has become tradition, Dadr'Ka will cut off communication with Dadr'Ba shortly after launch and focus exclusively on its future and its path to its yet unidentified O'M. By the time Dadr'Ka begins its journey Dadr'Ba should be settling comfortably on O'M and see Dadr'Ka pass by on its way to some distant point across the galaxy.

---

[104] Sounds like Ahn-Sue or on-su

Di'Zo almost wished he could be part of Dadr'Ka's crew, but as proud as they must be, he and the crew of Dadr'Ba will have their work cut out for them colonizing O'M and dealing with the hostile genetically flawed aliens.

The aliens are a cancer, infecting O'M and forcing it down a path to ruin, hopefully, they'll self-annihilate quickly, and shorten their suffering, perhaps with nuclear war, but Di'Zo must prepare Dadr'Ba if they don't. They could be on the slow path, the path of slow and gruesome poisoning of the planet and themselves. Whatever order, technology or civil society they possessed is devolving into chaos and anarchy. When Dadr'Ba arrives, the aliens may not be capable of putting up much resistance. Eliminating them would do the planet a favor and without a doubt, be an ultimate kindness.

If the alien's history is any indication of future action, a negotiated settlement will be impossible. If their society, if one can call it that, hasn't already broken down to anarchy, the establishment of a Dadr'Ba settlement similar to the one in Vr'Chm will be impossible.

A fundamental change in the balance of power (military, control of resources, energy, information flow, mineral wealth, water) of O'M is needed before a Dadr'Ba settlement will succeed. Predictive analysis shows that alien armed forces would surround them and if Dadr'Ba doesn't surrender, the aliens will attempt to destroy them.

Now that Dadr'Ba has reached the innermost region of O'M's Oort cloud Dadr'Ba will soon begin feeling solar wind, thus heralding its entry into O'Ms solar system. Dadr'Ba will be able to take advantage of the resistance, and braking effect offered O'M's sun's solar wind.

To avoid detection by the aliens on O'M, Dadr'Ba will begin operating in "stealth mode." By adjusting its magnetic field, increasing its ejectorate mass, and adding carefully calculated ion concentrations it will create a kind of force field around itself. Dadr'Ba will become invisible to radar while continuing to decelerate. It will follow a carefully planned trajectory using the system's outer planets as gravitational brakes and when near enough follow a carefully planned trajectory designed to keep Dadr'Ba on the opposite side of the Sun as O'M until the last possible moment.

As for dealing with the crew, the CA's psychologists have determined; based on internal intelligence from monitoring communications, social networking sites, and Nanobot Collected Intel; a more nuanced approach is necessary to help mold public opinion. So the central committee authorized the use of all available media, Vr'Chm, news releases, infomercials, and carefully edited documentaries to sway public opinion toward a more "compassionate" approach, a focus away from the aliens and more toward saving the planet from a scourge and curing its cancer.

Chapter 57, Su'Zi's Dadr'Ka

Su'Zi, P'Ko, and Tn'Ya silently stood on the crowded Ol'Tn street facing one of the large display panels above the street usually used in the Run with the Se'Ro'Bs but brought out now for "The Launch."

They had said their goodbyes in person just hours ago, and now the ship wide departure ceremony was displayed on every monitor. All the public places, Stadiums, Churches, Ym'Cha's, restaurants, taverns, bars, recreation centers and day rooms were packed with people. Even the crew members on shift had monitors set up to show the event. Special permissions were granted to allow those that couldn't break away to view the launch through a heads up display or through their TaC-B's.

Nobody seemed to want to stay home, and everyone appears to feel the need to be with someone, part of a group. Except everyone was quiet, needing to be close to others, but deep in their thoughts.

Much like the set up for the Run with the Se'Ro'Bs, the main street of Ol'Tn was a mass of people. Powerful thoughts and emotions pervaded the crew causing the resultant psychic energy to feel overwhelming, palpable.

The whole ship became one.

Dadr'Ba, on the verge of completing its two millennia journey, mere decades away from reaching O'M is giving birth. A select portion of the crew will now never see O'M, at least not this O'M. Their new O'M, or whatever they choose to call it could be a hundred light years away and take several millennia to reach. Most, if not all of Dadr'Ka's crew living today will never see it.

The involvement of the Church was especially poignant, the Church orchestrated the event and had many meetings, counseling's and public announcements in the weeks prior.

There was a Dadr'Ba wide moment of silence just before launch and then communication was permanently cut to the squadron of ships as they separated from Dadr'Ba and drifted away. Marking a new beginning, a new destiny. They will search for and find a proto-comet and will use their ship's engines to begin nudging the proto-comet sunward, all the while starting the mining and construction processes need to turn a massive chunk of rock and ice into an interstellar spaceship, and their home for the next several thousand years.

The moment of silence lasted longer than a moment... it seemed like a mini-eternity. Unintentionally, it felt like a massive, Dadr'Ba wide multiself, retirement and a birthing ceremony in one. Though no one died, there was a definite parting. There was an extensive sharing as those departing and those staying shared pieces of themselves with each other, changing in the process, both the multiself that remained on Dadr'Ba and the multiself that was becoming Dadr'Ka.

261

The psychic energy was so intense Su'Zi was certain that it must've moved even the hard-minded D'En.

P'Ko was losing both his parents, they decided together, his father Tu'Tan, having had become frustrated with his job, decided to start anew, and there was no way his mother Le'Ta would part with him.

Tn'Ya was only losing an uncle, and Su'Zi was losing her mother. Ln'Da, Su'Zi's mom never re-mated after the loss of Kr'T. Ln'Da and the senior Prz'Nr from the Prz'Nr crew the resistance rescued, the one P'Ko called Number One became fond of each other. Ln'Da decided to go away with Number One. All of the former Prz'Nr's stowed away on the ships bound for Dadr'Ka.

After much negotiation between the CA and the Church, Dadr'Ka would follow a modified version of the forward-looking only policy. Acknowledging that once launched all Dadr'Ba specific administrative matters that had been in effect on Dadr'Ba would become moot, a waste of time and clock cycles. The databases that the crew of Dadr'Ka brought with them to run and administer their new ship were correctly configured but empty of data.

Contact with Dadr'Ba and its people would become prohibited, but the Foundation of the Church, the Touch of God Event and the remembrance and honor regarding people's ancestry, was retained. It provided the foundation upon which the life cycle of the people rested and comprised the core of church doctrine.

By stowing away on Dadr'Ka, the escaped Prz'Nr's found a safe and final escape from discovery by the CASS. Dadr'Ka's new Commander and its new Chief of Security are both moderates that had fallen out of favor with the CA and the CASS and had already been serving a sort of internal exile.

There wasn't a member of the resistance that wasn't tempted to volunteer for Dadr'Ka. The decision was between; immediate escape from the persecution and fear from living under the CA and the CASS and putting up with the CA with its harsh rules, the CASS with its draconian enforcement for the remaining decades until they reach O'M and achieve the fulfillment of a generations long goal.

Very soon after launch, the former Prz'Nr's will be able to come out of hiding. The rapidly diverging trajectories of the Dadr'Ba and Dadr'Ka's small fleet would make it impossible to return the stowaways. Given the stowaways extensive mining experience they would be too valuable an asset to lose. Their unconventional method of boarding would soon be excused.

Su'Zi hoped that her Ma would find happiness with Number One on Dadr'Ka. Ln'Da had never been the same since Ba's death. She was outwardly happy for Su'Zi that Su'Zi found P'Ko, but Su'Zi sensed deep down an awkwardness. It was almost like Ln'Da was… Su'Zi couldn't describe it, but the nearest she could form in her mind was an uncomfortable very tenuous jealousy.

Su'Zi attributed it to the fact that Su'Zi, had found a best friend, a companion and hopefully, one day, a mate, and the wretched CA had taken her mate, and she was now alone.

Dadr'Ba is not kind to those in Ln'Da's situation, she was tainted, though no one treated her badly if anything they respected her sacrifice and showed her deference. There were just not that many compatible mates her age. Her situation placed her one step above a leftover.

Su'Zi wondered if Z'Shi had anything to do with getting the CA to authorize Su'Zi's mother and P'Ko's parents as crew members on Dadr'Ka. There were far more volunteers than necessary to crew Dadr'Ka, yet all the family and close friends of Su'Zi and P'Ko that applied got selected.

Su'Zi knew P'Ko and Z'Shi are in occasional contact, but P'Ko never mentions her, perhaps, out of respect for Su'Zi. Su'Zi couldn't help but feel uncomfortable with P'Ko's relationship with Z'Shi and Su'Zi knows that even with P'Ko's not fully matured psychic abilities he can sense it.

Su'Zi glanced at Tn'Ya hanging on P'Ko's other arm, to Su'Zi she seemed shallow. Tn'Ya's center is still focused on a deep devotion to P'Ko; P'Ko is Tn'Ya's center mass, something firm, a foundation on which she builds from.

Su'Zi had to admit Tn'Ya's has done quite well despite being plagued by an early life of insecurity and persecution.

Her willingness and ability to take charge as she does on occasion in the bedroom demonstrates a certain independence and strength. She thoroughly enjoys the freedom of action, the trust, and control that Su'Zi and P'Ko surrender to her. An opportunity that a weaker person might use for a kind of revenge, but Tn'Ya has never taken it too far or abused the power, instead, she's grown to be more confident as a person because of it and seeks to please, a kind of thank you for being trusted and empowered.

Her dependence on P'Ko still shows a side of her that's insecure and fears persecution.

So what or who is Su'Zi's center mass? When she was younger it was her father, Kr'T but after she had lost her ba there was nothing, Ma tried to be strong, but the reality was that Ma was cast adrift in a void herself. Religion helped, Ma attended regular church services at first, but over time spirituality grew within her, she attended church services less frequently and with Mi'Ka's aid and guidance became more spiritually independent.

Su'Zi's center, thrown out of balance by the loss of Ba at such a young age was helped when she and P'Ko found each other, but P'Ko as strong and reliable as he is, isn't strong enough or reliable enough to be Su'Zi's center.

Su'Zi's own strength and reliability surpasses P'Ko's. Perhaps that's it; Su'Zi needs to be her center. Having a troubled childhood and few friends, Su'Zi had to foster and grow internal strengths, that over the years caused Su'Zi to be strikingly independent yet powerfully drawn to P'Ko despite his weaknesses or perhaps because of his weaknesses.

Though Su'Zi can't imagine her life without P'Ko, her center is still within herself. Su'Zi found herself jealous of Tn'Ya, not because P'Ko showed any favor of Tn'Ya over Su'Zi, but of Tn'Ya's ability to make her center P'Ko and this left Su'Zi feeling isolated and alone.

———————————————

Su'Zi found herself laying prone looking out through the transparent metallic liquid, she had parted with P'Ko and Tn'Ya hours ago and couldn't remember how she got here.

She watched the skeletonous heroes and creatures of myth dance across the inky darkness like a slow rain falling against a black sky.

She paid particular attention to the ones that she and her father had made up so long ago, looking for a clue or a sign that her father, wasn't entirely gone.

She came to the slow realization that he's not entirely gone as long as she remembers him, as long as someone remembers him. She's seen some of her father's traits in her brother Sa'To meaning that some small part of him lives on in his son. She never speaks to Sa'To about Ba; there's no need to.

There's not a time when Su'Zi and Sa'To are together that their psychic interaction doesn't touch on Ba. It's like a special signal or acknowledgment between them when they meet. The equivalent of a verbal "Hi brother, remember Ba, how's your day going?"

She watched as the constellations progressed across the sky and in her imagination turned it into a great Run with the Se'Ro'Bs. The Se'Ro'Bs constellation chasing the rest, then without realizing it, she saw a team of constellations chasing the Se'Ro'Bs. The thought flashed through her mind of P'Ko coming up behind the Se'Ro'Bs, unable to stop in time and jumping over it.

She's not sure why she hadn't yet shown P'Ko this place, it's so special. Maybe she wants to protect it. P'Ko can sometimes be slow picking up on significant subtleties. If P'Ko didn't or wasn't able to appreciate the significance of this place Su'Zi didn't know how she would react.

She had never talked much with P'Ko about her father, yet she had thought about it many times, there was just never a time that felt quite right. There's time, she and especially P'Ko are young, they have much growing and maturing to do, and as the years go by they will become stronger, and wiser, together.

Chapter 58, Chn'Gi's Thoughts Nearing O'M

Chn'Gi, lay naked in the hot water of her bathtub enjoying the luxury of her status, at most five percent of the population of Dadr'Ba has a tub large enough to lay full-length. Most U'Te's and Dr'T's have to settle for a shower on an automatic timer or a shallow sit bath or go to one of the public baths.

The reading light on the nearby counter became her friend.

She didn't like it at first, it gave off an eerie blue-green shimmer producing a scary effect. If she scanned her eyes across it, it causes a dizzying flickering effect. The only way to avoid the weird effect was not to look directly at it or to blink your eyes hard before scanning away. Now that Chn'Gi has grown accustomed to it, it's a companion, and its light has become a warm glow, providing her a sense of security.

The mechanism behind its operation must be unique, the CASS must know about them and would recognize it immediately. Fortunately, the CASS doesn't surveilled bathrooms, at least not at her security level and doesn't raid or inspect quarters without suspicion.

So the fact that she has the light means that she must not be suspected, at least not yet. CASS' trust assessment is satisfied instead on surveilling the common areas of her quarters, which, along with their ship-wide network of informants, surveillance devices and undoubtedly uses a computerized analysis of it all to assign an anti-progressive risk index to every individual on board.

Her bedroom, supposedly, the only other area in her quarters without surveillance, she doesn't trust. Usually, the CASS uses cameras that are noticeable, but there's absolutely no reason to use conspicuous cameras unless for the deterrence factor and as a decoy to help hide the real unseen cameras and create a false sense of privacy in areas, like her bedroom.

Even though she grew up, spending her entire life with a camera on her, still it made her uneasy when she thought about it, dressing and undressing in her bedroom, knowing that "probably" someone was watching. Her bathroom has become her sanctuary, especially with the addition of the reading light, and the reading light is supposed to work better in small spaces.

Keeping the reading light and the reader in a sack safe in the back of the bathroom cabinet, along with some occasionally used sex toys was convenient and gave her reason and an excuse for a good soak and relaxing. Though she had to be careful not to spend too much time in her sanctuary to avoid raising the suspicion of the CASS and result in an "inspection."

She hadn't dared to pick up the reader in a long time, the effects it had on her from the last time scared her. Reading Or'Gn's history was like looking into a portal to the future and most of what she saw portended death and devastation.

Dadr'Ba had exited the harsh domain of interstellar space and its corrosive nothingness and was experiencing the "atmosphere" of O'M's solar system.

O'M's sun doesn't look like just another star anymore and is clearly recognizable as a guide star brighter and more inviting than all the others. The parallel to the first Touch of God and the Touch of God ceremony that they all experienced is undeniable.

She picked up the reader, this time; she's prepared; she and her team have learned much about the O'Mi's. She still prefers her pet name for the people that live there, and the name the Dadr'Ba's would have possibly called themselves once settled.

Chn'Gi picked the reader up off the stand near the tub. She wasn't worried anymore about the risk of getting it damp or wet; the thing is over a thousand years old and in all that time must have survived much worse than Chn'Gi's tub.

She began to look for the parallel goodness between Dadr'Ba's past and that of the O'Mi's and what the O'Mi's are going through. Her goal is to craft an argument for peaceful coexistence with the O'Mi's. Properly managed, there's plenty of room on O'M for everyone.

There she had to stop herself, "properly managed" for proper management there has to be a method of management, control, monitoring, and enforcement. The O'Mi's of aren't there yet, they're not a really "bad" people, there are some indications of hope and goodness. But they're not ready or capable of "proper management" of themselves let alone the planet.

Can the O'Mi's be taught? Or, as the CA has advocated, in some of its infomercials, accept "management?" Even Dadr'Ba's people resist the CA's management coupled with CASS' enforcement. How can the O'Mi's be expected to?

The CA has given hints that preparations are being made to handle the "O'Mi problem" but even at her security clearance level they're hidden, special access required, and need to know. She knew nothing more than the average U'Te or Kr about the CA's plans. All Chn'Gi knows about the CA's plans are what the CA sends out with its infomercials, documentaries and Vr'Chm depictions of O'M.

Everything that the CA and CASS are revealing, much under the auspices of Chn'Gi's team slant perspectives of O'Mi's as an aggressive, dirty, barbaric, evil cancer, squeezing all the goodness and life out of the planet.

Frustrated, Chn'Gi set the reader aside and once again plunged her head under the water wondering how long she could hold her breath.

Chapter 59, New Vr'Chm

The beach was pretty crowded in spite of being so far from the settlement. The buildings and the people near them appeared quite small.

They were trying to invent a game, one that involves the waves and sand, but doesn't give an advantage to either the U'Te or the Mi'Nr. Su'Zi and Tn'Ya were arguing about how many shells should be needed to be collected behind the waves to win. P'Ko, watching the two argue, thinking that there couldn't be a more childish thing in the world.

His favorite thing was to swim and to float; there's few swimming pools on Dadr'Ba and no large ones, and nothing with scenery or marine life. In most places on Dadr'Ba, swimming for enjoyment is impossible, nobody has a bath tub, and the public baths and pools are crowded. The other places you can float on Dadr'Ba, near the core and the counter rotating, or more accurately described non-rotating observation decks, are work areas, used for monitoring Dadr'Ba's progress, obstacle detection and whose observation decks are crowded with tourists.

Swimming in O'Ms massive ocean, even Vr'Chm, P'Ko found exhilarating, like floating in weightless space on the counter rotating observation decks of Dadr'Ba, but without the crowd and with more control and nothing can compare to the marine life, updated with the latest imagery from O'M it's breathtakingly beautiful and awe-inspiring.

The security provided by the CA Settlement Defense Force, a subdivision of the newly created O'M World Management Office, itself, a subdivision of the CASS, had done an excellent job of controlling the threat from the alien barbarians. The settlement perimeter walls are visible in the distance and further still P'Ko's well-trained eyes could make out the outer perimeter wall with its automated guard post/surveillance towers linked to a rapid response force of soldiers.

Ever since Dadr'Ba entered the solar system, heralded by the detection of the solar wind and the accompanying celebration, a marked change in attitude came over Dadr'Ba. Everyone was happy, excited in spite of the extra work necessitated by the loss of the crew members to Dadr'Ka. The engine output was increased, and the slight resistance of the solar wind helped to counter the gravity pushing them towards the sun.

This system like most others contains a good number of planets, some gas giants, which Dadr'Ba will use for gravitational braking. A high priority is to maintain "Stealth Mode" and when close enough, stay as close to the opposite side of the sun from O'M as possible to reduce the change of detection by the aliens.

By this time, they've developed capabilities that could detect and threaten Dadr'Ba. The advertised plan is to achieve orbit at a safe distance. Then to make non-threatening slow, deliberate, conscious contact, followed by diplomatic relations, negotiate space for a settlement. Then, hopefully, begin to teach these aliens how to manage the planet better.

Retirements had stopped decades ago, and the CA was faced with a gap in its graduate/apprentice pipeline. Classroom sizes had to be reduced.

The departure of Dadr'Ka allowed for the granting of birthing rights to those that had lost their parents, even though their children might not be full crew members by the time they arrived at O'M.

Slowly Dadr'Ba's crew will come back to full strength, not that it would benefit the overall mission, but the life and lifestyle aboard Dadr'Ba needs to be maintained, and it did no practical harm. Dadr'Ba still had adequate resources, the ship and its machines that were lost to Dadr'Ka would slowly be replaced. With O'M so near and the crew staying motivated, efficiency and production remain at all-time highs.

It had crossed both P'Ko's and Su'Zi mind, though they never discussed it, that with Su'Zi's mom and both P'Ko's parents having left, forever, not dead or retired, but never to be seen or heard from again. Left the question of being eligible for birthing. Many other couples applied for and were granted birthing rights, but P'Ko and Su'Zi both felt they weren't ready, they weren't mated, and though there was no reason for the CA to refuse, they never applied.

For P'Ko and Su'Zi, the excitement of coming O'M, its sun becoming distinguishable to the naked eye overshadowed thoughts of birthing and children.

Whispers among Dadr'Ba's crew began to spread about how things are going to work once they're settled at O'M.

The Biologicals would be thawed, and the slow process of recovering and adopting Or'Gn's biosphere to O'M would begin.

It could take centuries, perhaps millennia to work out and combine (replacement or introduction would only work only on a sterile planet) Or'Gn and O'M's biosphere, but there were plenty of people looking forward to and training to meet the challenge. Many of them educators, what with the reduction of students, jumped at the chance to participate in such a momentous undertaking.

The Church engaged early. It realized that arrival at O'M would change everything for them. Foreseeing this day, the Church dusted off old plans and began mentioning how natural death is going replace retirement. Birthing will become biological, and organic "children" will become little people instead of big childlike people, all very wondrous and amazing to the crew of Dadr'Ba. The existing crew will be honored and for the first time be allowed to retire, without departing, to enjoy a life of leisure activity, rewarded by society until disease, accident, misfortune or eventual fatal fatigue takes them.

Chapter 60, O'M Welcoming

Dadr'Ba's deceleration continued and adjustments to its trajectory for gravity assisted deceleration and orbital capture progressed flawlessly. Dadr'Ba was able to conduct successful gravitational braking maneuvers using gas giant planets in the outer solar system, the reverse of some of the maneuvers Dadr'Ba accomplished almost two thousand years ago when it exited the Or'Gn system.

There was a celebration when they had slowed enough to guarantee solar system capture. It was an irreversible milestone, like when Dadr'Ba passed the point of no return when there wasn't enough fuel to get back to Or'Gn.

There were others less significant milestones, for example, when they passed the point when there wasn't enough fuel to divert to another destination. Today Dadr'Ba became a permanent resident of the O'M system.

Now O'M was just months away. It would be visible to the naked eye had Dadr'Ba not approached from the far side of the sun.

Engine thrust and the fuel mining necessary to support the load is at near maximum capacity. The regulation of Dadr'Ba's internal temperature in interstellar space had become routine, but now they were beginning to feel the warmth of a sun. Operating a spaceship composed mostly of ice surrounding a massive fusion rocket engine, hotter than the surface of a sun, started to become a concern.

The solution Dadr'Ba's engineers worked out was to operate the standard cooling at full performance and to flow excess heat in the form of hot gasses out the engine exhaust. This solution increased the ejectorate mass, improving the performance of the engine while at the same time getting rid of the heat that would have threatened Dadr'Ba's structural integrity. The addition of partially processed waste water to the ejectorate created a shadowing cloud that completed the solar protective measures.

The result became a massive plume in front of and bent around Dadr'Ba. Dadr'Ba looked, at least in the visible light bands in standard resolution, like what it started its life as. A comet. A careful examination at high resolution or at other than visible wavelengths would quickly show something unnatural about Dadr'Ba. Analysis of its speed and trajectory over several weeks would remove all doubt that Dadr'Ba was anything but natural.

The drawback to these cooling measures was that the efficiency of the ejectorate reclamation, using Dadr'Ba's magnetic field to draw the positive ions around Dadr'Ba and back into its intake suffered. Dadr'Ba began losing many times more mass than it did while operating in interstellar space. It was worth the risk, they have the mass to spare and losing mass increases the efficiency of the engine, the engineers calculated that even with the increased fuel consumption and loss of potentially useable fuel and water, Dadr'Ba possessed enough reserves to safely reach O'M.

Dadr'Ba was getting close to what it deemed the habitable zone. The morale of the crew at an all-time high. Excitement grew as they passed the system's outer planets, coming close, using them as gravitation brakes.

Images of the system's planets were produced, and the crew wondered at their beauty. Each view hammering home the fact that they're very soon going to reach O'M.

After almost two thousand years and nearly a hundred light years of travel, most people having worked through light years of travel, to be within light minutes of O'M meant that they were as good as there.

Then.

The forward-looking collision avoidance sensors detected an oddly shaped object, near Dadr'Ba's path on an intercept course. Further analysis showed that it was under power and guided, it must be a probe.

Chn'Gi and the CASS teams studying the aliens discovered that they had been sending probes out to the outer planets. Dadr'Ba went to a heightened level of alert; they didn't want to be detected, at least not yet. The probes' diminutive size, in comparison to Dadr'Ba, along Dadr'Ba's significantly reduced speed would make the probe an easy target for Dadr'Ba's debris clearing systems.

This was an unexpected development and the Commander, and his advisors had trouble deciding how to handle the situation. Chn'Gi advised against taking any action, to let them think Dadr'Ba was a natural comet. Chi'Yo and the CASS analysts wanted it destroyed, even at the risk of altering the aliens to the nature of Dadr'Ba's existence. It was decided to prepare, wait and see, and try to detect and analyze the communications coming from the probe. Whereby providing valuable information about the aliens and their operations.

As the probe got closer, it altered its course in such a way as to make a flyby. The tension aboard Dadr'Ba relaxed a little. But just as it seemed the probe would pass innocently by perhaps only taking some pictures. Dadr'Ba engineers frantically attempted to interfere remotely, jamming the probe's ability to collect imagery and send data back to its controllers. Image and signal analysts sought to discover the nature of the probe using their own imagers and analysis of the probes electromagnetic emissions.

The probe performed a trajectory maneuver and began to spin itself and shortly after began to deploy some secondary probes on a slow velocity intercept course with Dadr'Ba.

The alarm in the collision avoidance control room sounded, and the collision avoidance systems automatically began targeting the objects. Dadr'Ba had allowed the probe to get too close, and its collision avoidance systems had trouble targeting the objects. The systems were intended and designed to intercept objects more directly in front of Dadr'Ba.

There was also a slight delay in the chain of command, the first echelon of the chain, was uncertain what to do. They attempted to get the collision avoidance systems targeted while waiting for a command decision; they didn't have to wait long. Commander Chi'Yo gave the order to eliminate the objects, including the mother probe, that at this time was roughly parallel to Dadr'Ba passing quickly.

The collision avoidance system had just completed lock-on to the nearest of the objects with its powerful directed energy beam to vaporize it when it detonated. The nuclear blast blinded the electro-optical sensors and burned off much of the blanketing fog that surrounded Dadr'Ba protecting it from the heat of the sun. The intense radiation from the second blast, a specially designed nuclear device, designed to direct its energy, mostly in one direction, toward its target; only a few seconds later interacted with the surface of Dadr'Ba, blistering its surface. The third blast a few seconds after the last was the last, though it further blistering Dadr'Ba's surface. The collision avoidance systems using the surviving electro-optical and radar systems were finally able to target and eliminate the remaining objects, including the mother probe/control module bus that delivered the devastation.

The nuclear blasts caused the explosive armor meteoroid shields nearest the blast at the front and back of Dadr'Ba to detonate. Fortunately, the shields were designed to prevent a chain reaction that would have caused all of the panels to detonate. But enough of the shields were damaged and detonated on one side of Dadr'Ba to off-balance it a little. That, along with the repeated blistering of one side of Dadr'Ba imparted a tiny bit of sideways momentum, enough to cause Dadr'Ba to become unbalanced.

Dadr'Ba's spin, that gave its occupants a sense of gravity, a sense of up and down, began to deteriorate. Alarms sounded throughout Dadr'Ba and the fuel being pumped into Dadr'Ba fusion intake was automatically interrupted, but even without primary fuel. It took precious seconds for the fusion drive to snuff out. Sensors blinded or damaged by the second and third nuclear blast made it difficult to quickly assess the damage.

Dadr'Ba's primary power blinked out and slowly and in a deliberate priority auxiliary power came online. Practiced, but never before used in real need, not since the Touch of God Event over eight hundred years ago.

Most of the casualties were among the Mi'Nr's the nukes had tweaked Dadr'Ba enough that its superstructure cracked in several places, and some whole mining sections got evacuated out into space.

Some quick thinking engineers narrowly avoided catastrophe, sacrificing their lives in the process, manually overriding the electrostatic fusion beam control plates to keep the dying fusion reaction centered in the now off center Dadr'Ba, keeping the fusion reaction from blowing Dadr'Ba to bits.

Over a kilometer of the center core of Dadr'Ba had been overheated on one side, killing hundreds of engineers and technicians. The greatest loss of life was among the Mi'Nr's, well over a thousand Mi'Nr's operating in the lower zones died after the atmosphere they were breathing was sucked out into space from cracks in Dadr'Ba's hull.

In all, over three thousand people lost their lives, more than one-fifth Dadr'Ba's crew died in the first moments of the disastrous unprovoked attack, without retirement.

Dadr'Ba's main engine was out of commission. Dadr'Ba's now unbalanced spin slowly degraded into a cartwheel, Dadr'Ba's superstructure barely able to keep from breaking into pieces. Their velocity too fast to achieve O'M orbit, they will fly by O'M and be whipped back out into a long period comet trajectory.

Chapter 61, The Beach

The normally crowded Hawaiian beach was deserted, there's usually a crowd, but the tsunami warning sirens have been sounding for what seems like hours. People are taking this one seriously. The eastward facing beach, is taking the full brunt of the late midmorning sun, but oddly, the southern horizon looks like a sunset, bright yellows, oranges and reds radiating out stretching almost to the zenith.

To the right not far down the beach, a mirage, but not the ordinary mirage like the shimmer you see extending horizontally along a desert plain or a dry Lake bed. This mirage is much smaller and closer, appearing like a miniature dust devil but containing no dust, only twisted shimmering currents of air like those seen above a clean burning fire, but more intense. Further down the beach in the other direction, another twisting shimmering, swirling, pulsating, mirage, then they were gone.

NASA, the Russians and the ESA (European Space Agency) had all been considering testing a comet and asteroid deflection system on Apophis a small asteroid that is due to come close, but not impact the earth in 2029 and come even closer with a small possibility of Earth impact in 2036.

The People's Republic of China (PRC) CNSA (China National Space Administration), developed their comet deflection system named Tulong[105], and with their burgeoning space program planned to leapfrog ahead of its competitors. Year's ahead of its competition and using a more aggressive and efficient system, designed to avert a mass extinction event with less than half the warning time required with any of the other systems being developed.

The CNSA decided to test Tulong secretly against a known comet with a well-documented trajectory, one that would be easy to measure Tulong's effectiveness on, and deployed Tulong to this isolated intercept point on the far side of the sun. The target comet is due to pass through this area of space in only a few weeks. The comet picked for the test of the CNSA system was a zero risk on the Torino[106] scale, which offered a wide margin of safety in the event the deflection system had the opposite effect on the comet's trajectory.

But all that planning went out the window when this new comet appeared, database searches came up blank, this was a new comet. Based on preliminary data, this comet came up a six or seven on the Torino scale. As the telemetry

---

[105] Sounds like Too-long, the name given the CNSA comet deflection command module.

[106] a Near-Earth Object Hazard Index, zero equals no risk, ten equals a collision is certain

data accumulated the Torino index increased meaning that this comet could become a ten by the time of closest approach/impact. It was about the right size, and in the right place to use the deflection system on. This "test" has just turned into an emergency. And the CNSA's Tulong system, is humanities one chance at salvation.

A decision had to be made and made quickly, the whole thing was made more complicated by the fact that the comet and the deflection system was behind the sun, making communication difficult and impossible for terrestrial and space-based telescopes to see what was going on.

It would have been so much simpler if they had been less concerned with world opinion and security and conducted this test in the open with the test within direct line of sight of the earth.

The decision makers at the CNSA needed a decision to be made, a decision that could impact not just the people of China but every man woman and child on Earth. By the time the decision package made it all the way up to the Central Committee of the Communist Party of China, there wasn't enough time to contact the rest of the nations of the world and explain to them the highly classified program, a program that technically violated the International Outer Space Treaty.

There wasn't enough time for diplomacy, and if successful the comet would miss by a fair margin and the CNSA and the PRC could claim credit for saving the world, if not, it wouldn't matter.

Given the little information obtained mostly from the systems' cameras and radars, the decision was made to attempt the deflection. The comet's velocity was much higher than typical, meaning that it is either a very long period comet or possibly even a rogue comet. They're working virtually blind, and to make matters worse, the twenty-two-minute time delay for its transmission to be received near the orbit of Mars meant turning the deflection system on, telling it to execute and then wait and watch, there is absolutely nothing that can be done on earth that would have any impact on the operation.

The risk of a mistake, if the thing were to shatter into pieces and become the apocalyptic shotgun blast instead of a slug was mitigated by the systems design. The initial "pulse" or "pulses" would be used to clear away the coma and perhaps even increase the pressure on the near side of the comet. The follow-on pulses in quick succession would use the comet surface itself as a push plate in what amounts to be a combustion chamberless rocket engine. The lack of a formal combustion chamber is mitigated by using carefully designed "pulse modules" resurrected from data "collected" about America's sixty-year-old Operation Plowshare and Project Orion. If the comet breaks up, the system is designed to detonate the pulse modules a little further way so as to have a better angle to push each piece in the same desired direction as if the comet had remained whole.

As soon as the Mission Planners at the Beijing Aerospace Command and Control Center (BACCC), working Project 251, got the go-ahead from the Central Committee, they went into high gear. BACCC Mission Planners, all skilled professionals, most in their forties with twenty or more years' experience with the space program had little difficulty making the necessary changes to the Deflection Systems programming; they didn't have much time, data transmission and acknowledgment was excruciatingly slow. Software testing was completed, and simulations run to eliminate or at least mitigate any possible adverse outcome. In the end, they were confident their efforts would result in a Torino Scale reduction from a six or seven or even ten to a one. And effect a million-fold decrease in the risk of impact, the risk will be worth the gamble.

The location, the far side of the sun, made communication with the deflection system difficult but provided an increased level secrecy deemed paramount for the highly classified project. The events taking place are hidden from terrestrial observation, even imagers on the various planetary probes would have to be queued to what's going on to take their sensors away from their primary tasking, the planets, moons, asteroids and comets right in front of them.

The events occurring now are in a virtually empty spot in the solar system.

Despite the communications difficulty, having been forced to switch to longer wavelength, lower bandwidth frequencies able to bend around the sun, the Project 251 crew completed the necessary programming changes to Tulong.

The system data was good and transmitted with triple redundancy. The live video however was poor quality, choppy, pixilated and low resolution, but the entire team was confident in Tulong's, high-resolution optical and multispectral image recording equipment and looked forward to seeing the events in ultra-high resolution as soon as it cleared the blinding glare of the sun. When Tulong would send the triumphant proof that the PRC saved the Earth from the impact of a mass extinction event comet.

The Project 251 control room was alive with activity; every system was closely monitored despite the time delay. The VIP's up in the darkened windowed command section above and behind the control room floor waited and watched anxiously. Everyone watched the historical events on gigantic screens lining the far end of the large control room. Events that would determine the fate of the human race unfolded twenty-two light minutes away.

Knowing that they are mere spectators watching events from a distance of four hundred million Kilometers didn't make the Project 251 team feel impotent. Each member of Project 251 had embedded in Tulong a significant part of their intelligence, their strength, their will, their time, their very lives. Each witnessed the events on the choppy, pixelated screen personally, like they were there doing battle against the evil dragon bent on destroying the human race.

With the excitement of sports fans watching their favorite team play against an arch rival, the Project 251 team watched the fuzzy stop action video as Tulong now in fully autonomous mode performed flawlessly.

As soon as the comet came within range, still a fuzzy ball in the distance made even fuzzier because of the poor video quality, Tulong deployed the pulse modules, they looked like a string of pearls on the wide angle camera. Tulong is operating on its own changed the camera zoom and panned over to watch as the pulse modules arched over towards the comet. The camera filters flicked on turning the screen black as the first pulse module detonated the next frame showed a huge dent in the comet's coma. Then the second pulse module detonated showing a still fuzzy freeze frame image of the surface of the comet glaring brightly in the light of the nuclear blast.

The room gasped, the surface of the comet appeared to be smooth, and one could barely make outlines or structures the third pulse module detonated, and the screen went black, the room went quiet for what seemed like an eternity.

The Project 251 mission commander immediately asked for a status report and as practiced each component system supervisor in priority order began to report. The reports all came back the same, the transmission was terminated, no data was coming from Tulong, and they were attempting to re-establish contact.

What happened next, no one expected, the members of the Project 251 team that witnessed the miraculous events on the big screen were sent to conference rooms. Guards were posted and they were told to wait silently until questioned by investigators. Meanwhile, the CNSA leadership had to decide what to do.

The team members that didn't witness the "sight" were sent home with instructions not to speak about the events that day to anyone. The project changed completely; it was no longer called Project 251 it became Special Project 649. All the members of the original Project 251 were assigned to other projects with orders not to speak to anyone about anything related to the project, not even other team members. Only a few of the original Project 251 members, after being "cleared," were allowed to participate in the after incident investigation, to try to reestablish communication with Tulong and to figure out what happened.

Slowly and deliberately everything checked out, Tulong deployed the pulse modules flawlessly and was observing from a safe distance. The first three pulse modules performed correctly, the triple redundant data checked out; radio telescope records were analyzed, and the investigators were able to confirm the detonation of the first three pulse modules but no more.

The investigation also focused on the video, on that image frozen in the flash of the second pulse module blast that showed the surface of the comet. Then the investigation appeared to come to a complete halt.

The Project 251 team with the image of the comet surface burned into their memories in the nuclear fire of the second pulse module feared the worst. Their fears soared when the SOHO, (Solar and Heliospheric Observatory) and the STEREO (Solar Terrestrial Relations Observatory) spacecraft blinked off line and presumably out of existence.

Weeks later and without warning, a cascade of failures of earth's satellites occurred. For the first tens of minutes, it was thought to be a massive solar event. But as it was being confirmed that there was no coronal mass ejection in our direction, communication, and all things electronic started to fail. Across the entire planet, power grids failed.

Attempting to work around the communication failures, governments began to declare states of emergency, placing their militaries on alert and activated guard and reserve units. Then centers of government, military installations, bases and command-and-control centers along with the cities and municipalities in their vicinity, disappeared, vaporized in gigantic mushroom clouds. The surrounding areas stretching tens of kilometers reduced to smoldering gravel, further away, blast effects, shockwaves, and thermal radiation, started fires, that turned into firestorms. Nobody seemed to know what to do and even if someone did know there was no way to communicate it.

The loss of life and property is mind-boggling, rescue efforts, by the few rescue units that survived, were futile, but it didn't stop them. The rescuers closed their minds to the millions needing rescue and helped anyone and anywhere they could.

There were rumors of massive earthquakes on the U.S. west coast and that the Yellow Stone super volcano was erupting. Many people began to believe the world was coming to an end.

Inexplicably radiation levels remain comparably low which led some scientists to speculate that the bombs, they "must" have been bombs, were anti-matter core fusion weapons.

With no centralized civil structure surviving, no communication and without the military to support the local civil authorities around the blast zones, and even some isolated areas untouched by the devastation devolved into anarchy.

Huge numbers of refugees began to flee the blast areas for the intact rural communities, communities lacking the resources to accommodate the millions of refugees. Little did anyone know, there was more yet to come.

Terrestrial telescopes in remote areas operating on generator spotted them. The telescopes detected NEO's (Near Earth Objects) on a collision course with earth, each about a kilometer in diameter, with a closing velocity approaching seventy-five kilometers a second. The masses of the objects couldn't be determined accurately but, estimated to be more than one-hundred million kilograms, possibly as high as five or six-hundred-million kilograms.

The first struck in the mid-Atlantic with enough force to cause a tsunami a hundred meters high to ring the Atlantic coastlines, the second hit in the mid-Pacific, for a similar effect.

This was no accident. Close on the heels of the impactors, a comet or what appeared to be a comet, a fuzzy ball with a thin coma passed by earth. The comet came to be known as Samil named after the Angel of Death.

It's estimated that over a billion people died on zero day and in the days/weeks and months that followed that billions more will die of injuries, disease, and famine.

Based on best estimates of Samil's velocity and trajectory, it's estimated that it will return in about sixty five years.

Samil didn't kill humanity; it turned the earth into a patchwork quilt of starving people clawing their way back from the brink of extinction. Some areas were virtually untouched while many others were pushed back a hundred years, others set back two-hundred years, still other areas all the way back to the dark ages, what remained was given back to Nature.

Epilogue

"Poh'poh[107], why are you so quiet?" It had been a near perfect day; the morning had been cool and clear and as the day warmed up a slight breeze blew. A perfect day to spend the late afternoon on the beach.

The family spent part of the morning weeding in the garden and part of it trimming and pruning in their small orchard, enjoying themselves in a picnic-like atmosphere. The only damper on what was otherwise a perfect day was skyward.

A new star had appeared, the newcomer at first was only visible at daybreak and right after sunset, not unlike the morning and evening star Venus. Over time, it drifted away from the sun and grew a small tail. As even more time passed, it drifted further away from the sun and increased in brightness, becoming visible in broad daylight by blocking the sun with your hand.

Now only days ago it separated itself from the sun and lost its tail and began to track a slow arc across the sky.

Poh'poh, had an overwhelming sense of dread, a feeling deep inside her. Even though this newcomer's behavior was different than the first, she couldn't shake it from her mind. She felt a sense of dread emanating from the thing, and when she sat quietly and focused her attention on it, she felt from it a message of warning.

She had been the same age as her grandson when the comet that became known as the angel of death first appeared. The devastation that accompanied that arrival had been burned into her memory forever.

After almost forgetting his question, Poh'poh noticed her grandson waiting patiently, looking up at her, a concerned look on his face. Realizing the futility of sugarcoating her answer, she sighed and said, pointing up towards Samil as it traced its way across the sky "Samil, the angel of death" and she drew him close, hugging him tightly as the tears rolled down her cheeks.

---

[107] Sounds like Poh Poh, rhymes with "so low"

Glossary

A

An'Su – sounds like "on sue" code name for the CASS special mission vessel

Apprentice – work earns only partial mileage credit.

Apprenticeship – lasts for ten years, sometimes 25 depending on the job. Once the apprenticeship is completed, individuals can compete for job assignments at a permanent job.
Children can apprentice under the parent early, as young as fifteen, however, earn no seniority credit. The benefit is that they may pass their certifications early during regular apprenticeship and earn full seniority credit earlier than had they not apprenticed under their parent.

A'Pa – sounds like "ah pa" anti-progress activities, that carries a capital punishment.

Asteroids – had been integrated into Dadr'Ba's composition during its reconstruction into a starship; the prisoners The asteroids provide precious metals and minerals needed for the interstellar flight but were lacking in the original comet. The easiest method to provide these essential materials was from asteroids that were carefully buried in strategic locations to maintain Dadr'Ba's balance under spin near the ends of the cylinder that makes up Dadr'Ba.

B

Beh'Bei, – passive action, hidden hand

BACCC – Beijing Aerospace Command and Control Center

Bio-mods – distinctive to U'Te's and D'En's gravitate toward?
>   **U'Te's:** Tattoo's, including facial and permanent eye makeup, coarser shorter hair,
>   **D'En's:** Lack of Tattoo's, height enhancement, finer longer, hair, whiter smoother skin – almost like porcelain but not shiny,
>   **Mi'Nr's:** Aside from distinctive bio-mods for their race, often flamboyant facial tattoos, coarse facial hair for men

Birthing: One-way parenting is possible but very rare.
>   The most famous was the original survivor who parented his spouse, but that was a true parenting it was more like saving someone near death because once revived, she retained most of her original

i

functions, not like the revived newborn that are devoid of functionality and once birthed need to be trained in even the basic functions of biology and taught how to understand, interact and function in the environment.

Bo'Ba – sounds like "bow bah" term for baby, not yet potty trained, unable to speak

Body mods – are a medical appointment requiring scheduling and sometimes taking weeks to accomplish followed by sex education by mentors. It used to be different before the Touch of God and the establishment of the CA whatever governing body that controlled Dadr'Ba didn't allow the crew individuality.

Bot – slang for robot

Bo'R – sounds like "bow-er" or borer, slang for miner

Bylaws – Nothing is wasted on a starship.
> Every act is to help
> All energy expended helps Dadr'Ba to reach O'M
> All support that goal
> There is but one O'M, and that is our goal

C

CA – the central authority the CA was born out of the ashes of the Touch of God and is the divinely chosen command organization of the ship. Leading and guiding Dadr'Ba and its crew O'M

CASC – Central Authority Security Council

Capsule Flats – tiny Nu'Tn apartments

Children – look alike, but subtle differences in facial expressions, makeup, and personalization of uniforms help to identify individual children as well as nametags and distinguishing markings on the uniforms to show age and grade school. At age, fifteen children can start a un-bio-moded apprenticeship with their parents.

Church robes – white robe black tunic with the star

Clone crew – the crew is all clones, but cosmetics, body piercing/adornment, and tattoos are popular even among the young, (young are not authorized permanent mods until coming of age at age twenty-five) variations in clothing also popular.

Clonely – a derogatory term describing the look of someone, similar to "homely" that refers to a pre-bio-mod person or post bio-mod person that looks too much like no bio-mods were done, basic, plain, ordinary, dull

CNSA – China National Space Administration

Coming of age Ceremony – marks graduation from school, the start of vocation and adulthood. At age 25. There's a group graduation ceremony where each sector conducts a ceremony televised across all of Dadr'Ba typically about 250 graduates they received academic recognition, and their apprenticeship assignments are announced.

Credits – The currency earned, a small stipend is supplied to every crew member to pay for "incidentals" mostly food spices and hygiene items. Extra credit is earned by exceeding one quota of quality or quantity. Mechanics are one category of worker they can fairly easily make extra credits simply by doing more preventive maintenance routines during a shift.

Crystal Tear – Miners are given a snowflake ice crystal tear near the eye to represent a frozen tear for lives lost in their profession. Like real snowflakes, each is unique. It is created by placing a probe near absolute zero against the skin; the Probe is ignited on fire at one end and then designed in such a way that the fire draws heat from the opposite in creating a pinpoint of absolute zero. That pinpoint causes a burn that is often mistaken as a tattoo. The color from the Crystal Tear has been engineered to indicate of the effectiveness of the Mi'Nr's anti-CASS surveillance nano-bot nano-bots. P'Ko's tear is unusual and is attributed to his U'Te skin. Note Su'Zi and P'Ko like many other Mi'Nr's put on makeup to cover their tear when visiting Nu'Tn.

Cs'Oc – sounds like "cassock" CASS operation center

D
Dadr'Ah – sounds like "dad er ah" the first gift of God

Dadr'Ba – sounds like "dad are ba" the second gift of God, Dadr'ah renamed named Dadr'Ba after the Touch of God

Dadr'Ka – sounds like "dad are Ka" the third gift of God

D'En – sounds like "Dee in" slang word for guardian, upper class, smartest, ruling class

Divorce – is strictly 50-50 split shared custody of children and what can't be split is sold with the proceeds divided 50-50 or confiscated by the CA with no compensation.

Dr'T or D'Rs – slang for "Dirty", Derogatory name for miners

E
eSuit – environmental suit

Echo click – miners, have mastered the ability to echo click to help find their way down dark passages.

ESA – European Space Agency

eTaC-M – sounds like "EE tack em" Enhanced Tracking and Communications Module, a communications device linked to the CASS command center and is used to track movements of personnel with special access to CA information. The eTaC-M is fused to the wearer's skull and has tamper protection built in, making it extremely difficult to remove without alerting the CASS or causing central nervous system damage to the wearer.

Exoskeleton – powered exoskeleton that in conjunction with and eSuit enables the wearer to function in cold high G environments.

F
Family status – is based on family contributions to Dadr'Ba in distance. The higher distance families get better quarters that get assigned on Memorial Day.

Food processing – is tied to waste processing; it's processed in farms, but nothing like a terrestrial farm, but called so in a strange way to help make the product of food that's created more palatable
Biological food processing involves large tanks interspersed with light tubes in which grow several species of genetically engineered plankton designed to produce all the essential nutrients for the sustainment of life; the algae-like creatures are then processed into consumer packaged bars and cakes for food. Cooks and chefs that can make these foodstuffs more palatable are in great demand.

For'Nr – sounds like "fore ner" slang for foreigner, miners name for anyone other than a miner

FOP – Forward Only Policy, a policy or tenant by the CA imposed on the crew requiring only forward thinking and actions, imposed by the law against **A'Pa** or anti-progress activities, that carries capital punishment.

G

Gender-neutral pronoun
>   Ne
>   Ne laughed
>   I called nem
>   Nir eyes gleam
>   That is nirs
>   Ne likes nemself

Ghost – online CASS monitor

GLC – Gene-Locked Clone

GP – Give Power, miner slogan

Graduation ceremony – is followed by a coming-of-age ceremony, which is a Touch of God reenactment followed by a social welcoming parade.

GRB – Gamma Ray Burst

H

HB – home brew, a drink that Mi'Nr's, usually mechanics make from a contraption of broken and spare parts, and some non-fuel grade substances found in the scree during the mining operation that is cooked and distilled then filtered through a barrel of the latest ore, it's then bottled and allowed to age. Each sector's HB is different, and each batch is different, and there is an annual contest between the sectors to determine which sectors HB is best

Hn'Gri Bo'R – "slang for hungry boar or borer" restaurant in Ol'Tn'Ka, a hangout for Mi'Nr's

Holidays and Ceremonies:
>   **Graduation Day** – a ceremony held at the same time about the
sector. Group ceremony in each sector, video distributed across all of Dadr'Ba. Academic recognition and job selection announcement. ToG ceremony, coming of age ceremony in church annex, followed by body mods, sex education, and social welcoming.

ToG ceremony – Touch of God ceremony is a rite of passage marking the point that juveniles become legal adults. The ceremony is the first step followed by bio-mods, including sexual organs. Until then there is no physical difference between boys and girls. As they are raised and mature most, tend to gravitate to one or the other gender. It's rare to have a nonsexual individual; it is frowned upon socially, morally, and religiously, and may interfere with the grandparent's chance at passing on.

Memorial Day – a one hour Dadr'Ba wide ceremony, key people cannot attend, but get extra credits for working during the ceremony.

Retirement - A reverse birth ceremony occurs, a person becomes a full adult (religious) and is expected to birth children themselves.

I

IL – Intelligent life

J

Jobs-

Shift work – For every ten shifts worked crew members get one shift vacation, no weekends. One holiday off and can bank a hundred shift's that are tradable (unsellable) and two hundred shifts parenting, not tradable, use or lose.

Jm'Pr – sounds like "jumper" All-terrain vehicles used by Mi'Nr's to get to places quickly.

K

Ko'Ka – Child, pre-teen

Kr'/Kr's – sounds like "kur" shortened form of worker/workers, D'En name for Mi'Nr's and U'Te's

L

Laws – Penalties for lawbreakers are: fines, restriction of movement, confiscation of property, hard labor, isolation confinement, or finally death, commonly referred to as forcible retirement

Leftover – "leftover" the label used to name a person incapable of finding a mate and therefore fated not to have children

Lele'Kolo – sounds like "lay lay ko low" P'Ko's Mi'Nr name

LIDAR – Light Detection and Ranging

Lr'Lng – sounds like "ler ling" rhymes with yearling, or learning, coming of age apprentice to a Mentor

M

Magneto Hydro Dynamic (MHD) generator – an electrical power generation system that uses the fast-moving ionized gasses in the fusion engine to generate power.

Marriage – is a legally binding partnership contract is for the control of property and credits and birthing of children.

Martial arts – are against the law practitioners swear an oath of secrecy

Me'K's. – Mechanic

Mentors – ostensibly provide sexual education and training, but often provide social, economic and other mentoring that often lasts a lifetime.

Mi'Nr – **Miners** are short, stocky individuals specially adapted to live and work in the most hostile environments on the ship. They can echo click see better in the dark and have thick dark skin and eyelids so they can better survive in the mines.

Mines – are very cold, dark places; especially old abandoned mines nothing is wasted on a starship. Any lighting and ventilation equipment and utilities are moved to the new mining areas. The old mining areas are abandoned.

MOC – Mission Operations Commander

Mp'Isr – Mining Personnel, Intelligence Surveillance and Reconnaissance

Old mines – have no light and very thin air. The lighting systems had been removed and moved to new mining areas

M'Vr – sounds like "em ver" the Run with the Se'Ro'Bs' Most Valuable Racer

N

NASA – National Aeronautics and Space Administration

Nightclubs – dancing is popular, but not advertised or talked about openly they operate only in restricted areas

Nor – him, not her pre-grad, non-declared sexual orientation

NSTR – Nothing Significant to Report.

Nu'Tn – Sounds like "new ton" New Town. It is where the gravity and temperature are comfortable for, and where the majority of U'Te's and D'En's reside. It encompasses most of Zone two and was constructed after the ToG event. Each of the ships sectors has one and are designated by their sector, Nu'Tn'Ah (sector one), Nu'Tn'Ba (sector two), Nu'Tn'Ka (sector three), Nu'Tn'She (sector four) and Nu'Tn'Go (sector five).

O

Ol'Dr/Ol'Dr's – sounds like "Older" -- first born child, most closely tied to the grandparents

Ol'Tn – sounds like "Old Tin" where a large portion of Mi'Nr society resides, and less fortunate Up'Lndrs are forced to live, due to bad luck or bad decisions. Each of the ships sectors has one and are designated by their sector, Ol'Tn'Ah (sector one), Ol'Tn'Ba (sector two), Ol'Tn'Ka (sector three), Ol'Tn'She (sector four) and Ol'Tn'Go (sector five).

O'M – sounds like and means "Home."

O'Mi – sounds like "homie" Chn'Gi's nickname for the aliens that reside on O'M

Op'Cm – sounds like "op com" Operation Commander

Oort cloud – Oort clouds are speculated to exist in the titanic region of space beyond the outermost planets, only loosely bound to the sun's gravity and contains many millions of comet asteroid or protoplanetary objects.

Or'Gn – sounds like and means "Origin" world, the planet where Dadr'Ba came from, not its real name, its real name is banned from use by the Central Authority.

P

PCF -- Prompt Cold Fusion, powerful shots of liquor known for their instant effects

Penitentes – spiked hardened snow or ice caused by the snow or ice sublimating under the interaction of overhead light or radiation.

PRC – People's Republic of China

Per – Pre bio-mod, or not male, not female, non-gender specific version of him and her.

Pets – are androids like robotic body creatures resembling dogs, cats, and birds.

Philosophy – is outlawed, it's feared that introspection and self-understanding may lead to the discovery of their true nature (androids). -- Created by bios who dominated them. The idea behind being created or manufactured is repulsive to the Dadr'Ba; they believe that they are "born" to their parents and grandparents and alive in every sense of the word.

Pre-Born – people (clones) freshly printed or clones pulled from suspended animation that has never been brought to life.

Prostitution – is legal.

Prz'Nr's – sounds similar to and means Prisoners

PST – phase synched transmission

Q
QECS – Quantum Entanglement Communication System

R
Races – There are three races aboard Dadr'Ba Mi'Nr's Ute's D'En's. They are genetically designed for a particular purpose and were mandated for certain jobs until the equal job rights rebellion demanding and winning allowance for the medical modification to Bios

Resistance sign – is to rub against the cheek as if to wipe away a tear

Religion – From the CA's point of view religion is formed to keep the masses quiescent and to think correctly; focused on faith and belief in Dadr'Ba's mission to reach O'M, and superficial spiritual and bodily gains. Religious items are in every home. Religious services are "highly encouraged."

Resistance – The resistance movement originated shortly after the Touch of God. Nearly all miners are members of the resistance. Few U'Te's are members, and very few D'En's are members of the resistance.

Robots – are plentiful, but none is humanoid. They resemble automated machines except soldiers.

Reset – orgasm, climax

Retirement – Although not in Dadr'Ba tradition a terribly sad event, there had been a lot of stress; although everyone goes through it eventually it's still a very personal, profound event. Knowing your parents as not only as loving parents, but also as adult friends for over 100 years makes for a very close and mature relationship.
Society and the community have evolved to make the passing of one's parents as smooth as possible. Retirees can settle their affairs during their five-week "retirement" and don't need an executor to settle their affairs.

 Retirement Ceremony – Death ceremony - Funerals are mostly private affairs. With such long lives people of a community of tens of thousands, people know people.
During retirement family and friends say goodbye to the people leaving. Never is there any attempt to get the deceased to change their minds. Once the decision is made and retirement has been applied for and approved there is no turning back. There is some apprehension, but the attitude is overall positive because it is believed that they will be returning. Because what has made them special in many ways has as already been passed on to their children and during the ceremony, as they pass they will pass their psychic imprint on to their children who is then expected to pass it on to their children, their grandchildren. In this way, their seed is passed to the grandchildren.
The ceremony date and time and place is a prearranged and is a private affair. There are two areas, one for the parents that are passing and their children and a second area for the witnesses, usually some distance away or in an adjoining room.

S
Sensitive words – censored by CA, philosophy, alien, O'Mi

Se'Ro'Bs – sounds like "say-row-bus" -- 'security robots' a very old early model of Soldier Bot, that went feral during the ToG event.

Sex – everyone on Dadr'Ba is infertile, at least physiologically. This is as is a result of the need to create the clone's resistant to radiation. Dadr'Ba is also a sterile environment. There is no risk of unwanted pregnancy or sexually transmitted diseases. Dadr'Ba is a sexually open society. As a result, with long-term relationships lasting hundred to two-hundred or more years, the social mores allow for sexual relationships outside of marriage. Three way joining amongst adults is certainly possible, but to do a three-way parenting hasn't succeeded.

Sex education – is conducted by mentors selected by the graduate. To be asked to be a mentor is a great honor and is rarely refused.

SIL – Search for Intelligent Life

SMT – Special Mining Team

Soldier – robots that are artificially intelligent, but clearly robots. They are bipedal with an extra set of arms that enable them to go down on all fours and still have arms for action and weapons use. They have eyes in the back of their heads, allowing for 360° vision are ambidextrous forwards and backward, very strong, but have a foul odor due to their energy metabolism burning fuel, rather than recycling. Soldiers have camouflaged skin information from the eyes feed into scale-like plates that can change colors to match the surroundings.

Spirit – online, monitor friend

Superstitions – are common, but mostly among the lower classes and lower educated. Mi′Nrs have many superstitions; U′Te′s have few in comparison.

Supply Shuttles – rarely operate in a pure remote control operation mode, there are spots scattered around Dadr′Ba that wireless remote control is unreliable and the autonomous systems, though good could be subject to interference, especially something as large as the shuttle carrying several tons of equipment and supplies. The autonomous system plugged into the shuttle sensors, controls and limiters have proven to be far more capable rather than a remotely operated or even on board person at the controls.

T

TaC-B, – Tracking and Communications Button, an upgradeable Tracking and Communications device with connections linked to the central nervous system, capable of providing sight sound and some sensory communications. It is somewhat difficult to remove/replace.

T′Bm – "Tee-Bum" Tunnel boring machine

T′Bm Me′K – "Tee-Bum mech" TBM Mechanic

TE – Temporal Entanglement

Ti′Ro – sounds like "tea row" a beginner or novice

ToG, Touch of God, was a massive Gamma Ray Burst (GRB) that struck Dadr′Ba about half way through their journey. It is the official religion of Dadr′Ba and speaks of an afterlife, being returned to God or an all-knowing holy collective, but most people have greater faith in an afterlife through their progeny, their offspring, by teaching them, programming them, imprinting them, sharing of themselves so that they, in a significant way live on through their children and grandchildren.

Touch of God Ceremony – marks graduation from school, the start of vocation and adulthood. At age twenty-five. There's a group graduation ceremony where each sector conducts a ceremony televised across all of Dadr′Ba typically about 250 graduates they received academic recognition, and their apprenticeship assignments are announced, followed by the Church-run Touch of God Ceremony.

Torino scale – a Near-Earth Object Hazard Index, zero = no risk, ten = a collision is certain

To′Ta – sounds like "tow-tah" teenager

TTP – Tactics, Techniques and Procedures

Tulong – name of the PRC's comet/asteroid deflection system

Tween – someone between graduation and an established career

U

U′Ne – sounds like "you knee" -- Pre bio-mod, or not male, not female

Up′Lndr – Up lander Name Mi′Nr's have given to anyone that lives/works at or above zone 2, Nu′Tn

Up′Ln – sounds like "up Lynn" Up land, term Mi′Nr's use to describe all those that live and work above the Mining zones.

U′Te – sounds like "you tee" short for utility, the term is in popular use even among U′Te's. However, U′Te's don't like to be called U′Te's by non-U′Te's, contrasted by the miners that have a certain pride in being called miners.

U′Tl – sounds like "you till" Utility vehicle use at mining camps

V

Van der Waals forces -- intermolecular forces of attraction and repulsion at molecular distances.

Virtual world's – Dadr'Ba has an extensive computer network with many virtual world areas for online entertainment. The resistance takes advantage of these to create virtual safe houses that are protected from eavesdropping and available for meetings with members from all over Dadr'Ba.

Vr'Chm – sounds like "ver chum" Virtual O'M the CA-controlled simulation of O'M used to introduce O'M to the people of Dadr'Ba and to assess how the people adapt to their new O'M world. Vr'Chm is played/operated/monitored in real time; they do collect metrics about what goes on to gauge the people's reactions to the situation the CA pushes on them but doesn't have a playback available.

Vacation – for every ten shifts worked crewmembers get one shift vacation, no weekends, and one holiday off, workload permitting and upon supervisor's/CA discretion. Crewmembers can "bank" 100 shifts tradable, sellable and 200 shifts parenting, non-tradable use or lose.

W

Waste processing – is Top Secret. It's quietly assumed that no publicity is made to the fact that the people on Dadr'Ba are in a real way eating their processed waste, processed textured and flavored but still... Nothing gets wasted on a starship

Work Schedule – for every ten shifts worked crewmembers get one shift vacation, no weekends, and one holiday off, workload permitting and upon supervisor's/CA discretion

X

Y

Yng'Gr – sounds like "younger" second born child most closely bonded with parents

Ym'Cha's – sounds like "Yum-Cha" Tea shop chain, there is one in Nu'Tn of each sector

Z

Zones:
Zone One – the core of the ship where the engine, engineering, and power production zone.

Zone two – the habitable zone, most comfortable for people.
Zone three – the fuel zone.
Zone four – the death zone, near the hull and the edge of space.